The Crystal Dynasty

A Kingdom Divided

Abigail Mader

CASPIAN OCEAN
DUNES OF DECESSUS
DARLINGTON
RINGWICK LAGOON
BELMONT
BELSHIRE
MIDDLEBECK FARM
SLEIGHTS
TEMPLE
WITTLESHIRE
STOWDEN
GERALDTON
RENLANDS
SNOWY MOUNTAINS OF AZEND
FALMOUTH
TEMPLE
TEMPLE
ET

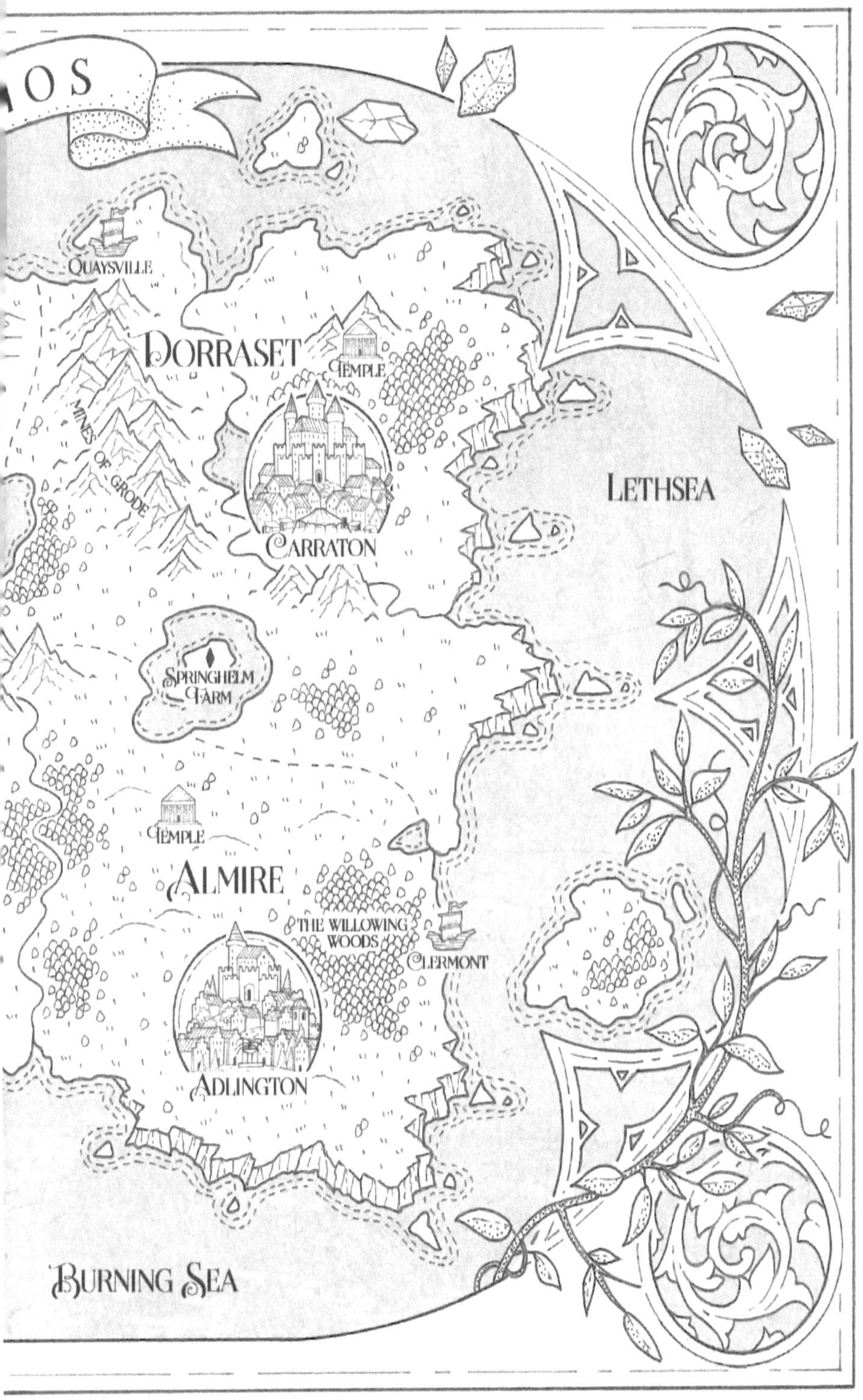

OS
QUAYSVILLE
DORRASET
TEMPLE
MINES OF GRODE
CARRATON
LETHSEA
SPRINGHELM FARM
TEMPLE
ALMIRE
THE WILLOWING WOODS
CLERMONT
ADLINGTON
BURNING SEA

Dedication

This is for all the bookworms out there who spent their childhoods devouring every book they could find, without wasting a single second. Those who hid under the blankets, reading by torchlight, transporting themselves to a different fantasy world every night.

This is for you.

Never stop reading. Never stop dreaming

About the Author

Abigail has been an avid reader since she was a child, getting lost in new worlds while crafting her own imaginative tales inspired by what she read. As she grew up, her love of fantasy continued, with authors such as Kate Forsyth, Robert Jordan, and David Eddings igniting her passion for writing. This led her on a long journey of creating her own fantasy world to get lost in, bringing about the book that sits in your hands.

Connect with Abigail on:

Website: https://www.abigailmaderauthor.com.au

TikTok: https://www.tiktok.com/@abigailmaderauthor

Instagram: https://www.instagram.com/abbiemader/

Threads: https://www.threads.net/@abbiemader

Content Warnings

This book has been written in a way that I followed my character's lead, seeing where they would take me. It's dark at times, with moments of sorrow, loss, and heartache, yet lighter moments too.

Knowing this, I'm mindful that certain themes in this book might be difficult for some readers.

These include signs of depression and moments of self-harm in one character, who, because of circumstances does reference to unalive themselves.

With another character, there are a couple of spicy scenes in the book. These are in Chapter 16, A New Reign and Chapter 21, Allies. If you don't like high spice, feel free to read both these chapters, but skip over any scenes that are too spicy for your liking (you'll know when you reach them).

However, I do recommend reading the last five paragraphs of Allies, as there are some key details for the rest of the book! Sorry I can't be more specific with page numbers, but depending on the format you are reading this in, I don't want to accidentally give readers the wrong pages to stop or start at.

Table of Contents

Prologue

Sitting comfortably in his chair by the fireplace, George watched as his grandchildren played a game of draughts. He could see their little minds working to outwit one another. Twins, at eight years of age, Aevah and Jacob got along well but were quite competitive. From experience, he knew the fighting would begin as soon as one realised the other was winning. With their bedtime approaching, George, wanting to skip the arguments tonight, called it time, much to their dismay.

"Aevah, Jacob, come along now. Time for bed."

"Oh, but Grandpa, we aren't the least bit tired!" Aevah exclaimed.

"And in the middle of a game," Jacob protested.

Both children looked up at him with wide-eyed smiles. They give the impression of being so sweet and innocent with their glowing faces, but both had a twinkle in their emerald green eyes that said they had a mischievous streak to match.

"Well, in that case, keep playing, but you'll miss one of my famous bedtime stories."

"Story?" Both children jumped up excitedly and dashed to the open fireplace to sit by their grandpa's feet, eager faces beaming up at him.

With a joyful expression, George sat in his chair, chuckling as he easily swayed his dear grandchildren, who looked up at him with anticipation.

"Let me tell you the tale of the most powerful crystal in all the land. This story has been passed down through the ages and continues to be shared to this day. It was told long ago that one of the greatest kings ruled the land. His name was King Henry, and all loved him in his kingdom. He took care of his people and his land, but he didn't do it alone. No, he had help. Help from a magical crystal."

"Like the one in our castle," Aevah interrupted.

"The same," George replied before he continued.

"An exceptionally rare crystal with a unique ability lived in the highest tower inside the castle. You see, this crystal not only harnesses energy from the sun but also connects with a person's soul.

"With this bond, the crystal sends its power far across the land, spreading positive energy to all, but that wasn't all. On the first day of spring each year at sunrise, the divine spirit herself would appear and bless the land once more. The country would celebrate in her honour with feasts and danced well into the night. And with the blessing came another year of bountiful harvests across the land."

"Is she real Grandpa? The divine spirit?" Aevah sat up straight, eager to hear his response.

"Once upon a time, she was very real. She has been absent for some time, and no one has seen her in over a century. Hopefully, she'll return soon and bring blessings to this land again."

"Oh, I hope she does," Aevah exclaimed, interrupting her grandpa again. "I would love to meet her!"

"Shh! I'm trying to listen." Glaring at his sister, annoyed, Jacob turned back to their grandpa just as he felt a push on his arm, almost knocking him over.

George raised his voice slightly, drawing their attention back to him.

"Now, where was I? Oh yes, King Henry. He possessed a gentle soul, and his spirit shone through the crystal. With his lands thriving and his people content, the King ruled over a kingdom filled with happiness."

"What happens if a person's bad?" Jacob asked his grandpa with a look of fear in his eyes.

"Then the crystal would mirror their mind. A ruler with an icy heart filled with greed would emit those energies into the crystal itself. Over time, these energies would spread across the land, causing hatred and greed among its people."

Both children gasped in horror. George quickly glanced over at the twins before continuing.

"The divine spirit made sure every ruler knew the consequences of greed and hatred, sharing both her knowledge and power with them. For generations, there was peace until King Henry's son, Garth, came along. Garth was banished and was told never to return. With a heart filled with darkness, the land would fall into disarray. King Henry placed his only daughter, Mary, as the heir to the throne. As Garth left, he told his father he would seek his revenge, wanting the power of the crystal and the throne for himself. And revenge came."

"What happened!?" Both children leaned forward onto their knees, their hands on their grandpa's legs, as they waited in anticipation.

"After Garth dyed his hair black with coal soot, he snuck into the castle dressed as a servant. He had made his way into the castle with ease while carrying a basket of fresh fruits. No one looked twice at him, assuming he was just a kitchen hand. Instead of going to the kitchen, he took a detour to the dungeons, where his men were hidden behind a secret wall. They lay in wait for Garth to lead them into battle. He greeted them before leading the way into the castle he once called home. They snuck through the servant's passageways as silent as mice, trying not to be seen."

"Oh, this is scary!" Aevah mumbled with a glimmer of nervousness in her little eyes. "Did they get caught?"

"No," said George with a faint smile and then explained. "Garth and his men continued their silent trip into the castle until they reached the hallway they were looking for. At the end of it was a simple wooden door. Two guards stood watch in front of it. Garth channelled his power and after releasing it, one of the wall hangings crashed to the ground at the end of the hall. The two guards turned instinctively to their left, drawing their swords. This was their fatal mistake. Before they knew what was going on, two of Garth's men came up behind the guards and killed them."

"No! Not the guards. How did he kill them?" asked Jacob.

"With his sword."

"Yes, but how?" Jacob was jumping around energetically with an imaginary sword, pretending to attack Aevah. "Did he stab them or cut off an arm?"

"Oh, it's too graphic to tell you, my boy," replied George, and quickly continued with his slightly less violent version of the story. "Let's just stick to who killed them and how his men hid the bodies."

"Garth opened the door, his men dragging the heavy bodies through, leaving them at the foot of the stairs. By the time someone found their bodies, it would be too late. Garth sprinted to the top of the staircase, his men right behind. With fifty loyal and strong men by his side, Garth prepared himself and his troops. As he opened the next door, they raised their swords and held their shields in defence. With a loud battle cry, Garth and his men charged into the next corridor. The king's guards came to meet them, swords ready in the defence position. Three guards were facing his fifty. He knew they were no match for them, but the narrow corridor made it difficult to move around. Garth realised more of the king's guards would soon be on their way, so he needed to be careful about how they attacked."

"Does this story have a happy ending, Grandpa?" asked Aevah with worry in her voice. "These poor guards are not faring well, and Garth is the bad guy!"

"Keep listening and you tell me. Now, these three guards would defend to the death and with not much space to swing swords, a good defence could prove difficult to get past. After all, these men are the king's guards. They are the best of the best and know every trick in the book. Four of Garth's men moved into position, ready to attack, with four more ready to replace them in an instant. In pairs of two, alternating their attacks, Garth's men worked on breaking the king's guards' defence, trying to find a weakness in their position. Back and forth, the men moved, alternating between pairs at a relentless pace until the first guard went down with a sword straight through the abdomen."

"Oh, no!" Jacob cried out in fear.

"Once the first went down, the other two were easy pickings, with space opening to allow Garth's four men to circle the two remaining guards. Four against two, it was mere minutes before the other two guards lay dead beside the first. Garth led his men to the end of the hallway, then around the corner to a much wider one with several doors, each leading to various rooms. At the end of this hallway was the last door that would take him to the tower he so desperately wanted to reach. To get there though, Garth needed to get past the king's guards that lined the hallway."

"Yes! More guards to protect the crystal!" Jacob yelled excitedly.

"They will stop him!" Aevah enthusiastically joined in.

"Maybe," said George before he resumed. "Twenty guards stood in rows of five, preventing Garth and his men from passing. Garth knew it wouldn't be long before more reinforcements joined the guards. With the element of surprise on their side, he raised his sword high and called out, 'Charge!' Loud and clear, his men heard his order and in agreement stormed towards their foes.

"The king's guards remained steadfast, refusing to budge as they expected the imminent collision. The clash of the two groups resulted in a cacophony of swords colliding as each side relentlessly attacked, searching for an opportunity to strike the exposed bodies of the men. Amidst the chaos, the king's guards kept their stern posture, keeping their shields strong and standing in unison without faltering. Their orders were to stand firm until reinforcements arrived, and they followed them without hesitation. Despite the skill of the king's guards, they were no match. Garth's men outnumbered them. With half of the other guards injured or dead, Garth broke free from the ranks and made it to the foot of the tower with two of his men close behind."

"No!" Both children shouted as they looked at their grandpa with terrified expressions.

George gave them a comforting look and continued telling the story. "Free from the fray, Garth came to a halt at the next door, turning the handle apprehensively and opening it wide before entering a dark circular room. The last man behind him closed the door with a thud, plunging the room into semidarkness. Directly in front of the three men was the start of a spiral staircase. Candles sporadically lined the walls. Garth, leading the way to the top of the tower, sprung up the stairs two at a time, eager to reach the top. He came to a standstill outside the last door. His heart raced in anticipation and eagerness at what was finally within his reach. Silence filled the air as his boots echoed on the hard floor."

"What happened next? Did he steal the crystal?" Aevah's eyes bulged with worry.

"No, surely the guards caught him and wrestled him to the ground, saving the kingdom!" Jacob mimicked wrestling an imaginary Garth to the ground as George and Aevah watched.

"Not quite right for either of you," answered George, with a hint of intrigue in his voice. "Although your ending would have been fun to watch, Jacob. Alas, Garth and his men walked into the room, coming to a standstill in awe at their surroundings. The spacious, sphere-shaped room greeted visitors with a high-rise glass ceiling that reached high into the sky, allowing the warm sunlight to filter through and illuminate the sparkling crystal. Four exquisite tapestries adorned the pristine white walls, each accompanied by a graceful arched window that offered glimpses of the outside world. In the middle of the room stood a pristine circular stand crafted from gleaming white marble. Placed in the centre, a regal golden holder rested a sparkling crystal radiating power. Delicate golden vines entwined around the crystal. The air carried a faint scent of purity, mingling with the subtle fragrance of the marble. Garth found his father waiting with three of his men on the opposite side of the table."

"Oh! The King will stop him!" Jacob exclaimed.

George, with a slight smile, continued with the story, not giving Jacob a hint of what might happen. "Both men looked at each other. The King, with sorrow in his eyes, stared at Garth, who only had pure smugness in his eyes. Neither of them spoke. Raising their swords, they came together with a clash of metal on metal. The dance for the kingdom had begun.

"Their men fought beside them, each determined to have their leader victorious, battling for power. As the fight waged on around them, father and son were oblivious to their surroundings, so focused on one another. Both men were skilled, matching each other's moves strike for strike. Then Garth made a mistake. Overconfident in himself, he misjudged his father's next move, raising his arm and allowing his father's sword to slice the skin open. The cut was not deep enough to be life-threatening but enough for Garth to take a step back, wide-eyed as blood seeped from the wound."

George took a moment to sip his drink, his voice becoming horse from the story. The twins were looking at him with curiosity on their little faces, eager to hear more, but a hint of sleepiness hid behind their half-closed eyes. He resumed, wondering if they could hold out until the end.

"The injured Garth, for the first time, heard the cries of the surrounding men and seeing one of his own down, doubt crept into his mind. As the panic rose in him, he did the only thing left at his disposal. He held out his hand to the crystal and began channelling its power. The King, too, began drawing the power, seeking to keep hold of the crystal's allegiance. The two men positioned themselves at opposite sides of the table, eyes focused on the crystal itself. Their hands stretched out to the crystal, and swords were forgotten on the ground. They visibly strained against the sheer will of the other for control. The King's face was crimson, with a bulging vein on his forehead. Garth, with bloodshot eyes, laughed manically at what was happening. Although the King had a bond with the crystal, his son, through pure strength, was trying to force his will over his father's connection. It appeared Garth had the edge as they struggled on, a battle of wills trying to control the crystal's power.

"With so much power being drawn at once in such a small space, a bright blue flash left the crystal with ripples of energy, lifting everyone in the room and throwing them backwards into the surrounding walls. With the flash came the echo of a voice saying, 'The land will be no more.' Then utter silence."

Both children gasped. "Who was the voice? What happened to everyone?"

"Let's find out," said George, shrugging his shoulders. "With the room immersed with silence, out came the King's daughter, Mary, from behind a tapestry.

"She moved through her surroundings, looking for the owner of the voice. Whoever the voice belonged to was no longer in the room. Everyone else lay still. The sight of her motionless father lying on the floor compelled her to rush to his side. Blood gushed out of the wound on the back of his head. The force propelled him into the wall, resulting in a deadly split in his head and an instant demise. In a state of panic, she couldn't accept he was gone and vigorously shook his lifeless body while crying out, 'Father!', desperately attempting to revive him.

"With no response, she cradled his head in her lap, weeping uncontrollably, unable to comprehend his death. The sound of voices in the distance began creeping into Mary's mind. As they got closer, her subconscious began tugging at her thoughts, pulling her from her state of mourning. With the voices getting louder, panic flared within her. All the guards remained motionless, but the voices from below grew louder and more distinct. A wave of fear washed over her as she glanced around in fright. Her heart and mind froze in shock at what she saw lying on the ground. Three crystal shards. As she picked them up, it was clear there should have been four pieces. As the voices grew louder, Mary jumped up in fright, before slipping back into her hiding place behind the tapestry, tightly clutching the crystals."

By now, the twins were lying on the floor, their inquisitive eyes still fixed on George, fighting the urge to sleep.

"Did she get away, the princess?" Aevah asked as a yawn escaped.

"She did," George answered. "Mary saw her brother's men enter the room and ran away with a few loyal companions. As time passed and winter came and went, the land underwent a drastic change. It started on the first day of spring when no divine spirit came to bless the land. The land fell into disarray. With spring well in the air, crops that should've been sprouting were instead not growing. As spring rolled into summer, then autumn, the people were becoming irritable as hunger set in across the land.

"With no food, thieving was abundant, and the death toll increased as the paupers of the land went hungry, and the rich took what little there was for themselves. Unable to watch the chaos unfold across her home any longer, the princess held the bonding ceremony herself. In connecting her spirit to the three crystal shards, she hoped to bring peace to the land once more. Thankfully, the divine spirit heard her plea and appeared one last time. The divine spirit blessed the three shards and Mary herself. However, she warned Mary even though the ceremony was complete, the crystal's power was diminished. The land would never be as it once was. The divine spirit instructed Mary to hide each fragment of the crystal far away, ensuring that it would never be put back together.

"Separated, the true power of the crystal couldn't fall into evil hands once more. Mary heeded the divine spirit's advice. With the aid of her companions, they travelled to three corners of the land, burying each shard. Mary used the power she held to hide them away. With her spirit linked to the shards, the land began flourishing once more. The crops that had struggled were growing in abundance, plants were spreading across the land like wildfire, and wildlife that had been struggling to survive was replenishing the land. Yet, something in the air had altered, a change that hadn't existed prior. Like something had broken. The princess decided never to return to the castle. Knowing her brother's ill intentions for them, staying away seemed the safer option. Instead, she remained in hiding with those few friends who had left with her. They alone knew the whereabouts of the shards, and for generations, have kept the secret in the hope no one will try to reunite them for evil once more."

George chuckled yet again, seeing both children sleeping soundly where they lay. One by one, he picked them up and tucked them into their beds. With an ache in his back, he began stretching. As he heard his back crack, he stopped, posture right again as a lightness swooped through him. He didn't feel old, but his body was feeling worse for wear, especially after a day of trying to keep up with Aevah and Jacob.

He slouched into the armchair by the fire, watching the flames dance in front of him. George thought about the tale he had just told the twins. A tale to them but the truth for him. How much longer were the crystal shards safe? The air was thick with uncertainty. Something or someone was coming. George, not knowing what was to come, could only keep watch and hope when the time came, he would be ready.

Chapter 1

Betrayal

The autumn skies were cloudy over the kingdom of Ethos. As late afternoon set in, a cool chill descended throughout the city of Carraton, the home of the royal family. Deep within the castle walls, King James and his wife Cecilia were getting dressed for dinner with his sister, Elinor. This was a special occasion, as they hadn't spoken to Elinor in over four years. Ever since he became king, their relationship fractured. Elinor became someone he didn't recognise. Gone was the older sister who used to care for him and shared stolen treats from the kitchen when they were denied dessert. The woman who remained, was bitter and jaded, as she hadn't been given the throne.

While James grieved their father's death, Elinor attempted a coup, seeking the support of her father's lords to become queen. The lords were loyal to his father and him. They dismissed her actions as mere theatrics and supported his claim to the throne. On the day of the coronation, Elinor left without a word to the city of Adlington. James had hoped that, with time, she would return to the kingdom she once loved and accept their father's wishes.

During Elinor's infrequent visits that initial year, though, her animosity towards him and his family was clear in every glance and every word she uttered. Her presence alone sent a chill down his spine, her eyes holding a coldness in them that when she looked at him, disdain curled her lips. It pained him to see what she had become. The once radiant princess, with fire in her eyes, is now a ball of anger holding resentment in her heart, turning every interaction into a battle of wills. During her last visit, even James couldn't pretend and make excuses for her anymore.

"Elinor no more! I won't tolerate the disrespect you show not only myself but my family. I love you, but it's time to set your grief aside, to heal and find peace within yourself," he exclaimed, his voice trembling with emotion.

Her eyes blazed with fury, and her fists clenched as if ready for a fight. "Set aside my grief! Brother, I don't hold grief in my heart. What I hold is anger at watching you play king."

"You need to let this go! Father chose me for a reason, and you need to honour his wishes like everyone else."

"Damn, his wishes! You are a weak and foolish king with no right to rule this land. You're nothing but a stain on our family's honour, and I will cherish the day you fall into oblivion."

"Enough! I'm done with you, Elinor. Leave and don't come back or so help me. I'll lock you up right now as a traitor to the crown." Although his voice was restrained, his tone was like ice, and his eyes burned with fury. Without a word, she stormed out of the room, leaving behind a trail of shattered glass.

The memory still haunted him to that day. Elinor left, with no visits or correspondence since. He reached out a couple of years ago, hoping to mend broken bridges, but he heard nothing back. As much as it pained him, he accepted that until Elinor could let her anger and resentment go, their relationship would remain fractured, thanks to the barriers built up around her heart. James was pleasantly surprised when he received a letter from his sister a month ago. The letter stated that she acknowledged her mistake, was in a better place now, and wished to visit him to apologise for her past transgressions. Excited to reconnect with his sister, he made arrangements for her to visit. He hoped this would be a chance for them to clear the air.

As he got ready for their dinner, James stood in front of the full-length mahogany mirror in the corner of their room, admiring his reflection. He wore a dark blue velvet tunic, embroidered with silver threads around the cuffs and neckline. Black pants and fine leather ankle boots completed the look. The only problem he had was his unruly chocolate-brown hair. He tried running his fingers through, pushing the tousled strands away from his face. He had inherited his hair from his father, the late King Frederick, along with his blue eyes and fair skin. While he didn't inherit any physical resemblance from his mother, his father always assured him he carried her kind nature — be it animals or people, tending to a fallen baby bird or giving out food to the hungry.

Despite his appreciation for the traits he inherited from his mother, he longed for her hair in moments like this. Perfect straight hair. Much more manageable than what he was dealing with right then. He turned his head, trying to see the tweaking strands that were out of place in the back.

"The way you keep staring at yourself, anyone would think you were vain." Cecilia's voice broke his reverie, prompting him to face her. Her arms encircled his waist as she looked up at him with a playful smile.

"And yet, you married me." He embraced her tightly, kissing her deeply as warmth and affection washed over him.

"Ew, do you have to kiss?" James chuckled as he faced his children, who were walking into their room without a care in the world. It would seem they had evaded their nanny once again since she wasn't with them. Twins, they were fortunate to be blessed by the spirit with a boy and a girl, who had grown into quite independent yet troublesome nine-year-olds.

"Well, Aevah, how many times do I need to remind you to knock first?"

"At least one more time," Aevah answered wittily.

"You look beautiful, Mama."

"Why thank you, Jacob. Now, why are you two not in your rooms?" Just as Cecilia walked them towards the door, their nanny came bustling in, flustered.

"I'm so sorry, Your Majesty, they once again disappeared when I turned my back." Cecilia handed them over.

"They do that sometimes." She looked them in the eyes, "Behave, and off to bed." Placing a kiss atop their heads, she bid them goodnight and turned to face James again. Flicking his fingers, James used his power to close the door – no more interruptions.

"Now, where were we?" As James continued to watch her, a rush of emotions surged through his body. As his gaze met hers, a shiver ran down his spine, sending tingles of electricity throughout his entire being. Her enchanting green eyes held a magnetic pull with their playful glint.

The golden gown she wore accentuated every curve of her body, highlighting her graceful movements as she glided across the room towards him. James ran his fingers through her auburn curls that cascaded down her back, framing her face like a halo. He leaned in and gave her a gentle kiss before his fingers brushed against her soft olive skin.

Taking his hand, Cecilia looked into his eyes. "Ready?"

The words jogged his memory, and a knot formed in his stomach. "Yes, to dinner." The thought of seeing Elinor filled him with nervous trepidation.

Cecilia sensed his apprehension and gripped his hand tighter. "It'll be fine, my love. Try not to worry. She's here to make amends, not to start a war."

"You're right. This dinner is about reuniting as a family. It's a joyous occasion. Let's celebrate."

The King and queen strolled through the grand hallways of the castle. The magnificent castle was a bustle of movement, as workers moved diligently through their daily duties. They exchanged candles, swept the floors, and transported important documents on elegant silver trays. Just ahead, a mishap occurred as a worker accidentally dropped his tray, causing a cascade of scattered documents. James swiftly moved to help the young man, stooping to help them gather the papers.

A warm smile adorned his face, offering reassurance to the startled young man. "No need to worry. It happens to the best of us."

"Thank you, Your Majesty."

As they continued, the intricate tapestries adorning the walls seemed to come to life, illuminated by the soft glow of lanterns. The air filled with the rich, tantalising aroma of succulent roasted pheasant, permeating every corner of the halls. As they neared the dining hall, his mind drifted to thoughts of his sister. He hoped this dinner would mend their relationship. Her letter spoke of reconnecting and starting afresh, but his mind kept replaying their last conversation. Unsure of what could transpire behind these doors, James braced himself and entered the dining hall, Cecilia right by his side.

Elinor was already there, waiting. When she saw them, she rose from her chair and crossed the room to meet them. Elinor was as tall as James, with the same chocolate brown hair that cascaded down her back in loose waves. She also had the same piercing blue eyes that drew you in and searched deep into your very soul. She wore a pear-green dress, making her eyes stand out more than usual. The tension in James disappeared at the warm smile on Elinor's face, relief flooding through his body. They greeted each other with an affectionate hug. James beamed, his face radiant with happiness, as Elinor and Cecilia embraced each other too.

"It's delightful to have you here again, Elinor. We all have missed your presence," James said with true happiness in his voice.

"Yes," Cecilia added, "the children have missed you just as much. They'll be bursting with joy to see you again."

"And I them. I'm sure they have grown since my last visit. And thank you for welcoming me back with open arms. I know I've caused you both grief in the past."

"The past is in the past, dear sister. Let's move forward and start anew. Nothing beats a family dinner to celebrate new beginnings."

James gestured towards the exquisitely set table, adorned with glistening silverware. The two women seated themselves and joined him in a toast. As they raised their glasses, each had a smile on their faces before the murmur of conversation began. They dined on succulent roasted pheasant with an array of freshly harvested vegetables, enticing their taste buds. Afterwards, they indulged in several desserts, including the Queen's beloved honey cakes, all washed down with some delicious fruit wine.

An indescribable sense of comfort settled over James. It felt like time had unfolded, taking him back to the carefree days of their youth. Stories poured out effortlessly as they reminisced about their past. Meanwhile, the encroaching darkness outside reminded them of the present. Night had arrived, and sadness tinted James's heart. He longed to prolong this moment, to extend the sense of familiarity. Yet, he knew that the night had its plans, so they bid farewell to the remnants of their childhood memories.

"Thank you for dinner, James and Cecilia. It was wonderful."

"You're welcome. It's always lovely to have you visit. I hope you'll stay for a while," James said.

"Yes, it would be wonderful to have you stay."

"I plan to stay for a few weeks. You'll get to enjoy my company for a while. If it's possible, I would like to go to a room and rest. The journey here was tiring, and it's taking a toll on me."

"But of course," Cecilia said as she rose from the table.

"We have prepared a room for you. I do hope you'll be comfortable. I'll show you and send one of our ladies up to help you."

James's eyes filled with gratitude at the news as they stood up from the table.

He watched the two women as they left and finished his drink. He then headed down to his study to look over a few documents before turning in for the night. Something always demanded his attention. Being King was difficult, but he did the best he could. Upon reaching his study, James entered and headed over to his desk, sinking into the cushioned chair. The study itself was a vast room, filled with the rich scent of aged books. One wall was adorned with shelves upon shelves of leather-bound books, their spines worn and weathered. The most impressive piece in the room, though, was the giant map of the world, spanning across one wall. Its vibrant colours and intricate details drew in the beholder, making them see a vast world ready to be explored. By the third wall, a crackling fireplace emanated warmth, its dancing flames casting a cosy glow around the room. Two inviting armchairs sat before it, their plush cushions beckoning him to relax and unwind.

In front of the giant map sat James's desk. It loomed large, constructed from rich cherry mahogany. A layer of black leather covered the top, with an indented circle on the far right to hold his ink pot. Next to it lay a beautiful white feathered quill from a swan. Turning in his chair, he faced the map. His eyes drifted to his own country. A small but significant country named Ethos. They were well-known for their skills in farming, mining, and fishing, which they used to trade with other countries for rich spices, gems, and exotic foods that were difficult to grow locally.

The country was a nation of kind, hardworking people James was proud to rule. They were like family to him, and he tried his best to help the many who still lived in poverty. He found a balance between firmness and understanding when enforcing the rules. Instead of punishing the hungry for stealing, he shared food from his kitchen with them and opened a food bank where people could donate food for the less fortunate. James, with his mind on his people, turned towards his desk. There were proposals from Lord Woodlock seeking his direction in trade agreements with other countries. It was becoming difficult to reach an agreement with Artea. Focused on his work, he picked up his quill and began signing documents. He was thankful he had such a good clerk who combed through them, ranking them by importance for him.

An hour later, James stood up and his body was tight after being hunched over for so long. He stretched until he heard a cracking sound in his back. As a lightness swept over his body, he headed over to his armchair and sat down. Flames danced low in the fire. James stood up and added a log to the dying fire to revive the embers before getting comfortable. He moved the logs around with the poker until the flames rose once more, engulfing the new log.

James settled back into the plush armchair, sinking into its comfort. He reached for his bottle of scotch and poured himself a generous amount. The amber liquid swirling around the glass reflected the flickering flames. Glass to his lips, he inhaled the rich, woody aroma, savouring the scent before taking a sip. Warmth enveloped his mouth, spreading a sense of satisfaction as he swallowed, a content smile gracing his lips.

Regardless of their past, James felt overjoyed in his heart that Elinor came to visit. He missed her presence within the castle and was looking forward to spending time together, riding horses through the open fields, and challenging her to a game or two of chess. She won often in the past, but he had become quite good of late. It would also allow his children to become closer to their aunt. The soft spot he held for his sister felt like a gentle warmth spreading through his chest. The memory of their shared laughter embedded into his very essence, leaving an everlasting impression of affection. Alongside that warmth, a bittersweet ache tugged at his heart.

James couldn't ignore the weight of her past transgressions. Within him, a conflict brewed between unconditional love and the undeniable truth. Despite it all, he couldn't help but forgive her. He recognised the complexities of her character, the layers that made her who she was. Their father's death played a part in her behaviour, grief clouding her thoughts and judgement. It just took her time to come to terms with the past and move forward.

Their relationship going onwards wouldn't be easy. However, he was prepared to embrace the challenges, driven by the unwavering love he held in his heart and the memories they shared. As a child, he looked up to Elinor, since she was the oldest. He missed those childhood days playing games in the courtyard. He enjoyed following her around the castle on her many adventures. Ever since he could remember, Elinor had a great love for exploration and was incredibly outgoing.

He was much more cautious and followed the rules. The mere thought of getting into trouble made him shake as a child. This kept him from Elinor's crazier adventures. James's thoughts brought him back to the present. He got up, knowing he would fall asleep in that armchair all night. It had become too comfortable with age. Reluctantly, he returned to his desk. While reading through the proposals again, he heard the echo of commotion coming from the hallways outside the study. He put down the quill and stood up, making his way to the hallway. Just as he reached the door, a guard came in with blood flowing from a wound on his side.

"My King, we're under attack! Rebels are inside the castle. They're heading straight towards us."

Adrenaline surged through his veins. When James reached for his belt to retrieve his sword, he realised it was in his chambers, as he had left it there before dinner. Panic crept into his mind. The guard gasped desperately for air with eyes wild with urgency. Blood stained the carpet. He could hear the clash of weapons and anguished cries, growing louder with each passing second. To protect the king, the guard returned to the fight, only to be stabbed by another guard. The traitor guard effortlessly retrieved his sword from the fallen guard, manoeuvred around the body, and entered the room. Ten more guards with unfamiliar faces followed suit.

Each wore the same armour as James's men, complete with the family emblem of a wolf's head. Their attire was the same striking black and red. These men, though, weren't his guards because he knew all his men's faces. They were his comrades, brothers in arms, who he had shared a drink with, and who stood by his side in his first year as king.

Panic formed in his mind. Who was attacking? Where were his family, and were his people ok?

"Who are you?" James asked anxiously. "You're not my guards."

In an attack formation, the unidentified guards stood motionless, swords drawn, watching his every move.

"Get out of my way. My family and people need me!" He shouted as he struggled to push past the men, but they blocked his path, aggressively shoving him backwards to where he initially stood.

"I'm sorry, but we can't let you leave until ordered otherwise," said one of the unknown guards.

"Ordered by who? As your king, I demand you let me pass or face the consequences of disobeying a direct order."

The guards continued to ignore him. Infuriated, and with no sword to defend himself, James resorted to the only other weapon at his disposal. Eyes closed to focus his mind, he tried to channel the power. He waited for the familiar tingling sensation as magic seeped into his veins. This time, nothing happened. Panic crept into his already turbulent mind as he tried again. No power came forth. Nothing. Not even a trace of it in his bones. Something was wrong.

How could his power be gone? Had the divine spirit somehow abandoned him and stripped him of his power?

No, he was letting his mind run away with him. Someone had tampered with his access to the power. There were two ways to limit a person's power: being cut off by the priestesses or using a magic blocker. The magic blocker was a tasteless powder that could be easily mixed with any food or beverage. Once ingested, it would strip off a person's defences, leaving them powerless for at least the next twelve hours. The person wouldn't notice this until they tried to channel their powers, just like the situation he found himself in.

"Who sent you?" James asked again. "Why are you here? What do you want?"

None of his questions received a response. Frustration etched his face as he paced the room. The magic blocker challenged his perception of reality. James no longer felt safe or knew who to trust. This was unsettling, leaving him feeling sick to his core. His mind churned with distrust and confusion. He yearned for a sword to seize command, but the motionless guards, armed and resolute, remained unyielding. He needed to escape the room, but fighting the guards was unwise. They were likely to harm him if he tried to pass. The question of who used the magic blocker on him echoed through his thoughts. They knew him, knew him well to pull off what they were doing. As he paced back and forth, his mind raced, searching for a way to outsmart his captors. Sweat trickled down his temple as he scanned the room for any escape route. Eyes locked on the fireplace, the guards, sensing his intentions, lunged forward, their eyes gleaming with malice. Their heavy boots thudded against the cold stone floor, closing in on him with every passing second. But he refused to back down.

James swung out with his fists, striking several of the guards. Blood spurted from a guard's broken nose before three of them were on top of him, holding him down. He tried with all his strength to get them off him. They slammed him face-first onto the hard ground floor. His nose shattered on impact. Pain clouded his senses as the guards relentlessly kicked and struck him while he lay on the floor, groaning. Satisfied he wouldn't get up soon, the guards stepped back, this time forming a circle around him. He pushed through agonising pain, sat up and clutched his ribs. Utterly broken, physically and mentally, James felt powerless. Thoughts swirled at just how this could have happened.

No one could penetrate the castle walls without being seen, but they had. An impossible feat unless they were already inside. Denial cursed through his bones as he tried to come up with any other possibility than the one he was thinking of. The only difference between tonight and any other night was his recent visitor. He had been a fool to think his only sister wanted to make amends. Despite knowing it in his heart, James's heart and mind battled with each other as he struggled to accept it. His sister had betrayed him. One small glimmer of hope remained, only to be shattered when she entered the room. Their eyes locked, a silent understanding passing between them.

"Hello, little brother."

Chapter 2

Confusion

James's blood boiled as he stared at her standing there with a smirk on her face. He stood up with every ounce of strength he could muster, defying the agony that threatened to bring him to his knees. A newfound determination overshadowed the pain he felt, fuelling his willpower to face her head-on. He held her gaze, his eyes burning with a fiery intensity that matched the rage building inside him.

"Elinor. What. Is. The. Meaning. Of. This?"

His breath came out in heavy, ragged gasps, pain and anger interjecting one another as he focused on staying upright. The normally calm and composed James was now a hurricane of emotions. His body quivered uncontrollably. The physical and emotional pain in his body threatened to tear him apart from the inside out.

"I'm taking my throne, and my place as queen." Elinor finally answered.

"Queen? Father chose me to be his successor after he passed. It was his decree."

"The decree of a tired old man who thought I wasn't ready."

"You weren't!" James shouted, "And still aren't! If this is your response."

"My response!" Elinor snickered at his remark, before hissing at him, "I'm the eldest!"

"That's not how it works, and you know it!"

"No, you're right. How it works is you came along, the perfect prince, who charmed his way to the throne." Elinor marked her responses on her fingers. "I gave him years of council. I made his court the powerhouse it became. I— "

James laughed. The sheer ignorance and arrogance of the woman before him were palpable. His laughter only seemed to infuriate her even more. He couldn't help it, though. She was delusional to think they would have given her the throne.

"You think it's funny? You only got the throne because you're a man!"

"Madness, damn you, Elinor! If that's what you really think, then you're an even bigger fool than I thought!" James shook his head at the pure ignorance of his sister right then.

"How dare you!"

"Oh, I dare. Let's get one thing straight, my dear sister. They didn't pass you over as queen because you're a woman. You lost your chance when you valued power over people."

"Power is how you keep your throne. Our father would have lost his kingdom long ago without it."

"If you believe that, then there is no hope for you." He tilted his head slightly, bewildered at how his sister just couldn't see the problem here.

"Oh, there's plenty of hope for me. You, however, have run out."

"Who are you? You're not the sister I once knew." James couldn't believe what he was hearing. Reasoning with her was futile. He knew she liked power, but never dreamed she would pull a stunt like this.

Betray her family just for a crown. He thought the attempted coup when their father died was a reaction to his death. Clearly, he was mistaken. He had misjudged her, blinded by his childhood memories of the sweet, caring sister he loved. Before him stood a cruel, vindictive woman with no morals. He saw it now in her eyes, the power-hungry maniac who would do anything for power. He had been a fool and was likely to pay for his stupidity with his life.

"This is the sister you never wanted to see," said Elinor, almost proud of her actions.

"No, the sister I knew and loved existed once, only to be replaced by the evil, scheming psychopath in front of me," James responded with blatant honesty.

Elinor stormed a few steps forward and slapped him across the face, whipping his head to the side. Cheek stinging, he turned to face her. Eye to eye, he stared her down with judgement on his face.

James glared at her as he spoke with venom in his voice. "Are you willing to spill my blood? Because that's the only way to the throne for you. And I won't stand by while you destroy everything our father built."

Elinor laughed hysterically.

"Do you think you have a choice? Look at you. Broken. Helpless. At my mercy." Elinor began inching towards him again, until their bodies were almost touching, and whispered in his ear.

"There's no stopping me, James. I've already won!"

A chilling silence filled the room. He felt a dagger piercing through his chest with ruthless precision before he could respond. The pain was immediate and excruciating as if the world had momentarily frozen in time. The sharp blade found its mark, plunging straight into his heart, stealing his breath, and sealing his fate in an instant. Blood spilt from the wound, staining his shirt in a deep crimson red, as life ebbed away with every beat of his weakening heart.

The pain was radiating through his body, but the physical pain couldn't match the devastation ripping him apart from his sister's betrayal. Unable to stand anymore, he collapsed to the ground as he fought for his life. Ragged breaths fell from his mouth as he tried in vain to speak. He could feel his body growing colder with every drop of blood that escaped. The pain was unbearable. Every breath felt like a thousand knives piercing through his chest. He knew the end was almost upon him and his thoughts ran wild. Memories of his beloved family, his loyal friends, and the kingdom he had dedicated his life to protecting flooded his thoughts, each one stabbing at his weakening resolve.

In his mind, he could see Cecilia's beautiful caring eyes and heard the sweet sound of their beloved twins' giggles. *What would their fate be?* His vision blurred into shadows, thoughts becoming muddled. He looked ahead with tears in his eyes and felt the last ounce of life drain from his body. With a smile, to a presence only he could see, he bid farewell to life as the hands of death took him away.

***

Elinor watched as the life drained out of James's body. No matter how long she stared at him, no sympathy stirred within her as his lifeless body, frozen in time, mirrored the emptiness in her. Her voice, a shard of ice cleaving the silence, she addressed her guards.

"Begin searching the castle. Bring Cecilia to me in the royal hall. Watch the twins' room. Spread the word that the traitor king is dead."

"Yes, my Lady."

Elinor turned to her most trusted advisor and knight, Adrian.

"Dispose of the body and secure the castle. Kill anyone you deem a threat."

Adrian bowed his head and set off to carry out her orders as Elinor walked into the hallway, another guard heading towards her.

"You, with me."

Elinor ignored those around her while striding through the hallways. Upon reaching the throne room, she strode straight in as the guards by the doors opened them for her. Taken aback, Elinor came to a complete standstill, staring in awe at the grandness of the room. With its high-rise ceilings, it exuded an air of grandeur. White marble pillars, adorned with delicate lines of gold, shimmered in the soft glow of the chandeliers above, casting a warm, golden hue throughout the space. The expansive room stretched out before her, its polished floors gleaming beneath her feet, as a deep purple runner led from the entrance, guiding your gaze to the imposing throne. Pristine white walls were decorated with fine golden flowers. When caught in the light, they glistened reminiscent of specks of gold. As you looked up, the ceiling revealed its mark of opulence, with golden embellishments that shone brightly as stars, giving the impression of reaching for the divine spirit herself.

And there, at the heart of it all, sat the majestic throne. Its presence commanded attention, a symbol of power and authority that was undeniable. The white leather upholstery was accentuated by a gilded outline that caught your eye. The house crest of a wolf's head, intricately embroidered in gold, stood proudly on the backrest of the throne, signifying the strength and nobility of the ruling family. A raised platform of steps served as the throne's perch, elevating its occupant into the seat of power. It exuded a sense of regality, a seat befitting a monarch. Elinor's heart raced with exhilaration as she maintained her composed appearance. A mischievous glint in her eyes gave away the excitement that coursed through her. Confident strides carried her towards the throne across the plush runner beneath her feet. Her stature was imbued with purpose and determination.

A rush of anticipation surged through her as she approached the majestic throne, causing her breath to quicken. Her senses heightened, allowing her to absorb every detail of the opulent surroundings. The room came alive, with the shimmering stars and the golden flowers glinting with newfound significance. It was as if the very walls whispered secrets of the power that now belonged to her. A smug smile curved her lips, a subtle display of triumph as she relished in the moment. The air crackled with an electric energy, and she could almost taste the sweet victory that lingered in the atmosphere. Her rightful place on the throne beckoned her, a magnetic force drawing her closer.

When she sat down, she felt the cool, soft material of the regal seat against her skin. A surge of satisfaction washed over her, sending shivers down her spine. The throne felt like her deepest desires had come true. Elinor's gaze swept along the grand hall before her as she settled into her newfound position. Visions materialised before her eyes. She saw herself commanding armies, making crucial decisions, and ruling her country on her terms. The glimmers of envy from those who once doubted her fuelled her determination to prove herself. Namely, the lords who hadn't backed her all those years ago. The day they laughed at her plans would haunt them for the rest of their lives.

All her life, she had to contend with the thoughts of men, doubting her abilities and dismissing her ideas. But she persevered, tirelessly working to improve herself secretly. She had learned the true strength of the shards and built a network of supporters who believed in her vision of power. She had refused to let the lords, James, and her father's scepticism of her abilities define her. With each passing year, her resolve had grown stronger. She had crafted her strategies, predicting every obstacle she would face that day. Determined to succeed, with the support of her loyal followers, she saw herself on the throne. And here she was. Their laughter had inflamed her determination, and now she stood victorious, ready to reshape the world in her image. Success was the best form of revenge. Lost in this reverie, Elinor was brought back to reality as one of her guards entered the room. With a sharp inhale, she rose from the throne, the physical sensation of power still lingering in her every movement. Her regal poise remained intact as she met the guard's gaze.

"My Lady, Cecilia, is being escorted to you as we speak. The children are safe, sleeping in their room."

Elinor pondered for a moment, digesting the guard's words.

"Keep watching them. If they wake up, let me know. I'll deal with Cecilia myself once they bring her to me," Elinor ordered and dismissed him with a wave of her hand.

"Yes, my Lady."

"Get up! Come on. Let's go!"

A pair of rough hands firmly grabbed the confused queen out of her bed and half dragged, half carried her through her chambers. Not knowing who these men were, or what was going on, Cecilia, in an attempt to escape their grip, began kicking her legs and tried pulling her arms free.

"Let me go! Who are you? I'm the Queen of Ethos and I demand you release me!"

With no response, she attempted to use her power on them, as feeble as it may be. When she tried, though, no magic formed. Panicking, she resisted her captors even harder, again kicking her legs towards their bodies and trying to pull away from their grasp. She fought against the strength of the two men. One guard gave her a sharp punch in the gut, which made her double over in pain. Cecilia stopped struggling and let them continue to march her through the castle.

Her heart throbbed in her chest, each pulse echoing her desperation for help. The sharp pain in her gut intensified with every step she took, making it difficult for her to keep up. Cecilia's body trembled with a mix of fear and anger coursing through her veins. Hope inside her grew stronger that her husband and the guards would appear any moment to save her. As they moved through the hallways, though, it became obvious things were amiss. The once familiar surroundings now seemed distorted, like a twisted nightmare. The air was heavy with tension, suffocating her with its palpable malevolence.

Occasionally, Cecilia caught glimpses of other guards patrolling the corridors. Their cold, emotionless eyes bore into her, sending shivers down her spine. These men weren't merely following orders, they relished in the torment they were inflicting upon those who had the misfortune to cross their path. Men engaged in sword-to-sword combat, and their cries of anguish filled the air while the walls echoed with the sound. Fear clung to the innocent as workers and children tried to flee the surrounding terror.

Two of Cecilia's guards moved towards her, and as they turned a corner, determination was etched on their faces. One of the two men who held her released her and began fighting her guards. Sparks ignited in the air as the steel clashed. The second captor sensed his man might lose. He let go of her as well and joined the fray.

Left alone, Cecilia seized the opportunity. She turned around and fled back down the hallway, trying to reach the secret passage without being seen. Without looking back, she ran for her life, trying to block out the yelling of the men behind her. She stopped in front of a tapestry that hung flush against the wall. She slipped behind it and tried the door, but it wouldn't open. Outrage rose in her at the thought of being taken by those men again. Tears streamed down her face as the fear took over. She yanked and pulled at the doorknob, twisting and turning it every way she could. Panic rising, she threw her body towards the door when she turned the doorknob one last time. It opened. Just as she stepped beyond the threshold and the sense of safety loomed ahead, a firm hand grabbed her shoulder, and a sharp pain radiated through her head as something hard struck her. Vision blurring, she would have collapsed had the firm hands not kept her upright.

Defeat seeped in her mind as she knew her captors had her once more. Vision clearing, sorrow came next as she saw what happened to her guards lying dead on the floor. The sound of distant screams and the smell of smoke trickled through the castle walls, further inflaming Cecilia's unease. It was as if the very foundation of the once majestic castle had crumbled, mirroring the chaos that now consumed her life.

Unanswered questions swirled in her mind, tormenting her with their relentless grip. *Who were these men? Why had they targeted her home? And what twisted purpose did they serve?* With each step she took, she silently prayed to the divine spirit for her husband's arrival, desperately clinging to the hope that he would come to her rescue.

They took Cecilia to the royal hall and upon entering, a small spark of hope ignited inside her as she looked around, half expecting James or her guards to be there. Instead, all she saw was Elinor sitting there on the throne. Seeing that, Cecilia became furious. With rage flooding her heart, she stood up, wanting nothing more than to reach Elinor, but her vision blurred again, causing her to sway just as the guards grabbed her arms, stopping her attempt. She took in a deep breath and frantically began pulling her arms away, struggling until they had her in a vice-like grip she couldn't escape from. Unable to get free, she glared at Elinor with nothing but hatred in her eyes and venom in her heart.

"What have you done? Where's my family?" Cecilia asked with a hardened expression. "Where are Aevah and Jacob? Where's James?"

"So many questions."

Elinor rose from the throne and moved towards Cecilia in an arrogant stride and circled her with a wicked glint in her eye. Looking her dead in the eye and without a hint of sorrow, Elinor served Cecilia with a blow that shattered her entire existence.

"They are all dead."

The words didn't register in Cecilia's mind. She couldn't comprehend what she was hearing.

"Dead. What do you mean, dead?"

"They are dead. A knife to the heart did the job wonderfully."

Her mind tried to explain something her heart couldn't understand. She stared into Elinor's eyes, waiting for the punch line, that this was some sick joke. But it wasn't. The look on Elinor's face told her all she needed to know.

Cecilia collapsed to her knees when her mind and heart caught up with what she had heard. Eyes wide with shock, she let out a piercing cry that penetrated everyone's soul to hear her agonising pain score through her. The thought of her family being gone sliced deep into her very core, and she couldn't stop the tears from flowing.

Blind rage surged through Cecilia's body as she got up with her sight on Elinor. Her body trembling, and the only thought running through her mind was to cause her uncontrollable harm. Every fibre of her being yearned to inflict the same excruciating agony that now consumed her. Even as she tried to lunge towards Elinor, she was again pulled back by the same guards that had just restrained her.

"Lock her in the cells."

With that same arrogant smirk, Elinor just stood there, watching.

Cecilia began kicking and screaming once more, trying to reach Elinor as the guards restrained her with an iron grip. She fought against their hold, thrashing, and twisting to break free. Unmoved by her resistance, the guards dragged her away.

As a last act of defiance to the woman she once loved as her own sister, she cursed, "You'll pay for this Elinor, mark my words. One day, vengeance will come. When you least expect it. I'll be there to plunge the dagger into your heart!" Pulled from Elinor's line of sight, Cecilia broke, falling back into hysterical crying.

Once they reached the cells, the guards pushed Cecilia into one of the cramped lower ones. Exceedingly small, the air was frigid, and the only light came from the narrow slits in the imposing steel door. A feeble light shone through, barely illuminating the barren room around her. The guards locked the door, sealing her off from the outside world. A pungent smell emitted around the cell. It reeked of animals and sweat, with the unmistakable odour of aged straw coming from the pile against the wall that was a bed. A solitary bucket in the corner awaited her, serving as her only means of relieving herself. Rooted to where she stood, Cecilia couldn't believe what was happening. Her entire world had just been turned upside down. So many emotions running through her mind. She felt numb until she thought about Elinor.

That name brought about a surge of anger and hatred that made her whole body shake all over again. Elinor was going to pay. That much Cecilia was sure of, even if it killed her to do so. She wouldn't let her destroy her family without making her suffer the way she was now. Cecilia's mind replayed the memories of James and the twins, sending her into the depths of despair. The images flickered in her consciousness, accompanied by a deep ache in her heart. Her heart felt as though it had shattered into countless fragments, each one stabbing at her from the inside. Slumped to the ground, Cecilia curled herself up into a ball. The deafening scream that left her body pierced her very soul to hear it. Primal and raw, the air filled with the anguished cries that only a mother's shattered soul could produce. With every scream, her voice grew hoarse, yet she couldn't stop. She had to release the pain, the anguish, and the unbearable weight of her reality. The tears flowed endlessly, soaking her cheeks and dampening her tattered clothing. Exhaustion took over, her cries became muffled, drowned in the sea of sorrow that engulfed her, ebbing away into silence. Only then did sleep finally come.

Chapter 3

The Takeover

Lloyd and Victoria Roberts stepped into the throne room. Victoria, with a face adorned with freckles and thick, curly red hair, walked alongside Lloyd, who wore short blonde hair and had a distinctive crooked nose. Their demeanour exuded an air of arrogance as if they were a couple to be reckoned with. Draped in vibrant silks, their garments shimmered in the sunlight, casting a radiant glow. Embracing the distinctive Belmont tradition of standing out, they embodied a culture that celebrated extravagance. Their bodies were embellished with glistening gold jewellery and vivid, colourful attire, a testament to their desire for vibrant self-expression. Their eyes, ever watchful, darted around relentlessly, capturing every detail of their surroundings. Though their bodies remained still, they absorbed the energy of the place, sensing opportunities to exploit. These two played a crucial role in Elinor's rise to power. As the first family to support her, they were instrumental in devising her takeover plan. Elinor watched as they both moved towards her, Victoria's face filled with glee, Lloyd utterly indifferent. Upon reaching the steps, they greeted her with a bow and curtsy.

"Congratulations, Your Highness! Everything is going to plan," said Lloyd with obvious contentment in his voice.

"Indeed. How are your tasks progressing?" asked Elinor with a slight smile.

"Guards are rounding up those who are likely to cause trouble as we speak," Lloyd answered.

"Excellent. Keep me informed, and if you see Adrian, tell him to come to me."

"Of course, Your Highness." Both responded in unison as they turned to leave.

While Elinor watched them leave, she thought about how much they had helped her over the years. Even with all the aid from them, Elinor wasn't naïve, she knew their loyalty only stretched as far as her success did. From Belmont, they came out of the womb as trained liars and swindlers. Deceitfulness ran in their blood. Cutthroat and lawless, they would rob their own if it gave them greater prestige and control. That's why she chose them to help her. She could rely on them to get the job done, no questions asked as long as they didn't betray her along the way. Although, she was confident they wouldn't. She held everything they wanted. Elevated positions and titles were the key factors. Without her support, they were stuck as small city dwellers, with limited opportunities for advancement. They saw her as their ticket out of mediocrity and into a world of wealth and influence. The Belmont natives had always been cunning but lacked the prestige to advance into the big leagues. This guaranteed her they had no unpleasant surprises in store for her.

Elinor departed the opulent throne room, her curiosity driving her to stay informed of the ongoing coup. Meticulously planned, nothing was going to be left to chance. Despite the late hour, the hallways were filled with a symphony of activity. The echoes of footsteps and hushed conversations resonated through the air. She observed the restless commotion of her people as she made her way through the castle, their urgency clear in their hurried movements. The scent of anticipation mingled with the familiar aroma of cleaning supplies, which invaded her senses. What were usually diligent workers in the hallways were now replaced by Elinor's guards. Tension engulfed the corridors as they gathered those crucial to the castle's operations, seeking to discern their loyalties. Anyone opposed to her rule would be identified and removed, paving the way for a new era under her reign as queen. Elinor realised just how much time had passed since she had explored the castle. As she walked through the ancient hallways, they echoed back memories of her childhood, sharing secrets long forgotten until now.

She delighted in wandering through the labyrinthine hallways, her curious fingertips traced the intricate patterns etched into the walls leading to secret passageways hidden across the castle. Her favourite was the one going to the kitchens. With each step, a tantalising aroma wafted through the air, beckoning her closer. Her heart danced with anticipation as she followed the hidden passage, feeling the cool stone beneath her fingertips, taking her to the enchanting realm of the bustling kitchens. Elinor found the bench holding the delicious treats, remembering all the times she snuck in when no one was looking. Each night, the cook hid a delectable cake or pastry just for her underneath a faded towel, knowing who was helping themselves to her baked goods. A silent agreement between them.

Despite her efforts, she couldn't convince James to accompany her. He always steered clear of trouble. This castle, with its hidden treasures and secret indulgences, had been her sanctuary as a child. And now, as she walked through its hallowed hallways once again, she couldn't help but feel a childlike joy resurface within her. As she got older, Elinor revelled in her classes, taking everything in. She was passionate about politics, and she developed a hunger for it. Her strength lay in debates with those around her. She loved challenging others while forming her ideas about how the world worked. Eventually, she joined her father's council, and always advised him, even if he didn't always follow it.

James engaged in politics reluctantly, driven more by a sense of duty than genuine passion. He favoured his time in the yard, where he dedicated himself to daily training with both sword and arrow. This left her shocked when her father declared him the heir to the throne. Bitterness consumed her. All her hard work was wasted. What angered her most was the fact that James appeared oblivious to what Elinor was experiencing. A rift he couldn't see formed, and her plan for revenge took shape. She refused to be a pawn in the power game any longer, nor would she passively observe as James, an undeserving usurper, basked in the glory that rightfully belonged to her. She left the castle and moved to Adlington. Elinor had lost all desire to be around him or the court that betrayed her. Her communication with James was sparse. Over the years, he often wrote and extended invitations for her to visit, but she rarely replied.

Elinor returned a few times that first year when James insisted. It was easy enough to fake pleasantries for a week or two, keeping up appearances that helped keep her plans for the throne secret. Yet, a blowout with James resulted in her never returning. The pig-headed fool declared her a traitor to the crown. That gave her the fuel she needed to carry out her revenge. She would dismantle James's reign piece by piece, sowing seeds of doubt and discord among the courtiers who had once praised him. Operating discreetly, she aimed to expose his weaknesses, exploit his flaws, and witness his kingdom crumbling under the weight of his ignorance. The once innocent princess had transformed into a formidable force, her heart consumed by bitterness and her mind set on one goal – to bring James to his knees and seize the throne that was rightfully hers.

And that she did.

Seven long years later, the royal seat was hers. There was no one left to contend with, since her niece and nephew were in her clutches. With the first phase of her plan accomplished, the next objective was to bring together the four shards, to possess full control of the country. But one task at a time, she didn't want to get ahead of herself. Elinor could see that not too much had changed while walking through the grounds. Just the decor in some rooms, and an outdoor play area designed for her niece and nephew. In the great hall, a portrait of James hung on the wall, standing tall and proud. She needed to take it down and replace it with her own painting soon. Besides the portrait, that room was still the same. Tall windows lined the walls to let in natural light through the day. Taking up most of the space at the back of the hall was a large, rectangular, wooden table with an ash-grey finish, accompanied by twelve matching chairs.

The remaining part of the room was filled with dark wooden bench tables for the court to sit at during mealtimes and important meetings. At one end, a sizeable old-fashioned open fireplace set the tone. Around the hearth, charcoal-coloured bricks covered the area, with logs stacked within. When lit, the fire warmed up the entire space on those cold winter nights. This space was dear to her heart, where all realm debates and decisions occurred. She thrived in a male-dominated court. With each debate, her voice resonated with strength and conviction, cutting through the air like a sword. Her arguments were sharp, her logic impeccable, leaving no room for doubt. The lords would shift uncomfortably in their seats, their faces reflecting a mixture of surprise and begrudging admiration. Much like the time she questioned the tax on shipments they received from overseas, she surprised the men at the table with what she considered a fair agreement at the end of their discussion. The debates and decisions within these walls were battles against the oppressive patriarchy, and in this grand hall, she emerged victorious, leaving an indelible mark on the kingdom. With a knock at the door, Elinor turned as Victoria came through the doorway, returning with the news.

***

Adrian was a tall, stoic man in his late thirties. He had short brown hair and furrowed brows from his work as a knight of the kingdom. That day, his role had him aiding Elinor in securing her place on the throne. He was one of the first to follow her and intended to see her crowned queen.

He found the takeover to be going well. A lot of planning had gone into it, getting the logistics right, working with Elinor for years, and making sure everything was set before they arrived. He didn't like surprises and was very thorough in his work, leaving no stone unturned. No loose ends. He ensured the castle was in lockdown, and rode down to the city gates, making sure they were closed. A dreadful fate awaited anyone who disobeyed. He had to be careful with the city guards. Too many were quick to accept bribes and discretely slip people in and out unnoticed. The dread of a slow and torturous death made sure people obeyed orders, and his reputation in swordsmanship and on the battlefield was legendary. He had fought in a war between countries for the previous king, playing a crucial role in their triumph, which earned him his knighthood. Since then, he worked closely with the king, safeguarding the country until his passing.

Although Adrian was a knight, and well respected by most, James was the only one he hadn't got along with. Their personalities clashed along with their values. James prioritised taking care of the kingdom's people first and doing everything by the book. Adrian, however, ensured the job got done and protected the one on the throne, no matter the cost. Their conflicting ideologies often led to heated disagreements. James saw his approach as misplaced heroics ruled by an impulsive nature. Elinor, however, saw Adrian's nature as positive and kept him as her knight when her father passed. So, seven years ago, he had left the castle in Carraton with her, accompanied by a few ladies-in-waiting and a couple of loyal guards. Ever since securing their new residence in Adlington, he made it his home.

Back in the castle, one guard approached Adrian, as they told him of a fire inside. He swiftly moved through the hallways, heading to the source of the fire. The air had already become filled with smoke, which filled his lungs just as fast as he breathed. As he turned the corner, heat surrounded him, getting hotter with every step. Running now, he reached the children's chambers, their room ablaze as flames licked the walls, devouring everything in their path. Guards ran out of the room as more entered, pouring water on the rising flames. One guard soaked his shirt, shielding it against his face, and pushed himself through the smoke. Adrian couldn't do anything against the heat. Coughing through the smoke, he searched the room, fearing the worst for the young children. With no bodies to be found, he stumbled back into the hallway, gasping as he inhaled the cleaner air like his lungs had been starved. As his breathing steadied, he watched the fire lessen and the flames dwindling into nothing. The acrid scent of burnt wood and singed fabric lingered in the air, filling his nostrils.

With cautious steps, he entered the desolate chamber, feeling the heat radiate over him. The crunch of charred remnants beneath his boots echoed through the silence. The room now stood as nothing more than a smoky, charred space. Moving slowly and mindful of the damage, he carefully cleared debris out of his way. An empty silence enveloped everything. There were no bodies in sight.

The lingering question was: Where had they gone? No one had seen them leave, and with their father dead, and their mother in the cells, who had them?

Two nine-year-olds couldn't have vanished on their own, and if they were hiding, they were doing an exceptional job. He had most of the guards discreetly hunt for them and made his way to Elinor. She needed to know they had disappeared.

"What news do you have for me, Victoria?" asked Elinor while gesturing towards the seats at the table as she sat down.

"It's going well so far, Your Majesty," Victoria answered and continued with her report. "Most of the people seem rather scared and confused about what's happening. Therefore, everyone is currently being very cooperative, but I've placed a few of our ladies in amongst their workers to monitor them when I'm not there."

"Excellent, that's good to hear. How's Lloyd doing?"

"Not as well. There are a select few that have discredited your claim and are calling for a revolt. They have been removed and locked up at your request."

"I expected as much. They need to be watched."

As Victoria left to continue her work, she promised to keep an eye out for disruptions and to deal with them swiftly and quietly. Due to the late hour and progress being made, Elinor headed to her chambers to rest. Her guards were in control and would notify her of anything important. Her next task had to wait until morning, and she wanted to be alert.

On her way there, Adrian stopped her, appearing dishevelled and smelling of smoke. He explained about the fire and detailed the extensive search of the castle and its grounds, revealing that the twins were nowhere to be found. Tension gripped her upon learning the children were missing. Upon reaching her chambers, she sent Adrian to freshen up and rest, knowing her guards were searching for the children. Stepping inside her room, her mind kicked into overdrive as Elinor paced anxiously. They didn't know where the twins were, but they would soon find them. They were her leverage against Cecilia. Although Cecilia thought they were dead for now, they would be the perfect bargaining chip to keep Cecilia in her place if she stepped out of line. Meanwhile, her focus remained on the castle. Going over the steps in her mind again, she was determined to ensure her plan unfolded perfectly. There was no room for error.

She didn't want an uprising from the people. The kingdom adored her brother, but even the kindest kings had their skeletons. Or so the kingdom would soon find out. The people were well aware of the tale of the shattered crystal. They knew it to be true, and to join them together again would be fatal for the land. Although no one was around at the time of the breaking, plenty of stories and historical documentation told the story of events. With the shards hidden, no one person had complete control of their power like before.

Over the years, Elinor meticulously planted and constructed evidence against James. Individually subtle, each piece of evidence, on its own, wouldn't raise eyebrows. However, when presented together, it portrayed a king who had been searching for the crystals all this time. Soon, she would present this evidence to the lords. After this, she would address the city's people, painting her brother as the villain and herself as their saviour. With their support, she aimed to eliminate anyone in the castle opposing her, gradually tarnishing her brother's reputation. They would see her as the true ruler of the land. A meeting with the lords was scheduled for the following evening. Elinor anticipated that some lords, particularly those seeking more power, would readily align with her cause.

Once her brother's supporters were gathered, they would address the rest of the castle's people. This included the twins' nanny. She might be of use in finding out where they were. Until then, no one could enter or leave the castle or its grounds without her approval. Within a few days, the entire kingdom would know she was queen, and it would be official. A knock at the door distracted her thoughts, as one of her ladies-in-waiting arrived to help her get ready for bed. After changing into her nightgown and washing up, Elinor settled herself into bed for the night. Closing her eyes, she tried to get some sleep. She had a big day tomorrow.

***

The next day the sun rose, with a beautiful clear blue sky. The birds were singing in the trees, and Elinor could feel it was going to be a good day. She had all her meetings scheduled, but first, she had one other thing to attend to. She wanted to see Cecilia. This would greatly influence the direction she took. Despite knowing the probable result of the meeting, she had unanswered questions. These questions only Cecilia could answer. As her ladies arranged morning tea for her and Cecilia, she started getting dressed for the day. Once ready, she ordered a guard to fetch Cecilia.

"I intend to break her."

Chapter 4

Prisoner

Startled, Cecilia woke up during the night. Darkness consumed her and panic set in as she questioned where she was. Cold seeped through her body, and everything came flooding back. Her thoughts turned immediately to George and the twins, grief-stricken, her resolve crumbling into dust. The straw pierced her body from all angles as she drifted back into an unsettled sleep. Loud voices startled her in the morning, followed by the slam of the door against the hard brick wall. Heart pounding in her chest, she recoiled backwards at the sight of the two towering guards who stepped inside. The slam of the door reverberated in her ears, mingling with clinking metal. As one guard grasped her shoulders, she felt an intense pressure when his grip propelled her forward, pulling her away from the cold, prickly straw that had been her only comfort. Hauled to her feet, she stood upright as her body trembled with trepidation. The other gripped her hands firmly, locking them into unyielding handcuffs. The heavy restraints tugged at her delicate wrists, causing her body to lean forward. They barely gave her a moment to adjust to the weight before the guard behind her forced her forward, intensifying the overwhelming experience.

"Walk!" The guard grunted before pushing her again with even more force.

Cecilia stumbled forward. As she moved through the castle, people around her avoided her. Those who caught her eye looked shocked before averting their scrutiny and hurrying away. Cecilia's head dropped and her shoulders slumped in defeat. With nothing left, she followed the guards. They led her into Elinor's chambers. Her glare fell upon Elinor, who stood by the fire with a sweet, innocent smile on her face. That look could melt the heart of anyone. Just an innocent young woman, but she knew differently now. She was a murderous madwoman. The pounding of nerves began thumping within at the woman standing before her.

Poised to speak, she thought better of it and stepped back. She needed to stay calm and contain her hatred to the best she could. At that moment, Elinor had the upper hand. Cecilia knew she had no alternative and had to play by Elinor's rules.

"Cecilia, welcome. Please take a seat. I think it's time we had a friendly chat."

As Cecilia sat down in the chair Elinor gestured to, Elinor sat herself in the opposite one. Both women sat with eyes locked onto one another, while one servant poured the tea. Elinor with the same friendly smile but with eyes that held an evil, knowing glint to them. Cecilia's straight face was void of any emotion except her eyes. They were like pools of fire waiting to burn Elinor to the ground. Elinor lifted her cup to her lips and took a sip. Cecilia cautiously raised her cup and also took a sip, despite the handcuffs constraining her. Undoubtedly, a power play on Elinor's part. Cecilia, however, wouldn't give her the satisfaction of asking for them to be removed. Instead, she continued to sip at her tea. It tasted heavenly after a night in the cells. The hot liquid was coursing through her bones, warming her right down to her toes. Although her body was warm, her heart felt like ice as she looked at the woman sitting across from her.

A woman she once cared for is now a living nightmare she hated passionately. Thoughts flashed through Cecilia's mind about how she could kill Elinor without an ounce of remorse — strangling her with the very handcuffs around her wrists. A pillow over her face as she slept or poison in her food. Maybe a dagger straight through her heart, just like she had done to James. The possibilities were endless. Elinor finally spoke as she set down her tea.

"Tell me, where are the remaining three crystal shards hidden?"

Straight to the point, then. Cecilia now knew the reason she was still alive. "I don't know, and even if I did, you would be the last person I would tell."

"I see," Elinor said as she rose and walked across the room.

Her steps slowed, coming to a standstill directly behind Cecilia. The hairs on the back of her neck stood up. She felt Elinor's hands grip the back of her chair. Heart pounding, she stared straight ahead. Cecilia's eyes bulged as unbelievable pain coursed through her body. Her chest tightened as if an invisible weight pressed down on her. Every muscle tensed in her body like they were being pulled in different directions. The pain radiated from her core, spreading like wildfire through her limbs, causing them to tremble. Vision blurred, her eyes filling with tears that threatened to spill over. This unimaginable agony consumed her entire being, rendering her immobilised.

"I know you're lying. I know you know where they are." Elinor sneered. "Lucky for you, I don't need them right now. I have a kingdom to win over. Heed this warning though Cecilia, my dear, because I'll only say this once. The next time I ask you where they are, you'll tell me, or I. Will. Kill. You!"

In an instant, the pain was gone, but the effects still lingered, along with Elinor's warning.

Her body shook as the tears fell. The rawness of her emotions consumed her, leaving her feeling weak and drained. Her trembling hands grasped at her tattered dress, trying to find some resemblance of comfort. Rough hands gripped her once more, their fingers dug into her skin like thorny vines and they dragged her to her new chambers, hidden down a dimly lit corridor lined with cold stone walls. A stark contrast to the warmth and light she had once known. She just stood there with nothing left in her. A mere shell of the person she once was with vacant eyes that showed no emotion, as if someone had drained them along with her spirit. As one guard removed the cuffs around her wrists, words flowed from the man's mouth, but her brain couldn't register what he was saying. His words were lost in the vast void that had consumed her mind. Her thoughts were a jumbled mess, unable to process the reality of her situation. She remained frozen, lost in the depths of her despair, and unable to comprehend the world around her.

The guard left, and the heavy door closed behind him with a resounding thud. Silence enveloped her, magnifying the weight of her solitude. Time seemed to stand still as she remained motionless, her eyes unseeing, her mind grappling with the enormity of her circumstances. It took a while, but awareness gradually seeped back into Cecilia's consciousness. The realisation hit her that she was finally alone. The room, devoid of any personal touches or comforts, felt like a prison. With eyes closed, she took in a shaky breath and a flicker of determination ignited within her. Though broken and battered, Cecilia knew she had to find strength within herself. She refused to let the darkness consume her. Summoning every ounce of strength, she took a deliberate step forward, the sound of her footsteps echoing in the desolate chamber. Now was the time for resilience, to stand against Elinor, to avenge her family, and to survive by any means necessary.

Cecilia took in her surroundings, wanting to know what she was working with. The room was much smaller than her previous chambers, enclosing a solitary bed, a humble wash basin, a simple dresser, a compact wardrobe, and a lonely table accompanied by a chair. There were no windows to allow natural light in or a comforting fireplace to warm the space. Instead, she found herself surrounded by four bare walls, with no hidden passages. The perfect room to stop her from wandering around without someone being able to follow her, which was Elinor's plan. Although she had the freedom to move around the grounds, she would be constantly followed. Her every move would be scrutinised, and she wouldn't be trusted in Elinor's eyes. Elinor would know the second she did anything out of the ordinary. Despite Cecilia's firm resolve, she wouldn't let that vile, evil woman win, no matter what the cost or consequences.

Determined to escape, Cecilia examined her personal heirlooms in the room. Certain items of hers could be helpful in the long run. As Cecilia rummaged through the dresser, drawers, and table, she discovered a few of her dresses and belongings, including her brush and mirror. She felt a warm tingle at the small connection to her old life. It was strange that it felt like it was her old life already. So much had happened in such a short time. The life she lived was truly gone. And in its place, uncertainty and anguish had taken root.

Cecilia, feeling dirty from the night before, disposed of her nightgown and poured cool water into the washbowl on the dresser. First, she put her hands in the water, icy cold water surrounded her skin. She longed for warmth, so she tapped into her power and felt a surge of heat. Steam rising from the bowl, she opened the little brown box to her left and sniffed at each bottle before settling on the lavender extract, pouring a couple of drops into the steaming bowl of water, and placed the bottle back.

With her face over the bowl, she inhaled, letting the aroma of lavender seep into her body, relaxing her mind. After a few minutes of enjoying the warmth on her skin, she picked up a washcloth and washed down her body, trying to cleanse herself and wash away the recent nightmare. Once as clean as she could feel, she wrapped herself in a towel; the fabric absorbed the water droplets from her body and headed over to the wardrobe to choose an outfit to wear. She settled on a plain, long-sleeved green dress. No frills, just a standard fitted day dress and channelled to fasten it. She couldn't fasten the dress on her own otherwise. Connecting the fastening at the back was difficult without assistance. Despite not possessing great power, Cecilia could still perform simple tasks and channel energy without the need for a gemstone. It had taken a lot of practice and insistence from her husband, James, to learn the skill. But now she was grateful he had made a big fuss about it. Elinor wouldn't know when she channelled. This was vital when she didn't know who to trust.

Once dressed, Cecilia took a walk. She needed to know what had happened in her home. As soon as she left her room and began walking, the guard at her door followed her. As she roamed the hallways with her guard, she saw Elinor had made many changes already. Elinor's people filled the hallways, with many unfamiliar faces running errands and doing jobs that used to be done by her people. She still saw a few familiar faces, but most wouldn't meet her eye. This tugged at her heart. Unable to handle any more, Cecilia headed back to her room. Upon entering, she was startled at the sight of one of the young serving girls from the kitchens.

The young girl curtsied. "Beg you pardon me Lady, twas just dropin' off yer apron from Mistress Katelyn. She be thrilled ye offered t help in t kitchens on t morrow, an already has t jobs lined up fer yeh."

The young girl curtsied again and left. Puzzled, she picked up the kitchen apron and noticed a note sitting in the pocket. It read:

Lady Cecilia,

Once again, I thank you for offering your services in the kitchen. Please arrive on time tomorrow at sunup.

Kind regards, Mistress Katelyn.

Brows furrowed, Cecilia sat down on her bed and read the letter to herself once more. Since she hadn't spoken to Mistress Katelyn or shown any interest in the kitchens, she assumed that was a gesture of friendship. The only way she could offer it, without causing a stir in the castle. She noticed the tray to her right on her dresser, with some bread, cheese, ham, and fruit, along with a pitcher of fresh water. A warm smile spread across her face and as she took a bite of cheese, she felt the weight of the note in her pocket, reminding her someone was on her side.

***

After a few hours of sleep, Adrian woke up early, eager to see how things were going. They were expecting several lords that day, including those from the far west. It had been weeks since Elinor had invited them to a celebration that no lord could resist attending. This ensured the timely arrival of important individuals for the meeting, creating anticipation. He expected to talk to the city guards to let the arriving lords in, but he figured they wouldn't arrive until after lunch.

If Adrian's assumption held true, many individuals who had embarked on arduous journeys would have arrived just outside the city a few days earlier. They would have taken up residence in the luxurious manors owned by the local lords, affording them the chance to engage in conversations and speculate about the current situation, while immersing themselves in thrilling hunting expeditions and drinks. Before meeting with Elinor, Adrian wandered around the castle, absorbing the atmosphere and gauging the progress of events. An air of uneasiness enveloped everything as people awoke to an uncertain new day. The word spread that Elinor would address everyone before lunch. She planned to ease everyone's minds by sharing the details of recent events. The challenging part lay in convincing the people of the King's betrayal. If Elinor could persuade them, she would gain complete control over the Kingdom. If not, it was uncertain what would happen next.

After making sure everything was in order, he provided a list to the guards who were allowed to enter. His stomach grumbled, reminding him to eat. Heading to the kitchen, Adrian found it bustling with activity, filled with the aroma of freshly baked bread and sizzling bacon. The clattering of pots and pans echoed through the air, accompanied by the occasional laughter and chatter of the kitchen staff. A silence fell upon his arrival. The air grew tense as their movements became rigid. As he sat down to eat, the cook's welcoming smile brought a sense of comfort. The plate before him held a hearty serving of scrambled eggs, crispy bacon, and buttered toast. It was satisfying, filling his empty stomach and easing the pangs of hunger. A glass of cool water quenched his thirst. Adrian listened to the conversations of the workers. Their tone carried a mixture of weariness and concern from the cheerful tones before his arrival. Aware of the negative effect his presence had on the atmosphere, he finished his meal, thanked the cook for her hospitality, and left.

Adrian set off to find Elinor and share his conclusions but found her heading towards Cecilia to speak to her. He took the opportunity to explore the castle and its grounds. It had been years since he had been there, so he wanted to see if any changes had been made during his absence. An intriguing castle, it had weathered stone walls hiding secrets within. A labyrinth of hidden passages waited to be found, some well-known to him thanks to Elinor, while others remained elusive, missing from the official maps. With a spring in his step, he began his search.

Adrian's fingers traced the ancient tapestries along the walls, the map in his hands guiding him to the entrances of these hidden pathways, ensuring their existence and functionality. As he walked, he discovered secret doorways disguised as ordinary objects, trick candle holders, when twisted just right, revealing hidden alcoves. Fake stones, meticulously placed, concealed secret corridors. And his personal favourite, an obscure switch hidden within the bookcase, opened a passage to unknown depths.

The dungeon held the greatest intrigue for him. As Adrian descended into its depths, a chilling breeze sent shivers down his spine. The stone walls seemed to whisper secrets as he ran his fingers along their rough surface. And there, tucked away in a corner, he found it. A wall so masterfully crafted that it deceived the eye. It appeared to be a solid rock, yet it held a secret. Curiosity beckoned him closer, and as he pressed his back against the wall, a rush of excitement coursed through him. He turned his head, and there it lay – a hidden bend in the wall, barely noticeable to the untrained eye. The narrow passageway promised adventure and mystery. According to Elinor, it would lead him to a wider corridor, guiding him to a hidden cave nestled in the hills near the enchanting woods. The thought of venturing into the unknown stirred a sense of wonder within him. The castle was a treasure trove of hidden secrets, waiting to be discovered, and he was determined to uncover them all, but not today. Aware of the time and his duties, he left the dungeons and headed back to Elinor's rooms. She was inside, preparing for her speech to those in the castle and its grounds, knowing many in the city would also come to hear her speak.

Chapter 5

Two Journeys

"There you are, Adrian. It's almost time to go. What news do you have?"

Adrian brought her up to speed, but they both knew Elinor's speech would be the biggest factor in what happens next. She needed to be persuasive and believable in her speech to the court. Depending on how they respond to her would determine what could happen next. If they believed her, they would welcome her reign as queen. If not, a revolt would likely happen. Her fate lay in the hands of the people. She felt prepared but nervous, careful not to show any signs of weakness which could derail her plan.

Having Adrian there by her side was a tremendous help. He put her at ease. Over the years, he had been her greatest supporter and was always there when she needed him. As she glanced towards him, he gave her a gentle nod, his eyes reflected an unwavering belief in her abilities. That silent encouragement bolstered her resolve, allowing her to push past her nerves and embrace her role of queen. As she turned, a subtle squeeze of her hand filled her with a calm reassurance. Upon reaching the podium, the expectant crowd awaited her. The atmosphere was thick with confusion and scepticism. The weight of their expectations weighed heavily on her, but she knew that this was her only chance to convince them of her brother's betrayal.

A spokesman addressed the people, announcing her arrival, and handed the proceedings over to Elinor. With one last glance at Adrian, their eyes locking, Elinor drew upon the strength he had always provided. Taking a deep breath, she began her speech with a clear and steady voice, her words carefully chosen to sway the hearts and minds of those before her.

"Today, I address you, the people of Carraton, with a great sadness in my heart."

The crowd began murmuring and whispering upon hearing this. Once it subsided, she resumed speaking, and the crowd fell silent again.

"An elaborate scheme has been in the making, with one person intending to unite the four crystal shards and use their power for their own gain. The person in question, I'm aggrieved to say, was my dear brother James. Your beloved King."

Elinor's statement caused the crowd to erupt into a cacophony of voices, their anger was palpable in the heated atmosphere. Shouts and accusations filled the space, blended with murmurs of disbelief and outrage. With a commanding gesture, she raised her hand, demanding silence. Tension hung in the air as the crowd pressed closer, eager to catch every word from Elinor's lips. Exactly as she desired.

"I understand this is a tremendous shock to you all, as it was to me, but know I speak the truth. Listen to my words, then speak your hearts after. I too was blind to his betrayal."

The crowd leaned in closer to hear her next words. A mix of distrust and confusion on their faces, heavy with tension and uncertainty.

"It started last spring when I noticed more patrol men being sent near my home. Their reasoning was to patrol against bandits and thieves. This struck me as odd. Our borders were safe, with my own men regularly patrolling it. They hadn't found any unusual activity involving either. I sent my men out on their patrols to keep watch over the king's men. What they discovered was men from these walls, summoned by our king, searching the country. And you have most probably guessed what they were searching for."

Elinor let her words hang in the air, watching as more faces turned from undeniable faith in their King to wondering if what she said was true. Not enough yet though to secure her reign. Indecision clouded many faces and the risk of being branded a usurper loomed if they were given too much time to deliberate. So, she continued sharing the king's betrayal, presenting fabricated correspondences between the king and his patrolmen. These exposed his clandestine plans to reunite the shards and rule the country with infinite power.

The people were listening. Through the devastated looks, slumped shoulders, and a taste of betrayal in the air, she saw it. She had them and continued to drive her truth home, putting on a mock sadness at how she had to kill James after he had revealed his plan to her. The crowd dropped their heads in sadness, with many crying, yet none calling treason. She informed everyone of her intentions to stay for a while and handle matters at the castle. The crowd mentioned Queen Cecilia, along with suggestions on how to handle her. After calling for her head, they seemed satisfied with her imprisonment. As she concluded her speech, a person in the crowd raised a question about the twins.

She had hoped to sidestep that conversation until she knew where they were. The plan involved leveraging them to get the necessary information from Cecilia. Then all three were to die once those crystals were in her hands. With their whereabouts unknown, and their deaths imminent, she continued with the deceit.

"I have grave news about my wonderful niece and nephew," she began. "A horrible fire erupted near their rooms, entrapping them inside. Unable to escape, they perished in the flames. I had hoped not to tell you this yet, as it is painful to say out loud."

Elinor cried into her handkerchief, forced tears trickling down her face. The people followed suit, mourning the memory of the beautiful royal twins.

"They'll be missed and will forever be in all our hearts. Know they are with the divine spirit herself now and we'll not forget them. I invite you all to join me tonight to gaze at the night sky and remember Jacob and Aevah."

Elinor bowed her head, seemingly thinking of the twins, yet her heart pounded in her chest, waiting for the collective response that would determine the path ahead. Aware that her destiny rested in the hands of these people, she maintained a façade of sadness, nerves still lingering beneath. She silently prayed to the divine spirit that her words had resonated, that they believed her, and that the people would choose to stand by her side. The courtyard bore the weight of sadness at her words. Elinor excused herself, leaving the people to process the information. Despite the heavy atmosphere, she believed that it had gone well. She headed back to her chambers with Adrian close behind her. As she left, a solitary woman watched, her mind clouded with doubt.

***

Adrian, Victoria, and Lloyd gathered in the adjoining room connected to Elinor's chambers to speak with her. They delved into the sequence of events that unfolded in the preceding days. Reports from Elinor's people posted around the castle had arrived that morning, displaying many positive results. Those who opposed her were under close surveillance. At present, she was reluctant to remove any more individuals, for fear of a negative impression if they continue to disappear. Instead, their efforts were directed towards discrediting the circulating rumours.

Victoria was working with the women in the castle and had an afternoon tea prepared for the head women in charge. She planned to learn about their roles and how to better their working environments.

She had also spoken to the twins' nanny on her whereabouts during their disappearance. Unfortunately, that was a dead end, as the nanny returned to her own quarters after putting the children to bed. Her alibi checked out. Victoria relieved her of her duties as a nanny and sent her to Mistress Fleur to find a new role for the time being. They didn't want to risk sending her away from the castle.

In terms of the men, Adrian was on his way to a training session after that meeting with the trainees affiliated with the Kingdom. The officers and soldiers of the kingdom respected him. It wouldn't be too difficult to convince those men to follow him. Lloyd's role was to meet with the castle's keepers, including those in bookkeeping, and the clerk. He needed to assess the castle's current financial situation and see what needed to happen going forward. It would take time to build trust will all the members of the castle, but they had to start somewhere. With plans in motion, only one other topic was left to be discussed.

"So, do we know what Cecilia has been up to this morning?" Elinor began.

"I believe she left her chambers late morning and went back around lunch. Her guard was with her the whole time, and she didn't speak to anyone. Well, she greeted a few of them she knew, but they all looked down and walked away," Victoria replied.

"The speech you gave this morning seems to be working," Lloyd added.

"Yes, we'll need to keep watching her," said Victoria. "It's likely she'll try to escape at some point."

"True, but she could also draw out those loyal to her. That'll make it easier for us to remove those few obstacles," Lloyd responded.

"With any luck. Well, we have a lot to do, so let's get to it," Elinor announced as she rose. Lloyd bowed his head, and Victoria followed suit with a curtsy as they took their leave. Once they left, Adrian moved towards Elinor.

"How are you fairing? You're doing a lot yourself right now."

"I'm fine Adrian. You don't need to worry."

The look on his face said otherwise. Concern flickered in his eyes, along with that twitch in his jaw when he didn't believe her but was biting his tongue to not contradict her. It had always been like that with him. He went above and beyond his duty as her knight to protect her. Before he became her knight, they had almost become more, but working for her father stopped him from crossing that line. When her father died, he doubled down and became her knight, leaving his life behind to move to Adlington with her. His love for her was clear. He just wouldn't admit it to himself even now. So, they did this dance every so often, when it felt like he was going to say something, and finally cross that invisible line.

"I'll head down to the training yard, then. Send word if you need me."

As it turned out, today wasn't the day.

"I will. Thank you, Adrian." Elinor watched him leave, frustrated with him for never saying what was in his heart.

She had told him how she felt all those years ago and she had no intention of voicing those words again. With a desperate need to clear her head, Elinor set off for a walk around the grounds. Lost in her thoughts, she barely noticed the murmurs of conversation as she walked past people. While she moved through the castle on autopilot, she reached the training grounds, stopping at the sounds below. Not sure what brought her there, she stood atop the balcony, looking down onto the sunlit yard. Even from there, the smell of sweat carried upwards from the men still training intensely. The yard was expansive, it had abundant space for manoeuvres and boasted an impressive selection of training items to work with.

As she looked down, Elinor saw several young men with wooden swords engaged in intense drills. Split into two lines, one row was on the attack, the other on the defence.

The sound of swords clashing reverberated through the air, accompanied by the occasional grunt of exertion. Unaware of her presence, she watched the young men practice. Most seemed half decent for their age, but one student caught her eye. He was lightning quick, and on the attack, leaving the defender struggling to block his attacks. Blow after blow against his opponent, hitting its mark. Sweat dripped from his brow, but he wouldn't let up, the intensity in his eyes like a fire burning within. His wooden sword was an extension of himself, his strikes precisely leaving the defender on the back foot struggling to keep up. Movements became lethal, he predicted his opponent's every move before he made them. The defender faltered as his arm trembled, leaving him open to an onslaught of strikes one after the other, overwhelming him. With a thud, the defender's wooden sword fell to the ground, hands up in surrender. The attacker pointed his own to their throat until he heard the words, "I yield." The attacker and defender shook hands as Adrian walked towards them. Elinor forgot he was going to be there. Before he could notice her, she walked back down the path.

"Well, if it isn't the royal Princess."

Elinor froze in place. She knew that voice. Turning towards the voice, she realised she was correct and answered kindly. "Bradley, what hull have you crawled out of this time? Apparently, sailing the seas hasn't taught you any manners, if that's how you greet royalty."

Wearing a grin, he pushed himself off the wall and stood in front of her. Towering over her, he gazed down with a glint in his ocean-blue eyes, a demeanour well-suited for his line of work.

"Please forgive me, Your Highness. After months of sailing the seas, I find myself forgetting proper etiquette in such a prestigious company. Would you like me to curtsy, or is it bow? Or how about I get on my knees for you? I'm sure you would like that."

Elinor rolled her eyes. She had forgotten what an arrogant prick he could be. They had known each other since childhood, being that his father was a lord. They played together as children and were of the same age. Childhood games like hide and seek, spying on the court during meetings, and running away when someone headed their way. She could still hear their laughter and feel the pounding of her own heart during those close encounters. Back then, they spent all their time together when he visited. Despite always finding trouble, as friends, they looked out for each other.

As adults, their relationship was nothing more than being acquaintances. They had spent little time together since her move to Adlington. Any brief encounters were mere pleasantries during events they both attended.

Was he the same person she grew up with or had the passing of time transformed him into a stranger? Elinor wondered.

Till that day, his reputation had preceded him, with rumours swirling about his arrogance. If the way he spoke to her was anything to go by, she believed them.

"Oh, I would like that a lot. You, on your knees with your head placed on a chopping block. Now that's something I would enjoy."

"How I missed your witty banter, Elinor. I look forward to hearing what else that pretty mouth of yours comes up with." After bowing, he walked away while chuckling to himself.

That man was something else. If she was certain of anything, it was that neither of them resembled the sweet, innocent children she remembered. The sound of Adrian's voice filled the air, drawing the attention of the young men. A glance in his direction, and she remembered where she was going before Bradley's interruption. With her back stiff, Elinor strode off towards her chambers, her heart thudding in her chest. Anger and fascination coursed through her veins, manifesting fists clenched at her sides and her nails digging into her palms. Her brows furrowed with a determination to maintain composure. The conflicting emotions flushed her cheeks.

Upon reaching her chambers, Elinor pushed open the heavy wooden door, its creaking protesting the force of her entry. The room enveloped her in its familiar embrace, a sanctuary where she could gather her thoughts and compose herself before facing the lords. She walked towards the large window, the evening sun casting a warm glow on her face as she gazed out at the bustling courtyard below. Her reflection in the glass revealed a face still flushed with the remnants of anger and curiosity. Her eyes, usually sparkling with mischief, now held a glint of determination. The intensity of her emotions had brought out feelings she hadn't felt in a long time. Not even for Adrian.

Inhaling deeply, Elinor released the tension gripping her body, feeling her muscles relax as she let go of the inner turmoil. Refusing to let a man distract her thoughts, she focused her attention on the imminent meeting with the lords. Such matters demanded her undivided attention and strategic thinking. Reinvigorated, she turned away from the window and approached the large oak desk in the room's corner, where she gathered her papers. The coolness of the polished wood beneath her fingertips served as a grounding force, anchoring her back to the present. As she prepared for the meeting, thoughts of Bradley crept into her mind. Despite the annoyance, a part of her couldn't deny the intrigue he had sparked within her. She pushed those thoughts aside, determined to prove herself as a capable and shrewd leader during the impending meeting. Elinor diligently rehearsed her speech, keeping her mind sharp and her emotions in check. The success of the meeting was non-negotiable, and she was determined not to let anyone undermine her efforts.

Chapter 6

New Beginnings

Adrian thoroughly enjoyed his time in the training yard, despite it being on the smaller side. Designed for young recruits, it had everything they needed to train. The adjacent small armoury housed archery gear and a variety of swords, ranging from wooden replicas to authentic ones. A line of cloth dummies, bearing marks from sword and arrow punctures, ran along one side of the yard. Despite its size, the yard efficiently accommodated their training sessions. It served as an ideal space for drills, while more advanced activities, such as long-distance archery, horse riding, running exercises, and training drills, took place in the adjoining open field.

He had been watching the young recruits and paired them up. One working on defence, the other on the attack. He wanted to see what they could do and help them hone their skills. The art of the sword was in his blood, and teaching his knowledge came naturally to him. It helped that the young men were a determined bunch. One student had already caught his eye. A young man named Tom, and at seventeen years of age, he had potential, reminding Adrian of himself when he was younger. The same fearless attitude, consistently giving one hundred per cent in everything he tried, never stopping until his opponent went down. He would go far if he continued with his current work ethic.

"Okay lads, that's time. Take a break, then switch places. I'll be back in ten."

He headed over to the fence where the men's training officer, Tyler, stood watching. He was a tall, grey-haired man in his late fifties who was a little fuller around the waist than when he was younger. With impressive strength and swordsmanship, he was an excellent teacher to his trainees and well respected by them.

The city's soldiers were the best by far for a reason. Tyler often took personal trips around the nearby towns and villages to find new recruits. He had a knack for picking young boys who would become excellent soldiers. Or perhaps his training techniques were the key. Either way, very few who trained with him failed. Being that Tyler solely oversaw the new recruits and lived in a tiny house just outside the castle's boundary, he played no part in the events of the previous night. When questioned where his allegiance lay, he replied "to the Kingdom and whoever wears the crown", before going straight back to work. Adrian believed he meant what he said. Tyler enjoyed his work, but beyond training his recruits, he had little interest in what had happened after they finished. Once the recruits completed their training, Lieutenant Banes took charge, deciding their roles as soldiers, guards, watchmen, or potential knights. What happened next was determined by Banes. However, everything changed after the events of last night. The Lieutenant loyal to his king, laid down his life in service to the crown.

That left Adrian down a lieutenant, and he needed a replacement. He wanted to pick someone from Carraton that the men knew rather than a stranger. Aware of the complications that would arise if he took on the role himself, Adrian sought out Tyler's expertise to help him find someone suitable. Tyler knew all the men well, having trained a large per cent of them himself, so Adrian hoped he could give him the names of a few suitable replacements. Adrian suggested they talk, so Tyler led him to his office. As they sat down, they engaged in idle chitchat. The room layout revealed Tyler's efficiency. His compact workspace was uncluttered, with scrolls and books tucked away. The table he used as a desk held his current projects in a tidy arrangement. He utilised the small room well and created an atmosphere of productivity.

"So, we're down a lieutenant after last night's event," said Adrian, eager to get the conversation started.

"Indeed, and I guess you're here to find a replacement?" Tyler replied.

"I am, and I was hoping you would know of a few suitable candidates."

"Lucky for you, I already have someone in mind," said Tyler reassuringly. "A man by the name of Julian Wood. I'll have him sent for."

Adrian didn't know the man, but he trusted Tyler's judgement. While they waited, both men headed back to the training yard. At that point, they were back to training with their roles reversed. Adrian, while observing, took on the role of guiding the trainees, pointing out mistakes and offering tips to enhance their defence and attack techniques. The trainees wasted no time in implementing his advice, resulting in quicker and sharper movements. Those who struggled to keep up cried out at the sharp blows they received. As he neared the end of the line, Adrian saw a man entering the grounds who could only be Julian.

He walked with an air of confidence, striding across the yard. About mid-forties. He was of average height for a man from Carraton, with short brassy hair and eyes like a hawk. Tyler made it clear to Adrian that Julian was highly intelligent, never missed a single detail, and currently worked as a soldier. He had the experience and discipline to become a lieutenant, as well as ambition.

Stopping in front of the two men, Julian nodded to Tyler and Adrian, respectively. For a brief second, surprise glimmered in his eyes before his cool indifference returned. "I was told you requested to see me, sir."

"Not me but Sir Fellows here."

At that moment, Julian couldn't mask the look of surprise on his face.

"If you have a few minutes to spare, I have a proposition for you if you care to hear it?" Adrian gestured towards Tyler's office, leading the way. Once inside, he motioned to one chair and closed the door. "Drink?"

"No, thank you. I'm still on duty, sir."

"A wise choice. One I should follow." Adrian poured himself a glass of water from the pitcher on the table, and sat down, taking a sip. "So, a few changes are being made in the way of command here in Carraton."

"I noticed, sir. What does that have to do with me? Is it my loyalty, sir? I can assure you, I'm loyal to the crown sir, mark my words—"

"Relax Julian. You're not here to prove yourself. It's quite the opposite. Thanks to your loyalty, I have a proposition for you involving a new role, if you want it."

"A new role, sir? I'm intrigued. Tell me more."

"How would you like to be the new Lieutenant of Carraton?"

"Lieutenant? Me? You're joking, sir?"

"Not at all. I've spoken to Tyler, and he believes you're the most suitable man for the job. Should you want it?"

"Truly? Lieutenant! Of course, I want the job. I graciously accept this offer, sir."

Standing, Julian leaned across the table clasped Adrian's hand and shook it firmly, his face beaming with pride. "Thank you so much sir, it's an honour."

Amused by his excitement, Adrian smiled back and shook his hand just as firmly. "The honour is mine. You'll make a fine lieutenant, I'm sure. I'll inform the princess of your decision and make a formal announcement tomorrow. We'll speak later, so don't stray from the castle."

"Thank you, sir. It's an honour to be given such an opportunity. I will not go far and will be ready when you need me."

Buzzing with excitement, Julian walked out of the office. Adrian, satisfied with the progress, headed back out with Tyler to continue with training.

***

As the evening approached, Elinor felt the weariness from the day taking its toll. After having read her speech multiple times, she was confident she was well-prepared and simply wanted to get the final meeting over with. As she waited for the hour to tick by, she enjoyed a light snack and a glass of wine while Adrian brought her up to date with the day's events. Elinor was pleased with how well everything was going. Adrian left to arrange the announcement of the new lieutenant for the following morning, during which she would meet the soldier. She trusted Adrian's judgement to pick the right person and was eager to meet the individual whom she would be working with closely.

With time ticking by, Elinor got dressed with the help of her ladies. The room buzzed with soft chatter as they worked to put her outfit together. Once fully dressed, she stood before the mirror in awe of her reflection. The gown, a shimmering silver-grey, gracefully embraced her figure, accentuating her curves. A corset top gave the dress structure, while a long, flowing skirt added an air of elegance to her ensemble. The sleeves running to her wrists were soft against her skin. Her ladies finished the look with matching silver shoes and a statement necklace. When caught in the light, a white gold necklace adorned with sparkling diamonds would draw the attention of anyone who looked her way. With a spritz of perfume as the final touch, Elinor was ready physically. Her foot tapped anxiously under her skirts. Mentally, she replayed the times when she had been dismissed for her opinions, usually by her father in front of these very men. The snide remarks at her poor ideas. This time, she wanted it to be different. This time, it would indeed be different. She would make sure of it. The men would see her as more than just a woman with ideas, but as a force to be reckoned with.

Her eyes were fierce. She glanced one last time at her reflection, seeing a woman who exuded authority and strength, ready to command the room with her presence. Elinor straightened her posture. A surge of confidence washed over her, and strode down to the great hall, with the sweet smell of floral following her. She knew the lords would already be there, awaiting her arrival. Some waited for her to slip up and make a mistake, to seize the power for themselves, but she wouldn't let them. It had been too many years since a queen had sat on the throne. Many men still feared a woman in charge. They had become complacent about having a king.

A prevailing notion persisted that queens were ill-suited for leadership, given their emotional instability and the demands of raising children. While some may not have agreed with all of their king's decisions, most would still choose a man over a woman. Thankfully, Elinor had the support of the more progressive lords, but from experience, she knew how easily some could switch sides when a better offer came along. Taking a brief pause outside the doors, she composed herself, displaying a confident demeanour. All six lords were expected to be present. By this point, they were likely aware that something major had occurred, although the specifics eluded them. The intrigue alone should have left them pondering, their curiosity piqued as they wondered what transpired and how it would impact them.

They all lived lavish lifestyles, accustomed to a land rich in opportunities and fortune. It would be unlikely for them to want to give that up, especially given the varying degrees of power among them. James, aware of the ambition within his court, had restricted the power and influence of certain lords, keeping their greed in check. Or so he believed. Many had their secret dealings unbeknownst to the crown, keeping their wealth and status thriving. Their titles stayed the same, but their wealth kept growing right under his nose.

Knowing this, Elinor had to show her authority and position as the queen in the eyes of the lords. She had to establish the true power of the court. Her goal was to surpass the power and status of when under James's reign. If she could get these lords on her side, the crown was hers.

After receiving a clear nod from her, the guards opened the doors, and Elinor walked inside. Commanding the room, she stopped at the head of the table, effortlessly asserting control over the men with a single glance. She was the one in charge. Looking around, she saw five lords were present. The sixth, Bradley, the son of Lord Woodlock. Eyes lingering on him for just a moment, she shifted her focus to the entire group. All the men had risen as she entered, and a collective nod and welcome greeted her as she began addressing them.

"Evening, gentlemen. Thank you for meeting me here today. I know many of you have travelled far."

As she took her seat, the men followed suit, arranging themselves with three on either side. On her left were Lords William Bennett, Thomas Stone, and Christopher Malins, while on her right were Lords Johnathon Goodman, Wesley Bishop, and Bradley Woodlock, standing in for his father, Lawrence.

Lawrence and Thomas were the ones she was worried about. With Bradley there in place of his father, Elinor hoped he would side with her, but after their encounter earlier, she wasn't sure. Thomas craved power and had been involved in covert smuggling operations. While kept discreet, most knew about it. He was sly in his dealings and had never been caught himself, letting his workers take the fall. Most were happy to do so, knowing the payment they would receive for keeping quiet. Those who resisted tended to disappear. He would be the one to discredit her the most, not wanting to jeopardise his operations. Unless she gave him an offer, he couldn't refuse.

The other men could fall either way. But she knew Christopher was on her side. They had been working together since her move to Adlington, and he had been supporting her claim. He was one lord James capped in their rise to power. With a new title and more land on the table, he was eager for her to take the throne. Ultimately, her speech and ability to win over the lords would determine her acceptance as ruler.

"My lords, I don't wish to keep you long, so I shall keep this brief. First, I have sad news about my brother."

"It's true then, the rumours?"

"Lord Stone?"

"That the king is dead, by your hand, no less? We may have only arrived here earlier today, but your speech this morning spread like wildfire. Your evidence against him was quite interesting. Well played."

"I dislike what you're insinuating, Lord Stone, but I assure you, what I said was true. James had been plotting against the kingdom for his own gain."

"Oh, I'm sure he was, my dear. Now, why don't we skip the fake pleasantries, and you tell us why we're really here."

Murmurs began swirling between the men before settling down with all eyes on her. Inside, Elinor seethed. They already knew and played her for the fool. What she was about to say next could well have her condemned for treason.

Keeping her voice steady, she ignored the insult about her part in James's demise and continued. "With the passing of the King, and I, the next in line, I put to you to crown me, Queen."

At that moment, the lords began deliberating among themselves, seemingly oblivious to her presence. They debated with each other, a mix of arguments for and against her rule, occasionally mentioning Cecilia for good measure.

As Elinor watched the chaos unfold, she noticed Bradley was the only one not debating. Instead, he watched her, his face a mix of awe and intrigue. Her cheeks involuntarily turned red. She shifted her attention back to the men and furrowed her brow at their remarks.

Before she could respond, Bradley rose and addressed the men. "My lords, as wonderful as it is hearing you all debating so passionately about the future of our kingdom, I believe it's impolite to continue in the princess's presence. Maybe we should continue this discussion privately and share our decision in the morning."

They looked somewhat ashamed. They exchanged a murmured agreement before unanimously deciding to continue with the conversation without her being present.

Relieved to avoid enduring their remarks about her abilities, Elinor rose with as much grace as she could muster.

"Thank you, but before I leave, I want to leave you with a few reasons I know will make you choose me as your queen."

One of her guards handed her a rolled-up parchment, which she placed on the table before her. All eyes turned to the parchment, yet no one made a move to retrieve it.

"Until tomorrow morning, then. Shall we say around ten?" Without another word, Elinor walked out of the room, leaving her fate in the hands of the lords.

Teetering on the edge of blind rage, she held her composure until she reached her chambers. Behind the closed door, she screamed until her voice was raw. Ripping the necklace from her neck, she hurled it across the room, the metal clattering on the hard floor. Tears blurred her vision as she stumbled towards the dresser, swiping everything off in one swift movement. Sobbing with rage as the contents of her dresser came crashing to the ground, glass bottles shattering on impact, mirroring the chaos in her mind.

Her chest heaved with each breath, while her heart hammered as if it might burst through her chest. The veins on her temples pulsed with tension, echoing the fury coursing through her. Trembling hands clenched into fists, nails digging into her palms, cutting her skin till the blood trickled down her palms. The nerve of those men. To speak so harshly with her right there, not caring about what she had to say. Her fate rested in their hands and there was nothing she could do.

"Wine, now!" She stood with her hand held out to take the goblet. Head back, she gulped down the whole goblet.

"More!" Elinor sat down on the end of her bed, kicked off her shoes, and knocked back another goblet of wine, followed by another. Without undressing, Elinor lay on her bed, staring at the ceiling, her mind turning foggy before sleep finally came.

Chapter 7

New Roles

The next morning, Elinor woke to a throbbing sensation in her head. Her vision blurred as she sat up, pain shooting through her temple, and her mouth was dry. With every swallow, it felt like a sharp object scraping against the back of her throat. As she licked her lips, the cracked layers snagged along her tongue. The wine may have knocked her out for the night, but now she was paying the consequences. With her eyes still half shut and her limbs heavy to move, she made her way to her bath, ready to wash away the memory of the previous night. Steam rose, causing a misty cloud to envelop her into its fold. As she removed her gown, one of her ladies pinned her hair up. The heat of the water cascaded around her body as she eased into the tub.

The warmth seeped into Elinor's soul, relaxing her muscles and calming her mind. To her left, a tray laden with fresh strawberries and blueberries sat alongside a jug of water. With thirst being her biggest problem, she drank deeply, washing away the remnants of last night. Immersed in the rose-scented water, she savoured the fruit while her ladies laid out her clothes for the day. Each bite of the delicious fruit delighted her senses with its sweetness and plumpness, its juices trickling down her chin. They were just how she liked them, freshly picked from the garden. She soaked as long as she could, trying her best not to think of her appointment with the lords. The thought made her feel nauseated, so she shifted her focus to the ceremony with her new lieutenant. It offered a positive distraction. At the urging of her ladies, she got up and dressed for the day.

After eating some biscuits to settle the queasy feeling in her stomach, she left her room and walked to the royal hall. Adrian was already waiting for her. Inside the chamber, several individuals and Julian's family stood, their chatter filling the air. Elinor, wearing a regal gown, welcomed them with a warm smile, positioning herself in front of the throne. The guards announced Julian's arrival, and as the heavy doors swung open, his gaze met Elinor's. He paused at the foot of the staircase leading to the throne. With a graceful bow, he showed his respect.

As he straightened, Elinor's voice resonated through the hall. "Julian Wood, today you stand before us to accept the esteemed position of lieutenant to our trained men. It will be your duty to collaborate with your comrades, assigning roles and ranks that match their unique abilities and skills, all while leading the noble royal guard. Tell me, are you prepared to embrace this role and the substantial responsibilities it entails?"

"I do, Your Majesty," Julian responded, his voice filled with pride. His words echoed through the grand hall, reaching the ears of all present. He kneeled on the marble floor, his head bowed.

"Then it's with great honour I bestow upon you the title of Lieutenant Julian Wood."

Julian rose, his face lit up with a joyful smile. Elinor descended the steps, her flowing gown sweeping against each stair. A warm smile adorned her face as she approached Julian, extending her hand. Elinor's touch conveyed both congratulations and well wishes for his new position. Engaged in small talk, they discussed his role. Their voices carried excitement and anticipation. With the formalities concluded, Elinor bid Julian farewell, leaving her new lieutenant to celebrate with his friends and family.

On the way to the great hall, Elinor and Adrian deliberated over what was likely to occur. She shared with him what her ladies had overheard, and though it seemed positive, that didn't alleviate the knot in her stomach. A part of her was regretting breakfast. If they didn't support her claim to the throne as queen, she didn't know what would happen. The idea of just killing all who opposed her and replacing them was appealing, but a little too messy. Either way, she knew she had Adrian's support, no matter what happened next. She stole a glance at him as they reached the hall. Pure focus lined his face. She gave him a smile filled with hope.

"I guess this is it. It all comes down to this meeting. If they say yes, everything we worked for will become reality."

As they entered the room, Adrian smiled with his eyes locked on hers. "They will. Don't worry about that."

His words offered comfort, soothing the knot in her stomach, yet had an edge to them as though he knew something she didn't. Before she could ask what he was hiding, the door opened, and the lords entered, one after the other.

"My Lady."

"Lord Malins."

Everyone greeted her and took a seat at the table, except for Adrian, who remained standing. Positioned at a suitable distance to not seem overbearing, but close enough to intervene if he needed to. That alone helped Elinor keep her calm exterior. She wore it like a mask, not revealing her inner turmoil. Yet, if they removed it, they would see a lost little girl, hoping that all her dreams weren't about to be ripped from her grasp. The room was silent, but the tension was palpable. Elinor's heart raced with anticipation; it was pounding so loud in her ears that she wondered why no one else could hear it. The sound reverberated like a drumbeat on the summer solstice. Unable to wait any longer, Elinor broke the silence, even though she was loath to do so.

"My lords, thank you for meeting with me. I hope you have good news regarding my claim to the throne."

"You'll be happy to hear we have, my Lady."

"Yes, we have. Thank you, Christopher, but before you get ahead of yourself, I would like to remind you of our conditions." Thomas pulled out a roll of parchment and passed it along to Elinor. "We agreed to support your claim, princess, but only if you meet our requirements."

Elinor unravelled the document and read it.

"Yes, I was getting to that, Thomas. Thank you for cutting in," said Christopher in an annoyed tone.

"Now, now, no need to get tetchy," replied Thomas with the same snarky tone. "We all want the same thing here. Some more than others. We are, however, all in agreement to support the princesses' claim, if we all get what we want. Fair is fair, is it not?"

As Elinor read through the demands, they were not far off from what she was expecting from them. Their requests included more land, better trade options, and a few extra titles, along with more control in their own territories for some. All were more than doable if they supported her claim. She couldn't overlook the fact that Thomas had made the most demands, while Christopher had only asked for what was in their previous agreement. One condition made her pause as she reached the last section. Lowering the parchment, she noticed that all eyes were fixed on her.

"Problem?"

"You tell me, Lord Stone. It would seem you have added your own condition in here that I find… unusual for want of a better word."

"Oh, and what condition would that be?"

"The final one."

"Refresh my memory. There were so many in there I forget which one it is."

Elinor tapped her fingers on the table, eyes like daggers as she glared at him. The man was infuriating and had a talent for knowing how to irritate her. She never liked him, and he knew it. All those times she questioned him and pulled rank over him were coming back to haunt her. He was toying with her for fun, as he made her squirm for his approval. Approval she needed if she wanted the throne. Her tone clipped as she read the last condition to their support aloud.

"I agree to wed the son of a lord that is present today. It will be of my choosing, but I must decide within six months of the official coronation. If I can't choose, the choice shall be made on my behalf."

The smirk on Lord Stone's face was apparent. The other lords at least looked a little guilty after the glare she gave them all. Lord Stone, though, he was practically gleeful. Her grip tightened on the parchment, her knuckles turning white. It was clear to her now that this was all a game to him. Forcing her to agree to his demands and play nice while holding the key to what she wanted most. Behind her, she sensed the anger radiating off Adrian, and she welcomed it. At least one person shared her frustration, as she was right then. With a glimmer of hope, she entertained the thought that perhaps Adrian might take matters into his own hands to kill Lord Stone and save her the trouble. In one swift motion, she slammed the parchment down on the table, and the resounding thud echoed through the room.

"I'm not a pawn in your game, Lord Stone. I will not sign this."

He chuckled, a cruel sound that reverberated in her ears. "Oh, but you have no choice," he sneered, his words dripping with disdain. "Not if you want that crown."

"How about I kill you where you sit and replace you with someone better suited to your role? I'm sure there are plenty who would take your place in a heartbeat." As she spoke, she drew on her power, wrapping it around his throat, restricting his breathing long enough to prove her point.

Wheezing from the loss of air, his voice was hoarse as he spoke. "Kill me and you'll follow soon after. Remind me, treason is still the death penalty, and anyone found committing such an act will face execution by beheading."

"It is, but I don't see how that affects me. I've committed no such crime."

"Evidence can suggest otherwise. Everyone here knows the truth, and then some. If I die, you die too. Think carefully before you try that little trick again."

Elinor looked amongst everyone at that table, staring into the pits of their very soul. No one uttered a word. Out of fear or agreement, she couldn't be sure. They had her right where they wanted her. They could call treason and have her killed before the end of the day if they wanted to. Or they could stand with her and help her take the crown. All she had to do was sign on the dotted line.

"The important phrase is, it is your choice, my Lady."

She looked at Christopher and saw the sympathy in his eyes. At least one of them showed some remorse at how this was going. She knew it was all Lord Stone's doing. The rest were following suit because it benefited them. If she wanted the crown, she had to agree to their terms now. Revenge would come later. At least for one of them.

Her mind swirled with thoughts of marriage, a topic that hadn't previously occupied her mind. With all her time and energy dedicated to becoming queen, this had not seemed a priority. She wanted to take the throne herself. Believing that doing this alone would secure her authority and establish her as the true ruler in the eyes of her kingdom. Having a husband, she couldn't be guaranteed that the lords wouldn't choose him over her. She had read many books in the royal library with this happening to past Queens on the throne. With little to no magical abilities for some, they became overshadowed by their husbands. Especially after bearing children. Powerless Queens. Elinor had no intention of letting this happen to her.

Although the demand for marriage was arcane to her, she knew why they requested it. She had no choice but to agree to the terms. The only little comfort she held onto was that she could choose. That and the fact she could kill them all off later, one by one. Sign now, and secure her throne, then take out anyone who caused her problems. An accident here, an accident there. No one would be any wiser. Elinor picked up the quill and signed on the dotted line.

"I agree with your terms."

A murmur of approval came from the lords, with them all rising and signing the document one by one. Bradley was the last, a penetrating look towards her before he signed on his father's behalf. She looked away, focusing on those around her, unnerved by his gaze. With his final signature, everything was official, and the lords raised their glasses in a toast to their new queen.

Raising her glass high, Elinor exclaimed, "To a new reign, and a promising future!"

"To a new reign and a promising future." All around glasses clinked together, and merry conversation began. Eager to tell the news to their court members, the lords filtered out one by one, congratulating Elinor. Bradley was the last to leave.

"Congratulations. My future queen. I'm looking forward to seeing how you handle this new role." Bradley bowed before kissing her hand and flashing a dazzling smile.

A tingle surged through her core at the kiss, the smile, him. She watched him leave, shuddering. Bradley Woodlock wasn't that person. Yet, the feelings lingered, the moment replaying in her mind. His dazzling smile disarmed her unexpectedly. She pushed aside the lingering emotions, remembering what had just transpired in this room. He was a part of it, even if he said nothing. As she turned, she recalled who else was in the room with her.

"Did you know? Your comment earlier implied you were aware of more than you let on. Did you know?"

"Yes," replied Adrian.

"You were aware! And yet, you failed to mention such an important condition they were about to throw at me? And what about Stone's blackmail? Did you know about that?"

"No! I knew nothing of the blackmail, believe me. Christopher forewarned me just before I met you outside the royal hall about the marriage proposal, but that is all I knew. I was about to tell you when they all entered. By then, it was too late."

"Too late? We walked together through the halls. You didn't think to speak up then? Or my chambers. You could have met me there. Delay the meeting for a few minutes. Anything. You let me be blind-sighted and look like a fool."

"I know. I'm sorry."

"Apologies don't help me, Adrian. You kept information from me. Right when I needed it most. You're supposed to be the one person I can depend on. And today you failed me."

"Elinor—"

"No! I don't want to hear it right now. I'm too angry with you. While I may have secured the crown, I've also lost my trust in you. Leave. Now."

She stormed over to the window. Clear blue skies and a shining sun. A stark contrast to the tempest raging within her when she should feel elated.

The door closed with a firm thud. When she looked back, she was alone. Head in her hands, tears streamed down her cheeks as her shoulders shook with each sob. The weight of her anger and disappointment settled heavily on her chest, making it hard to breathe. Her body trembled with both frustration and sorrow. Elinor got what she wanted yet lost at the same time. With the sound of the door opening again, her head snapped up.

"I told you to get out! Oh… What are you doing here?" Bradley stepped closer as she turned her back to him, trying to clean up her appearance with the handkerchief she kept on her.

"When I left, I heard raised voices. I came in to see if you are okay. I know that it didn't go the way you planned, but none of us knew what Stone was going to say after your outburst earlier. It's clear you can take care of yourself if that power of yours is anything to go by."

"I can, and I'm fine. No thanks to any of you."

"Clearly." His voice sounded closer. She gathered her composure and turned to face him, startled by how close he was. As he reached out, an invisible current sparked between them, and she felt a jolt as his fingertips brushed against her hair.

"You look fine to me."

Her gaze lingered on his face before stepping back. "Exactly, I'm fine. Now leave."

"As you wish." His hand dropped, and she watched him walk away.

The second man to do that today. For once, Elinor found herself at a loss. In a state of confusion, she paced the room before collapsing into the nearest chair, burying her head in her hands. Frustration riled through her as she massaged her temples. This was supposed to be a day of celebration. Instead, she was all alone, angry with one man and confused by another, all while being tied up in the lord's games of manipulation. All she wanted was to go to bed and start the day over.

Chapter 8

A Nightmare

Darkness swirled around Cecilia. She sensed a profound stillness in the air, a silence so deafening it enveloped her. With each step, a resounding thud echoed into the abyss. Fear prickled her skin like tiny needles.

"Hello?"

As her voice pierced the void, its echo carried into the depths. Tentatively, she moved forward, trying to navigate through the obscurity. Grey mist billowed from the ground, engulfing her and her surroundings. No distinguishable shapes or landmarks to guide her, just an endless expanse of darkness and mist.

"Hello, anyone. Is anyone there?" Her voice was barely a whisper, the remnants of the echo came back in quiet waves. She heard a piercing scream behind her, causing her heart to race as the stillness shattered.

"James!" Desperate to find him, she gathered her skirts and sprinted through the mist, her heart pounding in her chest. Yet, despite her frantic search, she couldn't see him.

"Mum, help us, please. Mum, where are you?"

"Aevah? Jacob?" She froze, desperately looking around. The sound of their cries reverberated in her ears, a haunting chorus that fuelled her desperation. She strained her ears, trying to discern the origin of the voices, but they seemed to come from all directions, disorienting her further. Panic clawed at her throat, threatening to choke her, as she fought to maintain her composure.

"Where are you? I'm coming, don't worry, mum is coming my little ones. Mum is coming."

Just as she took a step forward, another voice called out. "Cecilia, help me!" The plea sliced through her like a knife, sending shivers down her spine.

"James? Where are you? Where are our babies? I can't see anything in this godforsaken place."

Her entire body trembled as she struggled to keep a sense of control, desperately trying to pinpoint where her family was. With nothing to lose, she headed back through the mist and darkness, calling out to them. The darkness seemed to close in around her, suffocating her senses. Shadows danced and twisted, playing tricks on her mind. Her vision blurred, the misty veil obscuring her sight, leaving her disoriented and vulnerable. Another piercing scream echoed behind her, jolting her into action. She spun around, instincts propelling her forward, even as her legs threatened to give way. Sweat dripped down her forehead, mingling with her tears, as her breaths came in shallow gasps. Adrenaline surged through her veins, granting her a temporary burst of strength as she sprinted towards the source of the cry. But when she finally reached it, her worst nightmare unfolded before her eyes.

Cecilia dropped to her knees, tears streaming down her face.

"James, no, no, no…" James, her beloved husband, lay motionless on the ground, his eyes open, his mouth twisted in agony. A dagger nestled in his chest. Loss tore through her very being. Her screams of despair mingled with the agonised cries of her children, their innocent voices pleading for mercy. Time seemed to slow as she turned towards the approaching inferno. Trapped inside, Aevah and Jacob cried out, begging for help as the fire burned all around them.

"No!"

This couldn't be happening. The smell of burning skin filled the air, a mix of terror and determination consuming her, overriding the pain and despair threatening to consume her. Without hesitation, she sprinted towards the flames, her body bracing for the intense heat ahead, determined to save them. As she collided with the raging fire, blistering pain enveloped her, scorching through her flesh and her soul. Her skin blistered and cracked, the smell of burning flesh overpowering her senses. Yet, she pushed through the agony, fuelled by a mother's love and an unyielding desire to save her children. Amidst the consuming blaze, everything turned black. The pain, fear, and loss all faded into oblivion as unconsciousness claimed her.

Cecilia woke up startled. Her whole body was drenched in sweat, clothes and bed sheets clinging to her shaking body. She was in her bed, safe and sound. James slept peacefully beside her, his chest rising and falling in a rhythmic movement. Relief washed over her as she realised it had all been a nightmare. It wasn't real. Her family was alive. But despite the relief flooding her, her racing heart remained, and the remnants of fear lingered within her. She could still feel the adrenaline coursing through her veins, making her hands shake uncontrollably. The nightmare had felt so vivid, so achingly real. Taking a deep breath, she sat up in bed, trying to steady herself. Beads of perspiration trickled down her forehead, mirroring the intensity of her emotions. She used her forearm to wipe it away and reached for a glass of water that was not there.

As her breathing steadied, Cecilia turned her attention to James, his peaceful slumber undisturbed by the turmoil that had consumed her. She watched the rhythmic rise and fall of his chest. Gently, she reached out to touch his hand, drawing comfort from the warmth of his skin. His peaceful expression made her smile, a flicker of happiness amidst the remnants of her nightmare. As she settled back against her pillows, the dampness of her clothing irritated her and brought back memories of the nightmare. Unable to lie in the turmoil of her memories, she swayed her legs over the edge of the bed, her bare feet touching the cool wooden floor. As she stood, her sweat-soaked nightgown clung to her body. With each step, she willed her trembling legs to regain their strength, determined to shake off the lingering effects of the nightmare.

Cecilia walked over to the bathroom, her hands gripped the edge of the sink, steadying herself. With one palm against the top of the wash basin, the other lifted the jug and watched as the water cascaded into the basin, its gentle splashing creating a soothing sound. She extended her fingertips, feeling the lukewarm water encircle them before she willed it to transform into an icy coldness. As she touched the water, it sent a shiver down her spine. Satisfied, she cupped the frosty water, splashing it on her face, experiencing a sudden jolt that awakened her senses, banishing the remnants of her nightmare.

As she looked into the mirror, her reflection met her gaze. Her eyes, normally vibrant, now bore the weight of exhaustion, widening with a mixture of fear and anxiety. Her usually radiant skin was drab and weary. Attempting to find solace, she forced a faint smile and whispered to herself, desperately clinging to the hope that it was merely a haunting dream. A fabrication of her mind. She was alive. They were alive. But then she saw something that made her blood turn cold.

A reflection behind her. A reflection that wasn't her own, with a wicked grin and a bloody knife. It whispered in her ear, "Hello, Cecilia. I've been waiting for you."

The scream that left her body transcended into the waking world. Arms flailing as she tried to get away, it took her a moment to realise she was awake, and although just a dream, her family was gone. Cecilia's scream turned into a heart-wrenching wail as her hands clenched around her bedsheets, her body furled into a ball. Uncontrollable sobs left her torn-out soul. She felt like she was drowning, falling into the darkness with no one left to hear her pleas. Memories attacked her mind like relentless vultures, stabbing at her consciousness, replaying the vivid images over and over. Each scene taunted her with the agonising reality of her family's demise. Every muscle in her body ached with the intensity of her emotions. Her hands earlier clenched around the bedsheets, now gripped her flesh, nails digging into her skin, as though the physical pain could distract her from the torment within. Droplets of blood dripped from her arms as the surrounding darkness seeped into her very bones, pulling her further into the abyss.

"M'Lady? M'lady, are you okay?"

"What?"

"Are you okay? Mistress Katelyn sent me t check on you. You didn't come help in the kitchens today."

"No… I. I forgot. I'm fine, please tell Mistress Katelyn not to worry."

"As you say, m'lady. Tis dark in here an it be midday already. I brought you summat t eat an drink. Is they anythin else I can do?"

"No. Thank you." Cecilia sat up and looked at the young woman. It was difficult to identify her in the darkness.

"Tell Mistress Katelyn I'll be there tomorrow."

The young woman left without a word. All her energy sapped as though that small encounter was all she could handle. Her body felt heavy and weighed down by her sorrow. It required a great deal of effort to stand up and walk over to the tray of food on her dresser. Her trembling hands struggled to hold the cup of water. As she took a sip, the lukewarm liquid did nothing for her, nor the spoonful of porridge she consumed. With nothing but a hollowness within her, she staggered back to the bed and lay back down.

A blanket of grief washed over her as her once vibrant eyes turned vacant, fixated on the ceiling above. Cecilia let out a heavy sigh, closed her eyes and curled into the fetal position while clutching her arms as her body sunk further into the bed. Trapped in an endless cycle of nightmares and sorrow, the painful memories relentlessly replayed in her mind. Desperate to escape the torment, she dug her nails forcefully into her skin once more until she felt the slow trickle of blood beneath her fingertips. The sweet release of pain was the only outlet for the horrors within her mind. Night and day became as one as the passage of time eluded her. Her only sense of time came from the arrival of the familiar young lady with a fresh tray of food, and the same message from Mistress Katelyn. Each time, her response was the same before she succumbed to the dreams that haunted her.

"Get up Cecilia! This has gone on long enough."

Pulled from a restless sleep, Cecilia opened her eyes to find Mistress Katelyn in her room. The woman moved around, lighting candles, and rummaging through her dresser and wardrobe, laying out clothes to wear. Sitting up, she watched as Mistress Katelyn continued to bustle about, filling a bowl with water and soaking a washcloth in it.

"Katelyn. I wasn't expecting you. What time is it?"

Coming to a stop in front of her, there was no mistaking the pity beheld in her eyes as Katelyn looked at her. "Oh Cecilia, Lara told me you were in a sorry state, but I didn't expect this. Had I known, I would have come sooner. Come, let's clean you up and get some food in you."

Her words broke through the walls that kept Cecilia trapped in her despair, and she collapsed into the woman's awaiting arms, letting all the emotions from the past week out. As she calmed, Mistress Katelyn led her to the table and carefully helped her undress before adjusting her shift to sit in the chair beside Cecilia. She gently began washing her down the best she could, taking extra care of the obvious cuts across her arms. Cecilia sat in a trance-like state, quite unsure how to react.

Once Mistress Katelyn cleaned her to her standards, she placed a steaming bowl of porridge in front of Cecilia.

"Eat. You need your strength. I'm taking you with me to the kitchens before you starve yourself to death, or worse. I know you are hurting, but if you stay here much longer Elinor will seek you out, and that's not something either of us wants to happen."

"You're right. I can't let her break me."

With a new resolve, Cecilia forced herself to finish every last bite in the bowl. The food filled the hunger but did nothing to quell the void within her. She stood up, and with Mistress Katelyn's help, slipped into a close-fitting light blue dress, the colour soothing to the eyes. Lined with delicate white fabric, the dress felt soft against her skin while a belt added the final touch to her outfit.

Mistress Katelyn held up the little hand mirror. "There we go. You look better already."

Cecilia gazed at her reflection. Even though it was her reflection, she no longer recognised the person staring back. It was her face, but the eyes. The sparkle was gone. In its place, vacant eyes peered through. Eyes that lost all hope, hiding beneath the darkness. Deep lines etched a weariness that mirrored the burden she carried within. The glow of her complexion had faded, replaced by a paleness that spoke of sleepless nights and hidden sorrows.

Cecilia's fingers traced the lines of her face, feeling the burden of her emotions etched into every curve. The smile that once effortlessly adorned her lips now seemed forced, a mere façade to conceal the turmoil brewing within. Her cheeks, once rosy with joy, now appeared sunken and devoid of colour, mirroring the emptiness she felt inside.

A deep sigh escaped Cecilia's lips as she contemplated the loss of her inner radiance. She yearned to reclaim the spark that once ignited her spirit, to rediscover the joy and passion that had faded away. But it was gone. She pushed the mirror away, unable to gaze upon her reflection any longer.

With resignation weighing heavy in her voice, she uttered the words, "I'm ready."

Mistress Katelyn, with a faint smile, opened the door and led the way. Unsure of what to expect, Cecilia followed her only friend out of her room and down the corridor. As soon as she began walking, the two guards followed her to the kitchen. It made her uneasy, knowing they were just a few paces away. For years, guards had followed her. Their presence served as a reminder that she was safe. These guards, though, had the opposite effect, leaving her anxious and worried for her safety. Still, she held her head high, concentration on her face as she ignored the gnawing pit in her stomach. As they reached the kitchens, the guards hovered in the doorway, backs to the wall, arms crossed, watching her.

Cecilia turned away from the men, trying to ignore their presence, and took in the kitchen. It was a bustling space, with workers moving swiftly through their tasks. The air was thick with the aroma of sizzling meats and freshly baked bread, each station manned by skilled workers chopping and stirring. The pantry, a treasure trove of ingredients, overflowed with vibrant colours of fresh produce, enticing anyone who entered. The sheer scale of the work that went into preparing the meals captivated Cecilia. It left her with a newfound appreciation for the efforts of the workers. Before she could say anything, Mistress Katelyn pulled her along and set her to work washing dishes and cleaning the kitchen. Out of her comfort zone, Cecilia tried her best, fighting through the unease in her mind. Focused on the task at hand, she diligently washed everything placed in front of her.

It was hard work, with many of the workers giving her unsettling looks when they thought Mistress Katelyn wasn't looking. Regardless, she endured and kept at the tasks given to her. Every so often, her guards looked in to check on her, while also helping themselves to the food. Within hours, her arms became fatigued, and her fingers grew sore. Her emotional state was also being tested. The workers made her feel uncomfortable, their gazes making her skin crawl. Her body itched to leave, feeling dirty and unwanted. By the time she was free to go, Cecilia couldn't get back to her chambers fast enough. Anxiety peaked. All she wanted to do was lock herself in, safe and away from prying eyes.

Curling back into her bed, Cecilia shut down, closing off to the world beyond her room. She thought of the happy memories with her family. Of picnics in the woods and the way James could make her laugh so hard, she cried. Aevah's dramatic performances as she enacted her favourite stories, and Jacob's ability to create anything out of nothing. The tears flowed at the thought of never seeing those things again. Never hearing their voices, the warmth of their embrace, the twinkle in their eyes as they talk about the things they love. Memories turned into nightmares as sleep came, and the vicious cycle of grief began again.

She woke up the next morning to find Mistress Katelyn in her room once again, following the same routine as the previous day. The same trip to the kitchens, the same watchful guards. With one day under her belt, Cecilia became accustomed to everything, along with the pecking order. Although Mistress Katelyn was in charge, there was a social structure for the tasks. The more experienced older men and women did the cooking, with the middle-aged workers in charge of prep work. The younger workers oversaw the cleaning and running errands.

None of it mattered to her. The workers didn't acknowledge her unless they had to speak to her. The only positive from the morning was they stared less this time. With fewer eyes watching, the tension that gripped her body lessened, and she could zone out, focusing on cleaning. By the end of her shift, Cecilia's hands ached, and her skin was tender to the touch. This time, as hunger gnawed at her stomach, she asked Mistress Katelyn if she could take a tray back to her room. As she was about to leave, the guards stopped her, searching her tray of food. Satisfied with its contents, they followed her back to her room, positioning themselves outside once more. She closed the door on them and walked over to her little table, sitting down. As she looked at the contents, she felt overwhelmed. The morning's events caught up with her and drained her of the energy she had. The empty pit in her stomach told her she had to eat something, but her mind told her she needed rest. Cecilia took a few bites of the ham salad roll and sipped some water. Unable to eat more, she sat on the edge of her bed and kicked off her shoes, weariness settling over her.

Alone with her thoughts, the cycle of memories to nightmares began again. This time, though, she didn't pierce her skin until it bled. Instead, she clenched her arms, cocooning herself into a safe ball, fighting against the onslaught of nightmares. By the fourth day, Cecilia had got herself ready before Mistress Katelyn arrived. She ate her meals as small as they were, and the nightmares had lessened. Although she would never be her old self, Cecilia was accepting the life that was now hers. She had to stay strong. That was the only way she would get her revenge.

Chapter 9

Loyalty

Adrian was still in Elinor's bad graces after the meeting with the lords. To regain her trust, he worked with Tyler and Julian to establish a fresh chain of command for both the royal guards and the Kingdom's army. His main concern was ensuring that those under Julian's authority would obey him and that those in similar positions would collaborate with him. However, the way Julian got the job was not ideal, as the men respected his predecessor. Their numbers had decreased after that fateful night. Lieutenant Banes wasn't the only court member loyal to their king, who died protecting him. This tragedy created a sombre mood among the ranks. Adrian was certain many still shared Lieutenant Banes' sentiments, although they didn't express it. Introducing the new command structure had to be handled carefully. He didn't want to lose any more men.

Adrian leveraged Julian's esteemed reputation within the castle to rally support from the men. Rumours of his well-deserved promotion were already circulating among the soldiers, though tinged with a bittersweet tone. As the three men stood on the platform in the training yard, a multitude of men chatted among themselves, their postures rigid as they awaited the news. Adrian took a step forward, clearing his throat, which prompted the murmurs of the waiting soldiers to subside.

"Attention everyone. Attention! In light of the recent passing of Lieutenant Banes, we have found a suitable replacement for him. The late lieutenant was an exceptional man who has left a significant legacy behind, which we must uphold. I'm confident that his replacement will do the job well. Without further ado, I present to you, Julian Wood, your new lieutenant." Julian stepped forward. A small smattering of clapping began as he spoke.

"Thank you, everyone. I'm honoured to be stepping into Lieutenant Banes's shoes. I understand the significance of the legacy he left behind, and I'm committed to upholding it with the utmost dedication and professionalism. Together, we'll continue to serve and protect our kingdom. I look forward to working with each one of you in the upcoming months. If anyone has questions, please come see me. Thank you once again for your support."

The soldiers listened intently. Their attention was fixed on him. When he finished speaking, everyone erupted in cheers, thrilled for his promotion. His friends cheered the loudest, eager to work alongside him. A touching moment for many, they couldn't envision a more suitable replacement for Lieutenant Banes. After most of the men departed, a few lingered, stepping forward to offer their congratulations on his new role. With everything running smoothly, Adrian left to attend to his ongoing responsibilities.

***

Back inside the castle, Adrian went straight to the cells, where a little over a dozen people were detained. These were the individuals who had voiced their opposition to Elinor on the very first night. Upon reaching the entrance of the cells, Adrian descended the narrow stairs into the dark corridor, entering the interrogation room on his left. There were only two of these chilling rooms in the castle, and neither saw frequent use. In fact, not once during King James's rule did anyone set foot inside. The rooms mirrored each other in design, emanating darkness and an eerie coldness. Devoid of windows, the sole source of light came from flickering candles, casting unsettling shadows on the stone walls. Intentionally crafted to instil discomfort and fear in the hearts of those awaiting interrogation. Upon entering the room, one could see a spacious area with a rack, pulley system, and a foreboding trapdoor on the floor. The solitary table and chair against one of the stone walls were the only furnishings in the room. The table, intended for the interrogator's use, functioned as a surface to hold the tools of torment, while the chair provided relief during the arduous task at hand. Another disturbing feature was the trap door, which led into a cramped, coffin-like space where detainees awaited questioning. Although torture on its own, it left those confined within feeling as if they were buried alive, trapped in a narrow box enveloped in impenetrable darkness.

Adrian entered the room and saw a man he didn't recognise, someone who remained loyal to James. While Adrian didn't particularly concern himself with the man's identity, he wanted to know how many others might cause trouble for Elinor's reign. The man was currently restrained on a rack, yet Adrian didn't want to use it. His goal was to get information and have the prisoners leave peacefully. Those willing to peacefully resolve the situation and swear allegiance to their new queen faced only banishment. Conversely, those who refused would face the death sentence. Aware that there were likely many more people loyal to the late king, Adrian knew he had more questioning to do, hoping to reveal most of them through this process. Once questioned, the people who pledged their loyalty were being moved to Folkfield with their families, accompanied by a small unit of guards. There, they could start their lives anew, but returning to Carraton or causing trouble for the crown would cost them their lives. With his gaze fixed on the man before him, Adrian began his interrogation.

As evening set in, Adrian's weary eyes were bloodshot. It had been a long day of questioning, with barely a break in between. The dimly lit room was heavy with exhaustion and tension, filled with the acrid scent of fear, sweat, and the metallic tang of blood.

Adrian's mind replayed the haunting echoes of muffled sobs and desperate pleas that filled the room. Most of those he questioned wouldn't give up their secrets so easily. Instead, each question was met with blank stares or a selection of curses. For these people, he brought in the interrogator and let him have a turn at it. They soon cracked. Wanting the pain to stop, they divulged every little secret, desperate for relief. For those few, it meant the end of their life. Their loyalty to the late King James brought an end to their misery with a swift slice of the throat, blood draining from their bodies. With each secret extracted, his heart grew heavier, burdened by the weight of their confessions while his mind echoed with the haunting cries of the broken. The sight of lifeless bodies, now mere discarded husks, served as a chilling reminder of the ruthlessness of loyalty and the high stakes of betrayal. Those few who shared their knowledge pledged their allegiance to Elinor, and went back to their homes, packing for their new home. A stark contrast between loyalty and betrayal.

Weariness settled into his bones, and Adrian left the cells, intending to go back to his room and collapse. On the way, he ran into the one person he wanted to avoid. Bradley was walking straight towards him with a glowing smile on his face. Unable to ignore him, Adrian gave a nod and kept walking.

"Adrian, what a pleasant surprise." Bradley stopped in front of Adrian, forcing him to pause.

"Bradley. What can I do for you?" Despite feeling irritated, Adrian managed to maintain a bright smile on his face.

"I just wanted to check in, see how things are going, and if there is anything I can help you with?"

"Everything is fine. Thank you for your concern, but I have everything under control."

"Are you sure? It seems you've already dropped the ball, according to our dear princess. I wouldn't want anything else to go wrong for her because you refused to ask for help."

Adrian's fists clenched tightly in response to Bradley's words, a surge of irritation quivering within. Anger flared beneath his skin at knowing Elinor had confided in him. Assuming a defensive stance, he kept his posture straight and delivered a clipped response.

"I appreciate your concern, Bradley, but I assure you, I have everything under control," Adrian replied, his smile faltering slightly. "The princess's trust is my top priority, and I'll do whatever it takes to rectify the situation."

Bradley's smile wavered for a moment before he spoke again. "Well, if you ever need any assistance, please let me know. I'm at your disposal."

Adrian forced a polite nod, masking his annoyance. "Thank you, Bradley. I'll keep that in mind. Now, if you'll excuse me, I have some urgent matters to attend to."

With that, stepping around his nemesis, Adrian began walking at a faster pace than normal, needing to get as far away from him as possible. By the time he reached his room, he was visibly shaking. He needed to do something about Bradley, and soon. With a drink in his hand, he slouched into the chair as all thoughts of sleep were forgotten. His mind raced with indecision. With every shot of whiskey, his ideas became more unhinged, until he finally gave up and went to bed, where his dreams seamlessly carried on from where his thoughts left off.

***

Elinor surveyed her new chambers after finishing her duties for the day. She was finally in the royal quarters. There had been some damage done to the room. With repairs complete, the staff moved her belongings across, and this was the first time she was seeing them after the takeover. Stepping inside, she couldn't help but feel a sense of regality wash over her. The bedroom itself exuded grandeur. Beneath her feet, the soft, plush carpet welcomed her. Inside the large room was a magnificent four-poster bed made of dark mahogany wood. Sage green silk curtains draped gracefully around the bed, offering privacy and seclusion. Adorning one wall was a painting depicting the famous mountains of Azend, adding a natural touch of nature to the room.

Sunlight streamed through the large window, casting a warm glow that illuminated the room. The crackling sound of the fireplace provided a comforting ambience, inviting Elinor to curl up in the armchair and lose herself in a book. The sight of the flickering flames dancing in the hearth brought a sense of tranquillity and contentment. A vase of freshly picked flowers on the dressing table made the room smell like a blossoming meadow. As she entered the neighbouring bathroom, she admired the intricate golden faucets on the marble sink. The soft towels and bathing essentials arranged around the large bath beckoned her to indulge in a long, luxurious soak. In this moment, surrounded by beauty and luxury, Elinor couldn't help but be in awe. These rooms weren't just a physical space, but a sanctuary that filled her with regal charm, every fibre of her being revelling in her title as queen. As she walked back into her room, she noticed her guest setting up.

"Ah, my lady, beg the intrusion, but your guard let me in. I'm here for your final dress fitting."

"Of course. I received information that you would arrive soon. It's nice to see you again, Bethel. Please, the room is yours."

"Thank you, my Lady. I'll only be a moment."

Elinor sat down in her armchair and watched as the woman set up. Bethel was a short woman in her fifties with wild grey hair full of pins, and a tape measure around her neck was worn like an accessory. Tied around her waist was a multicoloured pinny apron filled with an assortment of pins, tape, thread, and scissors. The woman screamed chaos, but her work was undeniable. For dresses, Bethel was the best. The dress she had been working on was a deep purple, and this was the last fitting before she would take it away to turn it into a gown fit for a coronation. Being cautious of any stray pins, Bethel assisted Elinor in changing into the dress, ensuring she was ready for the last fitting.

"I would offer you tea, but I know your rules around beverages and clothing."

"No drinks of any kind when I work. It's not worth the risk, my dear. Why, I've seen one young woman insist upon a drink as I worked and ruined the whole thing by spilling wine on her beautiful gown. Arms up."

Bethel continued to measure and manipulate the material to how she wanted it, pinning sections and moving Elinor's body around as needed. Once done, she helped Elinor slip out of the dress once more. Her ladies helped her dress, as Bethel packed away.

"I'll have the dress to you in a few days, my Lady."

"Thank you, Bethel. I look forward to seeing the dress complete."

"Oh, it will be magnificent, mark my words. Good day, my Lady."

Elinor gave a nod as she left, reminding herself to thank Victoria for all her hard work. It had been Victoria who had brought Bethel in and was making the arrangements for her coronation to take place by the end of the week. Thanks to the lord's approval, they were able to proceed and make her position as queen official. With the Lord's presence in the city, Victoria had established who would attend from each of the families, thus finalising the numbers. An announcement was being sent to residents within the city as well. Those who wished to see their queen after the coronation were given the opportunity to do so. Victoria was also occupied with arranging a banquet for afterwards. Elinor had given her a list of her ideas, the food she liked, decorations and music, but was entrusting Victoria to see her vision through. With lots to organise, Elinor was grateful for Victoria's help. If she had to plan this on top of everything else, her stress levels would have reduced her to a ball of worry.

As the day drew to a close, Elinor climbed into her new bed, settling back into the soft plush pillows while her body relaxed as the silk sheets caressed her skin. The silence of her room was therapeutic after the hustle and bustle of the castle. Her mind was at peace with everything she had achieved. A new chain of command had been established, and court members were assigned new duties. The castle was full of capable people who could make simple decisions on her behalf. She had little interest in the details of which candles or oils were used to illuminate the rooms, or where the finest fruit could be purchased. Her sole concern revolved around ensuring that the rooms were adequately lit, and the fruit was of superior quality, entrusting those with expertise in these matters to decide. Moreso, after perusing the books alongside Lloyd earlier, the castle was being efficiently managed. To give credit where credit was due, her brother kept the castle operating smoothly. Elinor considered the day successful and looked forward to reaping the rewards in the coming weeks as everything fell into place.

It was difficult to comprehend the fact that her official reign as queen would begin after the coronation. The city's esteemed high priestess would conduct both the coronation and the bonding ceremony the following day. In a few days, Elinor would visit the temple of the priestesses and escort the high priestess back to the city. These priestesses were a distinctive community, worshipping the divine spirit in their own unique manner.

After the divine spirit disappeared many years ago, the priestesses have persisted in upholding her profound principles and ancient customs. Their unwavering devotion drives them not only to preserve her teachings but also to seek a way of bringing her back. Today, they help keep the peace by conducting sacred ceremonies and imparting their knowledge to those blessed with the power. Over the years, their harmonious collaboration with the kingdom has been a tranquil force. Revered by the vast majority across the realm, they epitomise serenity itself. Nevertheless, their journey has been marked by formidable challenges. Sceptics across the land emerged, denying the existence of the divine spirit and casting doubt upon the priestesses' unwavering faith.

Those people perceived the priestesses as deceitful individuals who yearned to exert control over the land itself. Regrettably, their actions caused significant turmoil within the order, resulting in an open rebellion against them when famine ravaged the entire region. Amid this crisis, the rebels besieged the temples, resulting in the loss of numerous priestesses' lives. Both young and experienced priestesses found themselves vulnerable amidst the rebellion. Almost wiped out, the surviving priestesses sought sanctuary in Carraton, the only haven left to them. Under the protection of the royal family, they kept hidden while the kingdom's army hunted the remaining non-believers.

Although the priestesses exist today in larger numbers than before, they will never forget the past. Their temples today, though now open to all, possess secrets known only to them, safeguarded like precious gems to protect them from any danger that may lurk outside. Their high priestesses have honed their mastery of power, dedicating more time to perfecting their strength and abilities in Earth's magic.

In the present day, the non-believers were few and scattered across the land, their voices drowned out by the chorus of those who witnessed the miracles performed by the priestesses. The people recognise the goodness brought by the priestesses and cherish their value. Even the royal family, intertwined with the order, holds strong ties to their ancient traditions. Without the priestesses, the bonding ceremony, a sacred rite, would be impossible. Even knowing this, apprehension rose in Elinor. Her relationship with the current high priestess was strained and this visit would determine if the high priestess would honour her position and complete the ceremony, or if her past actions were about to derail everything Elinor had worked for.

Chapter 10

The High Priestess

A few days after the meeting with the lords, Elinor ventured out of the confines of the castle. As she stepped into the courtyard, she felt the pleasant warmth of the balmy sun caressing her skin. She raised her hand to block the sun's rays before climbing into the horse and carriage in front of her with the help of her guard. As she settled back into the cushioned seat, her guard closed the carriage door, securing her inside. Despite the comfort of the seats themselves, the journey would be a bumpy ride nonetheless, once they left the smooth roads of the city and ventured into the countryside, where she was heading. Escorted by several guards on horseback, Elinor was making the journey to one of the sacred temples dedicated to the divine spirit. Today, there were five temples scattered across Ethos, each overseen by its high priestess. It was common practice for the new monarch to always visit before their coronation and bonding ceremony. The one closest to the royal family was just a few miles from the city. The royal family had strong ties to this temple, and the priestesses within it. James and Cecilia had formed a close bond with them since their day's training there as children.

Unfortunately, Elinor didn't have the same connection with the temple as her brother had. Being a strong-willed child, she had often clashed with the high priestess, disregarding their rules. One incident had involved her almost setting their sacred garden ablaze, as she had insisted on learning to control her powers in her way. She would like to say that after that incident, things had improved but that would be a lie. If anything, that had made things worse, and Elinor clashed with the high priestess more than ever. Yet, the time had come when she needed to play nice.

Only the high priestess could perform the sacred bonding ritual, and Elinor was aware that she wasn't held in high regard by this particular high priestess. The carriage was rickety as they rode through the rolling countryside. The dirt track was full of stones and holes, providing a rough ride that the carriage's wheels struggled to endure. Elinor experienced jostling with every turn of the wheel within the carriage and she was glad this journey was so short. With hands braced against the roof for the worst bumps, she remembered why she hated travelling this way. Given the choice, she would opt for horseback riding any day, finding it much better than this mode of transport. Just as frustration reached a breaking point within her, the temple came into view.

The place exuded undeniable magnificence, with the building itself standing as a masterpiece. Every detail spoke of grandeur, evident in the intricate carvings that adorned the walls and pillars outside. Each one told a story of the past, skilfully etched into the stone. Surrounding the temple, acres of lush green land stretched out, offering a peaceful ambience. A limestone footpath decorated with flowering shrubs graciously welcomed visitors. Diamond-shaped flower beds enhanced the front garden, bursting with a vibrant array of colours and a variety of flower species. Low lanterns illuminated the path leading to the temple steps, adding to the enchantment of the scene. A majestic staircase, constructed from the same limestone as the path, composed of a hundred steps ascended towards the temple, beckoning visitors. As one approached the building, towering pillars lined an arched walkway, serving as a gateway to the architectural marvel that awaited inside. Elinor stepped out of the carriage, and stood upon the limestone path, relief flooding through her. A priestess waited a few paces away, cloaked in their usual deep blue hooded robe, which veiled her face from view.

"Good morning Princess, the high priestess is waiting for you."

"Priestess. Thank you. Lead the way."

The priestess started walking, and Elinor followed while her guards stayed behind them, vigilant. As they approached the steps, more priestesses passed by, offering nods of recognition to Elinor. Within their hierarchy, the high priestess held an equal rank to the current monarch, hence a mere nod was the extent of acknowledgment she could expect. Despite her frustration, Elinor knew better than to challenge their customs. The priestesses had their own set of rules and questioning them would only sour her already fragile relationship with them. Upon reaching the temple doors, Elinor entered without her guards, as they weren't permitted entry under any circumstance. The priestess led Elinor into the vast foyer and gestured to the hall on their left. Familiar with her surroundings, Elinor strode confidently towards the high priestess's office, eager to get this meeting over with. Her escort rapped her knuckles against the solid oak door.

"Enter." At the sound of the voice, Elinor opened the door and strode inside.

"Princess Elinor. Please, take a seat. It's a delight to see you again. The last time I saw you, you were here engrossed in your studies."

"Has it been so long? I remember my time here. I certainly learned a lot."

"You were a bright student, yet stubborn at times. Your brother was better behaved," said the high priestess and continued in a respectful tone. "I want to express my condolences for his passing. He was a wonderful man and a great king. Both I and the other priestesses felt his loss deeply."

"Thank you for your condolences. Even under the circumstances at the end, all felt his loss."

"The entire kingdom suffered a significant loss because of his departure. Let us hope you can unite the people as he did, once more. Remind me, when did the funeral take place? I don't recall an invitation passing my desk."

"It was a few days ago, and no invites. Just an intimate gathering with family only, given the circumstances… with his betrayal to the kingdom."

"Yes, most receive a trial before being put to death," the high priestess clarified, her tone measured. "Your explanation of events, however, seemed to justify your actions, particularly given the imminent threat to your life posed by your brother."

Elinor smiled at the high priestess, trying to conceal her annoyance at the woman's tone and comments. The high priestess' low opinion of her was clear. Elinor, too, was unsympathetic to the woman, yet she recognised the necessity of her involvement in both the coronation and bonding ceremony. Although there were other high priestesses throughout the country, they were located too far away to arrive on time. However, like the current high priestess, Elinor had no confidence that they would help her. Annoyingly, they all adored her *dear James* and weren't particularly fond of her. Her time spent in the temple was far from pleasant for many who were present. As Elinor gazed at the high priestess, she had not aged a single day. Draped in a long sweeping deep blue gown, the high priestess boasted waist-length, jet-black hair. With her dark complexion and deep brown eyes, she possessed a striking appearance. Judging by her looks alone, one could never determine her true age. An average person would find it hard to believe her if she were to reveal it. The benefits of wielding magic were most apparent in defying age. Despite her youthful appearance, this high priestess was in her late sixties. Elinor knew that regular engagement with magic slowed down the ageing process. The oldest recorded magic wielder was a high priestess who had lived to be one hundred and sixty-two years old. While several kings and queens had also reached the impressive milestone of one hundred years, none had surpassed the longevity of that high priestess. To steer the conversation back to the reason she was there, Elinor bit her tongue, sidestepping what she wanted to say, and continued.

"I did what was necessary for myself and the kingdom. I regret my brother's death, although it was necessary. Now, I wish to thank you for seeing me today. I know how valuable your time is, and don't wish to take up more than I need to. So, I'm ready to begin the preparations for the bonding ceremony when you are, High Priestess."

"Certainly. The sooner we begin, the better for both of us, I think. As we spoke, preparations were being made to begin. If you follow me, we'll head to the sacred area."

Elinor felt a sense of anticipation as she followed the high priestess out of the room. They headed down a corridor before turning right, entering a vast open area through an archway. Two more priestesses greeted them, leading them through a set of doors to the outside. Following them down a sloping path, Elinor came to a secluded outdoor area. It was a sacred sanctuary where priestesses could come to reconnect with the divine spirit. Surrounded by trees, the area remained concealed, offering a haven of tranquillity for the visitor. At its heart stood a statue of the divine spirit, intricately carved from a tree. Water trickled gently through a meandering stream, while a lush carpet of soft grass adorned the ground beneath.

Because the divine spirit showed deep concern for the earth, a sacred outdoor space became the ideal location for reconnecting with her essence. Numerous priestesses would gather there, engaging in prayer and meditation to forge a deep connection with the earth's very soul. Before entering, all three priestesses ceremoniously removed their footwear and prompted Elinor to do the same. They then removed their deep blue gowns and entered the secluded area in just their slips. Elinor, knowing what to expect, swiftly followed suit and was already removing her dress. A fourth priestess was already waiting for them, candles lit and ready to begin the ceremony.

With great care, they placed the candles in the shape of a grand diamond. Elinor, avoiding the flames, stepped into the centre, settling herself upon the soft grass. The four priestesses positioned themselves at each point of the diamond, with the high priestess taking her place at the topmost point. Earth, water, fire, and air. Four priestesses embodied four elements. Elinor had gone over this process many times over the years, to prepare for this day. She wanted nothing to go wrong. No mistakes on her part. She was in two minds about how effective the bonding ceremony was these days without the divine spirit herself. However, she was reluctant to lose out on power through a lack of belief. So, she prepared well beforehand, learning the exact process, and her role.

The day's ritual was all about reconnecting her spirit with Mother Earth. By completing the ritual, one's spirit becomes more open to the elements and world around them. During the bonding ceremony with the shard, one's spirit becomes bonded with it, much like the shard is connected to the land all around. What flows through you, flows through the earth and land around you, and vice versa. In the past, when the crystal was whole, it wielded an immense amount of power under one's control. However, now with the broken crystal shard, the power, while still significant, was a mere fraction of what it once was.

Elinor, lying on the grass, went through the motions of the ritual. The priestesses were chanting, rising one at a time. The one of earth walked towards her and sprinkled a circle of earth around her body. Next came the one of water, following the same process. A gust of wind followed this, circling her before the candles went out and she went into a deep meditative state. Opening her eyes, the candles were lit once more, and the four priestesses were sitting in a meditative pose themselves. With heads bowed and eyes closed in a sitting position, they were each back to their original points from the start of the ritual.

"Welcome back, child of the earth. The divine spirit welcomes you into her fold."

Elinor sat up, looking at the high priestess with mild confusion on her face.

"It's complete. I'll see you at sunrise on the day of the bonding ceremony. Until then, leave in peace."

Elinor stood up and nodded to each expressing her gratitude before walking back to her clothes. In a daze, she began dressing herself once more, with the aid of another priestess who was waiting. Elinor's mind buzzed, contemplating what had just happened. Even though she had familiarised herself with the accounts of others and knew what to expect, the events had left her unsettled. While in a deep meditative state, she found herself transported to what felt like a tangible realm. A radiant glow emerged, beckoning her to various pivotal moments in her life. Like a floating speck, she felt drawn in different directions, catching glimpses of significant events from her past. She then explored her present circumstances and envisioned multiple potential futures dependent on the choices she would make.

In that fleeting moment, every detail became vividly real. The raw intensity of her emotions surged through her, tangible and overwhelming. The world around her pulsed with life, every action etched with purpose. And the events within the realm left an indelible mark on her soul. As she emerged from that ethereal realm, the memories slipped from her grasp like elusive wisps of a forgotten dream. The remnants of her experiences faded, leaving her scrambling to preserve even the faintest fragments. They lingered, yet remained elusive, like an intangible presence in the air.

A shiver ran through her body as Elinor trailed behind the young priestess, retracing their steps through the temple until they reached the entrance. At the bottom of the steps, her men awaited. With a sense of relief, she strode back to her carriage, eager to return home. Inside the carriage, she couldn't shake the warnings and fear from the ritual. Elinor wondered how accurate the visions were. Her future looked bleak in a few of them, and these involved her niece and nephew. This renewed her resolve to find them. And soon.

Rumours circulated about where they were, but they seemed to be unreliable and contradictory. She couldn't rely solely on hearsay; she needed concrete evidence. As the carriage rattled on, she pondered the possibilities. She knew time was of the essence. Every passing moment increased the risk of them eluding her. The thought of their escape, returning years later to kill her like in her visions, put fear into her soul. She would keep searching until she found them. They couldn't remain hidden for long. The question playing in her mind was who took them. None were missing from the castle since that first night, at least none who could successfully evade her men. Only one person had the skill to hide them away, and he was supposedly out of the country. Or so she had been told.

No one had seen George in months, but that meant little. The man was highly skilled in power and could easily keep his grandchildren hidden if he so desired. Upon returning home,

Elinor relayed her suspicions to Adrian, entrusting him to investigate further. If she was right, Adrian would uncover George's whereabouts. If not, it would be another strike against him. Her trust in him was still amiss. In the meantime, Elinor resolved to keep herself busy until the coronation. She wasn't about to let one lucid dream ruin her plans. With the memories slipping further from her grasp, it was easy to forget them and bask in her happiness.

The next day proceeded seamlessly. The food and entertainment had been organised with all the preparations in place for the coronation the following day. Guests were already present in the vicinity or within the castle itself, ready to arrive on time for the day's events. Elinor's dress, pressed and elegantly finished, hung in her chambers, adding to the anticipation of the forthcoming ceremony.

Around lunchtime, the high priestess arrived and made her way to the castle's sacred area, similar to the one at the temple. Accompanying her were several priestesses, offering support for the upcoming events. With the evening setting in, Elinor made her way to the great hall where a dinner was being held. The gathering served as both a small celebration of the impending coronation and a briefing on the schedule for the following day. Excitement reverberated through the room in anticipation of the upcoming event. Chatter and laughter filled the air, mingling with the delightful aroma of delectable wine and sumptuous food. Elinor's face radiated with joy, evident in the twinkle of her eyes and the contagious curve of her smile.

Chapter 11

The Coronation

The morning of the coronation dawned, and Elinor rose with the first light, preparing herself for the day ahead. Nerves overwhelmed her, a queasiness swirling in her stomach. Despite meticulous preparations, and her imminent crowning as queen before noon, a lingering anxiety stayed within her. She couldn't shake the nagging feeling that this was all a surreal fantasy. The nerves persisted, accompanied by a foreboding sense that something might go wrong at the very last moment, shattering her dream. She could only find solace when the crown finally rested upon her head. Until that moment, Victoria and Lloyd had been busy scurrying around the castle, ensuring that everything was prepared and flawless for her arrival. Her ladies now stood by her side, assisting her in getting ready and finding some peace. Even on such a significant occasion, she couldn't shake off her nerves.

A bath infused with lavender oils had been prepared for her, and she was doing her best to relax in it. As she observed her ladies bustling around her room, they busily attended to her dress and accessories, striving for perfection. Her gown was a masterpiece, adorned with a deep purple hue and elegant streaks of white cascading down the flowing skirt. Its off-shoulder design and long sleeves enhanced its overall appeal. When paired with the regal cloak and jewellery, the final ensemble would exude pure royalty.

Despite her frazzled nerves, she made an effort to eat something, although she had no appetite. Her lady Chloe reminded her to eat throughout the morning, so she nibbled on the toast and fruit, neglecting the eggs. After her bath, two of her ladies began styling her hair, creating loose curls and elegantly pinning up the top half to accommodate the impending crown. Next came the dress. Bethel had done a wonderful job. The corseted bodice hugged her figure perfectly, while the skirt billowed out gracefully. With the ensemble nearly complete, only a touch of makeup, the perfect pair of shoes, and a white gold necklace adorned with dazzling diamonds remained to perfect her appearance.

Standing before the full-length mirror, Chloe draped the purple velvet cloak with white fur trim around her shoulders. Surveying herself in the mirror, Elinor couldn't help but admire her reflection. She appeared every inch the queen, exuding regal poise. Just then, a gentle knock interrupted her reverie, and Elinor turned just as Adrian entered. His eyes widened in awe at the sight before him, a gesture of devotion conveyed through a respectful bow.

"My Lady. You look exquisite!"

Elinor couldn't suppress the blush that rose to her cheeks at his words and the way he gazed at her. She felt as though she was the only woman in the world.

Keeping her regal posture, she replied. "Thank you, Adrian. Now, would you like to do the honours of escorting your future queen to her coronation?"

With a twinkle in his eyes, Adrian offered his arm. "I would be honoured, my Lady."

As she hooked her arm through his, they walked together to the royal hall with Adrian engaging in light conversation to ease her nerves. She gripped his arm firmly as they proceeded through the packed hallways. Numerous castle workers lined the walls in the hope of a glimpse of their future queen.

As Elinor arrived at the doors, her presence was announced, prompting everyone inside to stand up. Simultaneously, a delightful classical melody began to play.

Adrian had entered first, making his way to the front of the hall, where he stood beside Lord Malins. Following him, Elinor entered, her head held high as she walked to the end of the aisle. With graceful strides, she glided up the steps before taking her place in front of the royal throne. As she lowered herself onto the throne, her gaze swept over the sea of people, her heart racing with anticipation. This was the moment she had been waiting for. To solidify her understanding that this was indeed happening, the high priestess of Carraton approached her. Elinor's skin prickled, nerves rippling through her as she awaited the words of the high priestess. A silent prayer to the divine spirit coursed through her, hoping that everything wasn't about to be swept out from under her.

"Greetings, my people. We're here today to crown Princess Elinor as the new queen. May her reign be long and just."

"Here, here," the crowd murmured.

"Elinor, do you vow to uphold the laws of the land and care for your people?"

"I do."

"Do you promise to uphold the traditions of the land and your connection to the divine spirit?"

"I do."

"Do you vow to serve your country and people, putting the needs of the many above your own?"

"I do."

"Then I announce you Queen to all. Be true and just in your rule," the high priestess announced loud and clear, as she placed the diamond and ruby-encrusted crown upon Elinor's head.

The royal hall erupted into cheers before dying down for the next stage of the coronation. As the voices quietened, the high priestess stepped to the side of the throne. At the same moment, four priestesses walked towards the throne, stopping at the base of the steps. They went up to the new queen one at a time with a gift from each representing the four elements.

The first gift was that of earth, presented as a living terrarium. In a small glass bowl, a harmonious combination of gravel, soil, moss, and plant life had been perfectly layered to create its living structure. The second gift manifested as water, embodied by a mini-functioning waterfall, powered by the elements. A stack of small granite rocks layered upon a granite bowl allowed water to trickle freely down the rocks and into the bowl. The third gift represented the element of air, encased within a small sphere where the wind itself moved within. Swirling forms could be seen whirling around the delicate object. Finally, the fourth gift symbolised fire, presented as an ever-burning candle that one could watch for all eternity through a glass case. The gifts were laid atop the steps, ensuring visibility for everyone present. Each priestess bowed her head before returning to where they previously stood.

After completing this part, Elinor stood up and expressed her gratitude to everyone present. With this, she officially ascended to the drawing room throne as the Queen of Ethos. As she rose, the entire room erupted in cheers once again, celebrating their new queen. As the cheers gradually subsided, Elinor thanked everyone once more for their support and vowed to be a benevolent queen to all. Having finished her conversation, she dismissed them and invited them to gather in the great hall, signalling the start of the festivities. As she descended the steps, her people continued to offer their congratulations before bidding their farewells.

As the rest of the crowd made their way to the great hall, Elinor and Adrian headed to the balcony overlooking the courtyard. This vantage point held significance, as it was where the royal family traditionally addressed the public for important announcements. The balcony, connected to the drawing room, provided a clear view of the courtyard and beyond, allowing the people below a glimpse of their beloved king or queen. Inside the drawing room, Elinor positioned herself in front of the rich royal blue curtains, awaiting her introduction.

The courtyard was already bustling with people, though there were still a few minutes before the designated time. Not wanting anyone to miss the moment, the guards stood ready, waiting for the chiming of the clock bells to draw back the curtains. As the bells rang, a guard announced her to the ever-growing crowd, this time introducing her as Her Majesty Queen Elinor the First, while the curtains gracefully opened. Stepping onto the balcony, a smile graced Elinor's face as she waved to her people. The weight of her crown became real as she looked upon her people. The realisation washed over her as she raised her hand to speak. She was their queen.

"Hello, people of Carraton! As your newly crowned queen, I wish to express my heartfelt gratitude to each and every one of you for your unwavering support. I vow to rule with fairness and integrity, prioritising the needs of our kingdom and its people above all else. Now, return to your homes and celebrate together at the dawn of this new reign."

The crowd erupted in cheers once again, and their enthusiasm fuelled Queen Elinor's spirit. She continued to wave to the crowd for a few more moments before bidding them farewell, urging them to return home and revel in their celebrations. After greeting her people, Elinor and Adrian headed to the great hall, where her guests had already begun to celebrate with a lavish banquet.

The splendour of the room took Elinor aback as she entered. Grand tables lining the walls were laden with delectable food. Platters of vibrant fruits, delicious cheeses, aromatic wines, and succulent meats were artfully arranged, enticing guests to indulge before the main feast. The spacious centre of the hall had been cleared, poised for dancing and performances. Enchanting melodies of music drifted across the room, mingling harmoniously with the laughter and conversations of the attendees. The ambience enveloped Elinor, immersing her in a world that felt entirely her own.

As she navigated through the crowd, her guests flocked around her, showering congratulations on her newfound position. Each person expressed their happiness to her and offered their assistance. Finally, she reached her seat at the royal table, and with a regal gesture, she announced the commencement of the feast. As everyone took their seats at their respective tables, the main courses were served. To start, the waitstaff placed an array of meat and fish dishes on the tables, accompanied by roasted vegetables and salads.

Afterwards, a variety of sweet and savoury pastries and tarts replaced these, along with an array of cakes to choose from as well. The waitstaff continued to replenish the already eaten items with more fruits and cheese delicacies as the evening progressed. Throughout, every kind of wine was served. As the guests enjoyed their meal, they were captivated by the music, dancing, and stories performed by the court entertainers. Once everyone had finished dining, the musical festivities resumed, with Elinor taking the lead in dancing, joined by many guests. This began a joyous evening of drinking and dancing. As the night wore on, Elinor bid goodnight to her guests, retiring to her chambers. Despite feeling worn out and having aching feet, she was relaxed, with a warm buzz enveloping her body.

***

Elinor woke up an hour before sunrise to prepare for the bonding ceremony. Feeling groggy from staying up late, she reluctantly got out of bed. Each step aggravated the throbbing in her head. She knew she shouldn't have had another glass of wine after the first one. The little voice in her head convinced her that one more wouldn't do any harm. It was her celebration, after all. Yet, one glass had turned into more than she could remember, and now she faced the consequences of a mild hangover.

Sensing the impending hangover, one of her ladies had thoughtfully brought along a remedy with her breakfast. As foul as it tasted, it did the trick. Grimacing, she gulped down the concoction as she pinched her nose in distaste. Elinor struggled to keep the repulsive liquid down, her stomach churning. Once done, she felt her stomach settle down, and she allowed her ladies to help dress her. They dressed her in a simple white and gold gown before wrapping her cloak around her, ready to head outside.

As Elinor arrived at the sacred spot nestled within the garden, her gaze fell upon the high priestess and the four priestesses she had encountered the previous day. They had already performed the blessings, preparing the area for the upcoming ceremony. Like at the temple, a wooden statue representing the divine spirit stood tall. Positioned at the heart of the spot was a raised circular platform, serving as a designated area for Elinor to stand and await the proceedings. Surrounding the platform, an assortment of blossoming flowers adorned the rest of the sacred spot, along with vibrant green grass.

In just her gown, Elinor stood poised as the high priestess approached, chanting, with the crystal shard held in the cusps of her hands. By now, the crystal emanated a faint glow. Extending her hands, Elinor took the crystal in her hands. As the sun ascended before her, Elinor elevated the crystal towards the sky. Its radiant beams bathed her in light, piercing through the shard, painting the sky with a vibrant rainbow.

Amidst the priestesses' melodic chants, Elinor proclaimed, "Divine spirit of the land, bestow upon me your strength and power."

The crystal intensified its glow, displaying all the colours of the rainbow. Elinor felt a surge of power moving through her veins, causing her body to tremble from the force within her. As the crystal shard dimmed once more, a tingling sensation flowed through her entire being. Then stopped. She felt different. Changed. It was as though she had become intertwined with the essence of the crystal, merged into one entity. She struggled to articulate the nature of this newfound connection. She felt a heightened sense of awareness of the world around her. It was as if a new way of experiencing the world had been opened up to her. She no longer just saw the world but felt it as well. This new perspective was a euphoric experience for her.

The surging power coursing through her veins now surpassed anything she had felt before. At that moment, she understood why kings and queens of the past had fought for it. It felt as though she embodied the very essence of the elements themselves. Not just to create a gust of wind or a light breeze, but to become a hurricane if she willed it. All this power emanated from one crystal shard. It begs the question as to how much power could one wield with all four. Still holding the crystal, the voice of the high priestess brought Elinor back to the present.

"It's done. You connect to all, and all connect to you. How do you feel?"

"I feel wonderful," Elinor answered, not wanting to share her true thoughts with the high priestess.

The high priestess told Elinor that she would see her on the first day of spring, taking the crystal to return it to the tower. Still basking in the glow of her newfound abilities, Elinor wanted to test her powers. Standing in place, she summoned the wind, embracing the energy cursing through her veins. Drawing more and more energy from the earth itself until her body vibrated from the power. As she released control of her desires, a small gust of wind began circulating, with a few leaves floating around her before the wind turned into a gale. Elinor reluctantly released the power while beaming within at just what she controlled. With so much power at her fingertips, her mind was filled with the endless possibilities now in her grasp. Lost in her thoughts, the sight of Adrian walking before her brought her back to reality.

"Speak to me."

"You were right. George somehow has them. I have men on their trail now, so they should be in our hands soon," answered Adrian.

"I don't share your faith in this matter. George will remain hidden for as long as he chooses to. Then one day he'll come, even if it's not for many years. He won't allow me to keep the throne," Elinor replied with resignation in her voice.

"Then we keep watch and make sure we're ready when he comes. And the best way to defend ourselves will be to find the shards," Adrian responded.

"That's it, Adrian. Now, the throne is mine. We need to find those shards," Elinor answered confidently and continued. "I already checked the royal vault for information on them, as well as the private safe in my chambers, with no luck. There must be something here. I want you to check through the private books and documents in the royal private library. Look at all the old stories on them as well. There may be a clue we need hiding in them."

"I'll get right on it," replied Adrian, as he left to get started on his new orders.

Frustration consumed her thoughts about George. He had always been a thorn that disrupted her plans at every turn. Well, this time, the thorn was about to meet its match. She would be ready for him when he came. As she channelled her power, she watched as a ball of fire burned in her palm. Oh, she would be ready for him.

Chapter 12

The Royal Crypt

With all the changes around the castle, Cecilia found herself struggling to reclaim her sense of belonging. Each passing day seemed like an uphill battle, trapped in the very place she used to call home. The once comforting walls were no longer a haven but a suffocating prison. Left with only Mistress Katelyn to call a friend, the days were tough, but the nights proved even more daunting alone in her room. With the rest of the castle preoccupied with Elinor's coronation, she felt compelled to leave her room and venture out to visit the royal crypt.

Elinor had concluded James's funeral in secret, only for Cecilia to find out about it days later. Once again, her grief spiralled out of control by losing the chance to say goodbye, leaving her bedridden anew. Now, in pursuit of solace and closure, she needed to visit James's resting place. Abandoning her morning duties in the kitchen, Cecilia left the castle with her two guards trailing behind her. The castle grounds housed the royal crypt, located underground.

As she neared the entrance, her heart raced furiously, and her palms became clammy with nervousness. She didn't know if entering the royal crypt was going to be a problem. While no one had forbidden her, a sense of apprehension gnawed at her, half-expecting the guards to grab her at any moment and drag her back to her room. Nerves reaching breaking point, Cecilia's complexion turned pale, with her hands trembling as she stood in front of the crypt's entrance. With caution, she pulled the handle down, and with all her strength, pushed the solid iron door open. As the door swung open, she found herself paralysed, unable to take a single step forward. Crossing this threshold would be the final admittance that James was gone. And she wasn't sure she was prepared to confront this inevitable moment.

Cecilia mustered the strength to take a step forward, moving one foot in front of the other until she crossed the threshold. Upon entering the main door, she found herself standing in a long, spacious hallway with wooden doors lining both sides. The walls, smooth throughout, were decorated with torch brackets at regular intervals, casting a steady illumination along the hallway.

With only a sliver of light filtering in through the open doors, Cecilia reached out and took hold of the first torch. She rummaged in her pocket, finding the flint and iron to ignite a flame. As the torch came to life, a soft yellow glow enveloped her, casting eerie shadows that danced upon the crypt walls. Determined, she began her descent deeper into the crypt. The further she went, the deeper the darkness became, and the air grew oppressively thick. Too long in this place could leave one feeling nauseous and lightheaded, the air laden with heaviness. As she walked through the hall, there were several chambers, each housing different royal families. Each holding statues of past kings and queens, situated atop their final resting places. Approaching the chamber designated for her own family, she paused just outside its door, a moment of reflection seizing her.

Heart pounding in her chest, Cecilia cautiously ventured inside. The sound of her shoes echoed with every step she took. Standing before James's grave, she felt dismayed that no one had given him a statue in his honour. Doubts clouded her mind, questioning whether he would ever receive one. Instead, there lay only a modest headstone bearing a simple inscription, a stark reminder of his humble memorial. Cecilia vowed that one day she would mark his grave as it should be and give him the dignified farewell befitting a king. After placing the torch in one of the brackets, she then settled on the ground. She sat in front of the headstone and talked to her husband as though he was right there with her. She reminisced about their memories and the dreams they had for the future, for their children, Aevah and Jacob. Absorbed within the moment, tears of both sorrow and joy streamed down her face as she reflected on the beautiful life they had together and what could have been.

"I hope I'm not intruding."

Cecilia spun round at the woman's voice behind her. Bewilderment upon her face at who stood before her.

"High Priestess. What brings you here?" Fear pierced her mind, not knowing what was about to happen. Once before they were friends, but considering recent events, Cecilia didn't know whom she could trust.

"To see you, my dear. It has been far too long." The high priestess walked closer and embraced Cecilia in a warm hug.

For a split second, Cecilia tensed before relaxing and hugged the priestess's back. With her guard down, she finally felt safe as the tears flowed.

"Oh Cecilia, I'm sorry for the way events are unfolding. I have little time. The guards are currently in a daydream, but it will not last long. You must listen carefully."

Cecilia pulled herself together at the serious tone in the high priestess's voice. "I'm listening."

"Elinor has her reign secured, but I know she faked her evidence against James, and she's planning to join the crystal shards together. But without proof, there's nothing I can do. The lords are backing her claim for their own benefit, so they are of no help either."

"But what can I do? I'm being followed every second of the day."

"Find a way Cecilia, get help. There are still those who support you within these walls. Get what I need and bring it to me in the temple, and I'll tell you where your children are."

"What?!"

"Your children. They are alive, and Elinor knows."

"But how?"

"Your father. I'm sorry, I can't explain everything now. Time is running out and I have to go before I'm seen with you. You need to get me that evidence so I can put a stop to Elinor and see your children brought home safely."

Before she could say another word, the high priestess disappeared, leaving Cecilia in a confused state. Her children were alive. Elinor had lied to her. That one thought surged within, sparking a profound joy that warmed her from the inside. She felt like bursting at the seams. At that very moment, she yearned to dance, sing, and perhaps even cry tears of joy to express the immense happiness she felt.

A cough from outside the door brought her back to the here and now. Her two watchful guards were always just a few steps behind her. Six guards in total took turns supervising her. Not one would speak to her unless she spoke to them first. The bubble of happiness within her began to deflate gradually as she contemplated the daunting task of evading them to gather evidence against Elinor.

As Cecilia looked upon James's tomb, a surge of anger enveloped her, fuelled by recalling how coldly Elinor described his death and the blatant lie she told about her children. The vow she had made replayed in her mind, intensifying her fury. Unconsciously, she clenched her fists tightly as her mind started plotting. Cecilia was determined to escape this prison with the evidence the high priestess needed and to reunite with her beloved children once more. She recognised the need for the perfect ally. A plan already forming, and she needed to secure an invitation to the upcoming ball. Without it, she would fail. Knowing Elinor's love of making her suffer, Cecilia thought a little reverse psychology here might do the trick. Convince Elinor that she didn't wish to attend, manipulating her into extending an invitation.

Cecilia gently placed her hand on James's grave, making a solemn promise to return soon. She fought back tears as she picked up the torch and left the chamber, making her way back to the castle. With a clear plan taking shape in her mind, she hurriedly returned to her room. Closing the door behind her, a sense of relief washed over her, knowing that no one was watching, and giving her the freedom to bring her plan to life. Every possibility swirled in her thoughts. She knew she needed help to pull off her ideas, though. Mistress Katelyn was the only person Cecilia could trust, and she resolved to speak to her in the morning. By then, her idea would be a more cohesive plan than its current state of disarray. Thus, she spent the rest of the day in her room, meticulously planning her escape. Not daring to write anything down, she continued to plan in her mind. If someone searched her room, any written escape plan would jeopardise her freedom and would result in her being sent back to the dungeons.

Famished from having skipped meals since breakfast, she left her room and headed to the great hall for dinner. However, instead of joining the festivities, she prepared a tray of food for herself and quickly returned to her room. The sight of everyone celebrating stirred something within her. Amidst the relentless pursuit of her plans, she had forgotten the significance of the day, it was the coronation. The lively singing and dancing served as a reminder. Luckily, she slipped in and out unnoticed. Back in her chambers, Cecilia enjoyed her meal in solitude, as she did every other day. Yet, this time, there was a flicker of something inside her – a small flame that steadily grew with each passing minute, as her escape plans took shape.

***

Cecilia and Elinor hadn't crossed paths since Cecilia's visit to the crypts, aside from occasionally passing each other in the hallway. While such distance suited Cecilia under normal circumstances, the present situation demanded otherwise. She needed to secure an invitation to the ball, and the only way to get one was from Elinor herself. Elinor had personally chosen the attendees with invites already sent out. Unsurprisingly, she wasn't one of them. Fully aware of Elinor's penchant to unsettle her, Cecilia devised a plan to obtain an invitation without explicitly requesting one. The plan swiftly took shape. While working in the kitchens, she overheard chatter among the young workers about the masquerade ball.

"Oh, t be a fly on the wall during the ball. Or better yet, be there in person. Imagine ey, the glitz an the glam ov it ey." Lilly daydreamed as she danced with her wooden spoon.

"Ah keep dreamin, you would neva be invited to such a fancy pants party ey," replied Sophie.

"Ah, like you would be any betta if you was invited, ey."

"I would be the Belle ov the ball, I would."

Hearing the two young women, Cecilia edged close enough to join in and add to their conversation.

133

"Oh, I'm glad I'm not invited. I would feel too out of place at an event like that these days."

The two young women looked at each other as if deciding how to respond. Sophie was the one to step forward and looked at Cecilia before replying, "ey I suppose you would."

They began gossiping as they moved further away from Cecilia. They laughed in between, glancing towards her a few more times before continuing with their work. Cecilia wasn't upset at the obvious disrespect they were showing her. On the contrary, they were doing exactly what she wanted them to. Aware of how fast gossip spreads, and the embellishments that tend to be added, she had no doubt her little conversation would soon reach Elinor's ears. Now, she merely awaited Elinor's anticipated response, hopeful that it would involve an invitation aimed purely at tormenting her further. Although Cecilia had been in minimal direct contact with Elinor, that didn't mean the woman hadn't been finding any opportunity to subtly remind her of her diminished social standing.

From Cecilia's new seating spot in the great hall, hidden away from view to her new role in the evening as a chambermaid, Elinor was doing a good job of making her life miserable. Between balancing her duties from helping in the kitchen in the mornings and running around in the afternoons cleaning rooms, Cecilia was feeling the strain.

She had become aware of a request being put forward as well to become a servant to Elinor herself, not a lady-in-waiting but a servant directly to Elinor. However, this hadn't yet happened because she was deemed in need of training for the role. Mistress Fleur, responsible for supervising all the young ladies who came through, was tasked with overseeing Cecilia's preparation for this role. Following a brief conversation she had with Mistress Fleur, Cecilia learned that her training would start when she called for her. Subsequently, she would start under Elinor's service after the masquerade ball. Given Mistress Fleur's extensive responsibilities in organising the ball and ensuring the young ladies were prepared in grace, dance, and social etiquette for such a monumental event, she was too busy to schedule set training days.

This left Cecilia with a very brief window indeed to escape and gather evidence, as there was no way she was going to be a servant to Elinor. That would be too much to handle. She waited for the gossip to spread around the court, and for Elinor to invite her purely out of spite and to humiliate her in front of the entire court. Given the opportunity, Elinor wouldn't pass up a chance to ridicule and embarrass Cecilia. It was a behavioural pattern she had since a child. If she felt wronged or didn't like someone, Elinor needed to put them in their place and show superiority over them.

Elinor's ways hadn't improved despite her age. Cecilia used this to her advantage. As much as it hurt her mentally to be treated so poorly by those around her, it would help her achieve her goal of escaping. Cecilia persevered, knowing it wasn't for much longer. Unable to freely move about, she relied heavily on Mistress Katelyn, who was busy being both a secret messenger and organiser for the whole undercover plan. She didn't seem to mind; she got a thrill at being so deceptive right under Elinor's nose. Mistress Katelyn was adamant she wanted to help Cecilia somehow after what had happened. No matter what, she would do it. This included getting matching dresses and masks made as a start, with these being a big key to the entire plan.

Now these dresses weren't cheap. Given the nature of the ball, dresses of a certain quality were expected. Determined to make this work, Cecilia and Mistress Katelyn pooled their spare money together to raise the funds needed. Though Cecilia lacked real money, she gave a couple of valuable pieces of jewellery they could sell. Mistress Katelyn sold the jewellery to a local merchant, and the money they had together was just enough. While the material wouldn't be as exquisite as the other ladies, it would nonetheless blend well amongst all the dresses there.

With so much to do and plan, Cecilia was grateful for Mistress Katelyn's assistance, and two other trusted members of her court, Anita and Sean. The married couple were longtime family friends of Cecilia's father and had contacted Mistress Katelyn to let her know they were there to help if needed. It turned out that Sean had spoken to her father before he left the city with the twins and promised to get her out of Elinor's grasp. This made it more real and set her determination into full gear. Once Cecilia had her evidence against Elinor, she would escape during the ball, with Sean waiting outside the city to get her safely away.

Sean would secure the guard's rotations for the night as well. This would be crucial, knowing when there would be small windows of opportunities for her to escape and move through the castle and its grounds. The longer her absence went unnoticed, the greater her chances of success. The idea was for them to be as far away from the city before anyone began looking for Cecilia, though the likelihood of achieving this was slim. Simply being beyond the castle grounds by that time would provide a strategic advantage. Whatever happens, would come down to how well Cecilia and Mistress Katelyn executed their roles. Sean would have no idea whether their plan had worked until Cecilia stood in front of him. Once through the woods, Sean would follow an escape route to their intended destination. Cecilia just hoped the plan went smoothly for everyone's sake. If they could pull this off, and get the evidence to the high priestess, they might stand a chance to turn the tables on Elinor and take back her kingdom.

Chapter 13

The Escape

George's suspicions had been right all along. He knew not to trust Elinor, no matter what James had said. She remained a cold, calculating witch in his eyes and always would be. For the past year, he had been travelling *overseas*, an excuse concealing his own secret operation of watching Elinor. Rumours had been circling for years about her plans for the throne, but they had gained momentum in recent years. Despite his efforts to bring this to James and Cecilia's attention, his warnings fell on deaf ears. James refused to listen while Cecilia heeded his words. Taking matters into his own hands, George went off the grid, faking a trip exploring the world while secretly keeping watch.

He spent months in Adlington, adopting various disguises as he unravelled Elinor's plans. Upon learning of her intentions to visit her brother in Carraton, George knew this was the crucial moment. He desperately needed to get back to the city to warn James and Cecilia, but Elinor had already departed. Determined to intercept her, George swiftly mounted his horse, pushing it to its limits to arrive ahead of her. Though his stead was fast, he reached Carraton mere moments too late. Passing through the city gates, he heard the gossip already circulating about the princess and her entourage.

Undeterred by the circumstances, he rode up to the castle. To evade detection, he skilfully used his powers to transform his appearance into that of an ordinary staff member returning to his duties. As he entered the stables, an eerie silence hung in the air, with no workers in sight. The emptiness of the courtyard heightened his sense of unease as he ventured further into the heart of the castle.

"Come on now, move it! Come along."

George pressed his back flush against the wall, keen to remain unseen. Cautiously, he sidestepped towards the corner. He turned his head carefully to look but ensured he stayed out of sight of whoever lurked on the other side. Six guards wearing the unmistakable crimson-blue colours of Adlington marched down the corridor, wielding their swords as they escorted a group of castle workers. Their destination remained a mystery to George.

Realising he was outnumbered and would be of no help right then, George opted to bide his time. Before he made a move, he needed to know what was happening. Keeping to the servants' passageways not to be seen while trying to figure out what was happening, he came across one lone worker hastily scurrying through the passageway.

"Hold on, their friend. Where is everyone?"

Startled, the man looked at him in panic as he cried out, "A coup! She's here for the throne," before running past George, no doubt trying to escape.

Fear momentarily paralysed him before he began to run, praying to the divine spirit for the safety of his grandchildren. His heart pounded as he raced onward, struggling to maintain a sense of hope amidst his anxiety. As he reached their chambers, he paused outside the doorway with bated breath. The thought of them not being safe in their beds filled him with dread. Gently opening the door, he was greeted with darkness, along with the peaceful breathing of two sleeping children. Relief surged through his body, causing his heart to nearly stop. Not wanting to startle them, he returned to his true form before walking over to their beds. Standing between them, he found solace in the tranquillity of their sleep, everything briefly feeling right in the world. Determined to keep them from Elinor's clutches, he began devising a plan to get them out. With no time to spare, he woke them with gentle shakes, each awakening to his urgent whispers.

"Aevah, Jacob, quick, follow me and keep quiet."

"Grandpa? Where are we going?" Aevah asked groggily as she struggled to fully wake up from her sleep.

"Quickly, both of you," George urged calmly. "Something is happening in the castle. We must leave before anyone notices you're gone.

Despite his desire to swiftly remove them from the castle without causing any alarm, he couldn't ignore the fact that they were still so young. He tried to remain composed, even though his heart was pulsing like a hummingbird's wings, his mind racing to devise a safe exit strategy for them.

"What's happening, Grandpa?" Jacob asked puzzled as he sat up in his bed, also feeling tired from being woken up.

"Nothing to worry yourselves about. I'll explain once we are out, but it's safer for you not to be here right now. Come on, we need to leave," George replied as he swiftly ushered his grandchildren from their beds towards the wall, guiding them back into the passageway from where he had entered. Hastening the twins into the dimly lit passage, he turned his attention to the beds, watching as his power ignited them. As the flames grew and intensified, he closed the door and guided them along.

"This way! Quiet now," George whispered once more.

It was imperative for them to remain silent. The twins gripped George's hands tightly as they trailed behind him through the servants' passageway, descending along the narrow corridor. Although safe in the passageway, the distant echoes of shouts and cries reverberated through the halls, reminding Aevah and Jacob of the chaos beyond. They squeezed his hands even tighter, their quivering bodies pressed close to his, fear etched across their young faces.

In silence, they headed deeper into the castle, George's mind racing with concern for what was happening around them, and if James and Cecilia were still alive. Approaching the end of the passage, George tiptoed towards the solid wooden door. He gestured for silence with a finger to his lips before pressing his ear against the doorframe, listening intently. Hearing nothing, he carefully grasped the door handle, making sure the lock didn't click as he slowly eased the door open.

The kitchen seemed eerily abandoned. Stations usually bustling with activity now stood vacant, dirty dishes stacked haphazardly on the bench, and uncovered leftover food attracting flies. With a growing sense of unease, he cautiously entered, his heartbeat quickening with each step. Something was amiss. Even with dinner over, the kitchen should have been tidied and prepped for the morning breakfast shift.

After a quick scout of the area, he was certain it was indeed empty, and he motioned for the twins to follow, guiding them towards the stables. As they entered, he made his way to his horse, but a movement in the adjacent stable caught his attention. Mindful of the children, he stepped in front of them so as not to frighten them any more than they already were.

"Who goes there? Come out of the shadows and show your face." George began channelling his power as the person stepped into view.

"George? What is going on?"

"Sean, my friend. Thank goodness! I was hoping you could tell me. The children are with me, and we need to leave now. I'm not sure how long the distraction I made will hold."

"Elinor happened. Just like you predicted. Come, let's get out of here and we can talk freely once we are safe. Do you have a horse? I just finished saddling mine."

"I do. I left mine saddled just in case I needed a speedy escape. And it turns out, I was right."

As the two men walked their horses into sight, George lifted Aevah onto his horse, while Sean greeted the children and picked up Jacob. They settled each child in front of them as they mounted their own horses.

"Where to?"

"The temple, of course," George confirmed. "They are the only ones I trust."

"Of course. Once we get there, you and I are overdue for a chat."

"That we are, but first, let's get out of here in one piece. Hold on tight little ones, we have a bit of a bumpy ride ahead of us."

Before riding out, each held their child firmly while wrapping them in their cloaks for warmth on the chilly night. The absence of additional layers left them relying solely on their woollen pyjamas for warmth. Exiting the stables, they moved at a brisk pace, keeping watch for any signs of guards. George remained vigilant, his power at the ready to defend them if needed. As they neared the castle gates, they found no one stood watch, only lifeless bodies strewn across the ground. George pulled Aevah closer, shielding her from the grim scene with his cloak, urging their horses into a gallop until they were safely beyond the gates.

As they reached the city, both men slowed down, trotting quietly through the deserted cobblestone streets. Most of the city dwellers were likely home for the night, with only a few people meandering about. This bodes well for them. The fewer people who saw them, the better. Getting closer to the city's gates, George saw they were still open and nothing was amiss. Both men adjusted their position on their horses, hiding the children from view the best they could. The cloak of darkness provided some cover, making their escape easier than it would have been in daylight. They cautiously edged closer, hoping to pass unnoticed.

Judging from the guards' casual demeanour, they seemed unaware of the turmoil unfolding at the castle. George briefly considered telling them but dismissed the idea. He couldn't risk anyone knowing he had the children. With only two men here, they wouldn't make much difference to what was happening. Trotting through the gates, George tapped his hat to the guards, heart pounding in his chest as they passed through unchallenged. Breathing a sigh of relief, he spurred his horse into a gallop, determined to put as much distance as possible between them and Carraton. Although they weren't being pursued, he knew that it wouldn't last for long. Riding hard across the rough terrain, Sean kept pace behind him until he saw the temple ahead. Aevah, who had been quiet the whole time, leaned forward and scanned the horizon ahead of them.

"The temple! Why are we here, Grandpa?"

"Because it's safer here for us. There are unfriendly people in the castle, and until your father gets rid of them, we are better off staying here."

"Unfriendly people? What do you mean? Where's our mother and father? And everyone else? What about them?" Jacob fired off each question in quick succession with his voice quivering as he spoke.

George brought his mare to a stop, while Sean stopped his own beside him and George looked at his beloved grandchildren.

"Don't fear little ones. Everything will be fine," he reassured them in a gentle tone. To lighten the mood, he continued, "It's a minor skirmish between a few villains and the entire king's guard. Care to wager who'll emerge victorious? I'm telling you, come morning, it'll all be over, and we'll be riding back home as if nothing happened. For now, let's look at this as your own little adventure, a nighttime visit to the temple."

His warm smile worked its magic, visibly easing their tension. Aevah nestled back against him as they continued. After a rough ride, George steered his horse down a winding lane towards the temple of the priestesses.

Under the canopy of a cloudless night, the stars and moon cast their soft glow upon the scene as George arrived at the temple. Bringing his horse to a halt, he dismounted and helped Aevah down, keeping her hand firmly in his grasp as he led the way along the path to the foot of the steps. Sean took the reins while George ran up the steps and banged on the door. One priestess cautiously cracked the door open, peering out before recognising George and swinging the door wider. She saw Sean and the children at the foot of the steps and turned to the priestess behind her.

"Wake the high priestess and send for the stable hand to see to the horses. Quickly now!"

"Will the horses be okay if they are left alone for a few minutes?"

"Yes, priestess, they are well trained."

"Then come in, all of you, quickly now."

As everyone entered, the priestess gave one last glance outside before closing the door. The candle's dim light made it difficult to see, but the priestess led them inside and attended to the children.

"My dear little ones, you must be tired. Go with priestess Sage. She'll find you warm beds for the night, and perhaps some hot cocoa to drink."

George watched them leave, noting the smiles adorning their faces, as the other priestess led the two men towards the high priestess's office before leaving them to await her arrival. Each man took a seat before her desk. George looked at his friend. In their youth, they had served side by side in the king's guard and had forged a bond akin to brotherhood over the years. Now retired for a few years, Sean and his wife Anita had set up a home on a local farm, making weekly visits to the castle. On these trips, he delivered fresh produce such as milk, eggs, and meat straight from the farm for the royal kitchens. Sean looked good for a man of his age, with his grey hair and subtle wrinkles the only giveaway of his true age. Thanks to the farm, he maintained an active lifestyle and remained in good shape. Unlike himself, who had gained a few pounds around the middle after slacking off in training in recent years.

"If Elinor succeeds, what do we do?" Sean asked, interrupting George's wandering mind.

"You'll go back to your farm and feign ignorance, keeping you and your dear wife safe. I'll take the children and hide. I have faith in my daughter and James. They won't let her take the throne."

"I hope you're right, George. I'll pray to the divine spirit to keep you and the twins safe."

Before George could respond, the high priestess entered along with the young priestess, who had greeted them at the door.

"Gentlemen, it's good to see you, or perhaps not under the circumstances of your arrival at this time of the night."

Both men stood and respectfully bowed as the high priestess strode to her seat and sat before them. "What has happened for you to arrive at such a late hour with the young prince and princess?"

"Elinor, High Priestess," George answered.

Both priestesses exchanged a glance. "I believe you have both met priestess Nala?"

"Indeed, High Priestess."

"She's my most trusted advisor here in the temple and has eyes and ears within the city and castle itself. We're aware Elinor arrived earlier today and will have reports by morning on anything that happened tonight. With you here now, though, it doesn't bode well for the kingdom, I presume. What has happened?"

Even though she exuded confidence, the high priestess couldn't hide the subtle undertone of concern in her voice following her last question. George exchanged a glance with Sean and nodded for him to take the lead. After all, Sean had been there from the start.

"Initially, everything appeared to be proceeding smoothly, High Priestess. Elinor arrived, dinner and drinks were served, and eventually, everyone retired to their respective chambers, from what I was told. Today was my delivery day, and I had hung back for drinks with a few old friends at the castle. However, as I was leaving, men from Adlington stormed through the halls, capturing or killing anyone who crossed their path. I ran to the stables to secure more men from the main gate. It was there that I ran into George."

"Yes, I managed to navigate my entry and exit from the castle discreetly, ensuring the safety of the children. It would appear Elinor's forces had gained the upper hand by the time we left, with the very guards Sean hoped to seek already dead at the gates."

"So, you came straight here?" the high priestess asked.

"Yes, High Priestess. Regardless of what may happen, we can find comfort in knowing that the children are safe for now."

"No harm will come to them under my watch, George. Now, I suggest you both get some sleep while you can. Once we have more information, we'll let you know. Until we determine what events unfolded at the castle, there's nothing any of us can do. I'll pray to the divine spirit, though, hoping Elinor fails." As the high priestess finished, she gestured their dismissal and began writing.

Priestess Nala led them out and found them a room for the night. Both men, exhausted from the day's events, climbed into their beds. George fell into an uneasy sleep.

With the emergence of the sunrise and the sound of a crowing cockerel, Sean heard a soft knock at the door. He got up to answer it while George sat up, eager to hear any news.

Priestess Nala stood at the door. She came with grave news. "The king is no more. Elinor has seized the throne."

Chapter 14

New Plans

Both Sean and the priestess wore sombre expressions, but George found himself gasping for air. His heart pounded, and his chest constricted, making it difficult to catch his breath. "Cecilia?" he croaked. His voice was thick with desperation.

"Alive, but a prisoner for now," the priestess solemnly replied.

The words hit George like a turbulent wave, crashing against his senses. He breathed a sigh of relief, knowing his daughter was alive. But the bitterness of his helplessness lingered, unable to aid her in her time of need.

"They also claim the children perished in a fire that began in their chambers," the priestess added, fully aware they were safe and well.

George's mind raced as he replayed the night's events. He wanted nothing more than to go back and rescue his daughter, but his dear grandchildren had to be kept safe.

Elinor likely knew the children hadn't perished in that fire and were no longer in the castle. Which meant her men would despatch a search party once they were ready. George and the children needed to leave immediately and make their way to a little secluded cottage not too far away from here. The protective spell on this cottage prevented anyone who didn't know it existed from finding it, which means Elinor. With no way of knowing who would look for them or how long it would take them to catch up, time was of the essence.

Priestess Nala went to ready the children and gathered supplies for the trip while George and Sean debated over Sean's involvement. Despite George's reservations about endangering his friend, Sean insisted on travelling with them to the cottage. After some discussion, George gave in, agreeing that Sean could ride with them and stay for a few days to make sure they were safe.

As they left their room, Priestess Nala escorted them to the gardens at the back of the temple. Waiting for them were the high priestess, along with the children, and several supply packs already attached to their horses. No one had told the children what had happened yet. George wanted them safely in the cottage before he told them of their father's passing. For now, they were told they were going to stay awhile in a quaint little cottage while problems at the castle were resolved. Neither seemed to suspect anything, trusting him with what he had told them.

The high priestess began walking and led them along a wooden trail to the high walls that surrounded the temple. George watched as she effortlessly drew back the vines with a wave of her hand and unlocked an old wooden door with a mere gesture using her powers.

"This is our emergency escape route. No one knows of it. In the likely event that men are already on the way here, you can leave through the woods and have a head start without being seen."

"Thank you, High Priestess. We will not forget your kindness."

"I hope to meet again soon under better circumstances. For now, leave, and keep our young royals safe. I'll do what I can to stop Elinor from here."

They bid each other farewell, with the high priestess blessing them all on a safe journey before they walked through the wooden door into the vast forest. Once more, George mounted his horse with Aevah, confident that the dense forest would give them the cover needed to keep hidden. With Sean and Jacob mounted and ready beside him, they set off on their journey westward at a steady pace, fully aware of the daunting twelve-to-fifteen-day ride that lay ahead. This timeframe included the necessary stops and camping each night. How quickly they travelled would come down to how well the twins coped. That and backtracking to cover their tracks.

By mid-morning, George and Sean decided it would be a good idea to stop and rest in a secluded clearing. The children weren't used to riding for lengthy periods, and they hadn't eaten since a quick breakfast at first light. Everyone dismounted, with George using his power to place a protective charm around them, keeping them hidden should someone, by chance, stumble upon them. They couldn't use the charm while moving, but it had a marvellous quality of keeping them hidden when they were in one spot. The charm needed a fixed surrounding to latch onto to hide them. Therefore, they could sit, rest, and eat for a time with no fear of being snuck upon. After they had eaten and rested, Sean surveyed the surroundings to check if anyone had followed them.

With the coast clear, they all set off again, planning to stop again before nightfall. While riding, they needed to cross the river, circle the next village, and then keep a straight course before settling down for the night. It was vital for them to avoid being seen by anyone, as the memory of their faces by even a single lone traveller could prompt an army of guards to pursue them.

They could only hope to make it to the next rest stop undisturbed.

The twins absorbed the sights and sounds of their surroundings as they embarked on the long journey, engaging in casual conversation. With the early autumn weather bringing warmth courtesy of the lingering summer heat during the day, it was a pleasant ride despite the sombre reason behind it.

Emerging from the dense woods, they found themselves on an open road encompassed by vast fields, offering breathtaking views adorned with an abundance of trees and exquisite flowers displaying a kaleidoscope of colours. The air was alive with the hum of bees diligently gathering pollen from the blossoms while hidden birds perched on branches, their melodious songs filling the sky as they sang to one another.

As they neared the river, George encouraged the children to bask in the beauty of their surroundings. He wanted them to continue as they were, enjoying the loveliness of nature with their childlike wonder soaking in the world's magic around them. They rarely could be this free and travel so liberally. He absorbed their playfulness, particularly on the crossboat as they watched the fish gracefully swim through the ripples of the water.

When they reached the next stop that evening, Sean once again patrolled the area to check if anyone had followed them while George placed a protective charm to keep them hidden. Being a pleasantly warm night, they chose not to make a fire and instead set up a small tent for the twins to sleep in after they finished eating. Snuggled close to each other for comfort, the twins drifted off to sleep beneath a blanket for warmth. Thanks to the priestesses, they had adequate supplies for the journey. Only their food sources would need replenishing along the way. With the children peacefully asleep, George and Sean followed suit shortly thereafter.

Soon after midnight, George saddled the horses and woke the twins, getting them ready for the next stretch of the journey, while Sean erased any traces of their presence from the grass. The twins ate some biscuits George handed them before sleepily climbing on the horses.

As they began the next stretch of their journey, the twins soon thereafter dozed off, resting against their riders for support. As they slept, Sean and George discussed the various potential challenges they could encounter and the measures required to safeguard the twins, the crystal shards, and the kingdom as a whole.

The first few days of their journey passed without incident, but as the week drew to an end, it became evident that they were being pursued. It took longer than George thought it would for them to find them, but find them they had. They were exercising caution about it. Clearly, they had been instructed to keep hidden for the time being.

Undoubtedly, Adrian was the one giving orders, orchestrating the search for Elinor. Both George and Sean were far from ordinary men; their keen instincts alerted them whenever they suspected that they were being followed. Armed with many tactics to mislead their pursuers, one of their strategies was to create false trails. They planned to lead their followers into a fruitless pursuit, particularly on the last day of their journey. Their final location had to remain a well-guarded secret, as the safety of the children depended on it.

George's ability to channel straight from the earth itself put them at a distinct advantage. This form of magic left no trace, unlike channelling through an object, which illuminated like beacons, making them easy to track. When a person draws power directly from the earth, it would move freely from the earth to the wielder and back again, with no discernible trail to follow.

However, an object can focus and contain power. When this power is contained in an animate object, trackers can trace it.

The use of objects was the most common among magic wielders because of its simplicity. Even individuals with minimal or no training could acquire the ability to perform basic spells and commands by utilising an object. On the other hand, channelling magic independently required meticulous training, as one had to learn how to control the power that existed within oneself. Failure to do so could result in a catastrophic outcome, wherein individuals risked burning themselves out, leaving behind nothing but a charred corpse in their place.

With George being one of the few who possessed the ability to channel freely, they could effectively conceal themselves. Each time they made camp, George would channel his powers, ensuring they remained hidden. This tactic forced their pursuers to backtrack and painstakingly scour the area for any hint of their whereabouts, retracing their own steps. By creating misleading trails to track, the men in pursuit found themselves struggling to pinpoint their exact location.

George and Sean both took turns galloping ahead, their horses' hooves pounding against the dirt road. They left false trails in their wake, confusing their pursuers at every turn. The frustration of their followers was palpable. With each false trial, the search party grew more exasperated, forced to track down every misleading path. Those men, spread thin, stood guard at the end of each trail while they scanned the horizon for any glimpse of George and Sean. It wouldn't have been so difficult for the men if they weren't also trying to avoid being seen. Being told to keep their distance was surely making things even more challenging when they couldn't see the people they were supposed to be hidden from.

With a clear view of their every move, George knew their posting locations and nap times, allowing him to start moving again when no one was watching. This tactic had worked very well, or so he had believed. However, by the tenth day, Adrian anticipated his tactics and had positioned men to intercept from the opposite direction. Caught between men both ahead and behind, George faced a daunting predicament. He now had to find a way around both groups of men while steering them to their new home, still a few days away, and without them knowing its location.

Safe in a thicket surrounded by thorny bushes, George sat on the ground with Sean and pulled out a map. He began examining their location.

"What are your thoughts, Sean?"

"It would seem they're closing in."

As they both looked at the map, George's mind retraced his knowledge of the area. He remembered that an old smugglers' tunnel was nearby, which would be the perfect escape route for them. Years ago, people had used it regularly to hide any goods as they travelled across the land. The smugglers hid goods away until they could sell them without paying taxes. The tunnel had been sealed off and mostly forgotten about after the King at the time found out about it. This made it the perfect escape route to use. Observing the map, George pointed to a route to the tunnel.

"If I remember correctly, wasn't the old smugglers' tunnel around here?"

Sean leaned in, looking closely. "I believe so. There's only one way to find out."

George planned a route, sticking to the trees to stay hidden and avoiding the guards. Sean scouted ahead to keep an eye on the guards' positions. They knew that getting caught would mean the end for all of them.

Approaching their destination, Sean took a last look around to ensure they weren't followed. Satisfied that they were in the clear, they proceeded cautiously until they arrived at the spot. George surveyed the ground and detected a faint trail. He led the horses along a path that years of overgrowth had concealed.

With a narrow dirt-packed path barely wide enough for one rider at a time and towering trees and lush shrubs enveloping the expansive surroundings, their chances of being spotted were slim. The dense underbrush and closely packed trees made it impossible for anyone on horseback to ambush them. Nonetheless, George and Sean remained cautious, knowing those on foot could still be hidden.

Upon reaching the tunnel entrance, a dense wall of ferns completely obscured the opening. Sean dismounted his horse and made his way towards the entrance, determined to clear the obstruction. With a firm grip, he pulled back the ferns, creating a passage wide enough for them to pass through. Holding the fern aside, he allowed George and the twins to enter along with their horse. Once they were safely inside, Sean closed off the entrance, remounted his horse, and circled back to ensure they weren't being followed.

Chapter 15

A New Home

Inside the tunnel, George and the twins awaited Sean's return. George retrieved a small lantern from one of his satchels, swiftly placing a candle inside and igniting it with a flick of his fingers, casting a comforting warm glow throughout the space. As soon as Sean returned back into the tunnel, he too produced his own lantern and candle, instantly brightening the previously dim surroundings. With their path now well-lit, George resumed their journey, leading the horses at a steady pace. He was sure that someone would recall the tunnel's location and eventually come searching for them. Concealed by the thick overgrowth and aided by the clever use of his power, making the vines and shrubbery grow, it would take considerable time and effort for anyone to uncover their hidden sanctuary.

It would take them two days of steady walking to reach the end of the tunnel. Once they were out, they would find more woods, but from there, their journey to their final destination would be relatively straightforward. If they could maintain a steady pace without too many stops, they would be just another two days away from completing the last stretch. George held onto the hope that the men following them wouldn't stumble upon the hidden tunnel entrance, ensuring a smooth ride for the last few days.

He could see that the twins were grappling with their own challenges. Never before had they been away from their parents for such a long time, nor had they experienced the demands of horseback riding and limited rations. Sean wisely made occasional stops in small villages they came across to gather food, yet George remained cautious about how much he distributed.

If they needed to stay hidden in one location for a longer period than he had planned, George wanted to ensure that they had enough food for everyone. Fortunately, finding water wasn't a problem, as small streams were plentiful in the area. Both he and Sean had stocked up on food and water before entering the tunnel. George knew that there wouldn't be fresh water inside and coupled with the strenuous couple of days they had of walking, he wanted to make sure they had ample supplies to sustain them.

The tunnel itself was quite wide and tall, providing enough room for a grown man to carry a child on his shoulders and a cart to be pulled through with ease. Its origins traced back to a natural cave, meticulously crafted by human hands into a functional passageway. Throughout the tunnel, there were small, recessed alcoves that were man made. A few of these still housed abandoned cargo boxes, remnants of a distant past. Serving as storage compartments, these alcoves were strategically positioned to keep the main walkway of the tunnel clear for horses.

As they ventured deeper into the tunnel, the air grew cooler and denser with humidity. Their lanterns shone a soft glow against the rough walls, casting eerie shadows that danced along the passage. Each footstep echoed in the confined space while the scent of damp earth filled their nostrils. The twins gripped onto George as they navigated through the dark and narrow space. George kept walking, leading them at a steady pace, quite at ease regardless of the poor visibility. Given the darkness, riding the horses was impractical, so George and Sean guided them on foot. Occasionally, George allowed the twins to take turns riding, offering rest for their weary legs. He would have let them take more frequent breaks, but he believed spending less time in the tunnels was better for both of them. When lunchtime approached, George stopped and turned, using the lantern's light to survey their surroundings.

"I think it's time we eat, little ones. What do you think?"

George guided the horses into a secluded cove, arranging the lanterns to provide them with light while Sean tended to the horses, making sure they were fed and hydrated. Jacob and Aevah settled beside the lanterns, finding solace in the comforting glow as they eagerly awaited their meal. Though the illuminating light granted them a sense of security within the cove, they couldn't shake off the lingering fear of the boundless darkness. Sensing their discomfort, George took steps to put them at ease. With a simple lunch of bread, cheese, ham, and biscuits, with water to wash it all down, George sat down beside the twins and tried to entertain them with some shadow puppets and songs.

After enjoying a late lunch, the twins felt more content and less frightened by the darkness. Following their grandfather's advice to *have a little fun*, they enthusiastically tried making shadow puppets using the light from the lamps. Despite their inability to create recognisable shapes, they laughed at each other's attempts, allowing them to momentarily forget their surroundings and unwind. Sean and George couldn't help but smile at the sight of the twins being joyful and carefree. As they made their way through the tunnel, they sensed the passing of time by how much the candles had burned down.

"Maybe it's time we stop for the night? I'm certainly tired, and the children look exhausted," Sean suggested.

"Yes, it has been a long day, and this tunnel isn't the most heartening of places."

Feeling the weariness seep into his bones, George wanted nothing more than to rest his aching feet. So, they halted at the next cove, cared for the horses, and prepared for the night ahead. George set another charm upon the cove to keep them hidden, just in case. He then set up sleeping bags and blankets. Aware of the risks posed by lighting a fire in the enclosed cave, they resigned themselves once again to a simple, uncooked dinner, opting for sustenance over comfort. They settled down for the night, grateful for the protective charm that George had placed around them, for they were all able to get a good night's sleep, ready for the next day.

∗∗∗

Early the next morning, George and Sean both woke up to the rhythmic sounds of hooves trotting down towards them. Listening carefully, they caught a snippet of the horsemen's conversation as they rode passed.

"Adrian believes they must have come this way, so we can trap them in the middle," the first guard ahead said.

"That's if they are in here. This place has been abandoned for so long, it wouldn't surprise me if it caved in long ago," another guard responded.

"There's only one way to find out," replied the first guard again.

Exchanging a silent glance, Sean nodded to George before discreetly slipping out of the cove to investigate. They still had a full day's walk ahead of them before reaching the end of the tunnel. While George waited for Sean to return with news, he woke the twins and swiftly began packing everything away, readying the horses for a hasty departure. As George packed, tension hung in the air. The sound of hooves grew louder, echoing through the abandoned tunnel. Wide-eyed, the twins

159

watched in silence as George strapped their belongings to the horses, each action filled with a palpable sense of urgency.

As Sean sneaked back into the cove, his face was etched with worry and his footsteps were hasty. He quickly whispered to George, whose heart was pounding in his chest. Their voices were barely audible over the approaching thunder of hooves. George's mind was racing with endless possibilities of what could happen.

George motioned to the twins with a determined expression to get on the horses.

"If anything goes wrong, you ride as fast as you can in that direction. Understand!"

"Yes Grandpa," both children said, their voices trembling.

Gripping their saddles tightly, fear mingled with excitement. The duo waited, holding their breath as the sound of horses grew closer and the vibration of their steps reverberated through the earth.

Chaos erupted in the tunnel as the two riders suddenly burst into view. George's eyes locked with Sean's, a silent understanding passing between them. Without hesitation, they jumped into action, running forward with a surge of adrenaline. Caught off guard by the unexpected resistance, the guards scrambled to react. Swords clashed with a metallic ring that sliced through the air. George and Sean fought with a ferocity born of desperation. Their determination fuelled every swing and parry.

Amidst the chaos, the twins watched from the safety of the cove. Their inexperienced eyes filled with a mix of awe and terror as they clung to each other. Their innocence was shattered by the violence unfolding before them.

The clash of steel echoed throughout the tunnel as George and Sean swiftly overpowered the guards. Sean inflicted a fatal wound on one guard, slicing him across the back before delivering a fatal blow to his throat, causing the guard to tumble off his horse. Meanwhile, George targeted the other guard's upper thigh and severed his tendon with a precise slash that pierced his femoral artery, ensuring that he would bleed out in minutes. The guard clambered off his horse. He staggered and grasped desperately at the gushing wound as blood poured uncontrollably. He had mere moments left as he collapsed against the tunnel wall, shock etched upon his face. George watched the last flicker of life draining from the guard's body until he finally succumbed, his head slumped onto his chest.

Exhausted and bloodied, George and Sean stood panting, their swords hanging from weary grips, chests heaving with exertion. George reached out, his hand finding Sean's shoulder in a silent acknowledgement of their shared triumph, thankful the high priestess had packed them such fine weapons.

With the danger subdued, George and Sean turned their attention to the twins. They pulled them from their horses, and George embraced them tightly, his arms a shield against the horror they just witnessed.

"It's okay now. You are safe." Both children trembled in his embrace, tears streaming down their faces as they clung to him tightly.

As they calmed down, George talked to them both about what had happened while Sean kept watch and secured the guards' horses. These were well-trained horses, and had they run, it would have given their location away if they had returned to their camp with no riders. As it stood, capturing these horses provided the twins each with their own horse. Sean patted each horse and moved them together. He then discreetly dragged the bodies of the two guards into the nearby cove once George and the children had moved further into the tunnel.

This time, Sean took the lead, mounting his horse and setting a steady pace, while George stayed at the rear. In the darkness of the tunnel, they needed to move as quickly as possible. They managed to shave off a couple of hours from their journey with their increased tempo. However, the looming problem now was what awaited them on the other side. As they got closer to the end, Sean slowed his pace and signalled for them to wait. He ventured out of the tunnel for twenty minutes before returning to guide them out and down a path into the nearby woods.

George and Sean discussed what was next, both wary of what lay ahead of them. With the realisation that guards could be close behind, they couldn't ignore the possibility of an imminent threat ahead. The fact they knew the tunnel was there posed a grave concern, suggesting the likelihood that there may already be a patrol of men sweeping this side of the tunnel. Thus, caution became their most valuable ally at this time.

Not wanting to waste any more time, they resumed their journey. Sean took on the responsibility of scouting ahead, while George skilfully concealed them whenever necessary. As they embarked on the last stretch of their expedition, the next day and a half proved to be lengthy and filled with tension. Yet, luck seemed to favour them, as they encountered no guards along the way. George and Sean couldn't help but entertain the hopeful notion that they might reach their destination undetected.

During a short afternoon break, the dynamics shifted dramatically. With just three hours left until they reached their new home, George decided to stop for one final rest and a quick meal. Despite the limited time remaining, the absence of any signs of guards left George feeling uneasy. It seemed too easy, considering their close encounter with the guards in the tunnel.

Sean volunteered to venture out once more, returning only when he believed it was safe. Proceeding with caution along the path that Sean had chosen, they remained vigilant, with him warning them twice about small patrols actively searching for them. Although visibility ahead was limited, it was likely that more guards were lurking nearby, making it crucial for them to reach their destination without delay.

Should they reach their destination without being detected, Elinor's task would become very difficult, as she would be left completely unaware of their whereabouts.

The presence of the two guards' bodies would inevitably reveal that they had passed through the tunnel. From there, they could have gone in any direction. However, if they were discovered at this moment, it would likely instigate an immediate attack. If they managed to escape, it would initiate relentless searches of the area. Even with the protection of his power, such a scenario would pose problems for them.

It became paramount then that they avoided being seen. They stayed away from the villages and the few farms they passed, continuing their journey discreetly. Sean made sure they were safe ahead while George covered their tracks the best he could. Neither Aevah nor Jacob made a sound this whole time, their eyes wary and their shoulders tense. George watched them closely as they rode, wishing he could provide more comfort, but their survival took precedence above all else. Once they reached the cottage, he vowed to fuss and care for them as much as they needed him to. For now, all he could do was to watch over them, silently praying one last time to the divine spirit that they would make it.

As night fell, the moon hung low in the sky, casting a pale glow over the landscape as their destination came into view. George felt his heart quicken with anticipation and his senses heightened as he surveyed the surroundings. This was the last stretch, and there were no guards in sight. Despite arriving a couple of hours later than planned due to the need to evade guards, they had made it. Hidden one last time, Sean did a last check of the area before he declared it safe for them to continue.

***

They rode across an open field, their little hearts pounding with expectation. The gentle melody of running water welcomed Aevah and Jacob as they turned the corner, drawing them closer to the ethereal glow of the moon illuminating a picturesque little cottage ahead. Intrigued by the scene unfolding before them, they were captivated by the faint scent of damp earth lingering in the air, accompanied by the distant whisper of leaves rustling in the night breeze. As they came to a small wooden bridge, they inched across slowly, their eyes filled with wonder at the shimmering river surrounding them.

The promise of a new home swelled within them, mirroring the rhythmic cadence of their horses' hooves. The distant hoot of an owl above them drew their glance up to the sky as they watched the majestic birds swoop overhead, flying towards their destination as if to tell them they were home. At that moment, their hearts filled with wonder, and all memories of the perilous journey were forgotten as they stood before the enchanting cottage.

"Aevah, Jacob, welcome to Middlebeck Farm," George beamed, his happiness evident to be back.

164

Chapter 16

A New Reign

Elinor was furious as she exclaimed, "You had them in your clutches, and they got away!" Do you have any good news for me, Adrian?" She knew George would evade them, but hearing it still enraged her.

"Not exactly, Your Majesty. We do have an idea of where they could be, and patrols are keeping a watchful eye out. We have distributed pictures of George and the children to the nearby villages and towns, offering a hefty reward for any information that leads to their capture."

Elinor dropped her head in her hands and let out an exasperated sigh before looking up. "The man can channel. Do you really think he's going to appear as himself to the locals?" she asked Adrian.

"No, but there's a chance he may slip up or one of the children might be seen, leading to their arrest. The odds of finding them now are slim, I know. It's still possible, though, and I'm pursuing new leads on the whereabouts of the shards. I believe I'm getting closer. I'm sure of it."

Her ears perked up at hearing his last remark. If Adrian could locate what she needed, it wouldn't matter if George was found or not. Fuelled with newfound determination, she dismissed Adrian and instructed him to continue with his task. The sooner those shards were in her possession, the better. Her reign depended on them. She was determined to be the only one with all the power. It was going to help her keep the throne, and she had no intention of relinquishing it to anyone.

Elinor revelled in her role as queen too much to entertain such thoughts. It was her destiny, and she savoured every moment of it. She was in control and everything she had worked for had now become her reality. To celebrate and begin her reign in style, Elinor had planned a masquerade ball for the following month, inviting all to attend. The ladies loved these types of gatherings. Herself included and they loved any opportunity to get into some sort of mischief. The masks provided the perfect opportunity for that. Invitations had been sent out a week ago, allowing the ladies ample time to plan their outfits. Elinor knew that many much like herself, would have their dresses custom-made for the occasion.

The evening promised to be more than mere dancing and celebrating. Elinor had several significant announcements to make, one of which held particular importance to the lords as well as to Victoria and Lloyd. Their unwavering loyalty had been instrumental in her ascent to the throne, and she acknowledged that she owed much of her current standing to their support. The castle operated smoothly under their guidance. By sharing the wealth, Elinor wouldn't only secure alliances but also strengthen her position as queen. Moreover, it would ensure that the crown receives more taxes, with newly appointed lords and ladies governing different lands. The royal vault was thriving presently, and Elinor was determined to keep it that way. She had no way of predicting what lay ahead and had no desire to be caught off guard by any unforeseen circumstances.

By claiming the throne, she remained acutely aware of the disgruntled individuals who opposed her rule. There were those who harboured grievances, ready to see her hanged for what happened to James. Strangely, this didn't worry her half as much as the disappearance of George and the twins. As the rightful heirs, their absence posed a tangible threat, and with George in hiding, he could make a move for the throne at any time. The mere thought of this caused her heart to race, especially if they rallied their own supporters behind them. Having the right allies was crucial to her cause, regardless of the methods used. The game of chess had begun, and as the queen, she held the advantage with the most strategic moves at her disposal. Her first move involved Bradley Woodlock, whom she invited to an intimate dinner for two.

The lords may have demanded that she choose a husband, but she would be the one to pick him out. While they believed they held the power, she understood the intricacies of the game and could be equally cunning as them. An alliance and marriage with the most influential traders in the land was most definitely in her favour. Before they knew what had happened, she would once more be the one with the most control. Yet, she had to admit that her choosing Bradley went beyond the alliance. The undeniable chemistry between them couldn't be ignored and these past weeks spent with him in the castle had been interesting, to say the least. Admittedly, at first, she was unsure. She had regarded him as just another arrogant lord. However, their last few encounters had made her soften up to him. There was something about him that captivated her – an intoxicating presence that left her yearning for more. This dinner provided the perfect excuse to spend time with him. Alone together.

Dressed in a long, flowing green gown with a daring neckline, Elinor appraised her appearance in her ornate mirror, admiring how the fabric accentuated her curves. The delicate aroma of Chloe's scented hair products enveloped them as she skilfully fashioned Elinor's rich chocolate locks into soft, cascading curls. As Chloe fastened the gleaming white gold bracelet around her wrist, adding a final touch of elegance, Elinor felt the cool sensation against her skin. She had the feeling that, like a moth to a flame, Bradley would inevitably be drawn to her before the night's end.

Satisfied with her appearance, Elinor, after being informed that he was waiting for her in her private dining hall, made her way to meet him. Entering the room, she saw him seated at the table, a glass of wine in hand. Despite its modest size, the dining room exuded an intimate ambience. Crafted by designers for the exclusive enjoyment of the king and queen, it provided a sanctuary for tranquil meals and romantic dinners. It was a snug and cosy space with only room for two at the table. A captivating canvas painting of vibrant wildflowers hung on the wall above them.

The sweet fragrance of the flowers filled the air. In the centre of the table was a stunning centrepiece made of gold hoops that held an intricately designed arrangement of dried flowers. On either side, two tall candles stood with their soft flames dancing in the dim light. As Bradley noticed her approaching, he stood up and set his glass down with a soft clink. With a graceful bow, he acknowledged his queen, his cheeks flushed as she drew nearer.

"My Queen, it's truly an honour to be here and enjoy your company this evening. You look as beautiful as ever," Bradley remarked, his voice filled with admiration, as he kissed Elinor's hand before helping her into her seat. After she was settled, he poured her a glass of wine before sitting back in his chair beside her, his gaze ravishing her the whole time.

"Why, thank you," Elinor replied, taking a sip of her wine. "You flatter me with your kind words."

"I speak only the truth, my Queen."

"Please, call me Elinor. There's no need for such formalities between two old friends who are enjoying dinner together."

He smiled and nodded, saying her name, "Elinor," with a dip of his head to the side.

At that moment, the first course arrived, a steaming bowl of savoury vegetable pottage. As they ate, they engaged in lively conversation, recalling their shared childhood experiences. They delved into fond memories with both having had an adventurous streak to them and often venturing out horseback riding, seeing how far they could get before the guards inevitably led them back to the castle. As the memories resurfaced, Elinor could almost feel the wind tousling her hair as she galloped across the open fields. The thrill of exploration reignited within her, infusing her heart with a lingering sense of adventure.

Intrigued by Bradley's life, Elinor inquired about his journey thus far, and the progress of their family business. In return, he showed genuine interest in her experiences in Adlington. Their conversation flowed effortlessly, accompanied by the clinking of cutlery and occasional bursts of laughter. With each sip of wine, their inhibitions diminished, fostering playful banter and undeniable chemistry. Elinor found herself marvelling at the natural rhythm of the evening, surprising even herself. While her initial intent was to manipulate Bradley and keep him under her influence, the genuine connection they shared rendered her original plan irrelevant.

Bradley exuded an innate familiarity coupled with an undeniable charm that naturally drew women to him. It was no surprise that he garnered adoration from many. Just like her, he had never found someone to settle down with and instead revelled in the company of others. She couldn't shake the suspicion that a part of him secretly desired the crown, with her being his potential pathway to it. Nevertheless, she couldn't deny how effortlessly comfortable she felt around him. Not to mention his striking appearance, boasting a muscular physique, sun-kissed curls, and mesmerising ocean blue eyes one could easily lose themselves in. As the night wore on, a warm tingling sensation within Elinor made her feel as if it was the perfect moment to invite Bradley to accompany her to the ball.

"I would be honoured," he whispered, his eyes filled with anticipation.

Leaning in towards her, one of his hands found its place at the back of her head, his fingers intertwining with her silky hair, creating a tender connection between them. Their lips met, igniting a surge of excitement within Elinor. What began as a gentle touch of lips soon deepened into a passionate embrace, her arms instinctively encircling him. The kiss elicited a thrilling sensation, causing a delightful tightening in her core as she melted into the moment, drawing herself closer to him without hesitation. In return, Bradley's arms wrapped around her, pulling her into an even tighter embrace.

Reluctantly, his warm lips parted from hers, leaving behind a lingering trail of desire. His lips ventured lower, tracing a path along the delicate curve of her neck, provoking a shiver that cascaded down her spine. Each kiss, simultaneously rough and tender, sent a tingling sensation through her body, akin to an electric current seeking its destination.

As his rough and possessive hand explored her trembling form, her senses surged with heightened awareness. The intoxicating scent of their combined desire filled the air, mingling with the musky perfume of their skin. A low, throaty moan escaped her parted lips, conveying a sound of surrender and deep longing.

Fuelled by her unspoken desires, his hand glided along the soft expanse of her thigh, eliciting waves of pleasure that surged through her. The sensation, both gentle and commanding, left her yearning for more. In response, she instinctively parted her legs, silently inviting him closer. Her body ached with desire, craving his touch in ways she had not anticipated for this evening. Although this diversion from her expectations was unexpected, it proved to be a delightful deviation. Each brush of his hands and lips against her skin sent electric currents racing through her. With her eyes closed every sensation intensified. Leaning back in her chair, she welcomed him eagerly as his fingers teased her entrance before delving deep inside of her. A cry of pleasure escaped her lips as she rocked her hips in rhythm with his movements, her breath quickening as the pressure built up throughout her body.

As his fingers thrust in and out of her and his lips trailed along her neck, she could feel her orgasm building. "Faster," she gasped, matching his rhythm as she rocked against him, her body ablaze with desire. Her own hand cupped her breasts, squeezing them firmly and pinching her peaked nipples through the fabric of her dress, sending waves of delicious friction coursing through her core. Gripping his arm tightly, her nails leaving faint imprints, she surrendered to the overwhelming rush of pleasure as her climax consumed her, filling her with pure ecstasy. Waves of euphoria washed over her, leaving her feeling elated and utterly blissful. As the intensity of her orgasm gradually subsided, she held his wrist, guiding his fingers with deliberate motions, prolonging the exquisite sensation. Once finished, she released her grip and leaned back in her chair, a satisfied smile gracing her lips.

"Now, that was satisfying and fun," she remarked, observing him savouring the taste of her on his fingers.

Bradley stood up and pulled Elinor into a warm embrace. "Most certainly," he said. "And you taste divine, by the way."

As he kissed her, she could feel his desire pressing against his pants. Elinor gently pulled away and intertwined her fingers with

Bradley's as she whispered, "Come with me," leading him to her chambers. As they entered, she led him towards the bed, gracefully taking a seat at the edge. With a seductive gaze, she inquired, "What shall we do now?"

With a firm grasp on her hips, he pulled her towards him, bringing her closer to the edge of the bed. "Lie down while I indulge in my dessert," he commanded. As he knelt between her legs on the floor, Elinor noticed a hunger in his eyes just before his tongue tantalisingly traced its way up her slit.

Elinor spread her legs wider, and she sank into the bed, emitting a soft moan as she felt his tongue. With the combined pleasure of his tongue and fingers, she became a tangled mess of desire. Her back arched, fingers gripping the sheets, letting out moans that echoed from deep within. She was on the brink, feeling herself on the verge of climax. Just as she was about to reach that peak once more, he stopped.

Bradley rose from the floor with a wicked smile. "I want the next one to be on my cock, Elinor," he declared.

A glint sparkled in her eyes as she rose to her knees, kissing him forcefully while removing his clothes. Once undressed, Elinor leaned back, admiring the sight before her. His face possessed a striking handsomeness, complemented by a physique equally pleasing to the eye. A tattoo of an ocean and his ship on his chest was a testament to his time spent at sea. Though his arms and torso bore a few scars, they only added character to his perfectly sculpted form. His sun-kissed skin stood witness to years of hard work in his family's trade. As Elinor's gaze descended, she noticed his erection firmly in his hand. Drawing her attention back to his eyes, she whispered, "It's your turn now." Eagerly, Bradley moved towards her, displaying lightning-fast reflexes as he tore her dress off, revealing her body.

He admired the breathtaking view before him, savouring every moment, before tenderly kissing every inch of her body. Starting from the crown of her head, he trailed down to her toes, his tongue, hands, and lips caressing every curve of her soft skin. Waves of pleasure coursed through her body at his touch, her hands exploring his body, tracing the arch of his back, and clutching his skin in response to the tantalising touch of his tongue on more sensitive areas. Their mutual desire overwhelmed them as they greedily explored each other's bodies, consumed by passion. Unable to wait any longer to be inside her, Bradley positioned himself on top of Elinor, stroking his erection as pre-cum glistened on his shaft.

Elinor licked her lips in anticipation as he teased her entrance, her core tightening at the sensation before he slipped inside of her. A soft moan escaped her lips as he fully penetrated her, filling her completely. Wrapping her arms and legs around him, urging him to thrust deeper. The sheer bliss of him being inside her overwhelmed her senses. As their rhythm synchronised, he quickened his pace to match her escalating response. Tightening around his cock, she soared to cloud nine as he drove her to the brink of madness between the feel of him inside her and the kissing of that sweet spot on her neck. The feel of his thick cock inside her pushed her to the edge of ecstasy, intensified by the sharp kisses on her neck.

As her body tightened around him, he couldn't contain the primal urge to moan her name while thrusting deeper into her. She arched beneath him, her nails tracing fiery paths down his back as the feeling of her orgasm built. Grinding against Bradley, she matched his rhythm, their movements quickening in unison until she let out a scream, her climax washing over her. Bradley continued with a few final thrusts before finding release himself. With a satisfied smile, he collapsed onto her, their lips meeting in a deep, passionate kiss. With one last gentle thrust, he withdrew

and settled beside her on the bed. Content and wordless, Elinor
snuggled into his embrace, drifting off into a deep sleep.

Chapter 17

The Visit

Adrian had spent the past week immersed in the royal library, dedicating most of his free time to research. Amid ancient scrolls and documents, he consumed a vast amount of information, diligently taking notes along the way. With the assistance of the castle's librarian and after an extensive search, he began to feel confident that he was finally sifting through the correct documentation. Initially, his solo attempts had only led to frustration, resulting in a pile of old and valuable books scattered across the floor after accidentally toppling them while searching through the tightly packed shelves. However, the cramped space made manoeuvring amidst the books and other items challenging, and he couldn't be entirely blamed for the mishap.

Following that incident, the librarian took it upon herself to help him in his quest. Initially hesitant, as he desired to keep his search a secret, she assured him of her discretion, particularly to prevent any damage to the precious works. Undeniably, with her help, the process became much more efficient. He felt a sense of confidence as he had stumbled upon something valuable for Elinor. Among the documents, it became evident that Princess Mary had departed alongside her loyal ladies-in-waiting and a small group of guards. These individuals had served both the princess and the crown, aiding her in concealing her whereabouts throughout the years. One lady, in particular, held a special place in the princess's heart – her first lady, Clemence Goodman. Renowned for her unwavering loyalty and devotion to the princess and the kingdom, Goodman played a significant role.

She bore the same last name as a prominent family member, including George's late wife, Maria. This family had always demonstrated unwavering loyalty to the crown, and now Adrian understood why. They had been safeguarding the knowledge of the princess and the whereabouts of the crystal shards. His body thrummed with anticipation as he jumped up, a tingling sensation coursing through him, energising him as he paced the floor, his mind racing. The Goodmans were currently within the castle walls. He contemplated detaining and questioning them, but would they divulge the truth? Additionally, such action might prompt others to hide pertinent information elsewhere. However, if he went to the Goodmans directly, they might provide the crucial information needed to find those crystal shards. His mind settled on a plan, Adrian gathered his notes and left the library to find Elinor. Finding Elinor in her quarters, he shared his breakthrough. As she read the documents herself, he witnessed a moment of realisation as her eyes widened, everything falling into place.

"How did I not notice this before? I've read this myself, yet I never made the connection. I guess I was younger back then and not actively searching for anything specific. It appears we've had a breakthrough. How soon can you depart for the Goodman's residence?"

"I can leave within a few hours. I simply need to gather provisions and get a few of our men, and then we can be on our way."

"Excellent! Take any resources you need. I want whatever they are hiding, by any means necessary."

Adrian acknowledged Elinor with a nod before leaving to make preparations. Time was of the essence, and he was eager to bring back good news as swiftly as possible. With her approval, and wanting to keep his intentions discreet, Adrian busied himself with gathering supplies while assembling a team of trusted men. He informed them of their impending departure but withheld the reason behind it. Once everyone was briefed, they embarked on their journey towards Albury, the location of the Goodman residence.

Once they had distanced themselves from Carraton, Adrian gathered his men and disclosed their destination and purpose. Adrian had already sworn the men to secrecy on behalf of the crown, and he trusted them implicitly. However, he exercised caution about speaking openly within the castle walls, mindful of the pervasive presence of prying eyes and ears. Too often, people have lost everything because the wrong person overheard them. If any member of the Goodman family were to catch wind of their plans, it would cause utter chaos. And so, Adrian and his men continued to Albury at a steady pace, with Elinor being the only other person who knew the true reason for their departure.

****

The journey to Albury was swift for the men, all seasoned riders accustomed to long distances, effortlessly keeping up with Adrian's pace without complaint. They wisely made regular stops to rest the horses, managing to trim the expected seven-day journey to just over six days. As evening loomed, Adrian called for a halt, instructing his men to set up camp for the night, a mere three miles from their destination. Situated within the dense woods, their camp was well-hidden, minimising the risk of accidental encounters. Once the camp was set, he sent two men to scout the manor, tasked with gathering information about the people present and checking for any unexpected visitors. There could be no room for error when it came to infiltrating the premises, with no one escaping.

If what he sought was inside, he couldn't risk it disappearing once again in another's hands. So, he stayed behind at the camp with his men, eagerly awaiting the return of the scouts. With their added information, the plan could be finalised. While they awaited their return, his men busied themselves around camp. Two of them were preparing a stew with the remaining scraps of meat and vegetables from their journey rations. Conscious of their proximity to their destination, Adrian continued moving forward instead of taking a detour to the nearby town for supplies. This meant the stew comprised whatever vegetables they had left, and the rabbit caught earlier by one of the men.

As the food simmered, a few others took turns keeping watch and occupied themselves by sharpening their swords. Meanwhile, Adrian and the rest of the group gathered around the fire, engaging in lively conversation and banter. As the night grew darker and some men settled down under their blankets, the sound of hooves approaching at a steady pace caught their attention. The men on watch stood, armed themselves, and moved towards the source of the sound. Suddenly, the sound of a familiar bird call echoed through the air, easing the tension, and signalling the return of the scouts. Emerging from the shadows, their silhouettes became visible against the warm glow of the fire.

"Welcome back!" Adrian greeted the two men. "How did it go?"

"It went well," Thomas replied. "Everything is in order, just as we anticipated."

"Come, take a seat by the fire and help yourself to some stew while you fill me in."

Gathered around the cosy fire, each enjoying a steaming bowl of stew, the two men took turns briefing Adrian about what they had witnessed and what they could expect in the morning. The layout remained unchanged, devoid of any unforeseen surprises. With this knowledge, Adrian strategically organised his men, ensuring a balanced guard's presence both at the front and rear of the manor. All but four of them would enter, with these four men keeping watch from different vantage points outside. Inside, the group would divide into two, with one entering through the front entrance, including Adrian himself, drawing attention from those within the manor. The others, sneaking in from the back, would remain unnoticed. This tactical manoeuvre aimed to expose anyone harbouring secrets and intercept anyone attempting to escape through the rear exit of the manor.

Should any escape unnoticed, the guards outside would catch any movement and track those that left the manor. The plan, meticulously devised, left everyone clear on their responsibilities. With everything in place, the guards on watch swapped out, and everyone else went to sleep. As dawn broke, Adrian and his men packed up and mounted their horses, ready to move. Timing their arrival during breakfast, when the manor's occupants would be less alert, they approached with caution. With Lord and Lady Goodman still in Carraton, only the workers and their children remained, making the manor an easy target. Adrian guided his men on the last stretch, halting out of sight a short distance ahead. Here, the men separated into their respective groups. The second group approached the manor from the back, taking a longer route while keeping hidden among the trees.

Adrian and his men stayed where they were for another half an hour to give the second group time to get into position. Once he felt enough time had passed, Adrian led his group up the long stone pathway to the manor's main entrance. Anyone looking out would see the riders coming clear as day. As they reached the manor's entrance, two servants met them. Adrian got down from his horse, handing the first servant a sealed letter.

"Notify the occupants that we are conducting a thorough search of this manor under the authority granted by Queen Elinor herself. We're detaining all individuals inside until further instructions. We'll apprehend those who resist, as they are defying a direct order from the crown."

He strode past the startled men and made his way up the terracotta brick steps before walking into the manor. His guards followed closely. The servant to whom Adrian gave the letter hastened to catch up, visibly flustered.

"Sir, please," the servant pleaded, "the Lord and Lady of the manor are absent, and it's only their children that's home."

"Then tell them what I told you," Adrian replied firmly. "Those who choose to cooperate will not face any harm."

Adrian walked away, leaving the flabbergasted servant standing in place while he instructed his men to begin their work. They detained everyone inside the manor and thoroughly searched every corner, yet they couldn't find a single thing. They combed through every nook and cranny not once but twice and even ventured outside, searching for any hidden entrances or trapdoors that could lead to an underground hideout. Adrian was confident that no one had escaped, as his men had been careful. They confined everyone in the manor to their quarters, with those who refused to cooperate being held separately in a guarded room. Fortunately, only a few Goodman guards attempted to put up a fight, but they were quickly dealt with. Even the three adolescent children remained in their rooms.

Everyone appeared cooperative, willingly answering questions posed by his men. However, none of them had any knowledge of what he was searching for. If they did, they were putting on a convincing act of ignorance. Determined to uncover the truth, he transformed one room in the manor into an interrogation space. Adrian questioned every individual residing in that household, aware that even the slightest detail witnessed by the servants could lead him to the hidden location. Although he held little hope that the servants would possess any pertinent information, he recognised that a chance encounter or observation could prove valuable. Yet, it was the guards and the children of Lord Goodman whom he believed held the crucial information. Altering his questioning techniques and tactics, he painstakingly interrogated them individually. Despite his thoroughness, he was met with nothing but silence. No one had the faintest clue regarding the whereabouts of the crystal shards. Frustration steadily gnawed at Adrian's patience. As he questioned the guards again, sweat dripped down his forehead, but they remained unyielding.

After two fruitless days, Adrian's search within the Goodman household had been in vain. He had hoped that by going straight to the family home while both Lord and Lady Goodman were still in Carraton, he would find something. With the advantage of surprise, he believed they wouldn't have been able to hide anything important from him. However, his plan had failed. There was no evidence of the crystals or their whereabouts in their home. Someone might have magically concealed them, but Adrian lacked the ability to detect such magic. Determined not to give up, he made one last attempt and called for a tracker. Occasionally, some individuals were born with an innate power and often trained to become trackers, assisting those who need help to find someone or something hidden by this power. In this dire situation, Adrian needed one, so he reached out to a friend for help. Noah was an expert in the art of uncovering concealed magic, a skill set acquired through extensive training and years of dedicated practice.

While awaiting Noah's arrival, Adrian and his men double-checked the floor plan, scrutinising the layout of the house and surrounding grounds for anything they might have missed. The crucial information they sought had to be concealed somewhere within these confines. Cecilia was the niece of Lord and Lady Goodman. The family had remained close all these years, making sure they could always monitor those who ascended the throne. All signs led them to this very manor. Given the role of the Goodman family as the original guardians of the hidden shards, it was reasonable to assume they possessed knowledge of their whereabouts. This explained why Lord Goodman opposed Elinor's claim to the throne, only relenting when the majority voted in her favour.

When Noah arrived at the manor, Adrian eagerly showed him around. Adrian's anticipation was palpable, his fingers twitching with excitement as he watched Noah open himself up to the power, sending out tendrils of magic throughout the manor and its grounds. The energy transformed into a swirling grey mist, permeating the grounds. Making it impossible for any hidden powers to go unnoticed.

As Noah worked, Adrian became increasingly anxious, his movements giving him away with the tapping of his feet and his constant pacing.

"Adrian, if you can't stay still, get out! I can barely focus with your nervous energy disrupting me," Noah warned.

"Apologies. I'll keep still. I just need this to work. It's because of me we are here, and if I go back with nothing… Well, you can imagine," Adrian replied, his tone fraught with concern.

"That the queen might need a new personal knight to do her bidding," Noah teased dryly.

"Hilarious," Adrian retorted sarcastically.

"Glad you think so. Now shut up or get out," Noah insisted, resuming his focus on the task at hand.

Without uttering a word, Adrian did his best to keep still at his friend's request. He observed intently, keeping his emotions in check as Noah worked. However, the mist revealed nothing, and Adrian's frustration mounted. With nothing left to do, he thanked Noah for trying and stepped outside to bid him goodbye. Unable to accept defeat, he found himself circling the grounds, his mind refusing to admit failure. Fuelled by nothing but a flicker of hope, he wandered the yard for hours, hands clasped behind his back, a solitary figure consumed by determination.

"Sir, there's nothing here. It's time to leave."

Adrian stopped in his tracks. His shoulders slumped as he turned to face Gerald. With a sombre expression, Adrian reached out and clasped Gerald's shoulder.

"Yes, it is. Let's go, Gerald. Tell the men we're leaving," Adrian replied, his tone resigned yet resolute.

He walked back inside the manor and informed the staff of their departure. He felt no need to address the young adolescents, leaving the staff to pass on the message. With brisk steps, he headed to the stables to get his horse. When his men were ready, they made their way back to the castle, a heavy sense of dread settling in his heart as he contemplated delivering the disappointing news to Elinor. He knew she would be upset, but he felt powerless to change the situation.

As they rode, Adrian's thoughts raced, contemplating where else or who else could possess the crucial information they needed. Upon arriving in Carraton, he knew he would have to start over and devise a new plan to uncover the information. Laden with the weight of the task ahead, Adrian spurred his horse forward, galloping towards Carraton with a renewed sense of purpose. There was no time to dwell on their recent setback.

Instead, he focussed on finding a fresh lead and ensuring the success of their mission, both for his own sake and for Elinor's.

Chapter 18

Plans

Cecilia found herself adjusting to her various duties within the castle, despite her intense dislike for them. Her role as a chambermaid proved to be both degrading and physically exhausting, with no support or friends to assist her along the way. While cleaning the rooms was bearable, certain ladies who visited the castle requested she attend to their rooms, ensuring they were present to supervise her. This meant she had to clean up spilt food or wine they purposely made in front of her, rearrange their belongings until they were satisfied, and endure threats of violence if she dared to disobey their every command. Among them, Lady Felicia Stone stood out as particularly tyrannical, with their last encounter ending badly for Cecilia.

As Cecilia diligently scrubbed the floors, her back throbbed with pain, her hands raw from the harsh chemicals and relentless scrubbing. Despite her discomfort, she continued, driven by fear of Lady Felicia's wrath. She watched her now, out of the corner of her eye, as she sat at the table with her husband, laughing and drinking their wine. As Cecilia worked, she felt a looming presence behind her, followed by the unmistakable sound of liquid sloshing and the sharp splash of wine staining the pristine hardwood floor.

"You missed a spot," Lady Felicia sneered, her finger pointing towards the puddle of wine seeping into the floor beside her.

Cecilia's heart raced with her fists clenched tightly as she fought to maintain her composure. With determination etched on her face, she knelt down and scrubbed the spot with fervour, her knuckles turning white from the pressure. Regardless of the woman's provocation, Cecilia remained resolute not to react. But Lady Felicia's cruelty knew no bounds. She kicked the bucket, spilling soapy water all over Cecilia's worn-out dress. The ice-cold water seeped through the fabric, chilling Cecilia to her core.

"Clean it up now!" Lady Felicia commanded with her voice dripping with venom.

Struggling to hold back her tears, Cecilia suppressed the urge to lash out. Gritting her teeth, she picked up a rag and began trying to soak up the water, squeezing it back into the bucket.

Lady Felicia watched with malicious satisfaction as her eyes gleamed with sadistic glee. "You're nothing but a lowly servant, Cecilia. Know your place!"

At those words, a surge of defiance coursed through Cecilia. She threw the rag aside and straightened, trembling with indignation as she faced Lady Felicia.

"How dare you speak to me like that? I'm done with your cruelty. I was your queen mere weeks ago and deserve some respect," Cecilia declared, her voice steady and defiant.

Lady Felicia's face contorted with rage before she lashed out, delivering a stinging slap across Cecilia's cheek.

Before Cecilia could react, Lord Thomas walked towards her, his demeanour stern. "Be very careful of what you do next, Cecilia. Your next move might be your last."

"At this point, Lord Thomas, death would be a blessing," Cecilia retorted, staring the man down with pure hatred. Lady Felicia laughed manically.

"Yes, it seems like you have little left to live for now, doesn't it? After your poor children perished in that fire, and your husband, oh your dear husband, a knife to his heart by his…"

Enraged, Cecilia lunged at the woman, but Lord Thomas grabbed her before she could cause Lady Felicia any actual harm. The beating she received left her barely able to move the next day.

After that incident, Cecilia kept her mouth shut when in their chamber, avoiding it where possible. Fortunately, her morning duties in the kitchen were far more enjoyable. Through her friendship with Mistress Katelyn, the other kitchen staff had almost forgotten her true identity. Almost. Although they were a lot more relaxed around her and made polite conversation, the constant presence of her guards served as a reminder of who she was. This situation posed a challenge to Cecilia's escape plan, as she was never alone. However, with the help of Mistress Katelyn, a plan began to take shape. Cecilia felt a profound sense of gratitude towards her friend and harboured hopes of one day repaying her kindness.

The upcoming masquerade ball presented as their only chance for escape. Should their plan fail on that night, Cecilia foresaw no other opportunities arising. Cecilia had received an invitation as Elinor's guest, and she planned to attend, catching Elinor off guard. She would never have expected Cecilia to slip away that very night, either. If they executed their plan successfully, Cecilia would be long gone from the castle before anyone noticed, and she would be out of the city before they even started searching for her.

Despite Sean's recent illness, Anita had taken charge of the planning. When Sean returned to work, he seamlessly resumed his responsibilities. However, his return didn't go according to plan. He found himself detained and questioned because of his absence from multiple trips to the castle. Anita had already informed the castle about his illness and had personally made the deliveries on his behalf. Despite the questioning, his story proved solid. Nevertheless, Cecilia couldn't shake the feeling that he was being monitored. This made them all more cautious, as they didn't want to arouse any suspicion.

In the privacy of their home, Anita and Sean took advantage of the time to devise their escape plan. Sean also gathered information on the guard's rotations, just as Anita promised, giving her a significant strategic advantage.

Mistress Katelyn continued to act as the go-between for Cecilia, getting information from Sean by arranging meetings outside of the castle walls. They would often meet in a local tavern during the evening. To remain inconspicuous, they never returned to the same tavern twice and always chose the dimly lit corners of the establishments. The atmosphere of these particular taverns was grim and uninviting, causing most people to pay no attention to others. Most customers kept to themselves, either drowning their sorrows alone or engaging in small-time gambling.

That night they had chosen *The Serpent*, a fitting name for one of the town's shadiest establishments where the cunning and deceitful would often spend their free time. Here, they could speak freely, confident that prying eyes and ears were absent. Mistress Katelyn and Sean discussed and devised their plans carefully. She would relay the information to Cecilia the following day when they worked together.

The next morning, Mistress Katelyn shared Sean's plan with Cecilia at the end of their busy breakfast shift.

"Once we pull off switching places, you'll have a brief window to move through the castle disguised as me, without raising suspicion. You need to make the most of this and get to the secret door near the west gate. Sean will be waiting there to help you." Cecilia mentally rehearsed the plan. Although it seemed simple, there was still a significant risk of things going awry.

"And what about you? If they discover we switched places—" Mistress Katelyn interjected, grabbed Cecilia's hands, and urged her to look at her.

"They won't, do you hear me? You're getting out of here and back to your children, where you belong. The rest of us here will be fine. Do not worry."

At Mistress Katelyn's reassurance, Cecilia let out a sigh, feeling the tension drain from her body. She was right. The plan was sound, and she needed to place her trust in those who stood by her side. Recognising her limitations, Cecilia understood she couldn't do it all on her own. Sean alone had gone to great strides to see her children safe and trusted him completely to do the same for her. After Mistress Katelyn informed her where Sean was during his illness, she couldn't help but weep tears of joy knowing her children were safe with her father. This revelation further fuelled her determination to escape. Now, the only obstacle in her path was gathering the evidence the high priestess had requested to incriminate Elinor.

With the ball looming just weeks away, this had become crucial for Cecilia. However, it proved to be quite challenging for her to get anywhere near Elinor's chambers or James's study, where she now worked. Every attempt she made to find a legitimate reason to be in those areas was met with immediate dismissal by those around her. She thought cleaning some chambers near those rooms might do the trick, yet her guards always waited outside, giving her only a small window of opportunity to pass through the hidden servant passages between those rooms. Unfortunately, her plan had failed because the delightful ladies of the court always occupied those chambers when she tried to clean them. Time was running out, but Cecilia refused to give up. Instead, she sought Mistress Katelyn's assistance in finding a suitable opportunity, and together, they were confident that an occasion would arise before the ball. In the meantime, Cecilia concealed her frustrations behind a façade of indifference and continued with her daily schedule. She eagerly awaited the day of the ball and longed for it to arrive soon.

***

The ball was just a little over a week away, and Elinor grew increasingly impatient for Adrian's return. He had departed a couple of weeks ago to visit the Goodman family, but so far, no news, whether good or bad, had reached her. Despite keeping herself occupied with preparations for the ball and attending to her daily responsibilities as Queen, Elinor found herself unable to suppress her anxiety about updates. Each time a letter arrived for her, she eagerly snatched it, scanning the signature first in hopes it was from Adrian. Frustrated, she would then lower the letter, knowing it was from someone else before composing herself to read its contents. With no word from Adrian and Lord Goodman behaving as usual, she had a strong feeling that no news had reached him either. Her own staff within the castle diligently attended to his family, ensuring that if any news arrived ahead of her, they would promptly inform her.

Regardless of the search's outcome, Elinor was aware it would strain her relationship with the Goodman family. Nevertheless, she believed that as long as she stayed one step ahead, she could manipulate the situation to her advantage. Hence, she eagerly awaited any news, desiring to know the outcome of events. The sooner she had that information, the sooner she could formulate the appropriate plan of action. Drumming her fingers upon the wooden desk, she looked at the stack of correspondence before her. Thoughts swirled in her mind, constantly distracting her attention and causing daydreams about various possibilities related to the situation. To entertain herself, she picked up the first letter, holding it up as she examined the handwriting on the envelope. Beautiful swirls adorned her name, offering an idea of its contents.

With the ball fast approaching, Elinor received many letters of interest from the esteemed lords of the land. The surge in interest in marrying her had increased tenfold, thanks in kind to the lord's influence. Ever since her agreement to wed a lord had been made public, word had spread like wildfire. The announcement of the upcoming ball had only intensified this even further, with many also asking to accompany her. This letter offered nothing different. The contents mirrored those of all the others, mundane praises about how amazing this nobody was. Bored, Elinor dropped it in the rubbish bin beside her and opened another. None of them managed to pique her interest, although a few were quite flattering to read, especially those that praised her beauty and charm. Though some of these letters made her feel vain, she couldn't resist indulging in a bit of positive reinforcement now and then. The next one contained the usual pomp and embellishment, making him seem like a worthy candidate for her hand in marriage. He, like many other suitors, provided intricate details of his wealth and status, making the reading process both tedious and enlightening. They had documented their worth on paper, unwittingly granting her access to their information for future manipulation. Perfect for her purposes.

It became common knowledge to the court that Elinor was in a relationship with Bradley, which explained her lack of interest in those men who flooded her with letters. She knew the letters would continue until she got married, as every suitor in the land wanted their chance at being king. Unlucky for them, she had already made her choice. Bradley was that unexpected person who just appeared out of nowhere and somehow became the only one to occupy her thoughts entirely. At first, she had her reservations, wondering about his motives and expecting him to be like every other suitor, seeing her as a means to a better life. Numerous men in Adlington had tried to win her affection, with some being around for extended periods as she enjoyed their company. Knowing their true intentions, they were merely used as moments of amusement for her.

With Bradley, however, the experience was unlike any other. He effortlessly captivated her, his charm and personality drawing her in completely. He was like a breath of fresh air, making her feel alive whenever he was near. As their romance blossomed, her initial doubts regarding his motives gradually dwindled with every passing day. He became more than a passing infatuation and someone she couldn't imagine living without. He was the man she wanted to marry, and for once in her life, she might get to marry for love rather than entering into a union solely for political alliances. As if summoned by her thoughts, Bradley walked into the room with a radiant aura enveloping him. With a grin, he approached the desk, bowing courteously before extending his hand to her.

"My Queen, would you do me the honour of dining with me this evening?"

Giddy with excitement, Elinor dropped the letter she had been holding between her fingers onto the desk and jumped out of her seat towards him.

"Of course. What are we having?" she inquired.

"Whatever your heart desires, my love," he responded, gently taking her hand and linking it through his arm, his gaze filled with longing as he looked at her.

With a sparkle in her eyes, she started walking out of the room. "Then I guess we should start with dessert."

Chapter 19

A Turn of Events

It had been a long and arduous journey home for Adrian. He had failed in his task and now found himself with the unfortunate job of explaining this to Elinor. As he crested the hill with his chestnut horse, the sight of Carraton came into view, and the afternoon sun illuminated the glorious city, casting a radiant glow upon its towering buildings. A stark contrast to his own despondent mood. A gentle breeze blew from behind, pushing him forward as if to hurry him along. With a shake of his head, Adrian tightened his grip on the reins and led his horse into a canter down the hill, following the winding brick path into the city.

His men followed suit, but upon entering the city, a few veered off, making their way home before returning to the castle. He pressed onward, riding through the bustling streets at a leisurely trot. It had been quite some time since he had simply wandered through the city. Today, it seemed to pulse with life, teeming with activity and bustling with workers and visitors alike. Bells rang as shop doors swung open and closed, merchants called out, sharing their wares, and the buzz of conversation reverberated through every street. Everyone seemed to have a purpose, a destination, or a task at hand. A kaleidoscope of colours surrounded him, from the vibrant attire of the locals to the rich assortment of food and produce adorning the stalls. Carraton, without a doubt, epitomised a thriving city.

As he rode further into the heart of Carraton, the grandeur of the city unfolded before him. Magnificent buildings stood tall, adorned with intricate architectural designs. The aroma of freshly baked bread wafted through the air, eliciting a low rumble from him. The city pulsed with remarkable energy, a vibrant tapestry of life and bustling activity. Riding through the streets, he watched children playing games in the cobblestone alleys, laughing as they chased each other down the narrow streets. Artists sketched portraits as people posed while musicians played music that stirred the soul. A swell of pride washed over him as he beheld the thriving city before him. Carraton wasn't merely a city; it was a realm of wonder, magic and dreams. A place where the heart's desires could be pursued without any constraint. Hopes and aspirations intertwined in the lively streets, painting a vivid scene of possibility.

Approaching the outskirts of the city, he continued along the brick path, passing by the scattered thatched houses until the castle came into view. Its towering walls portrayed an unconquerable fortress. Riding through the castle gates, all thoughts of the city dissipated from his mind, replaced by the reason he was there, reminding him who he needed to find. On edge, he dismounted his horse and walked it to the stables, where a waiting stable boy promptly took hold of the reins.

"Thank ye, sir, I'll take good care of 'im," the young lad assured Adrian.

Adrian nodded in acknowledgement. "Thank you. We rode hard these past few days. He'll need a good rest, along with plenty of food and water."

The young lad led the horse away, Adrian turned to leave, heading into the castle, and to Elinor's quarters. As he neared them, he noticed the absence of guards outside her door. Feeling a twinge of frustration, he turned around and began walking down the hallway, intent on finding someone to ask about her whereabouts. Soon enough, he spotted her lady Chloe, Elinor's companion, heading towards him.

"Lady Chloe, could you please tell me where I might find the queen?" Adrian inquired.

"Yes sir. She's out for the day with Bradley. They've taken the horses and went for a ride out in the countryside," Chloe replied.

"Thank you," Adrian reacted with a nod. As Chloe curtsied and continued, Adrian remained in place for a moment, pondering what to do next, feeling a surge of irritation running through his veins.

With weariness seeping into his bones as the exhaustion of the past few weeks caught up to him, Adrian decided that retreating to his chambers was the wisest course of action. There, he could freshen up and unwind until Elinor returned from her ride. With that in mind, he turned around once again and made his way towards his own quarters.

Adrian's chamber was spacious, yet with plenty of room to move about, reflecting modesty in its decor. He wasn't one for extravagance, so his room held only the basics that any man would need. A robust dresser stood against one wall, accompanied by a matching wooden wardrobe of mahogany wood. Positioned by the window, a simple writing desk offered a serene view of the outside world. The most extravagant feature of the room had to be the four-poster bed cloaked in silk drapes with enough pillows and blankets to decorate several beds. Apart from the bed, the rest of the room reflected who he was at his core, preferring order and simplicity over lavish embellishments and clutter.

In serious need of a bath, Adrian walked to the adjoining bathroom and began to fill the tub. While waiting for it to fill, he unpacked his travel bag, emptying its contents onto the floor and sorting them into sections. Items to put away, clothing needed washing, and pieces to dispose of. Once his personal effects were put away and his dirty clothes were in the laundry pile, he took off the clothing he had worn and added it to the pile. With the bathtub filled to the brim with steaming water, he poured a few drops of eucalyptus oil, then eased himself into the soothing warmth of the water. His muscles relaxed as he submerged deeper, savouring the heat after weeks of riding. Relaxed but still feeling unclean, he grabbed a washcloth and bar of soap, lathering up the cloth before washing the dirt and grime from his skin. Emerging from the tub feeling refreshed, he wrapped himself in a towel before finding some fresh clothes. Though he had no intention of rushing through the first hot bath he had in weeks, the weight of pending tasks lingered in his mind.

His top priority was to speak with Elinor without delay. Having instructed one guard to inform him of her return, Adrian felt a sense of urgency in sharing his news, especially with Lord Goodman present in the castle. After drying off and dressing, he paced his room, anxiously awaiting word of Elinor's arrival. She had been gone for a few hours already with Bradley, yet he remained confident that she wouldn't be too far away. While he could have found something to occupy his time within the castle, Adrian's thoughts were solely fixated on his impending conversation with Elinor. Until that took place, he found himself unable to focus on anything else. Adrian halted his pacing at a knock on the door. He rushed to open it so quickly that the guard outside was startled, his fist still raised, ready to knock again.

"Sir, the Queen has returned. She's going to her chambers to freshen up, then heading to her private dining room for dinner with Bradley," the guard reported.

"Thank you. I'll make my way to her quarters now. Unfortunately, this matter can't wait," Adrian replied with a sense of urgency.

The guard nodded to Adrian and left, leaving Adrian to close his door behind him as he set off towards Elinor's chambers. His thoughts immediately turned to Bradley and the amount of time he seemed to spend with Elinor. Adrian had been aware of their interactions before he left, and it appeared their relationship had only intensified during his absence if they were spending both the day and evening together. This should not have bothered him, yet Bradley consistently rubbed him the wrong way. His entire family exuded arrogance and entitlement, but Adrian could at least maintain being civil towards them. He and Bradley, though, had clashed right from the beginning. While Bradley's family had a long-standing lineage as the lords of the land, Adrian was merely a humble soldier. Despite his knighthood, Bradley liked to dismiss Adrian's status, which only exacerbated their strained dynamic. Between Bradley's snide remarks and pompous attitude, Adrian tried to be around him as little as possible. This had not been difficult over the past few years due to that they lived so far apart. Now, though, Bradley seemed to be everywhere, a constant presence that Adrian found increasingly difficult to tolerate.

The prospect seemed even more daunting if his relationship with Elinor were to deepen. Adrian had longed to put Bradley in his place, yet he knew he couldn't do much about it given Bradley's status as a lord. And if Elinor's evident infatuation with Bradley persisted, Adrian realised he would likely have to endure his presence for the foreseeable future. Resentment of their relationship threatened to boil over as he clenched his fists, storming down the hallway in annoyance before he pulled himself together, stopping outside her door.

Taking a deep breath, Adrian relaxed his hands and grappled with his emotions. He didn't hold romantic feelings for Elinor, nor had he experienced this in the past with the previous suitors. It was clear that his disdain was reserved solely for Bradley. With a renewed sense of calm, he knocked on the door, trying to convey a composed demeanour. Lady Chloe opened the door and let him inside just as Elinor emerged from her bathroom. She greeted him with a smile, which faltered into uncertainty as she observed Adrian's expression. His attempt to mask his emotions of indifference conveyed his frustration.

***

"From your expression and the lack of correspondence during the trip, I gather things didn't go as planned?" Although she knew the answer, a part of her had hoped for reassurance that all had gone to plan.

"No, my Queen, it didn't. We searched for days and questioned everyone in the manor but to no avail. We even brought in the aid of a tracer, yet nothing could be found."

She had been certain that what she sought must be within the manor's confines. As Adrian explained the events that had unfolded, Elinor paced restlessly in the room, trying to come up with a plan for what to do next. The thought of Lord Goodman discovering what had happened filled her with dread. Aware of the absence of evidence or valid reason to justify a search, she knew she had to think of something before he found out. As everything seemed to be falling apart, hope faded away, leaving frustration in its wake.

Elinor's narrowed eyes betrayed the simmering anger within her veins, pulsating with suppressed power. Suddenly, a surge of energy escaped her, whipping a whirlwind through the room. Before she could comprehend the unfolding chaos, furniture rattled against the floor, papers and trinkets swirling through the air and crashing to the ground. The atmosphere crackled with electricity, filling the air with an ominous energy. Amidst the turmoil, her clenched fists trembled with an unyielding determination. She embodied a tempest incarnate, an unstoppable force of nature.

As her anger intensified, her power surged in tandem, black tendrils flowing from her fingertips, slashing through the room with unrestrained force, ripping through everything in its path.

"Elinor! What are you doing?" Adrian grabbed her shoulders, his eyes filled with fear.

At his touch, she snapped back to the present, releasing the grip of her power. As her emotions shifted from anger to shock, the tendrils of magic disappeared in an instant – an unexpected display of power she had unwittingly drawn on. Standing motionless, she turned around slowly, absorbing the aftermath of what had just occurred. The room lay in disarray, akin to the aftermath of a tornado, with furniture strewn about and torn apart. In the midst of the chaos stood Adrian, his expression mirroring the confusion evident in his gaze, as if uncertain of who she had become.

"Adrian, are you alright?" She approached him tentatively, extending her hand, but he took a step back. "Adrian, please, speak to me." Her words came out in barely a whisper as she struggled to make sense of the situation. She couldn't believe what had just transpired. The loss of control was as shocking to her as it was to him. Never before had she experienced such a lapse. While there had been incidents of broken glasses and minor mishaps during her early attempts to harness her power, nothing compared to the magnitude of this event.

"I'm fine. But what just happened?" He conveyed one message with his words, but his body language revealed something different to her.

"I don't know. My emotions were running high, and the power just took over," she explained, her tone tinged with uncertainty.

"Elinor—"

"It won't happen again, I assure you. Now that I understand the capabilities of this new power, I'll keep it under control." Adrian simply nodded, though the worry in his eyes was unmistakable.

"Trust me, Adrian." She placed a hand on his arm, locking eyes with him in a determined attempt to convince him. As he met her gaze, his expression changed from worry to resolve, his posture stiffening.

"Of course, always. I'll send someone to clean your chambers. You may want to find an alternative chamber for the night, my Queen," he suggested with a bow before taking his leave.

After Adrian left, her thoughts became a whirlwind, and she felt the power pulse once more. Recognising it this time, she shook her head and pushed the energy aside, redirecting her focus to what she could control at that moment. With Adrian organising the cleanup and knowing she needed to keep her emotions in check, she sought a semblance of normalcy. Summoning her willpower, she composed herself and set aside what happened earlier with the power. Amidst the chaos in her mind, there was only one person she wanted to see – a person who could take away her problems and make her relax, making her feel like the centre of the universe.

Her feet carried her through the halls until she stood outside Bradley's chambers. He greeted her with that same cocky grin, the sight of which stirred a mix of emotions within her.

"Elinor, what an honour it is to be graced by your presence before dinner," Bradley said, stepping aside to gesture to her to enter his chambers. "Would you care to join me?"

Upon entering his chambers, she found herself captivated by the presence of the man before her, the earlier events fading into the background. As the door closed behind her, Bradley placed a comforting hand on her back, guiding her towards a plush armchair nestled beside a crackling fireplace. Seated, she watched as he poured two glasses of red wine, handing one to her with a gracious expression.

With a charming smile, Bradley raised his glass. "To a wonderful day and many more to come, my Queen."

Elinor raised her glass with a nod of her head, a smile gracing her lips as she reminisced about the joyful morning ride through the countryside they had shared. All thoughts of her power were pushed aside as she savoured the moment. Taking a sip of the wine, she revelled in the divine taste of the silky liquid on her tongue.

Time seemed to stand still as they engaged in deep philosophical discussions, exchanging thoughts on their favourite art and literature and arguing over the greats of their time. Elinor hung on to his every word, mesmerised by his eloquence and intellect. In his presence, she felt a profound connection, a meeting of minds that transcended the ordinary.

The hours slipped away unnoticed, the world beyond those chambers becoming a distant memory. Enclosed within their own little universe, nothing else mattered. Eventually, as the night grew late and the effects of the wine lulled her into a drowsy state, Elinor followed Bradley to bed. Wrapped in his embrace, she smiled contentedly as he placed a gentle kiss upon her forehead, drifting into a peaceful sleep.

Chapter 20

Secret Meetings

Bradley found it unbelievable how events were unfolding since his arrival in Carraton. He hadn't returned since his teenage days, and this time, he was only there because his father insisted. While his father and sister Adina flourished in the royal court, Bradley's heart belonged to the open sea and the distant lands awaiting exploration. From a young age, tales of sailors on grand adventures, fighting beasts of the seas, and seeing giant winged creatures across the sky had captivated Bradley. Not to mention the treasures they brought back after months on the open sea. As he grew, Bradley yearned for the freedom and excitement that only the open sea could offer while his family revelled in the luxuries of the royal court.

His father, a prominent trader, held high expectations for Bradley to follow in his footsteps and become a respected figure in the court. However, Bradley's heart beat to the rhythm of the sea. He spent hours studying maps, dreaming of the uncharted territories that awaited him beyond the horizon. At seventeen, when one of his father's trade ships left the dock, Bradley convinced his father to allow him to sail with them and learn the art of trade and negotiation firsthand. That day, Bradley set sail into the vast unknown. The salty air filled his lungs, and the sound of waves crashing against the hull filled him with a sense of exhilaration. He found his place, bargaining and trading with new people across the vast seas, establishing himself as a person of note. Over the years, he became highly influential in different lands, forming connections and forging alliances, bringing prosperity, wealth, and influence to his own family – great commodities in their line of work. While Bradley sailed the seas, his father and sister sold his products in their own lands for hefty profits. Together, they became the foremost traders in the region, specialising in exotic spices, delectable foods, dazzling gems, and rare materials from distant shores.

In the early days, anyone who dared to stand in their way ended up regretting it, as their trade diminished to nothing. Presently, very few dared to challenge them. Occasionally, some insignificant sailors would appear, only to vanish without a trace soon after. Over the past few years, there has been a shift in the family's business dynamics. He had begun preparing to assume his father's position as lord and assist his sister in running the family business from these shores. His father's health had been declining, prompting him to step down and allow his children to take the lead roles in the family. However, his father still maintained a firm grip on everything that transpired. With their shared ambition and greed, the entire family thrived on being at the top of the food chain. This meant that even as he relinquished control, his father continued to monitor their endeavours.

This led to his eventual arrival in Carraton, much to his annoyance when he first received the news. Unable to travel anymore, his father insisted he trust their workers with the next shipment delivery and head to Carraton in his place. After a fair bit of arguing with his father, he finally agreed. Little did he know that his father's insistence was about to yield the biggest payoff his family could ever imagine. Stepping back into the court, aware that Elinor now occupied the throne, promised to be a captivating experience. It was common knowledge that she had seized power by force, yet nobody had dared to challenge her. With her in control, the remaining lords could thrive in ways that had been impossible during James's reign.

Certainly, James may have been a ruler who upheld fairness and justice, but such virtues did little to fill one's pockets with gold. He suppressed the power of the lords excessively, prioritising the well-being of the impoverished over the interests of the wealthy. Elinor, on the other hand, embraced power and was willing to employ any means necessary to achieve her goals. A prime example of this was her ruthless ascension to the throne.

So, when he saw her at their initial meeting, he threw his support behind her, seeing it as his chance to earn her favour. What he hadn't expected was for them to forge a romantic connection and begin dating. He remembered her vividly from their childhood but hadn't given her much thought over the past few years. With her residing in Adlington and him occupied with travel, they hadn't crossed paths for many years.

Meeting her again, she remained as ambitious and cunning as ever. As soon as he laid eyes on her once more, he couldn't help but acknowledge the undeniable beauty that emanated from her. Her flowing chocolate brown hair, captivating siren blue eyes, and curvaceous figure made her an absolute sight to behold. She remained as driven and clever as she had always been, making every moment with her engaging. Spending time with her was far from a chore. They reminisced over countless cherished childhood memories, forging a unique bond, unlike her relationships with the other lords and their sons.

This meant he didn't even have to try to get close to her. It just happened naturally. Conversation flowed effortlessly, and their playful banter added an intriguing element. Like Elinor, he had never married. He didn't consider it a priority yet. If he were to entertain the idea of marriage, it had to offer him more than just a beautiful wife for pleasure. He could indulge in such pursuits anytime. No, if he were to commit, it had to be to someone worthy, someone possessing significant power, wealth, and success, much like himself. And Elinor exceeded those criteria by far. To hold such immense power and status was an opportunity he couldn't walk away from. If Elinor were to propose marriage to him, it would be foolish to decline.

His drive wasn't solely fuelled by ambition; he had genuine feelings for her. In truth, these past few weeks had seen his feelings for her grow beyond mere fondness, even if it hadn't blossomed into love. An undeniable spark ignited between them, growing more intense with each passing day. They complemented each other well, and she challenged his thoughts and ideas, making him question his own knowledge. Smart, witty, beautiful, and adventurous in the bedroom, she possessed all the qualities of an ideal wife. Yet, he couldn't profess to be in love with her, nor did he believe she felt that way about him. Thus, the arrangement suited them both. They needed each other for their own reasons, making it a perfect match in their own unique way. However, he perceived a problem in the form of her secrets – information he deemed essential, especially if he were to rule by her side. He refused to be kept in the dark, always being the last to find out what was going on. He yearned to be the one she confided in, sharing everything with him. To achieve this, he knew he had to earn her trust, even if it meant employing covert tactics. Using his network of spies within the castle, he ensured he stayed informed. Right on schedule, one of his spies entered his chambers.

The chambermaid, Anna, possessed a deep understanding of the secrets that unfolded within these walls, adeptly navigating through the hidden servant passages. It was remarkable how individuals openly confided in her presence. With her lacklustre complexion and typical flat brown hair, Anna seamlessly blended into the background.

"Anna, what news do you bring me?" Bradley gestured for Anna to take a seat, his own posture leaning forward eagerly to hear her report. As she settled into her chair and noticed the intrigue in his eyes, Anna began.

"The news starts with the Queen herself, sir, and what happened in er chambers just yesterday."

"Yesterday?"

"Yesterday sir. It seems she had a problem wiv er power see, an lost control when Adrian came by wiv news for er. Seems she didn like what e ad ter say if the damage in er room was out to go by."

"What time was this?"

"Early evening, sir. Just before she came to see you."

Bradley leaned back in his chair, his brows furrowed, a hand resting on his chin as he contemplated Anna's report. He had heard of instances where rulers succumbed to madness fuelled by power, often starting with a loss of control. If this happened to Elinor…

"That wasn all, sir. The reason she lost control will interest you."

As he refocused on Anna, he stared at her with curiosity. "Tell me."

Anna shared the details she overheard about Adrian's secret visit to Lord Johnathon Goodman's house, but she was unaware of the purpose behind it. However, she told Bradley that Lord Goodman had a scheduled meeting with one of his trusted spies at eleven that morning in the hunting grounds by the castle. If he wanted to uncover what Elinor was hiding, all he needed to do was locate this meeting and eavesdrop on their conversation. Checking the time, Bradley saw it was already past ten, so he got up and made his way towards the door.

"You're welcome."

He glanced back at Anna. "Yes, thank you, Anna. Your information is invaluable, as always." He reached into his pockets, retrieved a silver coin, and tossed it to her. "As always, I trust you to keep this encounter confidential."

Anna caught the coin and pocketed it. "Certainly, sir," she replied.

Satisfied with her response, Bradley continued, determined to hear what this spy had to say. At the stables, feeling impatient to leave, he saddled his own horse and took off to the hunting grounds at a gallop.

He slowed his pace as the sound of his horse's hooves echoed through the open area. As he dismounted, a soft breeze rustled passed, carrying fallen leaves. He strained his ears, but all he could hear were the birds chirping in the trees. This had to be the place. Bradley scanned the ground for any signs of recent activity until he spotted what looked like fresh footprints leading ahead. Deciding not to bring his horse further, he led it deeper into the dense woods, securing it to a sturdy tree. Retracing his steps, his senses heightened, his skin prickling in anticipation. Sneaking through the underbrush, he listened intently for any sounds. The voices of men pricked his ears. With careful movements, he inched towards the voices, staying hidden behind a thick cluster of trees. As the men came into his line of sight, his hands gripped the rough bark of the tree, pieces of it scraping against his fingertips. Concealed in the shadows, he was confident that he remained unseen. Yet, his ears caught every whispered word, the distant voices carrying on the wind.

"What were they doing in my home?" Lord Goodman's voice was laced with indignation.

"Looking for evidence of the crystal shards, my lord. Naturally, they found nothing."

"Of course not. Do they think me foolish enough to keep that information in my home? What about my children? Were they present at the time?" Anger morphed into worry in Lord Goodman's tone.

"Yes, my lord, but they are safe and unharmed."

"Good. That's good. I need you to get them out of there and somewhere safe."

"My lord?"

"If Elinor believes I know something, she'll stop at nothing to get what she wants from me, including harming my family. I will not put them in danger. See to it that they are safe."

"Yes, my lor—" The spy's sentence was interrupted by a sudden sound. "What was that?" The spy spun around, scanning the area as Johnathon tensed.

"What did you hear?"

Bradley's body froze, his eyes widening as he swore the spy looked right at him. He crouched down, his gaze fixed on the two men as his hand inched towards the dagger hidden in his boot.

The spy shook his head. "I thought I heard voices." Both men stood motionless, as though listening.

Although he was certain they hadn't seen him, his heart raced, his movements cautious as he backed away, one step at a time, further from them. Aware of the odds, he couldn't risk being seen. Once he deemed himself at a safe enough distance, he hastened back to his horse. Having got a good look at the spy and heard all he dared, he mounted his horse and galloped back to the castle, his own plans taking shape in his mind.

Unbeknownst to him, Elinor had already set her own schemes in motion, schemes he was determined to become a part of.

***

In a shady bar nestled deep within the city's slums, Adrian sat, his gaze fixed on the wall, clutching a generous pour of scotch. Following his encounter with Elinor earlier, he yearned for an escape from the confines of the castle. He sought solace in a place where anonymity prevailed, and the apathy of others shielded him from intrusion. Drawn towards the underbelly of the city, his feet led him to an area the prosperous preferred to deny existed.

Adrian ended up at *The Forgotten Well*, an apt name for the type of patrons who frequented the establishment. That night, he was one of them, hoping to drown out the memory of what had happened, and the potential consequences if it were to happen again. He knew all too well that losing control of the power never ended well for anyone involved, and Elinor wasn't one to admit when she needed help.

As he knocked back his scotch, he slid the glass across the bar. "Another." With a nod from the grizzled-faced bartender, another hearty glass of scotch was poured, and Adrian placed coins on the bar to pay for it.

Turning on the bar stool, he surveyed the room. What or who he was looking for, he wasn't entirely sure. The bar itself had seen better days. With its dim lighting and bordered-up windows, creating an atmosphere of neglect. Worn-out stools and chipped wooden tables added to the ambience of faded grandeur. Tonight's patrons sat either alone or in small groups, engrossed in card games, each bearing a demeanour that suggested they were no strangers to trouble. Catching the eye of one lone man, Adrian tensed upon his gaze. Preferring to avoid any trouble, he turned back to face the bar.

With another drink down, his thoughts drifted to Elinor and the fiasco that was the visit to the Goodman's manor. It was a problem that was bound to resurface and bite them in the ass. Elinor was supposed to have a backup plan in place if the mission failed, but evidently, she didn't – or she failed to tell him. Lately, she had been keeping secrets, and it seemed they were only digging themselves further into a tangled web from which he wasn't sure they would get out.

The tasks were progressing at a pace that exceeded his capacity to manage, and Elinor was making decisions without proper planning, leaving him to handle the resulting chaos. Additionally, there was a rumour circulating among the servants upon his return that Lord Goodman knew of the situation, but he couldn't confirm its accuracy. Thus, he found himself trying to find a way out of this mess while Elinor neglected her duties, preoccupied with Bradley. Since she told him to mend things with Lord Goodman, he had done his utmost to intercede in any correspondence with the family, the best he could do given the circumstances. Yet, to her, this marked the second offence he had committed in as many months, causing her once unwavering trust to falter. He couldn't help but wonder how much longer it would be until he became irrelevant to her, with Bradley becoming her preferred confidant.

For now, all he could do was wait and hope she sought his guidance soon. If not, he feared what would become of them both, and whether everything they had worked for would go up in flames, whether from her neglect or, worse, the power itself, engulfing them both in the process. With another drink coursing through him, Adrian began to feel a buzz from the alcohol. He steadied himself on unsteady feet and made his way out of the bar, back to the place he now called home.

Chapter 21

Allies

The following day, Elinor found herself in the countryside with Bradley, enjoying a moment of solitude. Well, as much as one could have with guards positioned at a distance, ensuring her safety. They sat on a blue-striped blanket, indulging in another delightful picnic lunch. It had become their routine to escape for the day, riding together before finding a secluded spot to enjoy their lunch. That day, the autumn sun beamed down with a gentle breeze caressing Elinor's skin, causing strands of her loose hair to dance in the air. The soft rustling of leaves and the distant chirping of birds created a soothing soundtrack to the serene ambience.

Perched on yellowing grass, resting against the sturdy trunk of a majestic oak, they beheld the vast expanse unfolding before them. Elinor savoured the crisp bite of a juicy red apple while surveying the city below. Carraton sprawled out ahead, its buildings and streets visible from this elevated vantage point. The fields and farms appeared minuscule, resembling intricately crafted wooden models, lending an air of enchantment to the scene. Beside her, Bradley was lying on his side, facing her, and propping himself up with his elbow.

He picked his way through a punnet of strawberries, his gaze unwaveringly fixed on her. "You look serious. Something troubling you?"

"Nothing much, just pondering a few matters. Nothing too important, just some loose ends I need to tie up before the ball."

"Such as what to do about Lord Goodman, given that your search of his home didn't go as planned?"

"Who told you of that?" Elinor fumed, her posture rigid as she fixed him with a seething glare, her eyes ablaze with anger. Her heart raced, panic threatening to consume her. If he knew, who else could be aware?

"Relax. I know more than you might think, but rest assured, Elinor, I'm on your side. Trust me." He sat upright, gently took her hand, and peered into her eyes, willing her to believe his reassurance. Sensing her body relax, he continued.

"I'm aware of it, and he knows it, too. During a walk yesterday, I overheard him having a private conversation with a messenger. I had hoped you would trust me enough to confide in me, but I understand your reasons for keeping it to yourself." Bradley paused, a puzzled expression crossing his face as if he were trying to decipher her thoughts, but she maintained a stoic demeanour, giving nothing away. Instead, she fixed him with a steady gaze. Undeterred, he pressed on, his words quickening with urgency.

"I've taken it upon myself to do some investigation, and I've learned about your quest for the crystal shards. If you allow me, I can aid you in locating them and rid us of Lord Goodman once and for all. All I ask is for your trust."

Elinor found herself caught in a whirlwind of conflicting emotions. She had always kept a small circle of trust for a reason. The fewer people who were aware of her plans, the better. The fact that Bradley knew about them and was essentially spying on her made her question her trust in him. She recognised that his actions stemmed from her deliberate choice to keep him in the dark. Were it anyone else, she would have swiftly eliminated them from the equation. One less person to concern herself with.

However, Bradley was different. He wasn't just anyone; he was the man she was courting and intended to marry, even if he was unaware of her aspirations. If she regarded their relationship as seriously as she believed, trust needed to be established between them. Though it didn't come naturally to her, she recognised the necessity of letting him in. It was clear she couldn't effectively govern a kingdom while keeping him in the dark. Given what he had just revealed, she had faith that he would be a dependable ally who would support her without hesitation.

The internal debate concluded, and contrary to her usual instinct to trust no one, Elinor blurted out, "I trust you. Tell me what you know." Bradley told Elinor everything he knew and had overheard, and together they devised a plan to ruin Lord Goodman's reputation.

The candid conversation with Bradley brought a sense of renewal to her spirit. Finally, she felt gratitude for finding someone who resonated with her on such a deep level. The idea of planning the downfall of one of her enemies together stirred a primal sense of purpose within her. She had exposed her innermost thoughts, unconcerned by any potential judgement from him. His alignment with her thoughts was unmistakable, revealing his willingness to go to great lengths to support her in keeping the throne, even if it ultimately benefited him as well.

After their conversation, Elinor experienced a newfound sense of liberation, a freedom she hadn't felt in a long time. She leaned towards Bradley, initiating a light kiss, which deepened as their passion intensified, her body yearning for his touch. He responded with equal fervour, their kiss becoming more intense as desire coursed through her veins. These moments shared with Bradley made her feel alive in a way she had never experienced with anyone else. As his hand found its way into her hair, gently pulling her head back to expose her neck, his lips traced a path along her skin. In turn, her own hands explored his body, before she pressed herself against him with a soft moan, relishing in the firm kisses trailing up her neck before he whispered her name in her ear. Leaning into him, she became aware of the bulge in his pants, a sensation that shifted her thoughts.

It was one thing to engage in passionate kisses and explore his mouth with her tongue, but she craved more. She desired to taste him, to feel the firmness of his cock in her mouth, and to run her tongue along his impressive shaft. With a soft moan, she broke away from their intense embrace, gently urging him backwards until he lay on the ground. Anticipation gleamed in his eyes as he propped himself up on his elbows, watching hungrily as she positioned herself between his legs. The bulge of his hard cock was already visible, straining against his pants. With deft movements, she eased his pants past his hips, allowing his cock to spring free. Giving him a seductive glance, Elinor leaned closer, guiding the tip into her mouth, skilfully caressing him with her lips before teasingly pulling away. She slid him back into her mouth, gradually taking him deeper with each deliberate motion, firmly sucking him before releasing him from her lips once more. On her third descent, she eagerly took him in deeply, taking as much of him in her mouth as she could. Her desire heightened as she continued to move up and down his shaft, her tongue gliding along his length, eliciting moans of pleasure as he tightly gripped her hair.

With a rhythmic motion, he rocked his hips back and forth, firmly gripping her hair as he thrust into her mouth. With each movement, the tip of his cock reached the depths of her throat, drawing forth moans of ecstasy. He savoured the moment, repeating the action a few more times before pulling away from her. "How wet are you right now?" he asked with his voice laced with anticipation.

As she caught her breath, she moved closer to him. "Very. Want to feel?" she teased in a sultry tone, lifting her dress and guiding his hand towards her. As his fingers tenderly stroked her entrance, desire swirled through her core before his fingers slipped away. She was wet and ready for him.

"I want you to sit on my cock and ride me until you come. Then you'll get on your knees, and I'm going to fuck you until you can't take it anymore."

His words sparked a deeper yearning within her, causing her core to burn with longing. The commanding and instructive tone with which he spoke heightened her pleasure in ways she had never experienced before. It was a refreshing change from how others had treated her. Without hesitation, she obeyed his command, straddling him. Adjusting her dress, Elinor took hold of him, sliding him against her entrance before taking him deep inside her. A slow, pleasure-filled moan escaped her lips as she arched her back, savouring the sensation. Gradually adjusting to the feeling of him inside her, she began to sway her hips back and forth, revelling in the feeling of him filling every inch of her. With each movement, she increased the pace, moaning with delight, thoroughly enjoying the feel of him inside her.

"Fuck, you feel amazing," he moaned, his hands tightening their grip on her hips, pushing her down even further onto him. A low moan escaped her lips as she felt his cock penetrate her even further. She clenched around him, the sensation driving her wild as she increased the pace, simultaneously rubbing her clit for added stimulation. Panting heavily now, she could feel she was close.

"That's it. I can feel your orgasm. It's close. Keep going and ride me till you explode all over me. I want you dripping down your thighs so much I can lick them clean."

Bradley matched her rhythm with each thrust of his hips, his hands squeezing her breasts as he enjoyed the sight of her riding him, lost in a state of pure bliss. Surrendering herself to the intensity of the moment, she called out his name as waves of pleasure washed over her. Collapsing into his embrace, she trembled with satisfaction, a delighted smile lingering on her lips as she kissed him. In a gesture filled with passion, she gently bit down on his lower lip.

"Ouch," he muttered, delivering a firm slap to her backside, ensuring she felt the impact. "And we're not done yet," he asserted.

"Oh, are we not?" she replied teasingly, rocking against him once more with his hard cock still deep within her, emitting a soft moan.

"No, we're not. On your knees. Now."

Slipping away from him, Elinor rose to her feet and took a step to the side. A mischievous glint sparkled in her eyes as she faced him. "I'm all yours," she declared in a playful tone before assuming her position. Bradley moved himself behind her, adjusting her position and lifting her skirts. With an alluring view before him, he grasped his cock and thrust himself into her without warning. Elinor cried out, barely able to adjust to him before he began pounding into her at a relentless pace.

With swift, deep movements, Elinor moaned in ecstasy as he filled her completely. The angle they found hit pleasure points deep within her, amplifying her satisfaction as her inner walls tightened around him. Just when she believed she couldn't handle any more, a new sensation overwhelmed her senses as his finger gently teased the entrance of her backside. Overcome with pleasure, she cried out loudly, another orgasm crashing over her as his finger slipped inside. Tremors ran through her body as these new sensations threatened to overwhelm her. The relentless pace, combined with his exploration of her ass, pushed her body to its limits, causing her to tremble with pleasure and lose control. Her arms gave way, her upper body collapsing to the ground while her hips remained raised by Bradley's firm grip.

"That's it. You're taking me so well. My good girl. You're so wet for me. I'm so close. Your tight, wet pussy is going to make me come," he murmured, thrusting deeply, his moans mingling with hers as he reached his own sweet release.

As she screamed into the grass, another orgasm washed over Elinor while feeling Bradley's cum filling her. He stilled his movements, releasing her hips. Exhausted, Elinor collapsed onto the ground, Bradley joining her. He tenderly kissed the top of her head before pulling her close and adjusting her skirts.

"Are you all right?" Bradley asked, brushing his fingers through her hair before delicately tucking the loose strands obscuring her face behind her ear.

Unable to articulate her thoughts, Elinor uttered a "yes," her voice wispy, before closing her eyes and taking his hand in hers, intertwining their fingers.

She relished in the overwhelming emotions that had just washed over her, her body content and at peace. They lay there for a while, neither of them moving, basking in the warmth of the afternoon sun as they drifted into a light doze. Elinor was the first to awaken, and as she looked over at Bradley, still sleeping, she couldn't help but reflect on everything he had said earlier and the intensity of their recent encounter. Her heart fluttered in her chest as she thought of Bradley's lips against hers, his hands roaming her body. A soft tingle lingered on her skin, as a shiver ran down her spine at the memory. Elinor's gaze shifted to Bradley's peaceful face, his features relaxed in slumber, his chest rising and falling rhythmically with each steady breath.

It was surprising how drastically her life had changed within a mere few weeks. During that first encounter with Bradley, she had been a lot more guarded around him. Given his arrogance and familial background, she had harboured suspicions that he was using her as much as she was using him. However, the more time they spent together, she found herself unable to shake the growing sense that he might have genuine feelings for her, perhaps more than she had believed. Likewise, she cared for him more deeply than she was willing to admit out loud.

The moment she heard his plan to assist her with Lord Goodman, conviction settled within her. Rarely had anyone ever gone to such lengths for her, except for Adrian, who, of course, had been handsomely compensated for his services. With Bradley, there lingered the risk of betrayal. He possessed the potential to share what he knew with the other lords. Yet, to her surprise, he chose to support her instead. It marked a positive turn for Elinor. Lately, she had struggled to determine who she could trust and how to navigate the complex web of alliances without succumbing to despair. Within the court, everyone had their own agendas, ready to betray her at the slightest hint of advantage elsewhere. The high priestess and her group of priestesses harboured a deep disdain towards her, undoubtedly scheming behind closed doors to secure her downfall.

Then there was Adrian, her most trusted advisor and knight. He had stood faithfully by her side from the outset, unwavering in his support, steadfast in his belief in her and her visions. Together, they had meticulously crafted strategies to reclaim what rightfully belonged to her. However, since the throne became hers, a subtle yet palpable shift had taken place, fracturing their once flawless working relationship. His mistakes and the growing annoyance she detected from him prompted her to question how much longer he would remain loyal, fearing he might soon turn against her.

That left only her lady Chloe by her side, the one person in whom she placed her trust. Throughout their years of friendship, Chloe had proven herself a steadfast guardian of her secrets, providing support during her most vulnerable moments. Elinor knew Chloe would always remain loyal. Since their teenage years, they shared everything as young girls often do, and Chloe found her place as one of Elinor's ladies in court. Due to her family's financial struggles, Chloe secured the position by forming a friendship while working as a maid in the castle, for which she was grateful. Even now, Chloe continued to serve without hesitation, remaining Elinor's confidant and, when necessary, her informant. Elinor now faced the daunting task of determining just how much she could rely on Bradley, taking the biggest risk of all. Was he a friend or foe, an enemy or a lover, an ally or a rival, Elinor wondered. The decision lay solely in her hands. She simply had to make it.

Leaning in closer, Elinor pressed a gentle kiss to Bradley's forehead. As he stirred in his sleep, a soft smile graced his lips, affirming to Elinor that they were embarking on a journey together, filled with love, passion, and limitless possibilities. With gentle strokes, she traced her fingers along his cheek, silently contemplating. When he finally woke, he pulled her close and kissed her. Locking her gaze with his, Elinor gathered her courage and her voice steady as she addressed him, "Bradley, there's something I need to ask you."

Chapter 22

Evidence

Cecilia was on edge as she prepared for her escape during the masquerade ball. She had everything in place, except for one crucial element: the evidence of Elinor's betrayal against the crown, which she urgently needed. With time ticking away, Cecilia realised this might be her last chance to scour for the evidence, especially since Elinor was out for a ride. Yet, the main obstacle in her path was her guards, who seemed impossible to evade.

Cecilia had identified two critical places to search for the evidence. The first was within Elinor's chambers, which she could access during her cleaning duties. The second was the study, a far more formidable challenge given she was strictly prohibited from entering. Her best option involved utilising the secret servant passageways that connected to Elinor's quarters. However, they fell short of reaching the study. The closest they came was the hallway, a few rooms away. While it didn't seem like a significant distance, it posed a considerable obstacle as her entire plan depended on remaining unseen.

In addition to avoiding detection, Cecilia had to rely on the hope that her guards would remain stationed outside Elinor's chambers and not check on her. She prayed to the divine spirit that they would stay outside. If they entered, it would mean the end of everything she had worked for. Her success hinged on a delicate balance of timing, secrecy, and luck.

Upon finishing her shift in the kitchen, Cecilia grabbed a bucket brimming with soapy water and a duster, ready to commence her cleaning duties. Inside the first room, she hastily went about her usual tasks, her frayed nerves pushing her to work faster than usual. Each time a guard came to check, she was startled, fearing they would somehow discover her plan and expose her. Determined to extend her window of opportunity without raising suspicion, she again dusted the same shelves and fluffed the same pillows, lingering within the room. Fortunately, by the time she reached the third room, the guards had stopped checking on her. It was time for Elinor's room. Her heart raced within her chest, causing sweat to trickle down her palms, almost threatening to loosen her grip on the bucket she was carrying.

"Watch it!" One guard yelled and leapt back as water splashed onto her dress, narrowly missing them.

Cecilia's nerves made her skittish as she entered the chambers that were once hers, the guard closing the door behind her while muttering curses. She let go of the bucket, instinctively wiping her palms on her dress, only to realise it was already damp. Instead, she wiped her hands against the back of her dress and proceeded forward, halting in her tracks, attuned to every sound. At that moment, her senses heightened, causing the fine hairs on her arms to stand on end. Over the distant murmur of the guards conversing outside the door, her eyes absorbed every detail in the room. Her mind raced, considering every potential outcome of her plan. Despite recognising the grim possibilities, she felt her feet carry her towards the concealed passageway, her hand extending forward as her nerves transformed into determination. Regardless of what lay ahead, she knew she had to act – not just for herself, but for her family. With the passageway now open, she hesitated briefly before mustering the courage to step into the corridor, ignoring her nerves.

She navigated the hidden passageway, winding through dimly lit corridors. Inside, she noticed several servants passing by, busy with their own tasks. Each encounter sent her heart racing, fearing that they might stop her and question what she was doing. Yet, as they passed without a word, the tension gradually left her body. Descending a flight of stairs and continuing along another narrow corridor, she finally reached the sought-after exit. With trembling hands, Cecilia pushed open the door, surveying the surroundings. Apart from a few workers going about their day, there was no one to be concerned about. Hastening towards the study room door, an unsettling feeling of being watched lingered. As she scanned down the hallway, she entered the room and closed the door behind her. A wave of relief washed over her as she leaned against it, her head lowered in exhaustion. Cecilia had successfully made it. With her heartbeat steadying, she lifted her gaze, fixing it on the desk. Moving at a quickened pace, she walked towards the desk, acutely aware of how little time she had.

Upon reaching it, emotions overwhelmed her like a tonne of bricks. Memories flooded her mind. Images of James working at his desk, the two of them sitting together, discussing problems. The late nights when she had to drag him away from his work to go to bed. Tears welled in her eyes as she traced her fingers along the smooth surface of the hardwood. Memories rushed in as she circled the desk, settling into his chair, determined to hold back the tears before they spilt. Entering his study, she hadn't expected this surge of emotions. His study. Yet, as she looked around, nothing remained to signify his presence.

She gently brushed her hand across the arm of the chair. James's chair. Finding solace in its familiar earthy scent. As she reached her hand towards the desk drawers, her nerves intensified, causing her hand to tremble. As she tugged the first, it wouldn't budge, so she tried the next. Frustration creased her brow as she stared at the stubborn top drawer and drew on the power. With a focused mind, she willed the lock on the drawer to open. Tentatively, she reached out to open the top drawer again. Alas, despite another determined tug, it remained steadfastly closed, defying her efforts.

Determination coursed through Cecilia's veins. Failure wasn't an option, not now. Gathering all her strength, she directed her focus once more on the top drawer, silently praying to the divine spirit to help her. This time, her plea was answered. With a startled jolt, she pulled the top drawer open so forcefully it almost tumbled out of the desk. Pushing it back in slightly, she began sifting through its contents, swiftly yet meticulously examining each item. Aside from spare ink, a collection of letters, and plain parchment, there was nothing of significance within it.

Cecilia closed the drawer and proceeded with the power to open the second one. To her relief, this one opened on the first try. As she rummaged through its contents, the door to the study opened. Distracted by her search, Cecilia remained oblivious until the resounding slam of the door echoed through the room, startling her. Frozen in place, her eyes widened as she saw who had entered.

"Cecilia?" Adrian approached her, stopping in front of the desk. "Whatever you're looking for. It's not here."

"How—"

"Don't lie to me, Cecilia. We both know you're not allowed in here. Your guards are also nowhere in sight, so unless the rules around your freedom have suddenly changed, no one knows you're in here."

With a whimper, Cecilia's body slumped into the chair behind her. Tears streamed down her face, dampening her dress as she struggled to contain her emotions. Adrian watched her silently, taking a tentative step closer.

"Cecilia," he began softly, but she interrupted him.

"This isn't how it's supposed to be." She shook her head, locking eyes with him, her tear-stained face pleading for understanding. She hoped he would comprehend the threat Elinor posed, the danger she represented with her growing power.

"Adrian, I can see it, and so should you. Elinor isn't the same woman as she once was all those years ago. The day she was denied the throne, she became someone else. Since the bonding ceremony, her behaviour has worsened, and I thought that was impossible."

"How dare you speak of your queen like that—" Adrian began, but Cecilia cut him off.

"She isn't my queen, and if you can't see her erratic behaviour, then you're blind! What about what happened in her room the other day? It didn't implode on its own. You're loyal, Adrian, and I respect you greatly for that. But it's misplaced."

"That was an accident—" Adrian's voice rose, but Cecilia's was louder as she interjected him once more.

"Adrian, please, I implore you, look at the old documents in the library. Read them carefully and you'll see what becomes of those who aren't pure of heart. Despite Elinor's status as queen, she can't possess any more power. If you truly care about her and the kingdom, you'll help keep Elinor away from the remaining shards."

Cecilia felt immobilised with fear as Adrian's narrowed eyes fixed on her. She held her breath, awaiting his next words. Although she hadn't intended for her words to be filled with anger, she had grown tired of people pretending that Elinor was the rightful heir to the throne. Witnessing everyone fawning over Elinor while treating her like dirt had become unbearable. She firmly believed that Elinor's reign would only bring forth greed, undoing all the progress she and James had achieved over the years. If only she could convince Adrian to see the truth and join her cause. However, this seemed unlikely. He was a loyal man, just not to her.

After what felt like an eternity, Adrian finally spoke. "I didn't see you. Now leave before I change my mind."

"Adrian—"

"Now, Cecilia!" he said in a sharp tone, causing Cecilia to flinch.

With a silent nod, she turned and left the way she came, not stopping until she found herself back inside Elinor's chambers. Her heart pounded against her ribcage with an urgency she couldn't shake. She hadn't found what she needed, neither had she been locked up by Adrian. Flustered and unable to concentrate, Cecilia felt the pressing need to get out of these chambers and back to her own. Grasping the bucket of water again, she swung open the door, only to jump back in surprise as her eyes met the look of the guards. For a fleeting moment, she had forgotten they were there.

"Done?" the one guard asked.

Cecilia simply nodded before she strode out of the room, the guards trailing closely behind. Upon returning to her own quarters, Cecilia realised she still had the bucket clutched in her hands. She placed it by the door and turned to face the room, walking forward as though in a trance. Her mind struggled to piece together what had just happened or how she was supposed to feel. Instead, her subconscious guided her to the bed, where she lay down with arms by her sides, staring at the ceiling.

Lying there, Cecilia's thoughts took shape, desperately seeking a new plan or idea to appear. Yet, all she could fixate on was her failure. She had one job, and time was slipping through her fingers. The impending ball loomed ever closer, and without the crucial evidence, Cecilia felt uncertain about what would happen. The high priestess placed her trust in her, and the weight of that responsibility pressed heavily upon her shoulders. With each passing day, the task of gathering evidence became increasingly harder. Her workload increased, leaving her with scarce moments of solitude. As the ball drew nearer, the frenzy of preparations intensified among the staff. Evidence or not, Cecilia remained determined to escape once the day arrived. Elinor had stripped away everything good from her life, and the only thing keeping her together was knowing her escape was imminent. Without this glimmer of hope, despair threatened to consume her entirely.

There were still days when she didn't feel like getting out of bed, despite all the progress she had made and knowing that her children were alive. This castle and its inhabitants drained her emotionally, leaving her feeling estranged from those she once loved and cared for, like a family. Without people like Mistress Katelyn, she might have given up from the beginning. It was a painful truth, she reluctantly admitted. Even thoughts of Aevah and Jacob failed to pull her out of the darkness on those sombre days. The loss of James weighed heavily on her mind, and in the loneliness of her room each night, she had no one to turn to for solace.

However, these past few weeks of planning had reignited a spark of determination within her, giving her the courage to carry on. Not securing that evidence, though, put a damper on that fire, with another part of her praying that Adrian wouldn't betray her. Her intuition reassured her she could trust him, but a part of her held her guard up, just in case. For now, nestled safely in her bed, she clung to the thought of escaping and the prospect of reuniting with her family. They might never be as whole as they once were, but they would be together again. A surge of happiness welled within her, and she held onto it tightly, banishing the encroaching darkness with a newfound sense of hope that she thought was lost forever. This wasn't the end. She would escape and be reunited with her children. While there would be future opportunities to bring Elinor down, perhaps none as crucial as this chance to regain her freedom.

Chapter 23

The Cottage

Even under the moonlight, one could see the charming two-story cottage. It held a special place in George's heart, for it had been in his wife's family for generations. Its existence remained known solely to those bearing the Goodman name, hidden even from the reigning monarchs. Through the ages, the Goodman family had played a crucial role in safeguarding the secret of the crystal shards, tracing back to the escape of the princess from the castle many years ago. This quaint little cottage had served as her refuge, enveloped by a spell woven by the departed princess herself and passed down through the intricate threads of family members. Throughout the years, the family had passed down the secret, hiding away the whereabouts of the crystals.

The only reason he was aware of its existence was through his late wife, Maria Goodman. However, she chose to reveal this information only after they got married, making him promise to keep it a secret. Maria had lived in the cottage since her childhood and only left when they got married, relocating to Carraton because of his work. In the early years of their marriage, they returned annually to visit and inspect the cottage, enjoying its tranquil ambience during vacations. However, after Maria's untimely passing, George seldom visited and when he did, it was always brief.

Cecilia wouldn't be able to recall the location, even if she tried all these years later. She used to visit as a child, often for short vacations. However, their visits ceased when her mother passed away when she was only six. The rest of the Goodman family also stayed away. As a nobleman, Lord Johnathon Goodman and his family had no use for it. Shielded by its enchantment, the family had no concerns about the cottage being uncovered, rendering it the ideal spot for him to hide his grandchildren.

Standing on the precipice of a new chapter, George couldn't suppress the surge of joy welling within his heart as he saw the expression on the twins' faces. With eyes widened with awe and jaws dropped in amazement, they reminded him so much of their mother, evoking cherished memories of their time together in this very place. The thought of getting to share this place with them, creating new memories, regardless of the circumstances, warmed his soul. With a decisive motion, George swung open the door, welcoming them inside. As they stepped into the dark room, he followed closely behind. With a flick of his wrist, the entire room lit up.

As the light flooded the space, revealing a spacious open kitchen and dining room area, they found themselves in its welcoming embrace. To their right, a staircase nestled against the wall beckoned upward, leading to the upstairs. Positioned prominently within the room, a medium-sized clay oven with a flute above it to carry excess hot air away commanded attention. Adjacent to it, a small pantry and a cool room built below the ground level that extends into the depths of the building, offering storage for provisions. At the heart of the space stood an aged yet sturdy cedar dining table, capable of comfortably seating six.

"It's not much, but it's home," George said, turning towards the twins and Sean with a warm smile.

"It's splendid," Sean replied, his eyes alight with admiration as the twins also took in their new surroundings.

"Come, let me give you a proper tour," George said, gesturing with the lantern he held.

Leading the way, he guided them through the cottage, starting with the kitchen area. Then, passing through a low archway, George and Sean instinctively stooped to avoid hitting their heads. Beyond, they entered the cosy living room, where high-backed chairs adorned with delicate floral embroidery on the backrests beckoned guests to sink into their plush cushions. Across from the window, a matching bench provided a comfortable spot to sit and gaze upon the outside world. A wooden table displayed a chessboard amid a game, while in the corner, a cabinet housed various threads and materials for embroidery. Above, an iron chandelier dangled from the ceiling, casting a warm glow from the flickering candles, illuminating the wooden beams.

Adjoined to the living room, a small study lay hidden, boasting the comforting presence of a log fireplace. Within its confines, numerous shelves brimmed with elegant leather-bound books, while plush cushions graced the floor beside inviting chairs. A petite slanted writing desk accompanied by a matching chair crafted from dark wood occupied a corner. Resting atop the desk was an empty ink pot, its contents long dried out, and aged papers that had turned yellow over time. Positioned to the right of the living room, a second door led to the bathroom, completing the cottage's modest yet inviting layout.

Turning back, they made their way up the stairs. This floor housed a spacious bedroom with an attached bathroom for George. Next to his room, there stood a locked door. He sternly warned the twins not to enter it. On the opposite side of the hallway, two more doors beckoned. George opened both before he turned to face Aevah and Jacob.

"Now, you've got two rooms to choose from," he said, stepping aside to let them look inside. Each room was almost identical, furnished simply with a small bed, wardrobe, a table, and a chair. The dim light made it hard to see much else, so Aevah decided to take the room on the left while Jacob opted for the one on the right.

Being so tired, both twins collapsed onto their respective beds. George took the time to cover them with blankets, watching them for a moment, a crease of concern etching his brow as he reflected on what they had endured these past couple of weeks. With the twins already in a deep sleep, he pressed a gentle kiss atop each of their little heads, before he murmured a soft, "Goodnight."

George headed back downstairs to find Sean, who hadn't followed them upstairs. Finding Sean in the living room, making himself a makeshift bed on the study room floor using cushions, a sleeping bag, and a blanket he had found. As George entered, Sean stopped and turned to face him.

"I took care of the horses for the night and rummaged around for an extra blanket."

"Thank you, Sean, but you don't need to sleep on the floor," George insisted.

"I'm only planning to stay one more night at most, and with all these extra cushions, it might be more comfortable than a bed. Are the twins already asleep?" Sean countered with a grin.

"As you wish. Yes, they're already fast asleep. Hopefully, they sleep well. Their little bodies need the rest," George chuckled in response. "Well then, if you're settled, I'll bid you good night."

"Goodnight, George," Sean replied, settling into his makeshift bedding with a contented sigh.

With a nod, George bid Sean goodnight and headed to his own room. Collapsing wearily onto the edge of his luxurious four-poster bed, he relished the softness of the blankets beneath him. The weight of exhaustion clung to him as he kicked off his shoes, their dull thuds echoing in the silence of the room. With a tired sigh, he shrugged off his heavy coat, its fabric rustling as it fell to the floor. The air within the cottage carried a faint scent of pine and warmth, enveloping George in a sense of security. Surrendering to the beckoning comfort of the bed, he allowed its softness to soothe his weary bones. As he closed his eyes, thoughts of a refreshing shower in the morning floated through his mind, knowing that his secluded sanctuary, shielded by an invisible charm, offered absolute safety. Within the unseen boundaries of the cottage, encased in an invisible cocoon, its secrets remained shielded from prying eyes.

To any passerby casting a glance at the cottage, all they would see was a ruin of a house on muddy marshland. Not a place one would dare to venture. Especially when there was a perfectly paved road nearby, offering a quick route to the neighbouring towns in either direction. Anyone brave enough to approach the perimeter would soon retreat, the desire to explore vanishing from their minds. Before they knew it, they would find themselves back on the path, resuming their journey without a second thought for the abandoned cottage. Fully aware of this reality, George settled into bed, drifting into a peaceful sleep until the first light of dawn.

***

As the morning sun rose, the rhythmic sound of an axe striking wood awakened George. Startled into wakefulness, he leapt out of bed and rushed outside in a state of panic. Power rolled through his veins, bracing himself to attack, but stopped as he reached the wood-cutting area beside the house. He let out a sigh of relief, releasing the power as he saw Sean busy chopping up fresh firewood.

"Curse you, Sean! You damn near gave me a heart attack," George exclaimed, his hands finding their way to his knees as he caught his breath and regained his composure. Straightening up, a wry smile tugged at his lips as he took in the mischievous grin on his friend's face.

"Thought I'd get a head start while you sleep the day away, old man," Sean quipped.

"Old! I'm barely a year older than you. Some of us don't wake up before dawn like clockwork every day," George retorted with mock indignation, a playful banter settling between them as they commenced their day.

Sean's grin persisted as he continued to chop wood, while George, now wide awake, went back inside the cottage. Inside, the atmosphere remained tranquil, with no sign of activity from either of the twins. With little else to occupy his time, George freshened up in his bathroom before he busied himself by examining the cottage, tidying up and checking for any necessary repairs. It had been quite some time since anyone had visited, and the place needed a thorough cleaning. An hour later, owing to George's magical abilities, the cottage looked much neater, requiring only a fresh coat of paint and some minor fixes. As George went about his tasks, the sounds of movement came from upstairs. Soft footsteps echoed across the floorboards followed by the distinct opening and closing of two doors. Then, the heavier footsteps of Aevah and Jacob descended the stairs, announcing their arrival in the kitchen. They looked around, taking in the changes that had been made.

"Morning, little ones. How did you sleep?" George inquired, setting down steaming bowls of porridge before them. Since there were no condiments like honey available, he sliced a couple of sour green apples to add some flavour. Placing the bowls on the table, he made a mental note to visit the nearby village for supplies.

"We slept well, Grandpa. Sleeping in a bed is far more comfortable than on the ground. Is this breakfast for us?" Aevah asked.

"Yes, it is," George replied with a warm smile.

"Oh, great! I'm so hungry!" Jacob exclaimed eagerly.

Both children excitedly settled into their seats and devoured their porridge as if they hadn't eaten in weeks. Across from them, George eased into his chair, a wistful expression on his face. He knew that once they were done eating, he would need to talk with them. It was time to tell them the truth about what happened that day at the castle. As they neared the bottom of their bowls, George refilled them, noticing their eating had slowed down to a more leisurely pace. Finally, as they polished off the last of their porridge, George cleared his throat, signalling his readiness to address the matter at hand.

"Now that your little bellies are full, it's time for us to talk," he said, getting up from his chair and gesturing for them to follow. With hesitant expressions painting their small faces, both children trailed behind him as he led them to the living room. Taking a seat in the centre of the bench by the window, he patted the empty spots beside him, inviting them to join him.

"Come, sit down."

Eyes widened with a blend of curiosity and apprehension; the children settled down on the bench beside him. Their little hands fidgeted nervously in their laps, fingers intertwining and twirling to find comfort. As he began to speak, his voice carried a gentle yet sombre tone, delicately balancing between honesty and protection. Each word was chosen with care, crafted to convey the truth while safeguarding their innocent minds.

It was undeniably heart-wrenching for George to explain that their father was gone, but explaining how it happened was even more painful. The betrayal of their aunt added to their anguish. Although they hadn't shared a particularly close bond with their aunt, they believed family always supported one another. Through tear-filled eyes, they mustered the courage to inquire about their mother. Fortunately, there was a glimmer of solace amidst the sombre news. George reassured them that their mother was alive and well, diligently working towards reuniting with them soon.

Curiosity consumed them. They yearned to uncover more details. Questions came from them, such as, would more soldiers come for them? How long would they stay in the cottage, and most importantly, how long would it take their mother to arrive? In an effort to ease their concerns, George reassured them they were safe where they were. He affirmed their safety within the confines of the cottage, urging them not to dwell on the events unfolding at the castle. With a calm demeanour, he explained how the protective enchantment encircling the cottage worked, ensuring them that no intruders could gain entry, and he promised that their mother would arrive as soon as she could.

With every passing sentence, the children's expressions shifted, mirroring the emotional journey their young minds were embarking on. Once bright and full of wonder, their eyes now carried a glimmer of sadness. Sensing their need for solace, George extended his arms, enfolding each child in a tender embrace. In the shelter of his embrace, he offered a small semblance of comfort amidst the turmoil, their tiny trembling frames seeking refuge against his touch. The room grew silent, leaving only the sound of their collective breaths hanging heavy in the air.

Peering down, George noticed they were asleep, undoubtedly overwhelmed by what he had shared with them. His heart ached at the sight of their innocent faces, bearing the burden of grief far beyond their tender years. He wished he could take it all away, but he knew he couldn't. All he could do was be there for them and help them work through their sorrow, no matter how it manifested. The weight of James's death weighed heavily upon George as well. James had not only been a great king but also a kind-hearted man who had treated his daughter with love and respect, which was all George had hoped for as a father. Witnessing firsthand how James cared for his children and prioritised their well-being, George couldn't help but admire the late king's reputation as a devoted family man.

James had always seen the positive qualities in those around him and it had been evident that he had hoped that he and Elinor would one day reconcile their differences. The betrayal from Elinor had blindsided James, shattering his expectations. The thought of how James must have felt upon realising what had occurred was unimaginable. A part of George wished James had been spared the painful truth, but he knew that was wishful thinking. He knew Elinor all too well, and she had a tendency for malevolence and a flair for dramatics. She would have made sure James knew his beloved sister had betrayed him.

She single-handedly tore apart an entire kingdom in just one day, and there was no doubt that she took immense pleasure in every second. George knew Elinor had to be removed from the throne, but such a feat would require time and patience. For the time being, his priority was to take care of his grandchildren and the safe return of his daughter to the cottage. Taking solace in knowing that the crystal shards were securely hidden, George clung to a fragile glimmer of hope. As long as they remained concealed, Elinor's powers would be limited, although the advantage diminished by her current hold on the throne.

Knowing that there was nothing more he could do at that moment, George left the twins to rest and went to find Sean.

Chapter 24

Supplies

George stumbled upon Sean rummaging through the pantry, searching for food. The scarcity of provisions was clear. It had been quite a while since anyone had visited the cottage. Sean, upon noticing George, turned to him and broke the silence.

"Ah, you're back. How did the talk go?" Sean inquired with his tone weighted with concern.

"Not great, but better than expected under the circumstances," George responded, his expression reflecting a mixture of weariness and resolve. "It will take time, but they'll pull through. I don't believe they'll ever truly get over what has happened. But they'll move on in a way."

"They're strong. Time will pull them through this dark time," Sean remarked, offering a sombre nod.

"Indeed, only time will tell, though, how each of them will cope in the long run," George concurred, sharing a sympathetic glance with Sean.

"I hate to change the subject so abruptly, but it would seem our food supplies are terribly low. I think it would be best if one of us makes a trip to the village up the road today for supplies. What's left will not provide much in the way of snacks, let alone a real meal," Sean explained, gesturing to the bare pantry, lifting a near-empty jar and examining its contents with a furrowed brow.

"Dare I ask what this contained once upon a time?" Sean asked as he waved the jar in George's direction.

"No idea," George answered as Sean tossed the jar into the rubbish bag at his feet, which was rapidly filling up with expired items. Glancing over at the bags of flour and rice, they seemed okay at first, but the holes in the corners hinted at a potential mouse problem. He discarded them as well because the last thing he wanted was to discover mouse droppings in his meals.

"Hmm, we definitely need to stock up on supplies, and not just food," George said, already mentally preparing for the trip. "I'll get ready and head to the nearby village to see what I can get for us."

George left Sean to continue sorting and made his way to his room. Inside, he began rummaging through his sturdy oak wardrobe, pulling out various jackets and inspecting them. None seemed to be quite right. Muttering to himself, he continued searching through the rack until he found a well-worn knee-length brown jacket, which he slung over his arm. Crouching down, he leaned further into the wardrobe and retrieved a pair of tattered brown boots. With the boots in one hand and the jacket in the other, George walked over to his bed and sat on the edge. He took off his sturdy black boots and put on the other pair, wiggling his feet around until they fit just right. Despite their age, the boots proved remarkably comfortable – exactly what he needed.

Picking up the jacket, he slipped it on as he made his way towards the oak mirror fixed to the wall. Gazing at his reflection, he adjusted the jacket to his liking. Then, using his power, he transformed his appearance. No longer did he see the familiar sight of grey hair and a wrinkled face. Instead, an unremarkable, friendly visage emerged, one that would seamlessly blend into a crowd. With gentle brown eyes, mousy brown hair, and worn-out attire, he became just another unassuming middle-aged man, passing through unnoticed, gathering household supplies.

Satisfied with his new appearance, George descended the stairs back to the kitchen. As he entered, Sean did a double take.

"George?"

"I was. Now, meet *Oliver*." With a mischievous twinkle in his eye, George executed a slight bow.

"Nice to meet you, *Oliver*," Sean responded with his grin widening.

"Well, I'm ready to head out, but I need to check the cart in the shed."

"Need a hand?" Sean offered.

"No, I'll manage. Once everything's ready, I'll take off. Keep an eye on the twins for me."

With a confirming nod, Sean resumed his tasks in the kitchen while George made his way to the stables. As he entered, the horses glanced up briefly, letting out a few neighs before returning to their food. The stables, although small, had a surprisingly spacious feel, providing ample room for four horses. Tucked away at the far end was the familiar wooden cart. George approached and attempted to pull it forward, but the wheels barely budged, resisting his efforts. A quick inspection revealed that the two front wheels had seized from lack of use. Fortunately, this was an easy fix. George used his power to loosen the wheels and brushed off the dust from the cart. With another gentle pull, the cart effortlessly glided along the straw-covered floor until it was finally outside.

Walking around the cart once more, George deemed it suitable and made his way back into the stables. He headed towards his horse, the majestic black Friesian beauty. The rhythmic sound of the horse's neighs and the steady tapping of its hooves filled the stable, conveying its eagerness to accompany George wherever he was going. Even in his transformed appearance, his horse knew who he was. As he reached Dusty, the horse stepped from side to side as he opened the door to his stable. Stepping aside, Dusty trotted out and affectionately nudged George with its nose.

"All right, boy. It's great to see you too. Are you ready to head out?" George asked while patting Dusty on the neck before leading him to the cart outside.

After securing Dusty's harness, George went back to the stables and brought out Sean's dependable brown mare, Mist. He saddled her up alongside Dusty and made sure both horses were properly secured. Climbing into the wooden seat at the front of the cart, George took hold of the reins and set off at a relaxed pace along the compact dirt track, making their way towards the local village called Sleights.

Merely an hour's journey from the cottage, George leaned back and admired the picturesque scenery. As he rounded the bend and merged onto the main road, the cart smoothly glided along the mostly even terrain, surrounded by browning fields and orange-tinged trees. Occasionally, glimpses of distant farmhouses emerged, their chimneys releasing wisps of smoke into the air. In separate fields, cows, horses, and sheep grazed peacefully, all confined by charming yet uneven waist-high stone walls.

With the journey familiar as the back of his hand, George enjoyed the ride under the crisp autumn sun. As the village loomed into view, it was a quaint and close-knit community, nestled amidst various local farms, and he couldn't help but feel a sense of contentment. Despite its small size, the village provided all the essentials one could ask for. Every morning, bustling market stalls would be set up, boasting a bounty of goods from local farmers and villagers alike. And that was precisely where he was now headed. Descending into the heart of the village, the first houses came into view.

The wooden houses had a rustic, homely charm, while the stone houses stood as elegant, sturdy symbols that exemplified the differences in their owners' status. The streets were relatively quiet, as compared to the bustling city streets, yet still abuzz with commotion as people went about their daily routines. The centre of the village thrummed with activity, filled with the calls of merchants hawking their wares and the cheerful chatter of locals catching up with one another.

As he rode nearer, he eased back on the reins, bringing the horses to a halt. Dismounting, he surveyed the lively crowd surrounding him. Amongst the sea of faces, his attention was drawn by an elderly woman exuding a warm and nurturing presence. Her wispy, curly hair boasted a distinguished shade of grey, and a dusting of flour covered her apron. With a gentle appearance, she met his eyes as she approached him. Returning her kind gaze with a warm smile of his own, he turned to greet her and introduce himself.

"Goods morning there, I don believe we met before? I be Mrs Daleman." She extended her hand, and George, now *Oliver*, shook it firmly as he introduced himself with his new identity.

"Mrs Daleman, it's a pleasure. I'm *Oliver. Oliver Turnbull.* I'm new to the area and in need of quite a few supplies for me and my children."

With a solemn expression, he described the tragic story of *Oliver*, a widowed father of two, one eight-year-old girl and a nine-year-old boy. By the end, he had captured the attention not only of Mrs Daleman but also of those nearby, all eager to lend a helping hand. Mrs Daleman sent the villagers off to gather everything their new friend *Oliver* needed, inviting him to wait at the local inn for a spot of tea and a late breakfast.

Making his way across the small oval, George spotted the inn directly ahead. It was the grandest structure in the village, with an abundance of rooms to accommodate weary travellers seeking a place to rest for the night. Upon entering, he followed behind Mrs Daleman into the tranquil dining space. Only one other couple remained, savouring the last bites of their morning meal of eggs.

"Take a seat 'ere, l be righ back wi some tea." Mrs Daleman gestured to the seat beside George, who complied, watching her scurry away out of sight behind a door likely leading to the kitchen.

Leaning forward, he rested his arms on the table, absorbing the warm and inviting atmosphere of the inn, leaving him with a feeling of belonging, even if only for a moment. As she returned, George helped set the teacups while Mrs Daleman poured them each a steaming cup of chamomile tea. As he took a sip, she began talking about the village and the people who lived there. Eager to keep the conversation on the village, George asked his own questions, trying to get a feel of the people who lived here, and how much influence the crown had over this area.

Thankfully, being a small village, they were left to handle things on their own, only having to pay their taxes to the crown when the tax collector visited in late summer. In the past, this was never an issue, with James never taking more from a family than they could afford. However, George had the sinking feeling that Elinor wouldn't be so considerate and would take what she deemed right for herself. Having enjoyed a few cups of tea and indulged in a satisfying breakfast of eggs and bacon, George rose from his seat.

"I'd love a tour of your beautiful village if you have the time?" George held out his arm as Mrs Daleman took hold.

"Of course, follow me."

Taking a short stroll, George pretended to be interested in the village he had visited countless times before, asking questions along the way. However, for *Oliver*, this proved to be an entirely new experience, and he found everything captivating, much to Mrs Daleman's delight. An enthusiastic storyteller, she loved sharing the village's rich history. After the leisurely tour, they returned to the oval, where the locals and vendors eagerly awaited them, offering not only an abundance of food but also a wide variety of toys, clothes, books, and puzzles for the children. George was both surprised and grateful for the villagers' extraordinary generosity. Although he insisted on paying the stallholders a fair price for the food, the villagers adamantly refused any form of payment for anything else.

As the villagers loaded his cart, now brimming with supplies, George tried to give the money to Mrs Daleman instead. He trusted her to share it fairly amongst the other villagers, but he had to convince her to accept the money first.

"*Oliver* me lad, no more be needed. Times be hard enough as is. Never be mind for e widower. Besides, I gets the feelin' we be seeing a lot of ye with young ans underfoot. If any ever needs a hand round here, we be sure te ask ye for one." While he tried to give her some money, she waved him away, stepping back and refusing to take any coin from him.

With everything loaded into the cart, George grasped the reins once more, bidding goodbye and expressing his gratitude to the villagers before setting off home. But before departing, he couldn't resist calling out to a few of the young children who were scampering about. As they ran up alongside the cart, he tossed the bag of coins in his hand to them.

"Keep it fer ye selves, since the grownups don't want it," George said with a wink towards the children and a nod to the now bemused Mrs Daleman.

He then continued on his journey homeward. By late afternoon, George returned, his appearance restored to its normal state so as not to startle the twins. Finding them both outside, completely covered in soil, he could tell they were thoroughly enjoying themselves in the flower beds with Sean. Their little faces lit up with excitement and wonder as they ran towards him, eagerly taking in the contents of the cart.

"Wow Grandpa, your cart is full, and I can see toys!" Aevah exclaimed enthusiastically, jumping up and down in excitement as she moved to grab a puzzle.

"No touching anything until you have washed up. You're both covered head to toe in dirt," George ordered playfully, eyeing Jacob as he noticed him attempting to reach for something behind him. Jacob grinned sheepishly before obediently putting his hands behind his back.

"I didn't touch anything," he protested innocently.

George laughed as he climbed down from the cart, urging the twins inside to wash up. While he tended to the horses in the stables, Sean began unloading the cart. Once the horses were back in their stables, George returned to help Sean bring the rest of the items inside before he moved the cart back into the stable where he found it.

As George started preparing a pot of steaming chicken soup and toasted sandwiches, Sean set about finding a suitable spot for the chickens and rooster that George had brought back. After completing his tasks, Sean went inside to freshen up. Meanwhile, the twins were busy sorting through the items they had received from the villagers, eager to have toys to play with. Once dinner was ready, George called out to everyone, and they all gathered around to enjoy a satisfying and comforting meal, the first they had had in quite some time. Following dinner, they moved to the living room, where George and Sean took turns entertaining the twins with stories until they eventually drifted off to sleep. With care, George and Sean each carried one twin to their respective beds, tucking them in for the night.

George and Sean retreated to the study, relishing a beverage in each other's company. Tomorrow it would be just George and the twins, as Sean would make his way back home. Having been away from his life in Carraton for quite some time now, it was time for Sean to return. George expressed profound gratitude to the divine spirit for Sean's presence. Without him, they might not have survived to reach this point. As the two men pondered over what lay ahead, George cherished this final evening with his friend. Tomorrow promised change – whether for better or worse, only time would reveal.

Chapter 25

Settling In

The delightful aroma of cooking porridge greeted Aevah upon awakening in the morning. Her hungry stomach growled, reminding her of her appetite. She leapt out of bed and made her way to the landing, where Jacob, also heading down for breakfast, caught her eye. Sharing a knowing look, the two descended the stairs, engaged in a friendly race. Determined to win, Aevah leapt the final few steps, securing a slight lead over her brother. Still running, she reached her seat just moments before Jacob. Laughing with joy, she reached for the honey pot and drizzled a generous amount of its runny goodness into her bowl of steaming porridge. After stirring in the honey, she tentatively tasted a small spoonful to gauge its temperature. Satisfied that it was suitable, she began to eat.

Jacob slumped into the chair beside her with a huff, grabbing the jar of strawberry jam. He scooped a large dollop onto his spoon and mixed it into his bowl before beginning to eat. Meanwhile, Aevah finished her bowl and observed her grandpa as he busied himself with cleaning up the dishes and tidying the kitchen area. It had been a week since they moved into their new home, and everything felt markedly different. Even waking up in her new room gave her a newfound sense of freedom. Unlike the castle, there were no strict wake-up times, dress codes, or expectations to remember everyone's names or perform curtsies. Here, there were far fewer rules, although her grandpa had his own set. Being in this new environment felt liberating compared to the castle. However, she couldn't shake the longing for her parents' presence. Her mother would be arriving soon, but the absence of her father left an unfillable void in her heart. During the day, she could sometimes forget that he was gone and pretend he was still with their mother. But at night, the harsh reality became harder to ignore. Her dreams replayed that night's events, leaving her feeling scared and alone. Yet, with the morning came sunshine and warmth, accompanied by the love of her grandpa and Jacob, and everything felt a bit more bearable, a bit more like it should be.

"Grandpa, can Aevah and I go explore again this morning?" Jacob asked.

"Not until your rooms are tidy, and you bring all your dirty washing down. I want to get it all done this morning while the weather's still fair," replied Grandpa George.

"Ugh, alright then," Jacob muttered reluctantly as he stood up and made his way to his room.

Aevah put her bowl in the sink and headed upstairs to her room. Comparing the two, she believed her room was cleaner, although a pile of dirty laundry by the door needed washing. She ignored a few scattered toys and attempted to gather all her clothes in her arms, but the load proved to be cumbersome. Several pieces slipped from her grasp and fell to the floor. Annoyed by the necessity of making two trips, she resigned herself to the task. On the way back up for the second pile, she crossed Jacob on the stairs, seemingly determined to carry everything he had in one go, even if it meant he couldn't see over the pile in his hands. With a sigh, Aevah grabbed her last batch of clothes, wondering how Jacob managed to navigate down the stairs without falling. With both loads of clothes in the washroom, a room they hadn't yet explored, Aevah watched with curiosity as her grandpa loaded a pile of clothes into a large metal cylinder tub.

"What is that?" Aevah asked.

"It's called a washing machine," replied Grandpa George.

"And what does it do?" Jacob pressed for a further explanation.

"It washes clothes," their grandpa stated simply.

"Ah, I see," Jacob replied, while Aevah discreetly rolled her eyes at the simplicity of the explanation. Both twins watched intently as grandpa George poured some powder from a nearby container into the tub. He added water and sealed the lid. Then, as if by some enchantment, the machine emitted a noise when their grandpa closed the lid and placed his hand on top. Aevah, startled, jumped slightly and turned to her grandpa, seeking clarification.

"Just a touch of magic to make the clothes twirl, so I can wash them without doing it by hand. It's a wonderful timesaving trick. In about an hour, the clothes will be fresh and ready to be hung out to dry. However, that part will have to be done by hand," explained Grandpa George with a smile.

Amazed at what they had witnessed, Aevah followed her grandpa out of the room, with Jacob right beside them, bombarding him with a flurry of questions.

"How do you use the power? When do people get their powers? Is it easy? Will you teach me?" Grandpa George raised his hand to halt the onslaught of the questions.

"Hold up now, one question at a time," he advised gently. Leading them into the living room, they sat on the floor, looking up at him expectantly for answers. After patiently answering all their questions and then some, Aevah felt satisfied with what he told them and was eager to begin practising the power herself, especially upon learning they both would likely possess the ability to channel. Grandpa George promised them they could begin their training under his guidance within the year. Filled with excitement and wanting to explore, Aevah tagged Jacob and ran outside. He chased after her, laughter bubbling as he tried to catch up with her.

***

Jacob chased Aevah down to the little river and along the stream's edge before watching her take a daring leap into the water. Though the water only reached just above her ankles, her swift movements caused splashes that drenched the lower portion of her dress. Jacob stayed by her side, running alongside her on the grassy bank until they reached a small pond, the farthest from the cottage they dared venture alone. Recalling the moments when the castle guards pursued them, neither of them wanted to be captured and whisked away. Besides, there was an abundance of activities right where they were. While the river originated deep within the woods, and since it lay beyond the boundary, they restricted themselves to the section of the river near their cosy cottage. For Jacob, just this area alone was teeming with experiences he could only dream of back at the castle. Here, he could splash around in the river without fear of being scolded for dirtying his clothes. Both he and Aevah revelled in the chance to get stuck in the mud and climb trees without a single worry in the world, seizing the day with boundless enthusiasm.

Jacob basked in the freedom of the great outdoors, perched on the branch of an apple tree. Leaning against the sturdy trunk, he savoured a juicy red apple in his hand. Just as he took a bite of the crisp fruit, he almost lost his balance in the tree as Aevah vigorously shook him.

"Look over there. It's a deer!" exclaimed Aevah with palpable excitement.

251

After his racing heart settled and he regained his composure, Jacob looked to where Aevah was pointing and spotted a majestic brown deer walking in the distance. Rising to his feet to get a better view, Jacob watched the deer going about its day. In that serene moment, he felt a profound sense of peace, devoid of any worries that typically crossed his mind in the bustling confines of home. The contrast between this tranquil setting and the busy pace of royal life was stark. Amidst their packed schedules, filled with lessons from tutors and rigorous royal training, there was little time for fun. Unlike his twin sister, Aevah, who adored books and learning, Jacob found his joy in exploring and climbing, which their nanny found quite bothersome. While his parents were relatively lenient as long as he completed his work and training, his nanny remained determined to mould him into the perfect prince.

Staying here in the cottage for the time being was going to give him a well-deserved break. He knew his mother would inevitably come for them once it was safe, but until then, he was happy to make the most of it. As much as he was enjoying his time there, he couldn't help but miss his home and his family, especially his father. The thought of never seeing him again weighed heavily on his heart. Nevertheless, he held onto the hope that one day they could return, and life would go back to normal, or at least regain some semblance of normalcy. For now, he resolved to make the most of their situation and enjoy the life he was living. Getting back to exploring with Aevah, they played until hunger pangs prompted their return to the cottage, their minds now consumed with thoughts of food. Together, he and Aevah hurried back, eager to satisfy their rumbling stomachs.

As the sun dipped below the horizon, casting an orange hue over the land, the scent of beef and potatoes filled the air, intensifying as they approached the entrance of the cottage. Taking a seat at the kitchen table, Jacob brimmed with eagerness to share their adventures outside. However, before he could utter a word, their grandpa turned his attention towards them.

"Out of my kitchen and go clean up. You're both covered in mud," Grandpa George commanded sternly.

After both took a moment to look at their mud-covered appearances, Jacob couldn't help but grin. He then made his way to the bathroom in his grandpa's room, while Aevah went to their shared bathroom. Once they were both clean and refreshed, Jacob returned to the kitchen. There, he found Aevah engaged in a conversation with Grandpa George, who was busy stirring a pot of stew. Jacob sat down and eagerly joined the conversation, wanting to share his thoughts about the day. They both enthusiastically chimed in, talking over each other as they told about their afternoon adventures. Grandpa George served three bowls of piping hot beef stew, filling the room with its enticing aroma. Jacob's stomach growled loudly, reminding him of his hunger. He eagerly began to devour his bowl, only to burn the roof of his mouth. Taking a moment to let it cool, he gulped some water to soothe the pain before diving back into the lively conversation with Aevah and Grandpa George, which seemed to stretch on for hours.

"Well, little ones, it seems you've had an eventful day, but it's time for bed," their grandpa announced.

Jacob watched his grandpa rise while Aevah attempted to complain, but a sudden yawn interrupted her, proving their grandpa's point. Feeling sleepy himself, Jacob stood up.

"Okay, Grandpa. Good night," he said, walking over to wrap his arms around him, hugging him tightly before making his way to his room. Aevah, after hugging her grandpa too, followed closely behind him. Standing outside their respective doors, Jacob exchanged goodnight wishes with his sister before entering his room and climbing into bed. Within minutes, exhaustion overtook him, and he drifted into a deep slumber.

***

As time passed, Aevah and Jacob fully embraced life at the cottage. Weeks melted into months, and months seamlessly transformed into years. The serene and picturesque atmosphere of the cottage provided them a haven, allowing them to indulge in playing, climbing trees, swimming, attempting to fish, and simply relishing their childhood. Despite their contentment, they eagerly awaited the day when they could eventually return home.

Chapter 26

Belle of the Ball

The much-anticipated day had finally arrived for Elinor – the masquerade ball. It promised an enchanting evening of dancing, drinking, music, and a touch of mystery. With masks adorning the faces of all attendees, an air of intrigue enveloped the atmosphere, fuelling excitement and anticipation among its guests.

As she glanced in her mirror, Elinor admired her appearance. The dress was a work of art in itself, boasting a stunning blood-red hue and a flowing silk skirt. Adorned with red lace and beautifully woven flowers cascading from the waist down the sides, the skirt exuded elegance. The bodice, featuring a graceful v-neckline, seamlessly complemented the skirt with its intricate detailing and sparkling sequins. Delicate patterned lace covered the top of the sleeves and wrists, while the underside showcased a captivating semi-transparent red shade.

The mask she wore matched the dress perfectly, with its blood-red shade. The patterned detail and sparkling rhinestones added an extra touch of elegance to the floral design. Her hair was down in loose waves, with the top half cleverly concealing the band of the mask beneath its voluminous strands.

Behind her, she felt a hand against her hip, as Bradley came up beside her, his reflection appearing next to hers in the mirror. He wore a mask of two colours: one-half red, and one-half black. Elegant black swirls adorned the red side, while stylish red swirls embellished the black side, both decorated with glitter to enhance their allure. Bradley was dressed in a white cotton shirt, paired with a matching deep red jacket and pants. The jacket featured white embroidered details on its high collar and front, as well as on the cuffs of the sleeves. With a long back reaching down to his knees, and a front cut just above his waist, the coat revealed his shirt underneath. Both the jacket and pants boasted luxurious velvet.

As Bradley squeezed her waist, his eyes met hers in the mirror. "Ready?"

She took in both their appearances, her hand adjusting her mask slightly before replying. "Yes, let's go greet our guests."

With her arm in his, Bradley accompanied Elinor as they exited her chambers and made their way to the ballroom where the masquerade event was taking place. This room was a large open space, with bare bones that were easy to transform to fit any themed event desired. Elinor was eager to see the room's appearance, as she had entrusted Victoria with its preparation for tonight.

Upon reaching the open doors, a symphony of laughter and lively music greeted them. The sight that met their eyes was breathtaking. Overhead, the candlelit chandeliers cast a radiant glow, illuminating the dance floor in a dazzling display. The enchanting melodies of the live music filled the air, emerging from a balcony above and tempting even the most hesitant of dancers to join in.

Elaborate gold-flecked mirrors lined the room, emphasising the guests' anonymity, while velvet drapes in gold and burgundy decorated the walls, exuding luxury. Spread out across the tables were bouquets of black and red roses, accompanied by decorative velvet masks that captured the eye. Masked statues were strategically positioned in alcoves and corners, heightening the splendour and mysteriousness of the event. The room created a realm where fantasy intertwined with reality.

As Elinor watched, couples danced gracefully in sync with the music, lost in a world of rhythm and movement. The clinking of glasses and the aroma of fine wines and delectable food permeated the air as guests indulged in the delights served to them.

With her arrival, the music momentarily ceased as she and Bradley were announced to the room. Eager to join in the festivities herself, her greeting was brief and warm.

"Welcome, esteemed guests! It brings me great joy to see each and every one of you here this evening. I must say, you all look absolutely fabulous, and I sincerely hope you enjoy the exciting events we have planned for tonight. We offer an exquisite selection of wine, delectable food, enchanting music, and, most importantly, the pleasure of each other's company. Without any further delay, I extend a heartfelt invitation to each of you to join me in a dance."

Leading the way to an open space, the crowd erupted in applause as the music resumed. As they took their positions, Elinor reached out and took Bradley's hand, gracefully moving to the rhythm of the music. Inspired by her lead, more guests joined in. Dancing was a rarity for her lately, so she relished this opportunity. Spinning around in Bradley's embrace, she felt a rush of joy and a sense of freedom. The world around them blurred as they spun in perfect harmony. Bradley's firm embrace made her feel safe and cherished as if nothing else mattered in that moment. The soft background music added to the enchantment of their dance. They laughed and twirled, their bodies moving in perfect sync with the music. Time stood still as they surrendered themselves to the magic of the moment, their hearts beating in unison. With his arms firmly around her, he gracefully dipped her backwards before pulling her back into his embrace and delicately kissing her lips.

At the sight of the kiss, Elinor could feel the gaze of her guests upon them, but she chose to ignore them all, remaining lost in the moment. As the night progressed, the dance floor transformed into a whirlwind of colour and movement. Conversations flowed freely as strangers became friends, their masks fostering an atmosphere of anonymity that encouraged openness and adventure among the guests.

After a few more dances, Elinor and Bradly took a break and began mingling with the guests. Elinor effortlessly slipped into the role of a gracious host, enjoying the evening as much as everyone else. As she finished a conversation with another couple, Adrian, dressed in his usual attire, approached Elinor and discreetly pulled her aside.

"Oh, Adrian, how lovely to see you here tonight," she greeted him warmly. However, her smile quickly faded into a puzzled frown as she noticed his inappropriate outfit for the occasion.

"And why aren't you dressed appropriately for this event?" she asked, disapprovingly tugging at his leather vest. Her eyes betrayed a hint of haziness from the wine.

"I'm on duty, my Queen," Adrian explained.

"Of course you are," Elinor responded, her demeanour unruffled by his explanation.

Adrian moved closer to her and discreetly pointed out Cecilia's presence while whispering about it. Elinor's eyes followed his gesture, widening at the sight of Cecilia lingering at the tables. Her body tensed, caught off guard as she hadn't expected Cecilia to show up, but she quickly dismissed the concern. Tonight was for enjoyment, and she trusted the guards to keep Cecilia out of her way. With pure hatred, she glared at Cecilia before turning away, relishing the satisfaction of seeing the horror on Cecilia's face as she realised Elinor was watching her.

Leaning back into Bradley's embrace, Elinor turned her head towards Adrian and commanded, "Make sure she doesn't cross my path."

Without awaiting a response, she gracefully glided away, resuming her dance with Bradley, much to the annoyance of the other men. Despite numerous requests for a dance, she declined them all, choosing to dance exclusively with Bradley. By the end of the night, there would be no doubt about Elinor's romantic interests in anyone.

Taking a break for refreshments, Elinor made her way to one of the tables, helping herself to some wine and cakes. As she surveyed the room, she noticed Lord Stone approaching. He poured himself a glass of wine, his eyes fixed on her as he took a sip. Elinor met his stare, waiting to see what he would do. Lowering his glass, he offered a forced smile.

"What a splendid event you've orchestrated this evening," he remarked.

"Thank you. I'm so glad you approve," Elinor replied, her tone laced with sarcasm.

"I've heard there are some announcements to be made tonight?" Lord Stone continued, ignoring her tone.

"There are."

"Would you care to share?" he inquired.

"With you? No. You'll find out at the same time as everyone else, Lord Stone," Elinor retorted.

"You're treading a dangerous line, my Queen. Remember who placed you on the throne. It would be a shame if you were to be removed," Lord Stone threatened, his expression darkening as he glared at Elinor. At his veiled threat, Elinor stood tall, meeting his eyes with sturdy resolve, prepared with her next remark, before Bradley appeared by her side.

"Everything okay here?" Bradley asked, placing his hand on Elinor's back, offering her an extra bit of reassurance.

"Everything's fine," Lord Stone interjected, flashing a smile at them both. "Enjoy your evening." With that, he walked away without a backward glance. Elinor glared after him, her brows furrowed in frustration.

"I despise that man," she muttered.

"Doesn't everyone? Unfortunately, we need him on our side," Bradley replied.

"For now," Elinor responded. Shaking off the moment, she turned to Bradley, reaching for his hand.

"Come, let's forget everything and dance," Elinor declared, her smile sly and infectious.

Following her lead, Bradley joined her for more dancing. Midway through the night, Elinor interrupted the musicians to make her announcements. Standing upon the balcony, she surveyed the room below. From the corner of her eye, she noticed Cecilia slipping away. Elinor was surprised she was still there. Then again, she hadn't expected Cecilia to attend in the first place, assuming she would decline the invitation extended merely as a formality. Disregarding Cecilia's departure, Elinor redirected her attention to her guests. As a multitude of masked faces turned towards her, she addressed them.

"To my esteemed guests, I would like to express my sincere gratitude for gracing us with your presence this evening. I promise not to keep you for long, but there are a few announcements I'm eager to share."

As her guests leaned in, their masks failing to conceal the excitement in their eyes, she sensed their anticipation. Each one harboured hope of earning her favour.

First, she expressed her gratitude to everyone for their tireless efforts and support during her transition to becoming queen. Afterwards, she bestowed gifts to those who had played significant roles in her journey, while also expressing her hopes for their continued support. Going the extra mile, she granted additional privileges to all but two lords, whether in the form of extra land, farms, or monetary rewards. She intended to ensure the contentment and loyalty of all, solidifying their allegiance to her cause. Whispers circulated among the guests, questioning why Lord Goodman and Lord Woodlock appeared to have been disregarded before Elinor broke the silence once again.

"Now, you may be wondering why Lord Goodman is absent from my list of gifts," Elinor began, her voice cutting through the murmurs of the crowd. "Lord Goodman and his wife have been apprehended for crimes against the crown." As shock registered on the faces of the crowd, murmurs rippled through the room, eyes darting around in the realisation of the Goodman family's absence. Irked by the noise, Elinor raised her voice with authority, making sure everyone could hear her.

"All land, housing, and belongings of the Goodman family shall be transferred to Lord Woodlock and his family in recognition of their service to the crown," Elinor announced, with a hint of satisfaction in her tone. "Furthermore, I hereby revoke the titles held by the Goodman family and bestow them upon Lloyd and Victoria Roberts."

At her proclamation, Lloyd and Victoria stepped forward, offering humble bows and curtsies to Elinor, expressing their heartfelt gratitude. The guests, still processing the sudden turn of events, responded with a lacklustre round of applause.

Before rumours and gossip could once again circulate, Elinor cleared her throat, capturing the undivided attention of all present. She understood the anticipated reactions regarding Lord Goodman and his family. By choosing to unveil this information now, in front of everyone, she aimed to serve as a poignant reminder to those lords who perceived her as merely a puppet. Elinor made it abundantly clear that she possessed the power to retract anything she had bestowed just as swiftly as she had granted it. Through her declaration, she intended to assert her authority, particularly over Lord Stone. Though his face was hidden behind his black mask, his clenched fists hinted at his seething anger.

"Amidst the negative, there's always a ray of positivity," Elinor proclaimed, purposefully locking eyes with Lord Stone. Her sweet smile was reserved exclusively for him as she clutched Bradley's hand. With enthusiasm, she declared, "Bradley and I are thrilled to announce our engagement!"

The room erupted with applause and cheers at her proclamation. Everyone except Lord Stone, she noticed, who scowled in response. His reaction only delighted her more, causing her to beam a radiant smile. She smugly watched as he and his wife left the ball, no doubt planning some scheme to undermine her announcements. She had no doubt that in the coming days, Lord Stone would appear with some counteroffer or demand to boost his own ego once again. For now, though, she enjoyed this small victory over him.

Returning to the midst of the guests, Elinor and Bradley mingled with everyone, graciously accepting their congratulations. They both embraced the warmth and joy of their guests' well-wishes. With the announcement regarding the Goodmans fading from memory, the atmosphere was one of pure celebration. Guests indulged in the delicious food, exquisite wine, and enchanting music once again. Elinor, too, fully immersed herself in the festivities, relishing the attention lavished upon her, particularly from Bradley, as they twirled and danced to the melodious tunes.

Overwhelmed with happiness, there was nothing that could sour Elinor's mood. As the night wore on, the energy in the room intensified. The music reached a crescendo, and the dance floor became a whirlwind of movement and fervour. The celebration continued into the late hours, with guests losing themselves in the captivating allure of the masquerade and the anticipation of the forthcoming royal wedding.

Chapter 27

An Eventful Night

Cecilia stood in her room, adorned in her exquisite masquerade attire. The air carried the delicate scent of perfume, mingling with the nervous anticipation pervading the atmosphere. The thought of what lay ahead intensified her already rapid heartbeat. Her hands trembled with a mix of fear and excitement, while her mind swirled with a whirlwind of emotions. This marked her long-awaited opportunity for freedom, albeit with the stakes so high. She knew that the consequences of failure extended far beyond her own life. With unwavering determination, she endeavoured to ensure every detail fell perfectly into place.

Bracing herself, she stood before the mirror, admiring her look one last time. The finished dress was beautiful, yet not so striking to draw unnecessary attention. A graceful black gown with a flowing skirt and elegant long sleeves enveloped her figure. Silver flecks intricately woven into the fabric shimmered as it cascaded effortlessly over her form. Tying the matching eye mask at the back, she marvelled at how it transformed her appearance. Cecilia hoped with every fibre of her being that she would remain unrecognisable in this disguise.

Turning away from her mirror, she picked up a small black purse and left her room, her guards trailing behind as she made her way to the ballroom. Every step quickened her heartbeat with nervousness, despite feeling prepared. The anticipation still unsettled her.

Approaching the grand doors of the ballroom, Cecilia stole a glimpse of the guests inside, engaged in dancing and conversation through the open entrance. With slow and steady steps, she entered the room, greeted by a breathtaking scene. Reluctantly, she had to admit that the room looked splendid. From the ornate masked statues to the elegant drapes and lavishly decorated tables, every detail exuded refinement.

The guests, adorned in a myriad of colourful masks, gracefully twirled around her, creating a vivid, dreamlike display. It was a mesmerising scene. As Cecilia blended into the crowd, her presence went unnoticed, just as she had hoped. None knew her true identity, nor she theirs. Except, of course, her guards. They alone were aware of the person concealed behind her own black mask, having followed her from her room.

Scanning the crowd, Elinor was nowhere in sight yet. A sense of relief washed over her, granting a sense of ease as she sought out a quiet corner. Finally, finding a spot at one of the distant tables, Cecilia took a seat and graciously accepted a glass of wine from a passing server. Aware of the opinions held in the room, she was grateful for the mask that obscured her identity. Apart from her guards, no one showed much interest in her.

It was a very awkward situation to be in and if it weren't part of a bigger plan, she would have stayed in her room for the night. But as she was there, Cecilia tried to make the most of it, enjoying the food and music while taking it easy on the wine, for she needed a clear head for the night ahead.

Shielded by her mask, and with many of the guests unaware of her true identity, she experienced a rare sense of anonymity. It allowed her to genuinely enjoy herself, even indulging in some dancing when a favourite song played. Retreating to the edge of the room, Cecilia indulged in another helping of food before settling back, immersing herself in the music. Contentment washed over her as she fondly reminisced about the countless parties she had both attended and hosted within these very walls.

She and James danced together, their movements synchronised in perfect harmony. If Cecilia closed her eyes, she could see him clear as day. The way his eyes crinkled when he smiled, the joyous laughter shared among friends. The woody scent of his cologne lingered as he held her close during their dance. Her memories evoked a bittersweet nostalgia, interrupted abruptly by Elinor's arrival, bringing her back to the present moment.

Standing out amidst the crowd in her striking dress, Elinor wore the most captivating ensemble of them all. A deep, blood-red gown, a subtle ode to the stone-cold killer she embodied. Cecilia couldn't help but watch Elinor as she perfectly played the role of queen, seamlessly mingling and laughing with her guests as if the evening were entirely ordinary. Elinor's graceful movements entranced everyone, particularly as she danced the night away with Bradley, commanding the attention of all present.

Cecilia found herself transfixed by Elinor's demeanour, unable to look away even when Adrian approached Elinor. A sense of shock paralysed her as Elinor's eyes locked with hers. Unsettled by the intense gaze, Cecilia instinctively rose from her seat and wandered around the room, purposefully avoiding Elinor's line of sight. With Elinor's focus already back on Bradley, Cecilia seized the moment to position herself inconspicuously. Her sole objective was to remain until Elinor made her anticipated announcement, at which point she could set her plan in motion.

Time passed slowly until the music eventually stopped, and Elinor gathered her guests together. This was the moment of truth — now or never. There would be no other chance to escape. Cecilia's heart pounded so fiercely that it bordered on physical pain. She slipped out of the ballroom, stealthily retracing her steps to her own room.

With the door slightly ajar, she turned to her guards and stated, "I'll be right back. I just need to freshen up."

One guard grunted in acknowledgement as she closed the door behind her. Looking around, she spotted Mistress Katelyn, impeccably mirroring her appearance, seated at the foot of her bed. Every detail, from their coiffed hair to their attire, aligned flawlessly, a testament to their meticulous planning.

"Are you ready to do this?" Mistress Katelyn asked, walking towards Cecilia in the centre of the room. She helped Cecilia in removing her dress.

"No, but I must be. This is my only chance," Cecilia replied, abandoning the gown with unsteady movements. Mistress Katelyn supported her to maintain balance. As they swapped the elegant ball gown for a plain brown dress and cloak, Cecilia redressed with Mistress Katelyn's help.

"My biggest concern is for your safety. If you're caught—"

"We've had this discussion before, Cecilia. I'll be all right, but staying here will only worsen matters for you. I can see the toll this place has taken on you," Mistress Katelyn interjected, her gaze piercing into Cecilia's eyes. Having witnessed Cecilia endure her lowest moments, she understood the aftereffects of staying any longer. Recognising the truth in Mistress Katelyn's words, Cecilia nodded in agreement, acknowledging her friend's genuine concern.

"You're right, I have to leave. I can't express enough gratitude for everything you've done for me," Cecilia conveyed, her hands gently clasped by Mistress Katelyn's own, giving them a reassuring squeeze.

"Go out there and embrace your freedom, Cecilia. Reunite with your children and gather an army capable of defeating Elinor. Then, we'll be even," Mistress Katelyn urged, her words carrying a weight of determination. Cecilia's laughter filled the room, a joyous sound she hadn't experienced in ages. The thought of finally breaking free from the confines of the prison she once called home filled her with excitement.

"I'll do my best to assemble an army," Cecilia responded, her smile radiant as she took a step back, focus shifting to her friend. With a sense of purpose, she tapped into her power. "But first, you need to look exactly like me."

Cecilia channelled all her energy into perfecting the delicate yet demanding weave, aiming to transform Mistress Katelyn's appearance to resemble her own. She had devoted countless hours to practising this skill daily, fully aware of her limited control over the power. Despite weeks of diligence, the illusion only lasted for a short while. Nonetheless, those precious moments would be enough for Mistress Katelyn to deceive the guards stationed outside and return to the crowded ballroom.

The next step was to lose the guards amidst the throng of people and discreetly navigate through the concealed passages used by the servants. Once there, Mistress Katelyn could retreat to her own chambers without arousing suspicion. With any luck, the guards would be preoccupied searching the ballroom for the imposter Cecilia, allowing the real Cecilia ample time to escape the castle. Her goal was to put as much distance as possible between herself and the castle before the inevitable pursuit began.

With the illusion firmly in place, Mistress Katelyn wasted no time swiftly walking out the door. Cecilia stood frozen by the door for a moment, her senses heightened, terrified the guards would notice. Listening intently, she heard no sounds but the fading echo of retreating steps. With a surge of determination, Cecilia turned and retrieved her small bag of belongings from beneath her bed. To keep calm, she recited the instructions repeatedly from Sean under her breath. Gently easing open the door, she found no one in sight. Moving with haste, Cecilia made her way to the tallest tower, keeping to the servants' passageways when she could. As a fellow worker, no one questioned her presence as she hurried along. Upon reaching the door of the tower, Cecilia kept hidden and used her power to dislodge a hanging candle bracket, causing it to fall to the ground. The sudden noise served as a diversion, capturing the guard's attention and drawing them away from her path.

Thankfully, her plan worked. Casting a quick glance behind her, she slipped through the door and made her way up the spiral staircase. As she entered the room, her eyes focused on the magical crystal shard that lay before her. The shard had an elongated shape, resembling an oblong with a triangular point at its apex. Within it, a luminous clarity radiated, casting a mesmerising pattern upon the circular walls. This particular shard was one of four pieces, and she had only ever seen them all together depicted in drawings.

Taking this crystal was a crucial part of her plan, one she had kept secret from everyone else. After all, one can't share information they don't know. While she trusted her friends and knew they wouldn't intentionally betray her, Elinor was a formidable opponent. If she wanted to uncover secrets, she had a way of making people talk. Hence, why she now worked alone, replacing the real crystal with a convincingly crafted fake. The duplicate was almost identical, instilling her with confidence that the switch would evade detection unless someone attempted to use it. Given that no one would do so until the annual bonding ceremony, she was positive that her deception would go unnoticed for the time being. With utmost care, she placed the real crystal into the pouch of her bag before commencing her descent down the stairs.

This proved the most daunting challenge yet. Cecilia needed to bypass the guard once again, despite already feeling weary from the considerable energy she had already channelled. She closed her eyes and rested her hand on the door, concentrating on her power. She visualised a protective shield surrounding the doorway, concealing her presence. Opening the door, she stepped behind the guard and closed it quietly behind her. Anxiety surged through her as beads of sweat formed on her brow, hoping that the shield held fast.

With painstaking precision, she manoeuvred the shield, inch by inch, until it formed a barrier between herself and the guard. A jolt of apprehension rippled through her as the guard locked eyes with her, though she remained invisible. Her heart raced with fear as he continued to peer passed her. Overwhelmed with panic, Cecilia hastened to the end of the corridor and turned left into the adjacent hallway, safely out of the guard's line of sight. Breathing a sigh of relief, she released the charm and pressed onward, though her weariness weighed heavily upon her, causing her movements to slow to a crawl.

As exhausted as she was, she didn't dare pause. Instead, she sought refuge in one of the servants' corridors and forged ahead towards the stables. Normally bustling with people, the area remained relatively deserted because of the ball, with most guards and workers preoccupied inside ensuring the event ran smoothly. Only a handful of guards lounged around, taking advantage of the relaxed atmosphere. While this situation worked in her favour, Cecilia couldn't shake the unease that gripped her at every faint sound. Upon entering the stables, she slipped into an empty stall, allowing herself a moment to catch her breath and plan her next move. Though she knew where she needed to go, anxiety and self-doubt were creeping in. If she made one wrong step, the guards could apprehend her.

By now, Mistress Katelyn should have returned to her chambers, meaning it wouldn't be long before her absence was discovered. Cecilia knew she had to keep moving and reach the city. Once there, she would have better cover to keep her hidden. The castle grounds were too exposed, with too many people knowing what she looked like. Mustering her resolve, she urged her legs into motion and began making her way out of the castle, keeping to the shroud of darkness for concealment. With every step, adrenaline surged through Cecilia's veins. Shadows danced around her as she navigated along the cold stone walls. The rhythmic thud of her own heartbeat drowned out all other sounds, amplifying her sense of urgency.

Glancing over her shoulder, paranoia gripped Cecilia. *Were they already onto her?* The thought propelled her faster, her determination fuelling her escape. As she neared the castle gates, her heart pounded like a war drum. The moon's pale glow illuminated her path, casting eerie silhouettes on the cobblestones. Swiftly, she darted between the flickering lanterns, a ghostly figure traversing the night.

A nearby guard patrolled, his echoing footsteps casting an ominous tone. Cecilia melted into the darkness, her body becoming one with the shadows. Holding her breath, she felt her pulse quicken as he passed, oblivious to her presence. Time stretched as she ventured further away from the castle, following the winding path towards the city. Within her mind, conflicting emotions argued, threatening her resolve.

Then, the distant hum of the city reached her ears, reigniting the will to survive as the city loomed ahead.

Chapter 28

Deceived

Adrian had been observing the ball from the sidelines, maintaining a watchful eye on the guests and Elinor as they navigated through the crowd. Throughout the evening, he ensured that nothing unusual occurred. So far, the festivities consisted of dancing, dining, and flirtatious interactions between various attendees, with some leaving early together. Despite this, Adrian remained relaxed for most of the night, as nothing raised any suspicion.

When he noticed Cecilia departing as well, he assumed that the remainder of the evening would proceed without a hitch. However, to his surprise, she returned, and everything took a different turn. Initially, he paid little attention to it, aside from finding it peculiar that she would come back, leaving her guards to keep an eye on her. Adrian continued with his evening, becoming carefree enough to savour the delicious food and indulge in a goblet of wine as the night progressed. Then the guards approached him, informing him that Cecilia had somehow vanished.

Becoming tense, Adrian went from a casual onlooker to a strategic thinker.

"For the time being, let's limit this information to the guards. Quietly secure the castle, and search anyone attempting to leave," he instructed one guard. Simultaneously scanning the room, he carefully examined the walls, statues, furniture, and any potential escape routes.

"Get one of the other guards on watch in here and search the servants' passageway. That's the only other way out of here beside the main doors, and if she had left through them, someone would have noticed." The other guard nodded in agreement and promptly left to carry out Adrian's instructions.

With the two guards gone, he looked towards Elinor, briefly considering approaching her before shaking his head and making a beeline towards a few other guards. He conveyed the same instructions as before and had them leave discreetly to begin a search of the castle. All the guards knew to report only to him, then swiftly made his way straight to the stables, making sure no horses had been taken.

As he entered, he was met with silence. There wasn't a soul about. With no one to ask, he took matters into his own hands, examining the ground and the empty stables for any recent markings that might suggest a missing horse. Although there were no visible hoof tracks, the soft imprints of footprints were unmistakable, gently etched into the dusty soil, guiding him towards the courtyard. Determined, Adrian hastened his pace, his heart pounding with anticipation as he traversed the echoing courtyard and pressed onward towards the city. With any luck, he could catch her before she disappeared for good.

As he made his way through the desolate city streets, a solitary figure caught Adrian's attention as it strode ahead. Maintaining a cautious distance, his footsteps barely disturbed the empty silence. The dim light revealed a silhouette of her face, confirming his suspicion. Continuing his pursuit, careful not to draw her attention. The city's darkened streets provided cover, heightening his senses with their eerie stillness. Each step he took was deliberate, almost mirroring her movements as he treaded on the edge of discovery. He shadowed Cecilia's path, remaining unnoticed by her. If she attempted to contact anyone, he would know. And if she dared to breach the city's confines, he was prepared to intercept her and return her to Elinor's clutches.

As Cecilia pressed on, she appeared to be making her way towards the west gate. Staying behind her, Adrian followed closely, concealing himself in the shadows, patiently awaiting her intentions. Given the lateness of the hour, all the city gates would be locked, and even if she went unrecognised, no one would let her out. It was unthinkable for a solitary woman to venture beyond the safety of the city walls at such a time.

As Cecilia approached the west gate, she unexpectedly veered off to the right, heading down a side road. Intrigued, Adrian followed suit, lurking in the shadows. He assumed she would enter one of the nearby houses, but to his surprise, she continued down an alleyway nestled between two rows of houses. Uncertain of what was unfolding, he felt the urgency to act. A surge of adrenaline tore through his veins as he sprinted, closing the distance between them with each silent stride. Just as he was mere inches away from her, he lunged forward – only to find himself grasping at nothing but emptiness. Cecilia had vanished.

Or so he initially believed.

She seemed to slip through a solid brick wall, leaving Adrian baffled as he approached. Regardless of one's powers, walking through walls was deemed impossible. His hand extended in confusion, fingertips brushing against the wall, only to encounter solid wood instead of stone. With urgency, he pushed aside the hanging vines, revealing an arched wooden door seamlessly blending with the surrounding brick wall. Concealed in darkness, the door would go unnoticed unless one knew where to look. Even in daylight, it would be difficult to spot. Tucked away on a dead-end street, few would dare to venture here. He made a mental note to inform Elinor about the door upon his return before slipping through it.

As Adrian forged forward, a flickering glow caught his attention, casting a dim light ahead. It seemed to emanate from a solitary candle or lantern belonging to Cecilia. He quickened his pace as best he could while navigating the darkness of the enclosed pathway. Without his own light, he moved blindly in unfamiliar territory. Whatever this was had to be fairly new. He had seen maps of the city and knew this wasn't here the last time he came. The purpose behind its construction puzzled him. However, he guessed that this dark and narrow passage couldn't stretch far, considering the familiar landscape surrounding them. Before he could ponder on anything else, he realised how close he was to Cecilia. With the light ahead mere metres away, he pounced like a cat in the night.

***

Deep within the city, Cecilia manoeuvred through the streets towards the secret door near the west gate. As she progressed, an unsettling feeling of being pursued crept over her, the skin on the back of her neck prickling with heightened awareness, yet she couldn't spot anyone trailing her. Nerves getting the better of her, Cecilia pressed on, deftly navigating the winding alleys until she reached the one she was searching for. With caution, she approached the corner, stealing a quick glance over her shoulder before advancing towards the door. Slipping inside, her fear subsided, knowing that freedom awaited at the end of the tunnel.

From her bag, she retrieved a small lantern and ignited it using her powers. A soft glow surrounded her, illuminating the path through the narrow tunnel. With its sleek walls and compacted dirt floor, navigating through the tunnel was effortless, even in the absence of proper light. This secret passageway had recently been constructed as an additional emergency escape route, known to only a handful of individuals. Fortunately, Cecilia was one of them. As the city guards scoured the main exits, she could slip away unnoticed, confident she would be long gone before they realised she had outsmarted them all.

As she walked, her sense of security faltered, haunted by the persistent feeling of being followed. Coming to a sudden halt, Cecilia strained her ears, searching for any sign of pursuit. The oppressive silence amplified her racing heart, intensifying her unease. A flicker of movement caught her peripheral vision, causing her heart to skip a beat. Spinning around, she braced herself to confront her unseen pursuer, only to find an empty passage bathed in the soft glow of her lantern. Paranoia gnawed at her sanity, questioning whether the threat was real or merely a figment of her imagination.

As she pressed onward, the suffocating silence seemed to mock her, its emptiness a taunting reminder of her vulnerability. Despite being on the brink of escape, an unsettling feeling lingered, refusing to dissipate. Alone in the narrow, dark tunnel, her fears tightened their grip. Cecilia's candle flickered as a slight breeze moved through the tunnel. She must be getting close to the exit. She stopped, shielding the candle's flame with her hand to keep it lit.

As a pair of hands gripped her arms, Cecilia gasped, her eyes widening in shock as she dropped the lantern, plunging them into darkness. Drawing upon the feeble reserves of power she could manage, she braced herself, ready to strike and run, until her captor spoke.

"Cecilia, it's over," Adrian said, his voice cutting through the darkness with force.

"Adrian?!" Her mind whirled with possibilities to escape as he began to pull her back the way she came. With no desire to return to that dreadful place, Cecilia sent a mild shock into Adrian. Not enough to harm him, but sufficient to make him release his grip. As his hands fell away, she moved to escape, only to feel his grasp upon her arms once more.

"No! Wait. Adrian, please listen to me. You know what she's becoming. You know what she will do. Or are you merely the blind lap dog she thinks you are?" Cecilia felt a tension ripple through Adrian's body at her words. Sensing his grip loosening, she pulled herself free, standing to confront him. In the darkness, unable to see his expression, she could only assume from his actions that he wasn't intent on dragging her back through the city.

"What do I do? She's going mad, Cecilia, just like those before her. Power has corrupted her soul," Adrian's voice carried a pained tone.

"Her soul was corrupted a long time ago. Too many of us turned a blind eye, myself included. But not anymore. She can't stay queen, and if she gets those crystals, Adrian, then we are all doomed," Cecilia emphasised, determined to get through to him.

In a bare whisper, his admission reached her ears. "I know." Cecilia, sensing victory, turned away from him and reached for her lantern. As she relit the candle, its glow illuminated his face, revealing a man who had just realised the extent of the mess he was in. Even after everything, she couldn't help but feel a pang of pity for him at that moment.

"Adrian, if you keep her away from those crystals, there might still be hope for her soul," Cecilia said as she distanced herself.

With each step, she silently prayed he would choose to walk away. Her heart raced in tandem with her footsteps until she broke into a sprint towards the wooden door at the end of the tunnel. Despite the jolt of pain from colliding with the door, she pulled it open and stepped to the other side. Relief flooded over her as she looked up at the star-studded night sky, feeling the cool breeze caress her face. A burst of laughter bubbled up from within her, overwhelmed with pure happiness at the thought of being free. At that moment, all her troubles were forgotten. With a lightness in her step, Cecilia made her way towards the cluster of trees where Sean awaited her.

Chapter 29

The Escape

As Elinor spoke with her guests, she couldn't help but notice Adrian. His expression looked vexed, characterised by a stern visage and stiff posture as he strode towards her.

"Excuse me a moment, ladies. I'll be right back," she said with a smile, then moved away, signalling for Adrian to follow. Walking through the crowd, she maintained a cheerful façade, telling those around her of her imminent return. She simply needed a moment to freshen up, all the while thinking about what could have Adrian looking so disturbed.

Exiting the ballroom, she stood by the entrance, waiting for Adrian. As he approached, she led him into a nearby small guest wing further down the hallway, attentively watching him as he closed the door behind them, anticipating what he had to say.

"Cecilia is missing," Adrian disclosed. Elinor remained composed, eager to hear more, harbouring a hope that entailed her now being locked up and under guard once again. Yet, as it became apparent that such wasn't the case, she felt her power rolling beneath her veins as her temper rose, waiting to be released.

"She escaped!" Elinor's face contorted in a mix of anger and disbelief, her nostrils flaring and jaw tensed tightly as she took in Adrian's words. With her power pulsing beneath her skin, begging for release, she fought to regain control, closing her eyes in an effort to calm herself. Inhaling deeply, Elinor silently counted to ten, willing the power surrounding her to disperse before responding to Adrian.

At that moment, disbelief clouded her thoughts. She had adamantly opposed Cecilia attending the masquerade ball, yet called her bluff by sending her an invitation. Now she found herself grappling with the repercussions of her decision. Despite the presence of the guards assigned to watch over Cecilia, they had failed in their duty, allowing her to escape.

"And what exactly are you doing about our missing ex-queen?" Elinor's voice dripped with venom as she spoke, her eyes still closed tight as she breathed heavily, awaiting his next response.

"A secret search is being conducted," Adrian replied evenly. "The castle and city are quietly locked down for the night, though it's unlikely anyone will attempt to leave at this hour."

"Then make yourself useful Adrian, and help in the search. I want her found now," Elinor commanded, her tone accepting no argument. Without waiting for a response, she strode out of the room, nearly colliding with Bradley in the process.

"There you are. I was beginning to wonder where you had disappeared to. Is everything alright?" Bradley asked, casting a concerned look towards Adrian, who was leaving down the hallway.

"Not really, but I'll explain later. For now, let's put on our happy faces and entertain our guests," Elinor replied, her voice tinged with urgency. With a radiant smile, she intertwined her arm with Bradley's, guiding him back into the ballroom.

Despite the underlying tension, the ball was an immense success. Everyone was thoroughly enjoying themselves. The music was enchanting, guests were dancing and exchanging jokes. Elinor observed with satisfaction as new friendships and alliances were being formed. Determined not to let Cecilia's sudden disappearance ruin the perfect evening, the ever-gracious host continued to dance and circle the room, pretending everything was perfect.

As the night wore on, several guests retired to their chambers. With the late hour, Elinor noticed Adrian standing by the door once again and decided to call it a night herself. She bid goodnight to the remaining guests and subtly nodded to Adrian. Walking alongside Bradley, she sensed Adrian following behind. Upon reaching her chambers, Bradley gently squeezed her hand before retiring to her sleeping quarters, leaving Elinor and Adrian alone for their conversation. Judging by his grim expression, it was evident that Adrian had unpleasant news to deliver.

"What has happened?" Elinor demanded as soon as the door was firmly shut behind them.

"We haven't located her yet. Our search for Cecilia continues, but she's nowhere to be found within the castle. Currently, our men are discreetly scouring the city, unless you deem it necessary to announce her disappearance to expedite the search?" Adrian's voice held a glimmer of hope as he offered his suggestion.

"This isn't good. No, keep it quiet. I want her found quickly and discreetly. She couldn't have gone far. With all the gates closed for the night, it's highly likely she's sought refuge in someone's house. Start by compiling a list of all those who were close friends with her and my brother, and prioritise searching among them. I want to be informed as soon as you have any information," Elinor stated with unwavering clarity.

Cecilia's capture was imperative, or else many of Elinor's plans could go horribly wrong. The last thing she needed was a rebellion to take place with Cecilia at the head.

"As you wish, I'll keep you up to date," Adrian replied before he left the room.

Following her talk to Adrian, Elinor retreated to her sleeping quarters, her eyes ablaze as she slammed the door with such force it rattled on its hinges.

"What has happened, Elinor?" Bradley's concern was palpable, offering a comforting presence.

Eager to unburden herself, Elinor joined Bradley in her bed, telling him everything she knew. As she spoke, her power went from spilling from her fingers to being locked back up inside her as her emotions settled down. With nothing else to do but wait, she and Bradley settled in for the night, Elinor clinging to hope for better news come morning.

***

Moving quietly through the trees, Cecilia strained her ears, listening intently for any sign of Sean's presence. Yet, all that greeted her was the gentle rustle of the breeze, causing the branches to sway in a hypnotic dance.

"Sean?" Her voice was barely a whisper, she called out, hoping for a response that never came. Silence engulfed her, not even a murmur in the wind. This was the designated spot, she was sure of it. But Sean wasn't here. No horses neighing. A sense of dread crept over her as she walked through the empty woods, desperately willing for Sean to appear.

As she pushed through the thick underbrush, doubts plagued her mind. They had planned this escape meticulously, leaving no room for error. Yet now, uncertainty gnawed at her inner thoughts. *Had they underestimated the vigilance of the guards? Were they already closing in on her whereabouts?* The dense foliage surrounded her, tugging at her clothes with each step, momentarily tricking her senses into believing she was being grabbed. With every beat of her heart, fear pulsed through her veins.

The woods enveloped her in an eerie silence, intensifying her angst. The absence of any sound only served to heighten her imagination, conjuring images of the guards closing in around her. Quickening her pace, she tried to outrun her escalating anxiety, her footsteps echoing through the silent expanse of the woods.

Finally, after what felt like an eternity, Cecilia emerged from the dense woods and found herself near open fields and a few local farms lining the road leading to the temple. Though her fear had lessened, a lingering unease persisted. While she had successfully navigated her way out of the woods, the danger still loomed. The temple was too far to reach on foot, especially with guards undoubtedly scouring the countryside in search of her. The shroud of darkness cloaking the landscape also made travel challenging, although it could provide some cover for hiding. Taking a deep breath, she weighed her options with a cool-headed resolve. Recklessness was a luxury she couldn't afford, yet the urgency of her predicament left her with little choice. With a farm just half a mile ahead, a bold plan formed in her mind – one that could either save her or lead to her capture. It was a risk she had to take, bracing herself for the pivotal moment when she would steal a horse and embark upon her dangerous journey.

In the stillness of the late hour, the farmhouse cast a shadowy silhouette against the night sky, the animals nestled inside for the night. Cecilia treaded cautiously towards the stable, her steps light on the dew-kissed grass. Before her stood the entrance to the stable, its arched wooden doors bolted shut for the night. Fortunately, they hadn't been fastened with a padlock. With the utmost care, she slid the bolt across, allowing the door to part just enough for her to slip through. Every movement calculated, she wasn't willing to take any risks.

Within the dim confines of the stable, her eyes adjusted to the darkness, revealing two horses standing side by side in their respective stalls. The familiar scent of hay and the earthy musk of the stable overwhelmed her sense of smell, making her wrinkle her nose. Standing between the two horses, she looked at each one. Uncertain of the temperament of either horse, Cecilia relied on her instinct, approaching the first horse with caution.

Continuing her exploration of the stable, Cecilia's eyes fell upon a well-worn saddle resting beside a small pile of grain. Before venturing closer to the chosen horse, she extended her hand, offering a handful of feed, its scent wafting through the air. With deliberate care, she reached out to the horse, her touch tentative as she gently stroked its neck, revelling in the warmth of its velvety coat beneath her fingertips, ensuring it posed no threat.

With the horse showing trust in her, Cecilia entered the stable and began to saddle her up. She then filled a small sack with grain, securing it to the back of the saddle. Despite knowing that taking this horse was necessary, a sense of guilt lingered within her. In an attempt to make amends, she left a silver coin in plain sight for the farmer to discover. Uncertain about the family's circumstances, Cecilia couldn't bear the thought of leaving them without the means to acquire another horse. With her conscience somewhat eased, she led the horse out of the shed and securely bolted the door behind her. Yet, as she stepped out into the open, her heart quickened once more, a prickling sensation of fear dancing across her skin. The vast expanse surrounding her transformed benign shadows into menacing creatures, every rustle urging her to flee. With nothing holding her back, Cecilia mounted the horse and steadied herself, holding the reins tightly. Urging the horse onward, she hastened their pace, galloping across the open field, her destination clear in her mind. The temple beckoned like a beacon of hope on the distant horizon.

Cecilia urged the horse on, pushing it hard until she felt they were a safe distance away. Though her instinct was to continue riding nonstop to reach the temple, she could see the horse was tiring and knew they both needed a rest. Bringing the horse to a halt, she dismounted and led it towards a nearby stream. After giving the horse some more food from the bag, she settled beside the stream, leaning against a sturdy tree. She felt overwhelmed by the events of the night. Her body was exhausted, and her limbs heavy. However, her mind buzzed with intensity, thoughts and ideas colliding like fireworks in the night sky. Her emotions, raw and unbridled, surged within her like a live wire, unpredictable and potent. Running on empty, her sole desire was for rest, safety, and the comforting embrace of her family. The image of holding Aevah and Jacob close to her heart stirred a newfound determination within her, giving her a much-needed boost of energy.

With the image of them still fresh in her mind, Cecilia stood up, preparing to sling her bag over her shoulder. As she held the bag, she glanced down, remembering what she had placed inside it. Retrieving the crystal nestled within, she turned it over in her hands, feeling the weight of her concern settle upon her. Amidst the turmoil of the night, she had momentarily forgotten her original plan. Though this wasn't the intended hiding place for the crystal, given the circumstances, it seemed as good as any. The urge to destroy the crystal and rid herself of its power, along with the other three shards, tugged at her conscience. Yet, she knew such an act would unleash catastrophic consequences upon the kingdom, and she didn't even possess the ability to destroy them. Cecilia did what she could and buried it, ensuring it would remain hidden forever. One less object of power for people to fight over. Using what little strength she had remaining, she dug a hole just over three feet deep and dropped the crystal inside. Covering the hole, she employed her dwindling power to conceal the spot, though whether it would hold was another question. Either way, the odds of anyone stumbling upon this spot seemed slim.

With her body teetering on the brink of exhaustion, Cecilia summoned the last of her strength to hoist herself back into the saddle, ignoring the persistent ache in her muscles. With the horse rested, she resumed her journey at a slower pace. As she pressed onward, Cecilia caught sight of the temple's silhouette, its form outlined against the faint glow of the moon. Relief flooded her being, urging her to quicken her pace as she sped up the horse onward, galloping toward the stone steps leading to the temple's doors.

Dismounting, Cecilia almost fell from the saddle, weariness taking over as she crawled her way up the steps. On her knees, Cecilia formed a fist and banged on the door repeatedly as hard as she could, even as her muscles burned. When the door swung open, she collapsed to the ground, tears streaming down her face as an overwhelming sense of relief washed over her. Strong arms gripped her, pulling her weary body inside the temple. Within its dimly lit confines, shadows danced along the ancient walls as voices murmured around her. Consumed by exhaustion, Cecilia found herself drifting into unconsciousness, her senses fading into a comforting oblivion.

***

Cecilia experienced the sensation of being aboard a ship, her body swaying in sync with the waves' rhythm. The gentle rocking induced a tranquil state in her drowsy mind, lulling her into a sleepy state. Amidst the serenity, sporadic turbulence threatened to disrupt her slumber. Suddenly, a violent jolt hurled her from her bed, sending her crashing onto the ground. As she tried to regain her bearings, she realised she was neither in a bed nor aboard a boat at sea. Confusion enveloped her as she attempted to stand, only to discover her inability to move. Lying on her stomach with her face obscured by her hair, panic set in as she struggled against invisible restraints. Limited to the movement of her eyes, which darted frantically, she desperately tried to make sense of her predicament. At that moment, a woman's voice broke the silence.

"Cecilia, you're all right. You're safe. Right now, you're only being held by the power because we're in a moving carriage. I'm going to release the hold on you, but move slowly, lest you cause an accident."

Instantly, Cecilia felt the weight lift, allowing her to regain her mobility. She first brushed her hair away from her eyes to improve her vision before cautiously sitting up, heeding the woman's words. As she looked up, she recognised the woman as Priestess Nala. With a smile, the priestess reached out and helped Cecilia settle back into her seat. Relief and confusion mingled on Cecilia's face.

"Priestess Nala, it's wonderful to see you, but I must know what happened. What—" Priestess Nala raised her hand, silencing Cecilia.

"Allow me to calm your mind, my dear, and then you can share with me what brought you to our doorstep," Priestess Nala spoke gently to Cecilia. She recounted how Cecilia had succumbed to exhaustion upon entering the temple, leading to her collapse. Concerned, the priestesses carried her to a room where she could rest while they sought guidance from the high priestess. Using her power, Priestess Nala briefly woke Cecilia long enough to gain an understanding of the night's events.

Among them was Cecilia's failure to gather any incriminating information about Elinor. Priestess Nala reassured Cecilia that this wasn't a setback, as the high priestess was already formulating her own plan to remove Elinor from the throne.

Upon realising that Cecilia had escaped, the high priestess decided to relocate Cecilia as far away from Carraton and the temple as possible. It was clear to her that Cecilia's presence posed a significant risk, likely resulting in a dangerous and potentially bloody pursuit to recapture her, a risk that the high priestess was unwilling to take. Thus, Cecilia found herself being transported to a place she never imagined revisiting. Adlington. This was where Elinor had lived for all these years. One could call it hiding in plain sight, but with Elinor in Carraton, it seemed the next best place to keep her hidden. At least, that was the belief of the high priestess.

The plan involved Priestess Nala accompanying Cecilia on her journey until they reached the next town. From there, Cecilia would continue alone, equipped with her horse, supplies, a new cloak, and enough money to ensure her well-being. Additionally, she was provided with a comprehensive list of contacts and priestess-friendly inns along her route. Assuming the identity of a priestess was the safest choice, allowing her to conceal herself and carefully strategise her path to the city.

"What then? What happens when I reach Adlington?"

"Then you embark on a new chapter of your life. Among your contacts is the address of an empty house belonging to the priesthood. It will serve as your sanctuary for as long as you need it," Priestess Nala replied.

Cecilia nervously bit her bottom lip. It wasn't a lack of trust in the high priestess, but the prospect of a prolonged stay in Adlington wasn't an option for her.

"And what about my family? How do I get back to them?"

"You can go to them when you are ready. However, I would caution you to wait a while before travelling to them. Elinor still has people searching for them," Priestess Nala explained. Cecilia's brows furrowed with concern.

"But where are they?" Cecilia asked, puzzled yet hoping she would be told it was all in her notes.

"What do you mean? Do you not know where your father went?" Priestess Nala's shock was palpable as the realisation hit her.

"No," Cecilia whispered, her shoulders slumped as reality sank in. With neither Cecilia nor the priestesses knowing where her father went, the task of finding and reuniting with her children just became damn near impossible.

Chapter 30

Hidden Agenda

The next morning, Elinor rose later than usual, finding Bradley already gone. The previous night's masquerade ball and Cecilia's disappearance had kept her up, so she slept in later than her typical routine. Enjoying a late breakfast, she indulged in a freshly baked loaf of bread, drizzled generously with honey. A delightful assortment of nuts and fruits complemented her meal, alongside a plate of smoked salmon and a steaming pot of tea, adding to the sumptuousness of the morning spread. During her meal, her lady Chloe approached, presenting her with a parcel and sharing the news of Adrian's arrival. Elinor had him wait in the study as she eagerly unwrapped her gift. Inside, she discovered an exquisite silver necklace adorned with a captivating pear-shaped emerald, accompanied by a note from Bradley expressing gratitude for the delightful evening together. A smile graced her lips as she placed the necklace on her dresser, intending to express her appreciation to Bradley later.

Remembering Adrian, she made her way to the study to meet him and discuss their next steps. Inside the study, the sun shone brightly through the window, brightening the room. Adrian stood by the window, lost in thought, and her sudden presence startled him, causing his body to tense up as she spoke.

"Morning Adrian. What news do you have for me?" Elinor asked sternly.

"Morning, Your Majesty. Still no sign. I've spoken to the watchmen on duty last night, and reported that none of them let anyone out at the time of her disappearance," Adrian replied. Elinor thought for a moment.

"Where are they now?" she pressed.

"Still at their posts for another hour."

"Bring them to me," she ordered. As Adrian moved to leave, Elinor added, "And gather the kitchen staff. I want them all questioned. She worked in that place every day. Surely, someone must know something."

"Yes, Your Majesty." With a respectful bow, Adrian left.

While awaiting the watchmen, Elinor paced the room, her mind consumed with the events of the previous night. If Cecilia wasn't found soon, well, that was a problem she didn't want to think about. Upon the watchmen's arrival, she interrogated them individually, yet each adamantly denied allowing anyone to leave during their watch.

"If you are lying to me, I will have you hanged before the sun sets today!" Elinor threatened the men.

"I swear, Your Majesty, no one entered or left this city after dark. There's a possible way out, but no one has found it before. It's more rumour than truth," one guard earnestly explained.

"I told Adrian all this earlier," the guard added. Elinor turned her gaze to Adrian, scrutinising his body language at the guard's statement. Without breaking eye contact, she dismissed the guards.

"He told you earlier? Then enlighten me precisely on what he shared because evidently, you failed to tell me," Elinor seethed.

To his credit, Adrian remained composed under her intense scrutiny.

"I fully intended to tell you, Your Majesty. I merely wanted to confirm it was real first," Adrian replied evenly.

"And what was your plan here?" Her tone was sharp as she awaited his explanation.

"The city maps. If there's a secret exit we're unaware of, it must be new. Therefore, it should be on the detailed city plans available here," Adrian explained.

Elinor watched him closely, searching for a quiver in his body, for any sign that he was keeping something from her. Yet she found nothing. With no option but to trust him, she went with him to the castle's library to search the cartography section. If he was attempting to deceive her, she vowed to expose him. Yet, she couldn't shake her own suspicions, wondering if James had devised another escape plan for his own purposes.

As they entered the royal library, Elinor took the lead, directing everyone to a secluded side room. This area, devoid of windows, was kept dimly lit to preserve the ageing maps adorning the walls. The room was lined with cabinets housing a collection of scrolls made of parchment, ranging from ancient to relatively recent. Each scroll bore meticulously detailed maps, encompassing not only the kingdom but also distant lands. However, Elinor was interested in the maps of her own city. She sought to compare the past with the present, hoping to identify any recent changes her brother James might have made.

One of the librarians, a little old man by the name of Erwin, diligently searched one cabinet for what she asked for. Due to his advanced age, his movements were slow, causing him to take longer than Elinor preferred to locate her desired documents. A slight sway accompanied his walk, and as he positioned himself before Elinor, he had to raise his head to meet her gaze. In his youth, he would have towered over her, but years of hunching over books had resulted in a curvature of his spine. This impediment prevented him from standing upright, giving the illusion of a shorter stature. Once he faced Elinor, he spoke, his words forming slowly in a whisper.

"My Queen… I have… the maps… you requested," Erwin began, his voice trembling with effort.

"Thank you, Erwin. Please, allow me to help you," replied Elinor, moving to take the two maps and spreading them out on the wooden display before her.

"No need… my Queen," Erwin interrupted, starting again. Elinor watched with frustration as he slowly placed the two maps on the display table. Her fingers twitched at her sides as she tried to maintain her composure and not take over from him.

Aware of how slowly Erwin spoke and moved, she tried to hurry the process along.

"So, Erwin, what we're looking for is a recent addition within the city itself, such as a doorway or an additional exit that my brother might have constructed in the last few years."

"Ah, yes… you mean the… the new… escape route?" Erwin replied slowly.

"Yes, exactly that, Erwin. Where is it?" Elinor murmured, leaning over the new map, her eyes darting across the detailed streets.

"Near the… near the west… gate… my Queen." Erwin's hand quivered as he pointed to the designated area on the map.

Elinor picked up the old map and aligned it with the new one, using her fingers to trace the outlines of both maps. Her eyes scanned the details until she finally found it. But there it was, a small door symbol on the wall, not far from the west gate. James had likely added this as an emergency exit, cleverly concealed, meant to go unnoticed unless one was actively searching for it.

Satisfied with her discovery, Elinor instructed Adrian to locate the door and explore it with a few men.

"Thank you, Erwin," she acknowledged, before leaving with a renewed sense of purpose.

As she made her way back to her study, leaving Erwin to put away the maps, Elinor recognised her duty to manage her kingdom amidst the ongoing search for Cecilia. A constant stream of documents required her attention, needing to be read and signed, alongside unresolved disputes that needed resolution. With nothing to do but wait for updates from her guards and Adrian, Elinor immersed herself in her responsibilities. Seated at her desk, she diligently attended to the pressing matters at hand, fully committed to maintaining order and stability within her realm.

With the bestowment of new titles and land upon the lords, there was an overwhelming amount of paperwork that needed to be signed to solidify these changes. Additionally, amidst the administrative duties, there was also the matter of planning a wedding. Despite having only announced her engagement to Bradley the previous night, Chloe had already informed her of various local bakers, dressmakers, and jewellers eager to meet with her. While the prospect of wedding planning seemed more enjoyable than the bureaucratic demands, Elinor knew that focusing on the paperwork was of utmost importance.

Thus, she diligently continued signing and reviewing the crucial documents, while entrusting Chloe with the responsibility of scheduling visits to the local establishments later in the week. With any luck, by that time, the issue concerning Cecilia would have been resolved, allowing Elinor the opportunity to focus wholeheartedly on the preparations for her impending wedding.

***

At Elinor's request, Adrian left the library accompanied by two other men and headed towards the west gate to locate the concealed door. Despite already knowing its whereabouts, he had to feign ignorance and pretend he was discovering it for the first time. Once they reached the designated street, Adrian divided the men, instructing each to go down a different alley while he followed the correct route leading to the hidden entrance. He briefly waited before rejoining with the other two men and guided them towards the secret entrance, revealing what he had found.

Together, the trio entered the door, and they each lit a lantern to illuminate their path. As they walked down the pathway, they eventually arrived at another door. As they swung it open, they stepped out into the woods, just beyond the confines of the city walls.

Closing the door behind him and stealing a backward glance, Adrian noticed its clever integration into the hillside. Its construction blended with the natural structure of the hill, while the dense vegetation hanging down from its edge further concealed it. Surrounded by the woodland, it remained inconspicuous to the casual observer, its existence a well-kept secret. Unless one was aware of its location, stumbling upon it would be nothing short of accidental.

Adrian and the guards embarked on an exhaustive search of the area, but given the considerable time that had passed, it seemed increasingly probable that Cecilia had already fled. Discovering footprints leading from the door into the woods provided a clue, yet their trail abruptly stopped. With the nearby roads full of tracks from men, horses and carts alike, finding prints of Cecilia would be like searching for a needle in a haystack – damn near impossible.

Knowing they could do no more, Adrian instructed everyone to return to the castle. He went in search of Elinor to deliver the disappointing news that there was still no sign of Cecilia.

Elinor's fury would be inevitable, of that he was certain. The silver lining, though, was that she remained blissfully unaware of his involvement in Cecilia's sudden disappearance. As long as Cecilia continued to stay away, Elinor would forever remain oblivious to the truth. It was a perilous game he played, one that weighed heavily on his conscience with each passing moment. Despite the guilt gnawing at him, he couldn't shake the conviction that his actions were necessary.

Years ago, he had witnessed a young princess brimming with potential and ambition, and he had once fervently believed in her ability to rule. But now, he witnessed a stark transformation unfolding before his eyes. While her stubbornness had always been evident, the changes were deeper, more profound. He had risked everything on her potential to become an exceptional queen, yet the bond with the tower's crystal had unleashed a power that threatened to consume her. It dawned on him that she couldn't possess the power of all the shards. Just one shard alone was causing enough destruction.

Throughout history, the temptation of having too much power had been the downfall of many great leaders. As proven in the past, the power of those shards caused more problems than they ever solved, leading to entire families being torn apart by greed and ambition. With Elinor, this unfortunate truth became evident as he witnessed firsthand the loss of control. Seeing the destruction within her room, he could no longer deny the severity of the situation. Her emotions grew increasingly erratic, instilling a fear of what actions she might take next.

The current problem he faced was determining what to do. On his way to meet Elinor, he was halted by the guards, who had just concluded their questioning of the kitchen staff. Although the workers knew little, they eagerly disclosed the details of the close relationship between Cecilia and Mistress Katelyn. They also mentioned numerous interactions involving the farmer, Sean, and his wife. Thanking the guards for their efforts, he proceeded towards Elinor's study. Despite his uncertainty about how to handle the situation, he resolved to fulfil his duty and speak to Elinor. Upon entering the study, Elinor raised her head but remained motionless. Her eyes bore into him as she rested her elbows on the table, hands cradling her chin. Her voice dripped with icy disdain as she addressed him.

"Adrian, what bad news do you have for me this time?" Elinor's voice cut through the air with a sharp edge.

"My Queen," Adrian bowed respectfully before delivering the news. "From the search of the tunnel, it would seem from the tracks left outside that Cecilia escaped from there."

"And?" Elinor's tone was laced with impatience, her unwavering gaze penetrating as she continued to stare at him.

Adrian held her gaze, his voice steady as he recounted what the guards had told him. An uneasy feeling settled in his stomach as he struggled to maintain his composure, wondering if Elinor suspected anything. With his hands clasped behind his back, he interlocked his fingers, a gesture intended to steady his nerves. Silence enveloped them, stretching into several tense minutes as

Elinor's eyes bore into him, without a hint of movement. Suddenly, she slammed her palms onto her desk and stood up.

"Summon Julian to me. I wish to speak to him," Elinor commanded. "He has been monitoring Sean's movements closely. He can bring me up to date with his activities and then bring Sean and his wife in for questioning." Adrian acknowledged her orders with a nod.

"And what would you like me to do, Your Majesty?"

"Nothing for now. Return to your chambers and await further instructions. I will have someone send for you when Sean arrives," Elinor replied coldly.

Taken aback by her dismissal, Adrian tried to hide his surprise, offering a nod before leaving to find Julian. As he made his way, he couldn't shake the sense that Elinor had her suspicions about his loyalty, though only time would reveal how everything would play out. For the present, he went and found Julian before returning to his chambers, trying to find a way out of this mess.

Chapter 31

A Secret Visit

Bradley could see the impact of the power on Elinor, despite her remaining oblivious to its effects. Each time anger surged within her, the power thrived, absorbing her emotions. Bradley, lacking the ability to channel this power, stayed clueless about its true nature, assuming it to be an energy source accessible at will. However, in Elinor's case, it appeared to possess a sentience of its own. Typically, individuals unable to wield this power could neither see nor feel its presence. He had heard of it as a radiant golden light that brought joy and fulfilment to those who experienced it. However, what surrounded Elinor was the opposite. It presented itself as an all-consuming darkness, like a looming shadow at your back, haunting anyone in its presence. The fear it evoked was palpable, leaving Bradley to wonder about its impact on Elinor herself, who seemed to embrace it, a notion even more terrifying to him.

That night, after the ball, it was the worst he had ever seen. Elinor seemed on edge the entire time, and he could sense the energy radiating from her. It made him uneasy. Concerned about Elinor's well-being, he ventured to the library the following morning. Immersed in research for hours, he delved into the lore of the power. He wanted to understand what to expect and whether this darkness surrounding the power was just a temporary phase or if it could pose a bigger problem for all of them, especially him, considering his stake in the future.

His ambitions were set on becoming king and ruling alongside Elinor, no matter what. Bradley understood that his grand plans would crumble if Elinor were to take her own life or harm others with her power before their wedding. Thus, he dedicated himself to extensive research on her abilities and the ramifications of mental instability. Unfortunately, his findings yielded disheartening results. It became evident that those consumed by the darkness within them underwent a gradual decline into madness, leaving devastation in their path. He uncovered accounts of a previous king who fell victim to this darkness, its repercussions spread across the kingdom due to the connection between the king and the crystal.

Fearing for the land, the priestesses intervened, determined to stop the king's destructive path and sever his bond with the crystal, thus ending his reign of power. After a fierce battle, the priestesses ultimately succeeded and cut off his ties to the power. Left with nothing but consumed by madness, the king tragically took his own life, bringing about the demise of his wife and children. Concerned that a similar fate awaited Elinor, he took it upon himself to intervene and decided to seek the counsel of the priestesses. With urgency pressing upon him, Bradley made his way to the stables, mounting a horse and riding swiftly toward the temple of Carraton, telling no one where he was going. He didn't know what he was going to say to them, but with an hour's ride ahead of him, Bradley had time to think.

Before he knew it, the temple loomed ahead, its majestic presence captivating him. Bringing his horse to a slow trot, he took in the wonder that was the temple. Although he had ridden passed the temple many times over the years, he had never ventured inside. Nearing the entrance, a surge of nervousness washed over him, causing his heart to skip a beat. Taking a deep breath, he dismounted from his horse and walked through the beautiful garden. Beneath the clear skies, gardeners tended to the flower beds, while priestesses strolled along the pathways. As he walked down the path, a priestess approached him, catching his attention.

"Good afternoon, Bradley. It's a pleasure to meet you. What brings you to our humble home?" The priestess's tone carried authority, yet her smile softened the sternness. Standing tall, hands clasped before her, she exuded an air of dignity. Startled by her question and commanding presence, Bradley fumbled for words.

"Forgive me, Priestess. I, uh, erm, I don't believe I know your name."

"I am the High Priestess, Bradley. Now, why are you here?" Her response widened his eyes in surprise.

"High Priestess, it's you I have come to see." Bradley looked around nervously. "Could we perhaps speak in private? It concerns the queen."

With a nod, the high priestess turned, while another priestess took hold of his horse's reins. Expressing gratitude, he followed the high priestess along the path, towards the towering entrance of the temple. Ascending the steps, he couldn't shake the feeling of insignificance against the grandeur of the surrounding pillars. The architecture's magnificence moved him, its intricate carvings and imposing columns seemingly reaching for the heavens. With each step, his apprehension grew, yet so did his curiosity. He had never seen inside these walls. Bradley had heard rumours of the temple's magnificence, but he never quite believed the tales. Experiencing it firsthand made him realise those who had been here weren't exaggerating.

Upon crossing the threshold, a profound stillness fell upon him. The brightly illuminated interior revealed a vast space filled with a sense of sacredness. The scent of incense wafted through the air, mingling with the whispers of prayers from bygone eras. Following the high priestess through the temple, Bradley's eyes were drawn to the intricately embellished altars and ancient artefacts displayed with reverence. Each step revealed another layer of history and spirituality, resonating with a profound energy that touched his soul deeply.

Having never possessed the ability to wield the power, he had never attributed much significance to the divine spirit or the priestesses themselves. While he harboured a degree of respect for them as individuals, he failed to discern any personal advantage in their presence. However, everything had changed drastically. The undeniable transformation occurring within Elinor compelled him to reassess his perspective. Standing within the temple's confines, he knew he was in the right place to help her.

The high priestess escorted him to her office, gesturing for him to take a seat as she settled across from him. Fixing him with her unwavering gaze, she began to speak.

"What news do you wish to share with me about our beloved queen?" the high priestess inquired, her tone firm yet expectant.

Undeterred, Bradley proceeded to explain the events of the recent weeks and the profound change that had occurred in Elinor. As he spoke, the high priestess's expression never changed, nor did her posture. After he finished speaking, she continued to watch him, not uttering a single word. Uncertain of how to proceed, Bradley found himself sitting there, observing her in return, waiting for her to break the silence.

"And what do you want from me, Bradley?" she asked.

"Your help," Bradley replied sincerely. "I have read the texts. This isn't the first time a king or queen has gone mad. Help me stop Elinor from suffering the same fate."

The high priestess looked lost in her thoughts as she pondered his words. "Are you aware that even with our intervention, there's no guarantee we can help her?" she cautioned.

"Yes, I am," Bradley replied without hesitation.

"Good. I will help you, for it is my duty to protect this kingdom. Yet, I'm curious to know your motivation in aiding Elinor. Is it love or fear that drives you?" the high priestess inquired.

"Can't it be both?" Bradley responded, a hint of uncertainty colouring his tone.

A smile graced the high priestess's lips at his answer. "For you, I'm not so sure," she remarked.

Her penetrating eyes made the hair on Bradley's arms rise at her response. She made him nervous, like she knew what he was thinking when her eyes bore into his. Before he could offer any further explanation, she stood.

"I require some time to prepare, as what you're asking for is quite challenging. It's not just me, but my priestesses as well, who will be facing a daunting task ahead. Allow me to take you to our secluded garden where you can wait. Once prepared, we shall ride together to Carraton and confront the queen's madness."

Unsure how to respond, Bradley simply nodded and followed the high priestess to a beautiful, secluded garden. Taking a seat at the picnic bench, he admired the tranquil scenery. Before long, another high priestess arrived bearing tea and biscuits, offering him a moment of solace amidst the waiting. With nothing else to occupy his time, he watched the birds flitting among the trees while savouring his tea. Several hours drifted by until the high priestess returned. He stood to greet her.

"It is time," she declared.

With a nod, Bradley trailed behind the high priestess as they exited the temple. Descending the steps, they then strolled along the path until they reached the outskirts of the temple walls. To his surprise, twelve priestesses on horseback were waiting. Bradley's heart quickened at the sight of them; the gravity of the situation became real. He followed the high priestess towards the front of the group where he mounted his horse, while she gracefully settled on hers. With a solemn expression, she turned to face him.

"Are you ready?" she asked.

"Yes," Bradley responded. With resolve, the high priestess spurred her horse into motion, leading the precession towards the city, the other priestesses following closely. Despite his lingering uncertainty about involving the high priestess, Bradley dismissed his doubts and urged his horse to continue. He may not know what would happen, but he knew he needed their help. Elinor's life depended on it.

Chapter 32

The Questioning Room

Trust proved itself unpredictable. People you once believed loyal easily veered into betraying you, much like anyone else. Ever since Elinor arrived in Carraton, she could see Adrian's loyalty waning with each passing day. It was subtle at first; she lacked direct proof of his betrayal, yet the signs proved unmistakable. The little things he said and the actions he claimed to have taken recently weren't adding up, raising doubts. However, the final straw came with the Cecilia debacle. That night, Adrian was spotted heading into the city and he was gone for an extended period. His prolonged absence suggested he trailed Cecilia. Knowing Adrian's character, he rarely wasted time on dead ends.

As Elinor pondered her situation, a sense of losing control over herself gradually took hold. The more anger consumed her, the more challenging it became to contain the power within her. Normally, the power remained passive, existing as ethereal strands of light, simply awaiting her command. Now it felt as though it was trying to gain control of her. Her eyes emitted an otherworldly glow, reflecting the turbulent energy within her. As her emotions surged, the darkness swirling around her intensified. Instead of floating lights, wisps of shadowy tendrils snaked and curled, mimicking her every movement as extensions of her essence. Crackling with sparks, the tendrils reacted to her emotions. A surge of pure, raw power coursed through her, begging to be unleashed.

The unsettling truth was, she craved it. She yearned to unleash that power upon those around her, instilling fear in their hearts. Her deepest desire was to inflict pain and death on any who dared oppose her. Teetering on the edge of chaos, she embraced it eagerly. Thoughts of Cecilia fuelled her anger, igniting her imagination. The mere prospect of confronting her filled her with a longing for a slow, torturous demise until she vanished from existence. As her thoughts grew increasingly sinister, a surge of power coursed through her, ready to be unleashed at her command. She savoured the euphoric feeling of the power, honing it, preparing to unleash it upon those deemed deserving of its wrath.

Just then, one of her guards knocked at the door, seeking guidance regarding the fate of the Goodmans, still imprisoned in the cells. Amidst the chaos of Cecilia's escape, the Goodmans had slipped her thoughts until now. Prior to the ball, Elinor had ordered their arrest, taking them from their beds in the night. The plan was to interrogate them the following day. While the information she sought might not have been in their home, she harboured no doubt they knew something. So, with Cecilia out of her control, she ventured to the cells herself. This power within her craved for release, eager to assert itself, and she was determined to extract the information she had been searching for. As Elinor neared the cells, she addressed the guard stationed outside the Goodman's cell.

"Get them ready for me. Oh, and keep Adrian in the dark. I don't want him to know anything. Understood?"

"Yes, my Queen," the guard obediently replied. Turning to the guard who walked to the cells with her, she inquired about Mistress Katelyn.

"She has already been apprehended, my Queen, confined in the cell over there," he informed, gesturing towards the cell as Elinor walked over.

"Open it." As he complied, Elinor looked inside, seeing a woman with fire in her eyes staring back at her.

"Oh, it's going to be fun breaking you," she remarked to Mistress Katelyn, who responded with a curse. Elinor laughed.

"Put her in the hole. Let's see how much fire she has left after a few hours in darkness."

As she strode back to the cell housing the Goodmans, Elinor couldn't suppress a smile at the sounds of anguish emanating from Mistress Katelyn. Elinor doubted that the fire within her would last long in the hole. Stronger wills than hers had been broken from the entrapment. It was like being buried alive, or so she had been told. Surrounded by darkness, the air thinning, few endured before their cries turned to screams and then to sobs, begging to be freed.

Leaving Mistress Katelyn to her punishment, Elinor entered the interrogation room, her mere presence freezing the atmosphere. It felt as though all the life and joy had been drained away. Seated before her were the Goodmans, each bound to a sturdy chair, their faces contorted with pure hatred. As Elinor approached, Lord Goodman cursed and spat in disgust at her, but his saliva missed its target, landing on the floor between them. A wicked smile curled upon Elinor's lips as she infused a fraction of her power into his body. Coiling around his every nerve, she struck, releasing a torrent of agony that engulfed him, searing through every fibre of his being.

His anguished screams were a symphony to her ears, reminiscent of a wounded animal howling in the darkness, begging for release from the endless torment. Enjoying the experience, she prolonged the pain there for several minutes, watching as his head flung back and his face contorted in agony. The twisted pleasure she derived from his suffering sent a chilling shiver down her spine. Each scream fed her sadistic desires, as she revelled in the grotesque harmony of torment. With each passing moment, she marvelled at the profound effect the pain was having on him. His clothes clung to his body, drenched in sweat, while his muscles fought against the pain, his eyes ablaze with red intensity.

Elinor savoured the dominance she wielded over him, the torment she inflicted becoming an intoxicating dance, a twisted tango between predator and prey. The control she held over him filled her with a perverse delight, relishing in the twisted pleasure derived from his suffering. As the man's cries waned, teetering on the verge of passing out, she released him from his torment. A haunting silence enveloped the room, broken only by his ragged breaths. Observing his trembling form, she lingered in the remnants of her sadistic euphoria. A cruel smile graced her lips as she embraced the depths of her darkness. And in that moment, she welcomed it wholeheartedly, ready to seek her next victim and indulge in the chilling ecstasy that only their anguish could provide.

Standing behind Claire Goodman, she trailed her fingers down the woman's tear-streaked cheeks. Claire quivering, already a picture of despair. Turning her attention to Lord Goodman once more, she posed the burning question that consumed her thoughts.

"Where are the crystal shards hidden?" His silence spurred her to strike once more, this time at Claire. The woman's agonised screams were a delight to her ears, as was Johnathon's reaction.

"No! Please, I beg you. Leave her alone. I'll tell you what you want to know," Johnathon pleaded, straining against his restraints in a futile attempt to reach his wife. The sight of Claire writhing in pain, her screams piercing the air like her very soul was being ripped from her, proved unbearable to him. At his plea, Elinor stopped, shifting her focus to Johnathon.

"Tell me," she commanded.

So he divulged the secret of the crystal shards, it was bound to one man alone. Only he possessed the ability to disclose the whereabouts, by the way the power was formed. This she comprehended. She understood how the power worked, and often in these circumstances, only the original wielder could break the links they formed with the power. What vexed Elinor was hearing the key to everything was George. As it turned out, his dying wife passed the bond to George instead of Johnathon, her brother, as it normally would. With George in hiding, she found herself back at square one in her search. Taking out her anger on the two individuals before her, she found abnormal solace in their pain. With a back-and-forth motion, she unleashed her power upon them, one after the other. While one person howled in agony, the other pleaded desperately for mercy, willing to do anything to end the suffering of the other. Their pitiful pleas fell upon deaf ears. The only thing she desired, they couldn't provide. Unaware of George's whereabouts, they were rendered useless to her. Thus, she continued to experiment with her powers, pushing the limits, if they even had any.

She began by subjecting specific areas of their bodies to various forms of torture. Elinor tested burning, freezing, fractures, and even simulated stab wounds. What made her power remarkable was that despite experiencing these sensations as if real, their delicate skin remained unmarked. Pure pain devoid of any physical evidence.

As her confidence grew, Elinor increased the intensity of each pain, eventually causing them to feel it throughout their entire beings. Their squeals and cries became a symphony, pleasing to her ears. By the end, both of them appeared severely battered, their will to survive devoid, their faces drained of life and colour. Only the chains keeping them upright prevented them from collapsing onto the floor.

As she continued her torment, one of her guards informed her of Sean and Anita's arrival. Relieved to finally have them in her clutches, she ordered that they be taken to the room where Mistress Katelyn was now being held after several hours in the hole. These three had long been thorns in her side.

"Get them ready. I'm almost done here," she commanded, circling the couple, and observing them. Claire's eyes were vacant, her body limp in the chair, while Johnathon, head bowed, breathed heavily. Elinor's footsteps echoed ominously, eliciting a flinch from Claire and a sly smirk from Elinor.

Exiting the room, she left them with a chilling farewell. "I won't be long," she declared before closing the door, leaving them to stew in their fear.

Elinor stepped into the adjacent interrogation room. Sean stood shackled against the cold brick wall, his arms suspended above his head by chains, feet firmly planted on the ground, each leg individually restrained. Anita was chained to the chair the same way as the Goodmans, facing her husband Sean. Between them lay Mistress Katelyn, her hands chained but not restrained to the ground, her uncontrollable sobs echoed through the room. The depths of the pit had taken its toll on her, leaving her spirit shattered after being confined in darkness, limited movement, and stale air. Not to mention listening to the screams of Elinor's victims. Mistress Katelyn now appeared a mere shadow of her former self, lacking the spirit to entertain Elinor as her fellow captives could. Elinor resolved to break each of them for what they had done.

"What do you hope to achieve here, Elinor? None of us can give you what you want," Sean challenged. In response, Elinor sent a jolt of pain through his body, eliciting a cry of shock and causing his body to convulse involuntarily.

"Address me as Queen Elinor," she commanded sternly.

Another surge of pain hitting every nerve in his body, longer and more intense this time. Despite the agony, he refrained from crying out, much to her annoyance. Instead, he gritted his teeth and tensed his muscles, trying to withstand the torment. Sensing his defiance, Elinor focused all her energy on him, engaging in a battle of wills. Determined to get a reaction, she increased the level of pain every few seconds, toying with him until he succumbed. With each increase, she could see the change in his body, from the mild tensing of his muscles to violent spasms, his brow glistening with sweat, his face contorted in agony, blood dripping from his mouth. Finally, he reached his breaking point. His scream reverberated throughout the room, a satisfying masterpiece to her ears.

Content, she released her hold over him and turned her attention to the two women. Without uttering a word, she directed her power towards them. In an instant, they went from stillness to writhing in agony, their bodies contorting in torment. Mistress Katelyn, displaying the most movement, convulsed upright, emitting anguished cries as her body spasmed uncontrollably. Turning to Elinor, she pleaded for mercy.

"Please! Stop," she implored, the anguish evident in Mistress Katelyn's eyes as she reached out a trembling hand. It appeared that Anita had lost consciousness. Despite the ongoing pain, there was no sign of a reaction from her. Elinor grasped Anita's hair, forcefully turning her head to examine her. Though still breathing, Anita remained unresponsive.

"Leave her alone!" Sean's cry pierced the air.

With a sinister laugh, Elinor unleashed her power upon all three captives, intensifying their agony as she had with the Goodmans. Both Sean and Mistress Katelyn cried out again as she upped the level of pain. Mistress Katelyn curled into the fetal position, fists clenched tightly as she battled against the overwhelming pain. Meanwhile, Sean thrashed against the wall, tugging at his shackles in a desperate bid for relief. Anita, previously silent, soon joined the cacophony of screams as Elinor delved into her subconscious, waking her from her slumber. Stiffening in her chair, Anita joined her fellow captives in begging for it to end.

With all three ensnared in unrelenting torment, Elinor should've felt satisfaction. Instead, an unsettling emptiness lingered within her, as if true vengeance hadn't been met.

Done toying with them, Elinor's curiosity was piqued to explore the extent of her power. *How much destruction could she unleash?* With that in mind, she instructed her guards to bring the Goodmans into the room. Both appeared defeated, their once vibrant spirits now diminished to mere shadows. Haunted eyes and pallid complexions reflected their profound despair as they took their places on the ground, offering no resistance, awaiting their fate.

Once they were settled, Elinor positioned herself in the centre of the room. A palpable silence filled the room, yet an uneasiness radiated from them as though anticipating her next move. Driven by a desire to show her capabilities, Elinor tapped into the vast reservoir of magic coursing through her veins. The power surged, a swirling vortex of ominous energy soaring above her, tempting her to delve deeper into its depths. Only pure destruction awaited if she dared yield to the darkness.

So she stood, arms outstretched, embracing the darkness within, feeling the power surge through her. It whispered to her, its touch gentle yet commanding, caressing her in its embrace. She basked in the exquisite sensation of power taking hold, every ember igniting within her being. It was euphoric; the power seeped into her essence, infusing her very bones with its strength. At that moment, she felt unstoppable, as if she held the world in her hands. The crackle of energy danced at her fingertips, while the scent of raw power filled the air, tantalising her senses with the promise of life and death.

"Do it," a voice urged, barely a whisper.

"Do it now. You have the power. You need only unleash it."

Captivated by the haunting voice, Elinor surrendered to the overwhelming urge for vengeance. Relinquishing control, she allowed tendrils of darkness to surge forth, whipping through the air with ominous fervour. The chilling sound of their movement echoed through the room, sending shivers down the spines of those present. Amidst the chaos, her manic laughter rang out, a symphony accompanied by the agonised screams of her victims. With no mercy, the power tore through everything in its path, leaving behind only turmoil and destruction. Indifferent to what stood in its way, it consumed all, driven solely by its desire to dismantle the world until nothing remained but ash.

In the aftermath, only Elinor survived, a solitary figure amidst the wreckage, with nothing but desolation stretching out before her.

Chapter 33

Madness

Adrian found himself growing increasingly impatient as he wondered what was taking so long for Sean to reach the castle. An hour had already passed since his expected arrival. The weather was pleasant, ruling out any weather-related hindrances. Unless they had encountered difficulties in locating Sean, there seemed to be no valid reason for the delay. Suspicion crept into Adrian's thoughts, hinting at the possibility of purposely not being told. Elinor's waning trust only fuelled his paranoia, especially when she told him to wait for someone to report to him.

Driven by frustration and an increasing sense of distrust, Adrian made his way to the stables to check if anyone had arrived without his knowledge. His suspicions proved valid as he learned from the stable hand that the guards had indeed arrived an hour earlier, escorting Sean and his wife as prisoners to the cells, as requested by the queen. Panic surged within him, his heart quickening with apprehension and Adrian wondered why anyone hadn't informed him.

With a sense of urgency, Adrian rushed to the cells, seeking clarity on the unfolding situation. Recalling his previous conversation with Cecilia in the castle about Elinor, and afterwards, when he allowed her to escape through the secret tunnel, Adrian grappled with the possibility of his involvement being exposed. While he believed Cecilia wouldn't have divulged their conversations or his assistance in her escape, he couldn't be certain. Aware of Elinor's growing suspicions, he couldn't afford for anyone to accidentally mention his name to her. He was walking on a precarious tightrope that could snap at any moment. Determined to protect his secret, and ultimately his life, Adrian hoped to intervene with whatever Elinor had planned.

As Adrian approached the entrance to the cells, he was taken aback by the sight of Bradley making his way towards him, with an entourage of thirteen priestesses trailing behind him. Among them stood the high priestess herself, holding the crystal shard from the tower. Determined, Adrian positioned himself in their path, demanding an immediate explanation from Bradley.

Before Adrian could voice his questions, Bradley spoke, asserting his actions as necessary for the kingdom's well-being. He appealed to the changes he perceived in Elinor, expressing genuine concern for her and the realm. However, Adrian's attempt to interrupt was promptly halted by the high priestess.

"Adrian," she interjected, her gaze piercing, "you've been by Elinor's side since the beginning. Can you honestly say the Elinor of today is the same from all those years ago?"

Her question hung in the air, daring Adrian to say otherwise.

"No, she isn't, but—" Adrian's attempt to respond was abruptly halted as a sudden surge of power emanated from one of the interrogation rooms, causing a collective sense of unease among them. Terrified screams pierced the air, followed by an eerie silence that hung like a shroud. Without hesitation, Adrian sprinted down the hall, with Bradley and the priestesses close on his heels, until they reached the door leading to the source of the disturbance.

With adrenaline coursing through his veins, Adrian reached the door first, his heart pounding in his chest. With a forceful tug, he yanked the door open, the handle nearly coming loose from its fixture. Stepping into the room, his senses were assaulted by the overwhelming stench of death and the sickening metallic tang of blood that coated the walls and pooled on the floor.

Before him lay a scene of utter devastation – a gruesome tableau of violence and suffering. Broken bodies were strewn in every direction, their limbs grotesquely arranged like a jigsaw puzzle. The sight of such carnage threatened to overwhelm Adrian, his stomach churning as he struggled to comprehend the horrors before him.

Limbs lay violently torn apart, forcefully separated from their sockets and strewn chaotically across the room. Once neatly encased organs, now lay splattered, their grotesque display mirroring the chaos of the scene. Faces, once recognisable, now had scars of brutality, some severed from their bodies in a ghastly dance of destruction.

The once pristine walls now bore the grim artistry of crimson paint, each droplet of blood echoing upon impact with the ground, a steady rhythm of *drip, drip, drip*. Puddles of deep red blood pooled beneath. Amidst the carnage, a lone figure stood untouched by the violence that had consumed the room. Elinor, the sole survivor, with a perfect circle of cleanliness surrounding her amidst the gruesome mess. Her laughter, tinged with madness, filled the air as she turned to meet Adrian's gaze, her eyes reflecting the depths of her derangement.

"Hello, Adrian. You've missed all the fun," Elinor greeted, her tone laced with a chilling nonchalance.

Adrian, taking tentative steps forward, surveyed the room in stunned disbelief. Before him stood a woman who had left no soul alive in her wake – guards and captives alike, now reduced to a morbid collage of carnage. As Adrian locked eyes with Elinor, he caught a glimpse into the depths of madness lurking within her deep blue eyes.

Unable to comprehend what he was witnessing, Adrian's voice escaped him in a mere whisper, "Elinor, what have you done?"

***

Elinor locked eyes with Adrian, her expression a mix of feral intensity and wild madness.

"What needed to be done!" she said, her gaze briefly flickering passed him to the cluster of women behind him. Leading the group was none other than the high priestess herself, gripping a crystal shard in her hands. It bore a striking resemblance to the one Elinor had in her own tower. Clearly, these priestesses had come up with a plan that she was unaware of. Undeterred by the lifeless bodies strewn about, Elinor approached the high priestess. As she advanced, the high priestess and her devoted followers began encircling Elinor in a tight formation. Halting, Elinor locked eyes with the high priestess, unable to contain a burst of laughter.

"What's your plan, High Priestess? Are you here to thwart me? To end my life? Go on, then. I would like to see you try," she declared, her head held high, openly challenging the high priestess to make a move. She watched as the high priestess initiated her chanting, the other priestesses joining in, their hands entwined. Still chuckling, Elinor spun in a circle, making eye contact with every priestess, until her gaze ultimately connected with the high priestess once again.

"Fools!" Elinor's desperate cry pierced the air, charged with raw intensity as she unleashed her power. Sinister tendrils, imbued with darkness, coiled around her form, poised to strike. With a thunderous crack, the tendrils surged forth, aimed at the thirteen women. Yet, just before impact, they collided against an unseen, impenetrable barrier, eliciting a faint shimmer and a static

317

shock. Stumbling back, Elinor's frustration boiled into rage, driving her to exert more force against the invisible barrier. The tendrils, now slowly caressing the imperceptible wall, searched for any weakness, an opening to get through. Her power yearned for the smallest gap, a hairline fracture in the barrier no matter how minuscule.

If her power could get through, it would tear those women apart. They had opposed her since her childhood training among them. Their insufferable demeanour persisted even after she ascended to the throne. They believed she remained oblivious to their spies within her walls. These spies watched and waited, relaying all their information to their esteemed high priestess. Yet unbeknownst to them, one of their so-called spies worked for her too. Every piece of information they gathered was authorised by Elinor before being shared. They were only privy to what she allowed them to know, a cunning blend of truth and deception.

As she spun in endless circles, Elinor noticed the diminishing gap, the circle shrinking. The thought of them overpowering her, stripping her of her abilities, instilled a deep-seated terror within her. She staunchly refused to entertain such a fate, resolving to fight back with all her strength. In the absence of an opening, she vowed to break through the entire barrier with sheer force alone. With every ounce of strength within her, Elinor pushed back with increasing intensity. Inch by inch, the barrier moved back towards the priestesses. Their chants grew deafening, echoing off the walls. Many of their faces contorted with strain, sweat dripping profusely. They were being pushed to their limits. Elinor wasn't faring much better. Her veins felt ablaze, blood trickling down her face from where she couldn't say. All her focus was fixed on breaking through that barrier, no matter the cost.

The barrier started to vibrate, a testament to the intense struggle waged by both sides until it shattered beyond repair. In the aftermath, every woman, including Elinor, collapsed to the ground. When consciousness returned to her, Bradley hovered over her, his lips forming her name, but no sound reached her ears. Instead, a persistent buzzing filled her senses. Struggling to sit up, she was engulfed by a searing pain coursing throughout her entire body, as if she had been torn apart. Surveying her surroundings, she noticed most of the priestesses slowly getting up, while others remained motionless. Gradually, the buzzing in her ears faded, allowing the sounds of the room to filter back in.

"You need to go to the infirmary, Elinor," Bradley's concern-laden voice reached her ears, but she brushed him off, needing to know what happened. Before the high priestess lay the shattered remains of the crystal, scattered all over the floor.

"I don't know what game you're playing, Elinor, but replacing the crystal shard with a fake was impressive," the high priestess seethed. "Now six of my priestesses are dead, and you still have your powers. Granted, not in their entirety as before, but still more than you deserve."

Elinor met the high priestess's wrath with a smirking expression, absorbing her accusations without flinching. Though clueless about the high priestess's insinuations, she remained resolute in her silence, allowing the high priestess to draw her own conclusions. To test the validity of the high priestess's claims, Elinor delved deep within herself, attempting to harness her power once more. She was right. The amount of power she previously possessed had vanished. What remained was nothing but pitiful. A stark realisation that sent a panic coursing through her veins. Nevertheless, she kept a mask of indifference on her face.

Standing up, Elinor positioned herself defiantly before the high priestess, Bradley steadfast at her side. "What a pity for you. Your little plan failed. I may have less power than before, but I am still queen."

"Not for long. As high priestess, I have the authority to challenge your claim to the throne. I call for a vote of the lords to determine if you are fit to be called queen."

"Hah! Go ahead. The lords are currently within these very walls. Let's see whom they choose," Elinor retorted, her gaze piercing the high priestess before walking out of the room. Adrian lingered by the door.

"Round up the lords. Bring them to the throne room. I want this resolved immediately," she demanded, urgency and frustration tinging her voice.

Without waiting to see if her orders were heeded, she strode briskly forward, her eyes fixed ahead. The sound of her footsteps echoed through the corridor. Every muscle protested with agony, each step intensifying the pain, but Elinor pressed on, driven by a desperate need to escape the high priestess's scrutiny. Finally reaching the hallway above the cells, her resolve crumbled. She sank to the floor, her body succumbing to exhaustion and pain. Bradley, ever at her side, caught her, his arms providing a steady anchor as he lowered her into a sitting position.

"Elinor, you need the infirmary immediately."

"No. Take me to my chambers. Find my ladies and send them to me, then you can get me something for the pain," Elinor said firmly, her tone looking for no argument. "If I am to face the court to determine my fate, then I will do it on my terms."

Acknowledging her command with a nod, Bradley helped Elinor as they made their way back to her chambers. Once inside, Elinor settled into the armchair with Bradley's help. She waved him off when he attempted to fuss over her, instructing him to carry out her orders instead. As Bradley left to fulfil her requests, Elinor leaned back in her chair, closing her eyes to combat the waves of pain coursing through her body. She focused on regulating her breathing as she recalled the evening's events.

The switch of the real crystal shard for a fake was an obvious betrayal, and it wasn't hard to figure out who was responsible. Now, the pressing question was: where had Cecilia taken it? Despite her seething anger, Elinor begrudgingly acknowledged that Cecilia's defiant act had saved her from the brink of losing not only her powers but potentially her life as well. It was a small act of mercy amidst the chaos. Had it been the real crystal shard, with its connection to the thirteen priestesses, their combined power would have far surpassed Elinor's own. But even with their formidable link, their collective power merely equalled hers. At best, they could only diminish her power, not obliterate it as the high priestess had undoubtedly envisioned.

Both Bradley and Adrian appeared at the same time as the priestesses. Though one of them had brought them there, Elinor wondered who it could be. Before she could delve deeper into her thoughts, her ladies-in-waiting arrived, followed closely by Bradley, who bore an herbal tea mixture for pain relief. While her attendants busied themselves with making her presentable, she drank the tea, disregarding the burning sensation it caused upon swallowing. As the pain relief took effect, Elinor felt a sense of lightness as her aches and pains subsided, although not completely gone. Aware that the lords were likely awaiting her, she proceeded towards the throne room. Meanwhile, Bradley, having delivered the tea, had already made his way there to secure favour with the lords before the evening's proceedings commenced. Upon her arrival, Elinor was announced to an already crowded room, indicating that news had spread rapidly. Many workers and court members were present, eagerly anticipating the outcome of the vote.

At the forefront, the six lords were in attendance, accompanied by their families who stood behind them. On the opposite side stood the high priestess, followed by her remaining six priestesses. Elinor passed them all, ascending the steps to her throne, every eye fixed on her. However, beneath her composed demeanour, anxiety surged within her, prompting her to tap her foot against the floor to regain control. Despite her earlier display of confidence, doubts regarding the lords' allegiance lingered in her mind.

She was confident that Bradley and Lloyd would support her. However, she doubted Lords Thomas Stone and Wesley Bishop would stand by her side. Lord Stone had his own reasons for not joining her, while Lord Bishop appeared swayed by Thomas's influence, clinging to his every word. This meant she only had two remaining allies: Lords William Bennett and Christopher Malins. Elinor placed her trust in Christopher, praying he wouldn't be swayed by anyone now, especially when she needed him the most. As for Lord Bennett, she could only hope he would align his vote with Christopher's unless Lord Stone got to him first. Ready to get this vote done with, Elinor rose to address the crowd.

"To my esteemed court and lords of the kingdom, I have called upon you today as our high priestess desires to cast a decisive vote. This vote determines whether I shall continue to reign as your queen or if she will anoint herself to take my place."

Whispers rippled through the crowd as Elinor's words hung in the air, gazes darting between her, the lords, and the priestesses. It was common knowledge that in such deliberations, the decision ultimately rested with the lords. However, it had been more than a century since a scenario such as this had last presented itself.

As murmurs intensified, Elinor cleared her throat. "As the high priestess has summoned this vote, it's her right to address the lords first," Elinor said, before settling back onto the throne.

Her foot tapped anxiously as nerves surged within her again. She watched as the high priestess stepped forward, commanding the attention of both the crowd and the lords.

"My lords and esteemed members of this court, I approach this chamber with grave purpose. It is not lightly that I seek this vote, for the circumstances demand urgency and transparency. There exist aspects of Queen Elinor's reign you have not been privy to until this moment."

The high priestess spoke with unflinching frankness, withholding no detail as she laid bare the truth. From Elinor's ascent to the throne to the recent disturbances within the prison cells, she left no stone unturned. Every aspect was explained, painting a damning portrait of Elinor as the malevolent queen, intent on destroying their realm and seizing its power. Elinor seethed inwardly, her blood boiling in her veins, yet she was helpless. Hindered by her diminished powers, she could do nothing but wait, biding her time until she had the opportunity to speak.

As the high priestess concluded her passionate speech, Elinor rose from her seat, her gaze sweeping across the room. In a rare moment, she found herself at a loss for words, grappling with how to counter the accusations hurled by the high priestess. Yet, to her astonishment, it turned out that words were unnecessary. Lord Stone strode forward with unmistakable confidence, ascending the steps towards her. Upon reaching her side, he locked eyes with Elinor before addressing the gathered crowd.

"Why thank you, High Priestess, for your eloquent words. Or should I dare say, lies? It is common knowledge you have held a grudge against our beloved queen since she was a child," Lord Stone's voice boomed, reverberating throughout the room. The crowd stirred once more, their murmurs blending with the high priestess's retort.

"No! I speak the truth—"

"Now, now, High Priestess, your time to speak has passed. The decision lies with the lords, does it not?"

"Yes, but—"

"No, High Priestess, your voice has been heard. It's now time for the vote," Lord Stone interjected, his commanding tone resonating over the crowd.

Elinor stood, a flicker of uncertainty clouding her thoughts, yet hope still glimmered within her. She strained to comprehend the unfolding events as Lord Stone pressed on.

"I now present it to the lords. All in favour of keeping Queen Elinor upon the throne, raise your hands." As his words echoed, all six lords raised their hands in unison.

"Those against?" Every hand dropped.

"Then there you have it. All rise for Elinor, the Queen of Ethos," Lord Stone proclaimed, leading the other lords in applause, prompting a confused reaction from many in the crowd. Stepping aside, Lord Stone yielded the floor to Elinor to address her court. With a self-satisfied grin, Elinor looked at the crowd before her.

"Thank you to the lords here today for recognising the lies and deceit the high priestess tried to spread among you," Elinor acknowledged, her gaze shifting to the high priestess and the remaining priestesses. With venom in her voice, she directed her words at them.

"Now, High Priestess, Priestesses, I advise you to leave or face the consequences for your crimes against the crown," Elinor declared, her gaze unwavering. At the ice-cold look from Elinor, the high priestess frowned, appearing on the verge of protest before abruptly turning on her heels and walking away. The other priestesses followed her lead. As she watched them leave, Elinor scanned across the room and noticed Adrian was gone. Before she could ask anyone, Lord Stone came up beside her, leaning in to whisper in her ear.

"You're welcome," he said before stepping away, descending the steps with a satisfied smile on his face.

A shiver ran down Elinor's spine. Despite still holding the throne, she felt acutely vulnerable without her powers or the crystal. Now, she found herself at the mercy of the lords. As the crowd erupted into cheers, Elinor maintained a composed façade, though turmoil churned within her. Though she bore the title of queen, in the eyes of the lords, she was nothing more than a pawn in their game of power. Yet, she refused to be a mere string-puppet. With narrowed eyes, she observed the lords revelling in their victory, particularly Lord Stone, his demeanour exuding arrogance as he engaged in conversation with those around him. He was in for a surprise, for this queen harboured no intentions to ever bow down to the whims of men. Striding down the steps, Elinor muttered to herself.

"Let the games begin."

Epilogue

The morning air carried a sharp chill, despite it being spring with the flowers already blooming. It felt as if winter refused to be forgotten so easily. Gradually, the woodland creatures awakened from their winter slumber, venturing towards the water's edge for a refreshing drink and a morning wash. As the deer walked along, it sensed the presence of a young boy trailing behind, attempting to remain hidden and muffling his complaints whenever he rustled the leaves. Ignoring the boy and his presence entirely, the deer continued its path towards the river. It paused at the riverbank, lowering its head to drink. While quenching its thirst, it heard the distinct sound of an arrow being pulled back, followed by the whooshing noise as it flew through the air. Eventually, a solid *thunk* reverberated as the arrow struck a tree just ahead. Unfazed, the deer calmly finished its drink, casting a knowing gaze at the boy, before gracefully retreating to its dwelling. It was evident that the boy's marksmanship left much to be desired.

"Damn, I missed again!" Jacob grumbled as he trudged towards the tree, his frustration clear in his stomping feet. Yet another failed attempt at hitting his target with the bow had left him disheartened. It wouldn't have bothered him as much if his sister hadn't been such an exceptional shot herself. She frequently emphasised her skill, often by showcasing the birds and animals she had successfully taken down with an arrow. In contrast, he struggled to hit a stationary target, let alone one in motion. Although he had once caught a rabbit, even if it was accidental — he had been aiming for a deer and hit the rabbit instead. Nonetheless, a hit was a hit, and they had rabbit for dinner that night thanks to him. Upon reaching the tree, he extracted the arrow from its trunk, taking a moment to examine it. Satisfied with its pristine condition, he returned it to its bag before resuming his hunt. Determined to secure fresh meat for dinner, he vowed to make it happen, even if it was the last thing he did.

***

It had been three years since they settled into life at the cottage, and Aevah had grown accustomed to her daily routine. Sundays meant their weekly trip to the local markets, where she, Jacob, and her grandpa would travel the hour on their horse and cart to sell the fruits and vegetables they had grown. For Aevah, it was an exciting day out, a chance to witness the bustling energy of the markets. She enjoyed browsing through the various wares and soaking in the vibrant atmosphere, which contrasted with the peaceful sanctuary of her usual surroundings.

Today was going to be an especially memorable trip because she had her own goods to sell – the most delicious honey cakes one could taste. They were perfectly baked using her mother's recipe after several disastrous attempts. One involved way too much honey – something she would never have believed, and another in which she almost burned the kitchen down, creating charcoal lumps instead of yummy cakes. It was safe to say she was banned from the kitchen for a few weeks after this ordeal.

With her cakes packed in the cart, Aevah sat and read her book while she waited. She was impatient to be off but knew her grandpa would not be rushed. To keep her mind distracted, she read about pirates, sea monsters, and mystical caves. Lost in the pages, she jumped when her grandpa spoke.

"Where's Jacob?" he asked.

"He's out hunting, Grandpa."

327

"Oh okay. Just run out and see if you can find him. If not, I'll leave a note, and we'll go as soon as you're ready, Aevah."

Eager to be on her way, Aevah dashed off in search of Jacob. The brown and green of the surrounding trees seemed to blur as she hurried along the familiar path. With enthusiasm in her voice, she called out for Jacob, eager to embark on their cherished weekly adventure together.

"Ssh, you're scaring the animals away!" Jacob's head appeared, poking out of the bush ahead of her, his expression angry, feet stomping towards her. Oblivious to his annoyance, Aevah hurried him along.

"Jacob, we need to leave now. Grandpa is packed and ready to go, and why are you hunting? We can get fresh meat from the markets. It's not like you'll catch anything, anyway."

"Gee, thanks."

"Oh, you know I didn't mean it like that," Aevah said, rolling her eyes.

She linked her arm with her brother's and led him back to the cottage, eager to leave. Once they reached the cottage, Aevah released Jacob and hopped onto the front of the cart next to their grandpa. After stowing his belongings, Jacob joined them, climbing up beside Aevah. With everyone ready, Aevah felt the jolt of movement as the cart started to roll.

As they trundled along the winding road, Aevah's heart fluttered with excitement as the village came into view. The quaint village unfolded before her, with charming two-story cottages made of weathered stone, standing proudly on the outskirts. The grass bloomed with colourful flowers, and the distant murmurs of bustling shops and a cosy inn in the centre contributed to the lively ambience. Nestled amidst individual farms, the small village boasted ample fields, with several townspeople keeping their own animals on the outskirts. At the heart of the village, a charming little covered cove had been built for the market stalls, ensuring that rain or sunshine, everyone could still bring their wares to sell. The small, meandering road that passed through the village led them directly to the covered cove. As their grandpa George halted the horses, Aevah jumped off, her face beaming with excitement.

Jacob, eager to be off, dashed away to attend to his own tasks. Meanwhile, Aevah and her grandpa, upon reaching their designated area, began to unpack. Surrounding them, the bustling locals had already arranged their stalls, their produce enticing the passersby. The atmosphere buzzed with activity as people were already buying produce, browsing stalls, haggling prices, and chatting about the latest happenings in the country. Eager to sell her goods, Aevah set up her own little area, with her grandpa following suit. Many customers were excited to try her honey cakes, particularly the children. Before she knew it, she was fully immersed, with her grandpa George assisting her in handling the money. In her element, Aevah embraced the world of sales, holding her own with the best of them.

***

Venturing out on his own, Jacob made his way straight to the wood shop. In that quaint little shop, an elderly gentleman named Larry and his son, Ben, worked together, skilfully crafting unique pieces of furniture, exquisite jewellery, intricate animal figurines, and captivating games for everyone to enjoy. Their craftsmanship knew no bounds, and Jacob found great joy in observing their work, occasionally even attempting to create something with his own hands.

As Jacob entered the wood shop, the air became saturated with the aroma of varnish and wood filings. Over at another workbench, Ben could be seen diligently sanding down a sizeable piece of wood, preparing it to create a stunning oak table for a resident in the area.

"Hello, Ben!" Jacob cried out excitedly. He walked in, fizzing with excitement, but slowed down as he neared Ben. He had learned to be careful where they were working.

"Good morning! I wondered if you would be in today. Care to give me a hand?" Ben, already anticipating Jacob's eagerness, grabbed a block and wrapped a piece of sandpaper around it for Jacob to use. Moving to the opposite side of Ben, Jacob copied his movements, sanding down the other half of the wood. This workshop was Jacob's happy place. He came by every Sunday without fail, and sometimes more when he could convince his grandpa to bring him through during the week. He loved working with the wood, learning the art of whittling, carving, and joining pieces together. Lately, like that day, he was discovering the importance of sanding the wood and how to do it correctly.

Woodwork was truly an art form, and he had the privilege of learning from the finest instructors. Larry, in particular, had lent a hand in crafting a stunning necklace for Aevah's birthday. The necklace was an exquisite oval piece with a hollowed-out centre, perfectly designed to cradle the precious gem she cherished and kept in her jewellery box. He had to sneak it out one morning and return it without her noticing that evening after Larry had inspected it. Ensuring it would fit perfectly in the hollow part was crucial. It was a simple yet stunning piece that would complement her beautifully. He even enlisted Ben's assistance in carving a rose on the back, knowing it was Aevah's favourite flower. He kept the necklace in the workshop, as bringing it home risked Aevah finding it and ruining the surprise.

Approaching their thirteenth birthdays, but in the eyes of the village, it was only Aevah's day. His birthday was the following month, supposedly making him fourteen. Since he was already taller than his sister, their grandpa suggested having different ages would make them less remarkable than being twins. This arrangement was solely for the benefit of the villagers. They would be celebrating their actual birthday together at home. In the beginning, it was tricky to remember, even with their names being different when visiting the village. Their appearance adjusted with the power as well, just in case. Now, though, it was second nature to them both. He and his sister both understood the risks and although three years had passed, it didn't mean they were any safer.

Refocusing on his work, Jacob sanded down the wood, following the advice given by Ben. Time seemed to slip away, and before he knew it, morning had turned into afternoon. His grandpa and sister appeared, all packed up and prepared to depart. They waited for him to complete the task at hand before everyone hopped back onto the cart, making their journey back to their cosy cottage home.

***

Back home at the cottage, life continued as normal as it could be for Aevah and Jacob. With George's guidance, they delved deeper into their family's history, honed their powers, and stayed dedicated to their studies. George knew the day was coming when they would need to be prepared to face the world and return to their true home in Carraton. Thus, he taught them the skills they would need to survive the world they were born into.

Rumours swirled about Elinor and her reign. He had heard so much, with some being so far-fetched, they couldn't possibly be true. However, what he did know was that she had married Bradley, and together they ruled while resisting the very lords that had placed her in power. He also knew she continued to search for both them and the crystal shards. Unlucky for her. As long as he was alive, she would fail. Bound to his life, the secrets would remain undisclosed until his death.

Hence, he dedicated himself to teaching the twins all he knew, preparing them for that inevitable day. Even in his absence, they would never be alone, as there were families eagerly awaiting their return, including their own mother. Sadly, with how everything played out, he didn't get the chance to reunite with her and bring her to her children. They missed her terribly, but they held onto the knowledge they would see their mother again. As for himself, he couldn't be certain. If it was the will of the divine spirit, he would see her one last time before his final days. Regardless of how his journey would end, he vowed to ensure the safety of his beloved grandchildren.

His extensive network of connections spanned vast distances, their families safeguarding a well-kept secret for countless generations. The legacy would not end with Elinor; instead, it would continue with the twins. Just like their parents, their hearts were pure, and they were the rightful successors to the throne. Until the moment arrived for them to forge their own path, he vowed to protect them, guide their training, and defend them with unwavering determination. They represented the future of the realm, and he was determined, in one way or another, to witness one of them ascend to the throne.

Acknowledgements

This book has been a long time in the making, and I can't believe it's finally here. I will not lie, the road here has not been easy, and I've wanted to give up a few times, but I persevered and boy, am I glad I did. To be able to hold my own book in my hands and share it with the world is a feeling like no other.

To get to this point though, I had help from some amazing people.

Firstly, I want to thank my hubby, who has the unwavering conviction that I could write a fantasy book in the first place, believing in me without fail. For that alone, thank you. Your belief carried me through more times than you probably realise.

Then comes my son Damon who always listened to my ramblings about different parts of my book and its progress. I'm not sure how interested you were most of the time, but you always humoured me.

To my Nana, thank you for always believing in me and asking every week when the book would be published. I am excited to say here it is, and happy reading.

To my editor Carien. What can I say but thank you from the bottom of my heart. I literally could not have done this without you. Not only are you my editor, but now a lifelong friend. Thank you for taking a chance on a first-time indie author and helping me bring my fantasy world into the world for everyone to read.

To all the writers who came before and sparked my love for stories in the first place, thank you. You ignited my love for all things fantasy, and without your stories to fuel my imagination and to get lost in, that little girl might never have dreamed of creating her own magical world.

To my readers who have ventured into my fantasy world, thank you for believing in the magic of storytelling. Your own boundless imaginations help drive my creativity to spin the tales I tell, breathing life into the characters and world I've lovingly created. I may have written the words, but you are the creators, bringing my words to life with every page you read. That is the power of storytelling.

It's my sincerest hope that each and every one of you forms a connection with the world and characters I've brought to life. They each have a cherished spot in my heart, and their story will be continued in Book 2. There are still many exciting things to come!